The Sanction

THE
SANCTION

MARK SENNEN

CANELO

First published in the United Kingdom in 2020 by Canelo

Canelo Digital Publishing Limited
Third Floor, 20 Mortimer Street
London W1T 3JW
United Kingdom

A CIP catalogue record for this book is available from the British Library.

Print ISBN 978 1 80032 005 5
Ebook ISBN 978 1 78863 981 1

Look for more great books at www.canelo.co

Printed and bound in Great Britain by Clays Ltd, Elcograf S.p.A.

It is only one who is thoroughly acquainted with the evils of war that can thoroughly understand the profitable way of carrying it on.

The Art of War by Sun Tzu, fifth century BC

Prologue

Kabul, Afghanistan. Thirty-five degrees centigrade in the shade. The buzzing of flies and an acrid smell in the air. Something burning. Something bad.

That'll be the truck, she thinks, the burning. The bloody remains of the people in it, the bad. Men and women and children and goats and chickens. Passengers and goods on the way to the market. Talking and laughing and bleating and clucking until the truck rolled past a roadside bomb. An IED. An improvised explosive device. But there was nothing improvised about it. The attack was carefully planned, the bomb meticulously prepared. And the word *improvised* does a disservice to those who died. As if killing can be a spur-of-the-moment decision, as if it has no consequence and leaves no mark. She knows from personal experience that's not true. Killing is a calculated business. In her profession there's nothing improvised about it.

In truth she shouldn't be here in Afghanistan. None of them should. The campaign ended years ago. A homecoming with no fanfare and no celebration because these days wars don't end with parades and tickertape and shiny medals pinned on proud heroes. They don't actually end at all. And that's why she's back on a second tour of duty. Supposedly she's a military adviser, a trainer, somebody providing support services, but that's crap, a sham fashioned for political expediency. The reality is that without foreign troops the thin veneer of normality would peel aside and the entire country collapse into anarchy once more.

Right now she's lying prone on a rooftop five storeys up. Behind her a rusty air conditioning unit stands idle. The unit casts a shadow which shields her from the afternoon sun. The sun is the enemy out here. The heat saps energy and drains water bottles, but it's the light which bothers her. One glint off a buckle or a flash from an eyelet on a boot and you're made. And once you're made then you'd better move fast if you want to live because the insurgents have the ability to rise from the ruins of the city like a miasma. As quickly as they come they can dissipate in the same way, slinking back into doorways, morphing into innocent civilians, returning to their hidey-holes until the night comes. But she won't be outside the base after dark. That would be nothing short of idiotic.

Beside her is her spotter, Richard Smith. Known variously as Ricky or Smithy or Itchy. Itchy because he can't stop moving. He's always fidgeting and fussing and at this particular moment she wishes he'd keep still because she can't concentrate while he's constantly in motion.

'Pack it in, Itchy,' she says. Her words are friendly, half in jest. Itchy's been like an older brother since they've been paired together. Always there for her, nothing too much trouble. 'Tell me what's out there.'

Itchy has a pair of binoculars and a spotting scope. Good eyes. An innate sense for picking out the tiniest of anomalies in a scene that would look normal to most people. Itchy is thirty-three, more experienced than she is, battle-scarred, world wise. This is his third tour and it shows in the handful of grey wisps sprouting among his dark hair. An old man's brain in a young man's body. He's seen too many things that can't be forgotten, although he never brags. You can always tell the true veterans by the number of stories they tell: the fewer stories, the more they've seen. Eventually they stop saying anything at all.

Itchy moves his eyes from his scope to the binoculars and pans from left to right. Like her, he's lying beneath a camouflage net of tan and grey. He's the lookout, there so she can keep her head down and her eye fixed to the telescopic sight on her rifle. In a sniper team the spotter is the most important component.

Anyone can pull a trigger and fire off a shot, although not many with the accuracy she can achieve.

'Nothing,' Itchy says after he's completed his sweep. 'We're good.'

'Keep looking.' She adjusts her position slightly and blinks, refocusing the image in her right eye. Eight hundred metres away a patrol is heading up to an intersection. Some unlucky bugger on point, the others following. The patrol's radio chatter crackles in her earpiece. Cautious. Nervous. She can't blame them for being nervous though. Not with the high buildings looming over the rubble-filled streets. This place is a maze with a dozen wrong turnings. A dozen ways to die.

If she and Itchy were the enemy, half the patrol would already be dead. Luckily they're on the same side. The closest thing the grunts have to a pair of guardian angels. From this decrepit building they can see a good portion of the locality. They can take out a target at a thousand metres and the first thing the hostile will know about it will be when the bullet hits them.

'Smith?' a voice in her ear says as the patrol checks in. 'Sit rep.'

'Nothing moving,' Itchy says in response. 'All clear ahead.'

'Taking five,' the voice says. 'A breather.'

The patrol back up to a wall. The point man hunkers in a doorway twenty metres away. Through her scope she can see water bottles being passed round, straps on helmets loosened. She reaches for her own bottle and takes a gulp without moving her right eye from the scope. Through her left eye she sees the world close to. Empty streets. A stray dog with three legs scrabbling in a patch of dirt five storeys below. A blur of helicopter fuzzing the air on the horizon.

She refocuses on the cross street near the patrol and something catches her eye. A low dwelling with washing on a line. She didn't realise anyone still lived in this part of the city. But it isn't the clothes flapping on the line that have caught her attention. Something just slipped beneath the washing line. *Someone.*

3

He's small. Not a combatant. A boy perhaps thirteen or fourteen years old. His clothes aren't much more than rags, but he's got a smile on his face as he leaves the little walled area and steps onto the street, heading for the intersection.

'Itchy?' she says, but he's already on it.

'Charlie,' he says, clicking the radio. 'Got a kid to your three o'clock. Just a kid, no drama, copy?'

Nothing but static in her earpiece.

She adjusts her position so she can see the patrol again. They're still in the shadow of the building. Against regulations, helmets have been removed. Three of the patrol are sitting on the ground. She sees one man laughing. Somebody is eating from a ration pack. They haven't heard Itchy. She tries her own headset in case Itchy's radio is down.

'Charlie, do you copy, over?'

Still nothing.

'Shit,' Itchy says. 'He's carrying something.'

She looks back at the kid. Itchy's right. The boy is holding an object in his hands. A metal ammunition box. And, come to think of it, perhaps his smile is more of a grimace than an expression of happiness.

'Bloody hell, I can see a wire. It's an IED.' Itchy is moving now. Out from under the camouflage net and standing as if he could wave or shout even though the patrol is nearly half a mile away.

'Get down, you idiot,' she says.

Itchy could call control and try to route a message through them, but there's no time. The kid will reach the intersection in ten seconds. When he turns left he'll be within a couple of metres of the men. If the box contains a bomb then the patrol are dead. What remains of them will have to be scraped off the street and sent home in a tub.

'Charlie, do you copy, over?'

Five seconds.

'Charlie, come in, over.'

4

Three.

Two.

'Take him,' says Itchy.

One.

'What's up?' comes the answer, the radio net working once more. But the response is too late. It's now or never.

Her finger touches the trigger. There's a crack from her rifle and time freezes. The bullet will take nearly a second to reach the target and will drop as it arcs in flight. There's a left to right breeze. She's had to compensate for the height of the building she's on, the drop and the windage, but all that comes easy to her. She's one of the best snipers in the British army and on this tour has already notched up more than half a dozen kills. Missing the target is unlikely.

In the fragment of his life remaining, the boy half turns. He knows nothing of the bullet approaching him at over nine hundred metres per second, which explains why he's still smiling. He knows nothing until the bullet strikes him just below his right ear, passing through the lower half of his skull and destroying the brainstem. He collapses to the ground.

The sound arrives at the intersection a full two seconds after the bullet, and the patrol leap up in response.

'Hostile eliminated,' she says as the men take cover. 'Your three o'clock. Five metres.'

There's a chaotic buzz. Point is on the wrong side of the street but he realises what's happened. He runs from the doorway and widens the angle so he can see down the intersection. He ducks behind a wall and makes a hand signal. One member of the patrol skirts back the way they've come and watches the rear, while another covers the forward position. The rest stand motionless while the patrol leader approaches the boy.

'Shot,' says Itchy. He pats her on the back. It's what he always does when she hits the target, whether it's on the practice range or in the field. Whether the bullet has hit a bullseye or a human being.

'There's an ammunition box,' she hears the patrol leader say over the radio. 'I can see a wire near the top.'

Careful, she thinks. There could be a delay on the device or perhaps there might be a hidden operator ready to punch a remote button when someone gets close enough.

The patrol leader is within a couple of metres now. He lowers himself to the ground to minimise the possible blast effect and crawls forward.

'Oh God,' he says. 'Oh shit, shit, shit.'

She wants to scream at him to get out of there, but she lets someone else do the talking.

'What is it?' Point says.

'Sweets,' comes the reply. 'The box is full of sweets. The wire was a tie holding the lid shut.'

She stares down the scope. The patrol leader is obscuring the ammunition container, but then he stands and she can see he's right. The contents of the box have spilled over the ground. Sweets and chocolate and cakes. Something catches her eye and she swings the rifle to cover the movement. The washing balloons out as a woman pushes under the line. Her hands are to her mouth and then she's on her knees in the dirt, screaming, crying, begging. One of the other soldiers comes forward. He speaks to her and translates.

'She's the boy's mother,' she hears across the airwaves. 'He was bringing us a present to say "thank you" for being here.'

'And we shot him,' someone else says. 'We shot him in the fucking head.'

Chapter One

Two years later

In her dreams the boy sometimes lives. Not often, but enough times to suggest there may be an alternate reality. A place where her life turns out differently. A place where the boy's story doesn't end with a headline and a blurred picture of a smiling face. Each night she wakes in a cold sweat and stares into the dark and clenches her fists so her nails dig into her palms. She prays to whatever God is listening, to whatever demonic force might be willing to make a pact with her. A straight swap. Her life for his. She listens for an answer but there's only the sounds of a car passing by outside, a siren blaring somewhere in the distance, the rain spattering against the window. At some point she falls into another fitful slumber, tossing and turning until the alarm bleeps and her hand reaches out to silence the unwelcome intrusion.

She struggles out of bed, washes, dresses, eats. She sets off for work but the morning sun doesn't warm her. Instead she remembers the cold of a mountain pass thick with snow. The sounds of gunfire. The thud of a heavy retort as an explosion rips through a crowded market. The stench of charred flesh and the streets echoing with the screams of men and women and children. The never-ending racket of helicopters. The eerie silence that descends at sunset and the sleep which doesn't come easily after witnessing so much death. She remembers the joshing and the horseplay and reading dog-eared paperbacks while lying on a bunk in the daytime heat. The boredom. The fear. And the screams again. Always the screams.

In her dreams the boy sometimes lives. But mostly he dies.

–

Plymouth's main shopping street measured five hundred metres, give or take a couple of strides. The street sloped gently upwards and ran west to east as straight as an arrow. If you had an eye for such a thing you could find several good hide sites, but the standout one was at the top of the multistorey car park down at the western end. You could lie there with your weapon poking through the metal guardrail or alternatively place yourself in a vehicle, open the front passenger window, and sit in the back seat. With a small gel bag on the sill the window would provide the perfect rest. The trajectory of the bullet over a range of five hundred metres meant there'd be a drop to account for but the buildings rose, chasm like, either side of the street, so crosswinds were minimal. If the target was walking to the west, towards the car park, you'd have plenty of time to make the shot. If they went into a shop you could simply wait until they emerged. No doubt about it, the car park was a standout position.

Rebecca da Silva stared up at the multistorey. She didn't have to think about such things any more, but she'd been in the army for eight years and situational awareness was in her blood. Quite literally, since her father had served in the army too. Back in the nineties he'd been with the special forces in the Gulf War. 'You thought Afghanistan was tough?' he'd sneer, as if patrolling the streets of Kabul was akin to taking a stroll in the English countryside. 'You should have tried SCUD hunting in southern Iraq. *That* was tough.' She would nod and pretend to listen, all the while wondering if it was genes or upbringing that had led to her following in his footsteps. Perhaps it was serendipity or divine intervention. Perhaps it was plain rotten luck.

Silva was twenty-eight years old. Her father was British through and through, but her mother was born of Portuguese immigrants. Her parents had divorced when she was ten and at some point in her teens she'd adopted her mother's maiden name. Partly it had been an act of solidarity with her mother, partly a rejection of her father. Her Portuguese side was evident in her light coffee-coloured skin and her dark-brown hair. Her eyes were a mixture of her father's and mother's, a grey-green that was the shade of the sea after a fierce storm. She was small, but lithe, strong and agile. In Basic Training, her instructors had been surprised she'd come in the top ten per cent on the loaded march. Her heart, she knew, carried a good portion of her mother's easy-going southern European attitude, combined with a dash of the fiery temper which had undoubtedly hastened her parents' separation. What was inside her head came from her father: a calm, stubborn orderliness that she'd done resisting and now used to her advantage. In the army both sides of her character had been invaluable.

Nowadays it was all she could do to remind herself that the military part of her life had ended when the judge advocate had sentenced her to twelve months in prison and dismissal from the service. The charge was negligence and, as her lawyer had been keen to explain, her situation could have been very much worse since initially there'd been talk of manslaughter or even murder.

She blinked as something moved against the brightness of the sky. *Someone*. There was a kid up there in the car park, held up by his father so he could look down on the street. The boy wasn't much older than a toddler and he pointed at Silva and waved. For a second she wondered if she knew the kid, but then she realised it was the uniform he was interested in. Silva forced herself to give a half smile and waved back. As the boy laughed with delight, emotion welled up in her stomach. Sadness, regret, self-disgust.

-

Stephen Holm wasn't usually asleep at four in the afternoon, but then he didn't often work a twenty-four-hour shift. When he'd stumbled back to his flat at seven that morning he'd tried to remain awake by fortifying himself with a cup of extra-strong coffee, but despite the caffeine boost he'd found his eyelids heavy. The long hours in the windowless situation room at MI5's headquarters in Thames House had led to something akin to jet lag, and eventually he'd given up and gone to bed. For a few minutes he'd lain in the dark and tried to calm his mind and then he was out like a light bulb. Hours later he awoke in an instant as his phone blared out. He grabbed the phone and thumbed to answer.

'Where?' he said, sitting up, aware of his clammy skin as the duvet slipped off his upper body.

'Tunis,' the voice in his ear said, adding in a sympathetic tone, 'Sorry, Stephen.'

The voice belonged to Martin 'Harry' Palmer, Holm's friend in SIS, the Secret Intelligence Service, better known to the public and journalists as MI6. Palmer worked the North Africa desk and was Holm's contact at SIS and his sometime drinking partner. They'd known each other for years, since way before either of them worked for the security services, and Palmer was an old hand to whom Holm could express his frequent dissatisfaction with work and life in general. If he wasn't a friend then he was as close to one as Holm had, and Holm always appreciated the way Palmer managed to sound calm even when chin-deep in shit, his tone being similar to that of a weather forecaster reporting the possibility of a short rain shower: *Pack an umbrella or a lightweight mac. Don't worry, it'll be brighter by the afternoon.*

'Tunis?' Holm threw off the rest of the duvet, climbed from the bed and staggered from the bedroom. He headed down the hallway of his little flat and into the living room. The location given by Palmer had momentarily thrown him, and he tried to work the angles and come up with something that made sense. Nothing did so he picked up the remote for the TV and blipped it on. 'How bad?'

There was a momentary pause before the answer came. 'At least four UK citizens so far. Three other fatalities, a dozen critically or seriously injured. The total death toll could well rise into double figures.'

'Right.' Holm was staring at the TV screen, taking in the news footage at the same time as his mind began to run the numbers. The casualty figure was bad but manageable. The location – Tunis – was a nasty surprise.

Holm moved back into the hall and towards the bathroom, wondering if there was going to be time for a shower, thinking no, a squirt of deodorant would have to do. 'Random or targeted?'

'Targeted. It appears the attackers were after the head of a British-run women's charity. She was killed along with a journalist who happened to be interviewing her at the time. The other dead are tourists: British, American, French and German.'

'Shit.' Holm worked the facts. American. French. German. Non-UK dead complicated the matter. For a moment he scolded himself for forgetting these were people no matter what their nationality. 'Have we got anything from the Yanks yet?'

'No, but BND has been in contact. They're pretty upset at the misinformation you sent yesterday.'

'Misinformation?' BND. The *Bundesnachrichtendienst*. The German intelligence agency. Holm could imagine the director fuming at the killing of one of his citizens, irate that the warning the British had issued was so bungled. 'That's unfair.'

'Fair or not, most of Europe went on high alert because of you lot and yet nothing happened. Then you cancelled the alert and when the attack happens it's somewhere completely off the radar.' There was a pause before Palmer continued. 'You might like to start devising some elaborate excuse for the Spider on why you fucked up on this one, OK?'

Holm shivered as Palmer ended the call. The Spider. Real name Fiona Huxtable, Holm's immediate boss and the deputy director of MI5. The Spider lived on the fifth floor at Thames House and spun sticky webs that could trap the unwary. Like many female arachnids, she enjoyed eating the male of the species alive, although in Huxtable's case it didn't involve sex beforehand.

He tossed the phone onto the sofa. In the bathroom he splashed water on his face and groped in the cupboard for a can of deodorant. The aerosol hissed out as he sprayed himself and he was struck by the thought that no amount of deodorant was going to prevent the stink Huxtable was going to kick up over this.

–

Silva turned away from the car park and back to the job in hand. She walked round the corner to where depressing flats stood above tired shops. She opened her postbag and took out a bunch of letters. Flat 2. She stuffed the letters into the slot, heard them fall onto the mat, let the flap clang shut, turned away.

The uniform. Red and blue, and she really hoped the boy in the car park aspired to be something more than a postal worker.

Next address. More letters. A dog growling behind the door. She shook her head as she heard the dog rip into the mail. Not her problem. She moved on. In the next flat a baby was crying, and over the child's distress a couple argued. Obscenities flew back and forth. What love there ever was drained away by poverty and circumstance. Silva didn't care. She drifted up the street and the day drifted with her. Just like every day. Work the round, deliver the mail, end the shift. In the evenings she retreated to the little boat she called home. It sat on a berth at the end of a pontoon in a rundown marina where nobody bothered her. She could cook herself a meal and try to sleep. Wake the next morning. Do it all over again. Day after day. Week after week. Month after month. She took all the overtime she could and enjoyed the fact the job involved walking everywhere. She relished the constant movement, finally understanding Itchy's affliction: if you kept moving you didn't have to think. You lived for each step, each swing of the arm, each twitch of the head. Seventeen strides to the front door. Push the flap, shove in the letters, walk away. Twenty-five strides to the next house. Push the flap, shove in the letters, walk away. Walk, push, shove. Each bag of mail represented ten thousand steps. Ten thousand little segments of time when she wasn't still, wasn't thinking.

Monday to Saturday she worked, but Sunday she was forced to take off, so on that day she ran. Wind or rain, she ran. Often she pounded the same streets she'd been walking the day before, but sometimes she took her motorbike out onto the moor and ran up there. From the vantage point of a rocky tor, she could see the city of Plymouth sprawled below, the ocean beyond. Warships lay anchored in the sheltered waters of the Sound or moored up alongside in the dockyards. This was the largest naval base in Western Europe. Nuclear submarines came here to be repaired and refuelled, and there was a huge armament facility on the far side of the river. The military had been inexorably bound up with the place for centuries, and conflict had shaped the city. She'd wandered here after prison, searching for a cheap place to moor her boat for a few nights while she was visiting Itchy, and ended up staying. Out here in the far west she was as anonymous and unloved as the city was, but like the city she bore the scars of war deep inside.

The Afghan boy, yes, but the others too.

She remembered her first kill as if it was yesterday. He was a figure rising from behind a wall, gun in hand. The four hundred metres between the end of her rifle and the man in the sights compressed until he was no longer a distant enemy soldier. The scope magnified his features and she could see he was somebody's son, somebody's father, somebody's husband. She slipped her finger from the trigger and raised her head. Her perspective changed from a restricted view of the man to a vista that took in a tree-lined road leading to a small fort. An armoured vehicle headed down the road, a squad of men marching behind. If she didn't take the shot the man behind the wall would shoot at the patrol. Lives were in her hands. During

13

training, her instructor had cautioned her not to overthink it, not to dwell on the morality of the act. Still, she was aware she was, for that one moment, God.

She lowered her eye to the scope once more, pulled the trigger, and the man went down. A figure crumpling in the haze, a mirage blurring the air as he died. Was that his spirit departing his body or merely a spiral of dust kicked up as he fell? She didn't know, but later, lying on her bunk at the base trying to get to sleep, she thought back to the moment of the man's death and wept. Then the next day she tried not to think of it again. She stuck the memory in a little box and pushed it to the far recesses of her mind. It's what soldiers did.

Silva could count the number of local friends she had on one hand: Itchy, also discharged from the army for his part in the death of the Afghan boy; a woman who was a doctor whom she'd met on a run; a girl at the Royal Mail who'd been in the navy. Life in the military provided a ready-made family, but once you left you were on your own, all of a sudden shorn of the common thread which had sustained friendships through the most horrific of circumstances. Civvy Street seemed mundane and trite after the streets of Kabul, everyday worries trivial or even offensive when you considered the situation in other parts of the world. When you had pulled a trigger and ended an innocent young life.

Away from Plymouth she had a few acquaintances scattered round the country, but they weren't much more than numbers and faces on her phone. They weren't people she could call up and talk to. Aside from her mother, there was really only one person who she'd ever been able to do that with and she had no idea where he was. She didn't even know what country he was in. Besides, she'd burned her bridges with him. Ended it. Her decision, no regrets. None. At least that's what she told herself every time he slipped into her thoughts.

More letters into letterboxes. Bills and court summonses and bad news. The occasional birthday card or a postcard from abroad. Somewhere hot and sunny where you didn't have to stay behind hard cover or crap yourself when you walked down a street because your opposite number had found a standout position.

She came round the side of a block of flats and the car park loomed above her once again. The boy had gone and there was nobody up there now. Nothing but a mass of concrete and rows of cars and, above it all, a brooding grey sky the colour of gunmetal.

–

Holm stood by the sink for a moment longer. He examined himself in the mirror, trying to see beyond his reflected image, to somehow see the future. There was nothing but a creased brow and a face with a dozen craggy lines, lines which he knew had deepened in the past few years. Was that life and ageing or were the marks indicative of a more serious malaise? He wasn't sure, but either way the job wasn't helping and the current debacle marked a new low point in a career that had recently been short on highs. Perhaps he should just resign himself to the fact he was past it. His mind simply didn't work in the same way as it once had. His creative juices had been sucked out by the constant stress of trying to stay on top of the latest threat. If you made a mistake, people died. And as Palmer had said, he'd fucked up on this one.

Big time.

He met his gaze in the mirror and wondered how in hell it had come to this.

–

Stephen Holm was a senior analyst at the Joint Terrorism Analysis Centre. Part of MI5, its role was to sift through intelligence and assess the threat level posed by various groups and individuals. Holm's route into JTAC had been circuitous. He'd started his career as a beat bobby on the Met before moving to CID where he'd been attached to Special Branch. He'd joined Special Branch long before 9/11, when the word *terrorist* invariably referred to the Northern Irish situation. That had been a dirty war, but the enemy had been familiar. They had the same colour skin, worshipped the same God and spoke the same language. They understood there were certain rules both sides had to abide by. If 9/11 changed that cosy view forever then the British equivalent – 7/7 – brought it to the streets of London with a literal *bang*. JTAC had been formed in the aftermath of 9/11 as the security services realised they were way behind the curve, and Holm had moved across from the police to Five around then, taking up a position in international counter-terrorism. His assignment to JTAC had come at fifty, and in the intervening years JTAC had had many successes and a few failures, but nobody kidded themselves the war was even close to being won.

No, Holm thought to himself, not even close.

There'd been whispers of a possible attack earlier in the week. Some vague intercepts from GCHQ. A person of interest making an unscheduled journey. A word from Palmer that he'd picked up a nugget from a deep-cover contact in Belgium. All these things suggested something might be about to happen, yet none pointed to an exact target or date. Nevertheless, Holm had a gut feeling of impending disaster but – as he often said to junior colleagues – you couldn't go to the Spider and offer her a mere hunch. You needed a juicy morsel if you wanted her to bite.

He'd scuttled round all week trying to extract information from various sources, even tapping an informant he usually reserved for times when an attack was believed to be imminent. The informant, bribed with a cup of sweet black coffee and a fifty-pound donation to a local homeless charity, had mentioned a mosque he'd attended in west London. There'd been a visiting cleric from Palestine. A meeting of a youth group where pictures of atrocities committed by UK, American and Israeli forces had been passed round. Talk afterwards.

'Hotheads and idiots,' the informant, a moderate who had no truck with extremism, said as he bent to sip his coffee. 'You want their names?'

Holm had nodded, but knew this wasn't it. This was just lads being lads. For all the religious fervour a leader could drum up among young, impressionable minds, he doubted the bravado was any different from that found among young men who followed other creeds or even no creed at all. There were morons in any country, from any culture, of any colour. He'd taken the names anyway, cross-referenced them and drawn a blank.

When Thursday evening ticked over into Friday morning, the chatter died to nothing. Bleary-eyed junior analysts kept casting him glances, and at a little after four a.m. Holm called it safe and sent everyone home. He remained in the situation room for another couple of hours and then checked out himself.

Safe.

Stupid idiot.

Holm gave himself another squirt of deodorant for good measure and returned to the bedroom to get dressed.

Chapter Two

Silva had just a handful of letters left to deliver when heavy rain began to fall. There was a rumble of thunder in the distance as she passed a shop with televisions in the window display. Water streaked down the glass, blurring the TV images. She pulled her waterproof around her, fastened the hood, and made sure the flap of the postbag was closed. A few steps ahead, the boy she'd seen at the car park earlier smiled at her as his father dragged him from the wet street into the store. The pair stopped in the entrance and stared at a huge screen. A red bar ran along the bottom of the image, the word *Breaking* flashing on and off. The father shook his head, bent and said something to the boy, and then they were gone, deeper into the store.

Silva looked at the screen too and found herself moving forward. A wash of warmth from an air curtain greeted her as she stepped into the shop. There were others looking at the screen now. An elderly man. A young couple. A woman in a business suit.

'Beggars belief, doesn't it?' the old man said to nobody in particular. 'We need to wipe them off the surface of the earth.'

Chaos flashed on the screen. Blue lights strobing, soldiers running, ambulances lining the street. The camera panned and showed the remains of a cafe. The entire front had been destroyed in a fusillade of bullets, the street littered with tables and chairs and debris. A pool of red stained the pavement near a pile of something pink and raw, and the camera quickly panned away. Silva felt a drop of cold rain slip from the hood of her waterproof and fall onto her neck. She pushed through and stood at the front.

'Where's this?' she said.

'Tunisia,' the businesswoman said. 'Thank God.'

The cafe on the screen emerged from a recent memory. A cup and saucer and cinnamon sticks with the coffee. Fancy little biscuits. An evening spent in the fading heat of a day not more than three months ago. The next morning, hugs and kisses and a promise that they'd catch up soon. A flight back to the UK, Silva staring through the aircraft window as Europe glided below, wondering what it would have been like had her parents led normal lives. Had their wanderlust rubbed off? Was that why she never felt settled?

The camera moved to the right. Three body bags lay at the front of an office block where a plate glass window had crazed into a spiderweb pattern. Next to the window stood several police officers, sub-machine guns cradled in their arms. The news ticker at the bottom of the screen scrolled to the left. The head of a British women's aid charity had been assassinated in an attack on a cafe in Tunis. Other expats and tourists had also been targeted. Seventeen people injured, at least seven fatalities. The raindrop ran from Silva's neck down to her chest and she shivered. She'd been to the cafe, she was sure of it. Then her phone rang and she was stepping away from the crowd, out into the street and the rain. She pulled the phone from her bag and saw the caller. He never rang her, not at work. In fact he never rang her at all. She realised her hand was shaking as she moved the phone to her ear.

'Dad?' she said.

'It's your mother.' The voice hesitated, stumbled over words, muttered a series of broken phrases. Although good at barking orders, dealing with emotion had never been her father's strong point. 'She's... well, she's dead.'

'I know,' Silva said.

She ended the call and dropped the phone back into the postbag. She left the flap open and rain patted in among the letters as she began to walk. After a few strides an involuntary spasm ran through her and she started to jog. She ran away from the main shopping area and headed towards the seafront, her feet moving faster. Trotting, running, sprinting. At some point she lurched to a stop and looked down at the bag. Everything inside was sodden. She dropped the bag onto the pavement and removed her waterproof coat. The red and blue. The uniform. She folded the coat neatly and placed it on the pavement and ran up to the expanse of grass that overlooked Plymouth Sound. Out to sea, sheets of rain swept across the water, lashing down on a solitary grey warship moored in the centre of the bay. For a second a shaft of brightness shimmied across the sea but then it was gone as dark clouds rolled in from the west. Silva ran across to a nearby bench and slumped down, breathless, on the wet surface. She pulled her knees up to her chest and rocked herself back and forth as the rain continued to fall, not wanting to stop moving, not wanting to think.

–

Holm found a clean shirt but his suit lay crumpled where he'd thrown it when he'd arrived back from work. He pulled on the trousers and jacket and grabbed a couple of chocolate biscuits from a cupboard in the kitchen. A swig of milk straight from the carton in the fridge and his breakfast – at four fifteen in the afternoon – was done.

Half an hour later he was emerging from the depths of Victoria tube station and striding towards the river. He headed up Millbank, dodging people coming the other way. It was rush hour now and most folk were going home. Throngs of workers. Crowded buses. Nose-to-tail traffic. As Holm neared Thames House, he looked across at a couple of young mums with babies strapped to their fronts. Nearby a trio of city types shared office banter and a teacher led a group of foreign schoolchildren on a tour. This was the soft underbelly of the country, awash with easy targets. Many a time he'd discussed with colleagues how lucky they were that most terrorists were fairly stupid. How else to account for the relatively low number of attacks? Sure, the security services had had great success in foiling a number of plots, but it didn't explain why there weren't more.

At Thames House he went through the rigmarole of passing through security and made his way to the situation room. When he'd left in the early hours there'd been empty chairs and blank monitors, but now every screen was ablaze and nearly every chair taken. People talked into phones, fingers clattered across keyboards and a buzz of half a dozen different languages filled the air.

To one side of the room a junior operative, Farakh Javed, hunched over a laptop staring at some black and white images. Javed was an analyst in Holm's department who'd unfathomably latched onto Holm as some kind of intelligence guru. Javed had a bouncy shock of black hair and an engaging smile. He was very bright and very gay – a fact, he'd told Holm, his second-generation Pakistani parents weren't happy with. Holm secretly sympathised with them. Live and let live was a motto he tried to abide by, but he had to admit he was slightly uncomfortable with Javed's overt sexuality. He put it down to his age, lumping Javed in with a jumble of things he found difficult that included smartphones, self-scan supermarket checkouts and music streaming.

'This is good,' Javed said without looking up, somehow sensing it was Holm at his shoulder. 'CCTV from a building near the scene. We've already got a match on one of the attackers.'

'Really?' Holm began to feel a glimmer of hope. He glanced down at the screen where Javed had zoomed in on an image. A young man stood with an automatic rifle in his hands. He wore a chequered *shemagh* round his head, but part of the covering had slipped away to reveal his face. The man had a beard and his features were indistinct, but Holm knew only a few data points were needed for the facial recognition software to pick a match. 'Who is he?'

'Mohid Latif.' Javed half turned to Holm. 'And he's British.'

'British?' Holm looked closer. 'Bloody hell.'

'Yeah, that's what I thought. A British citizen carrying out an attack on foreign soil and we missed him. The Spider's going to blow her top.'

'Is Latif on our radar?'

'He's on a long list. A very long list. Three years ago he was questioned by police regarding the distribution of some pamphlets.'

'And we did nothing?'

Javed didn't answer, merely made a face and shrugged.

'Where's Huxtable?' Holm said. He couldn't see the deputy director anywhere in the room.

'Prowling.' Javed raised his hand, palm down, and wiggled his fingers. A spider creeping forward. 'And hungry. I hope you've got something for her.'

'Christ.' Holm felt his knees weaken and moved to a spare workstation. He slumped down in the chair and logged in using a fingerprint scanner. 'There was nothing, Farakh, nothing.'

'Sure.' Javed held his hands up. 'You don't have to convince me, sir. You couldn't have done any more.'

You. Holm noted the word. Javed was distancing himself. He didn't want to be caught in the sticky web that was awaiting Holm.

Javed got up from his station and walked off, and Holm turned to the far wall where a towering bank of screens showed news reports, live operation maps, stock prices and currency rates. A glance at one of the screens told Holm the Tunisian dinar was under pressure. The markets were spooked. Tourists had only just begun to return to the country after the atrocities a few years back at the Bardo National Museum and the resort of Sousse. Now they would stop coming once more and the foreign exchange the country needed would dry up.

Holm refocused on his own screen. He needed to rustle up some kind of supporting document. Bullet points. A graphic or two. Concluding remarks. He bent to the keyboard and flicked his fingers over the keys.

'Stephen.' His name sounded cold and harsh, an icicle spiking into his right ear. He turned to see Fiona Huxtable beside him. 'Nice of you to join us.'

Holm had more than ten years on Huxtable but he couldn't help thinking of his boss as a stern headmistress, him as the naughty schoolboy. The image was one he was sure she cultivated. Her stick-thin body was always bulked out by a thick tweed jacket and skirt, but whatever she wore did little to disguise her angular figure. *Bony*, a colleague of Holm's had described her as, and he hadn't only been talking about Huxtable's appearance.

'I came as soon as I heard.' Holm began to rise out of politeness, but Huxtable's hand pressed down on his shoulder and held him in his seat. 'Seven dead. Not good.'

He didn't know why he'd said that. The casualty numbers only served to compound his error and that it was *not good* was bloody obvious.

'The latest figure is nine.' Huxtable's gaze flicked to a nearby screen and then back at Holm's monitor. She appeared to be reading the three bullet points Holm had managed to think up. 'Unsubstantiated reports? Is that the best you can do, Stephen?'

Holm opened his mouth to say something. He was aware of Huxtable's hand still resting on his shoulder. A reminder she was in control. That he was in her grasp.

'My office in one hour with something better than this crap.' She removed her hand. 'And don't even think of mentioning you-know-who, OK?'

With that she was gone, leaving Holm in a sweat as he struggled to add something meaningful to his document. Something that didn't involve *you-know-who*.

Chapter Three

You-know-who was the cause of all of Holm's sleepless nights and most of his problems. He blamed you-know-who for his increased drinking, the loss of half of his hair, for his marriage break-up, for the fact he lived in a one-bedroom flat with a fridge stuffed with ready meals, for his lack of supportive colleagues at work, for his failure to progress up the ladder in the last few years. And now for this farce which could well lead to his dismissal. Of course he'd be offered the chance to take early retirement, the easy way to sanitise the whole unpleasant business. *After many years distinguished service… blah, blah, blah.* There'd be a short announcement in the internal daily briefing, a glass of sherry in Huxtable's office, the meeting possibly graced with the presence of the head of MI5, Thomas Gillan. Back in the situation room a couple of bowls of hastily purchased snacks would be placed on a desk, and an envelope would be handed over. Inside a card signed by everyone and an Amazon gift voucher because nobody could be bothered with leaving presents these days. A few words would be said. There'd be some reminiscing about the good old days but nobody would mention the reason he was leaving the service. Nobody would mention *you-know-who.*

You-know-who. MI5 code name RAVEN. Street name – almost certainly an alias – Taher.

Taher…

The name hissed through Holm's thoughts, the two syllables drawn out as if part of a Siren's song calling him to his doom.

Time and again he'd been beguiled by the name, led astray, his attention diverted from other mundane but important tasks. He could almost hear the whispers at his leaving do. A nod and a wink as he turned his back to reach for a bread stick.

'*The poor boy lost it, don't you know? Became obsessed.*'

'*Obsessed?*'

'*Yes. Focused on chasing one individual instead of disrupting the network. Old style. Couldn't update himself to deal with the reality of the post-9/11 world. Analogue not digital. Social circles rather than social media. So sad.*'

A pause. Then a joke at Holm's expense.

'*Not that the old boy had much of a social circle. Somewhat of a loner, wasn't he?*'

Muttering in agreement. A laugh. Some management speak and then a segue into a safer topic, perhaps football or cricket or the extramarital dalliances of a celebrity couple that someone in Five had inadvertently picked up on a phone intercept.

Somewhat of a loner.

With a tinge of bitterness Holm had to admit it was true. He hadn't played the game in either the police force or the security services. No union, no Masonic handshake, he hadn't gone to the right school or university, and he definitely wasn't what they called clubbable.

He batted away the daydream and focused on his document, but nothing came to mind except a bunch of lame excuses, none of which would wash with Huxtable.

Sod it.

He looked up from his terminal and across at the screens. One news channel showed the centre of Tunis teeming with military personnel, another a beach full of parasols and sun loungers but devoid of tourists. A third focused on the glossy black door at Downing Street. A caption said the prime minister would shortly be making a statement.

'It was you, Taher,' Holm whispered to himself. 'I know it was.'

As soon as he'd spoken he looked up to check nobody had overheard. The mere mention of Taher's name would have Huxtable frothing at the mouth. For her, Taher was a sign of Holm's failings. The single-mindedness that had served him well when he'd been in Special Branch was frowned upon here. Phrases like the bigger picture, a connected world, and – Holm's favourite meaningless platitude – one bullet doesn't end a war, went down well. Holm's old-fashioned ideas did not. You didn't wear out shoe leather these days and you didn't cultivate informants in smoky back-room bars. You didn't chase after a man the security services were beginning to think was a myth deliberately propagated by the terrorists to confound their enemies.

Holm had to admit there wasn't much to go on. The first time the intelligence services had come across Taher had been in text messages found on a number of mobile phones that had been discovered in the UK, France and Belgium. Local ISIS operatives mentioned a free agent who was revered as some kind of emerging jihadi superhero. For a number of years he'd been rumoured to have been involved in almost every atrocity that had taken place in Europe. If he wasn't actually there, then he was the one doing the planning and supplying the means and the money. However, recently the leads had dried up, leaving behind nothing but speculation. Even Holm's most trusted informant had changed his tune.

'You want to believe, then you believe,' he'd said. 'But I've come to the conclusion Taher is no more than a straw man you've created to justify your failures.'

It was true that almost everything about Taher was unsubstantiated: his age, background, country of origin. Was he a refugee or home grown? British, French, German, Belgian? Did he wear his beliefs on his sleeve or was he in some form of deep cover? Was he in a relationship? Did he have a job? Where did he get his money from? Was he, in fact, a composite of more than one individual?

For a couple of years Huxtable had tolerated Holm's obses-sion because he was her spin of the roulette wheel, the couple of quid bunged on the lottery, a tenner on a long-odds outsider at the Grand National. Besides, what else could Holm usefully do? He was regularly sidelined on operations because he was too long in the tooth. He was passed over for younger men and women, graduates who had multiple languages and high-level computer skills. Holm spoke decent French and, in his pursuit of Taher, had picked up a smattering of Arabic. His German was limited to ordering beer and his Russian and Chinese non-existent. He could just about use a computer but when his colleagues began to talk of IP addresses and proxy servers and the dark web his eyes began to glaze over. Was tradecraft dead, he wondered. Didn't anybody follow a hunch any more?

Holm shook himself and concentrated on his screen. The hour had slipped by and there were no more bullet points. He logged off from the terminal and rose from the chair.

–

The man the security services knew as Taher sat in the back seat of a minibus bouncing along a rough track some fifty miles to the south-west of Tunis. After two hours of driving the stifling air was getting to him. The vehicle's air con was broken and the windows were jammed shut against the dust. In the next row of seats were two of his foot soldiers, Mohid Latif and Anwan Saabiq. Saabiq reached up and slid a finger under his *shemagh* to scratch his neck. The skin was slick with sweat. A laugh came from the driver's seat up front, hardened eyes flicking up to the rear-view mirror.

'Bloody Europeans,' the man said, his English heavily accented. 'If you can't stand the heat, that's what you say, no?'

Taher met the man's eyes but remained silent. The driver – Kadri – was Tunisian, nothing more than a hired thug, and he wasn't there to ask questions. Taher had seen the way the man had caressed the assault rifle he'd used in the attack. It was as if the gun was a pet or a woman. Kadri was ex-military, knew how to handle himself, but the way he'd held the weapon suggested he derived pleasure from killing. For Taher the use of guns and explosives was only a means to an end; for Kadri it was something approaching a fetish. Still, Kadri had been employed because they needed a local guide for the mission. Taher and the others didn't speak the language and, once you were away from the tourist areas, foreigners stuck out a mile. Kadri could mutter a few words, thrust out a handful of dinar or raise a fist, and trouble faded away. They'd never have been able to navigate the heaving streets of Tunis without him, never have found the route which had taken them south from the city into desolate, rolling hills populated with scrawny pine trees and little else. In short, the mission could not have succeeded had Taher been naive enough to believe he had all the answers.

Rely on others. Depend on no one.

His uncle had taught him the wisdom of the little phrase that made no sense, and Taher had always thought the sentiment it encapsulated was appropriate to his situation. Surrounded by those who venerated him and would die for him, he was nevertheless alone in the world. Aside from his uncle nobody knew the real Taher. He was a mystery, his name an alias. Perhaps, more correctly, a cipher. A jumble of letters that represented a man but had come to stand for something much more. His followers whispered his name with reverence and awe. *Taher...* the man behind Paris and London. Had he been in Berlin too? Barcelona? Sydney? Bangkok? Rumour had it he'd been a fleeting shadow in all those places and more. In truth the legend had grown larger than the man, and many attacks were linked to him even if he'd had no part in their planning, financing or execution. At first Taher had shied away from the notoriety, but he soon realised the legend was someone the security services chased in vain. When they shone a light into the dark, the shadow faded away, and the brighter the light, the quicker the shadow dissipated.

Who was this man, people wondered. It was something Taher himself often worried about too. Who exactly was he? A freedom fighter? A religious zealot? A soldier of fortune? A thrill seeker? A psychopath? When he looked into his soul he knew there was a little of each in there, his identity a jumble of motivations. He was human like everyone else, and surprisingly, considering the number of people he'd killed, he had human feelings. Guilt, self-doubt, anger. Even, sometimes, love.

They'd followed a cattle truck for the past few miles, unable to overtake, but finally Kadri pulled off to the right and took a tiny track down to a motley collection of buildings.

'My brother's farm,' Kadri said. He laughed. 'Goods for, how you say, *export*, yes?'

There didn't seem to be any animals or crops, just a main dwelling with sheet tin on the roof. An array of solar panels in a dusty field to one side. Some hefty steel doors on a brick outbuilding. Whatever Kadri's brother farmed, it wasn't going to end up on any supermarket shelf. Taher knew better than to ask. They were overnighting here and then Latif and Saabiq were journeying to a training camp close to the border with Algeria. Taher was heading for the tourist resort of Al Hammamet, from where a boat would take him across to Italy. He'd travel through mainland Europe and enter the UK secretly. In a few weeks, when they'd completed their training, Latif and Saabiq would do the same.

In front of him, Saabiq turned round, unease written across his face.

'Are we good?' Saabiq said. He nodded at the ramshackle homestead. 'Safe?'

Taher nodded. Much as he despised Kadri, at least he knew how to stay calm. Saabiq was a worrier and worriers made Taher nervous. Latif, the other man he'd brought with him from the UK, was far more reliable.

The vehicle lurched to a stop and Kadri wrenched open the door and climbed out. He pulled the side door across.

'I told you, nothing to it.' He spread his arms and then pointed to the dwelling where an older version of Kadri was pushing aside a tattered curtain and waving. 'Now we can have a beer and some food and afterwards you can sample some of my brother's stock.' His eyes flicked to the building with the stout doors. 'Fresh, young, and – how do you say – *tight*?'

The older version of Kadri – his brother, Taher assumed – came across to help with the bags. He spat on the ground and grinned.

'You boys up for that?' Kadri said, laughing. 'Some booze and some pussy? Or would you prefer a fucking prayer mat and your right hand, hey?'

With that, Kadri bellowed another laugh and turned to embrace his brother.

Taher leaned back in his seat and closed his eyes.

'Taher?' Saabiq. Right in his face like an annoying little insect that needed to be swatted.

'What?' Taher blinked, pushed Saabiq away and climbed out of the minibus. He wanted to find somewhere to pray, have something to eat and get his head down.

'I was wondering…' Saabiq gestured across to the low brick building. He looked more nervous now than he had before the job. 'Do you think Kadri would be offended if we skip the pussy?'

Taher didn't care one way or another. Offending Kadri was the least of his worries, but now the man was turning from his brother.

'My brother's farm,' he said, boasting. He indicated the building with the heavy doors. 'You like it? You want? Don't worry, English boys, these girls are clean. And you no pay. *Gratuit*. Free.'

'No.' Taher waved Kadri off. 'We'll pray and eat and sleep.'

Taher shepherded Latif and Saabiq away to their quarters, thankful they were in a small byre separate from the main dwelling.

Hours later Taher woke in the darkness. A desert chill had descended and he was about to pull another blanket over himself when he heard the cries of a child. Saabiq and Latif lay alongside him, both fast asleep. Taher pushed himself up from the hard floor and made his way outside. A clear sky blazed with a million stars, and a dim light filtered through the ragged curtain that served as a door to the main building. He walked across and pulled aside the curtain. An oil lamp hanging from a roof truss illuminated the living space. Kadri sat slumped on a chair, his trousers by his ankles, a young girl with her face in his lap, Kadri's paw of a hand on the back of her head.

'So you do want, yes?' Kadri said, looking up as Taher entered. The Tunisian laughed. 'You can have this one when she's finished or my brother will sort you out. Mansour?'

Kadri shouted into the night as Taher strode across the room. He looked down at the girl. She was twelve or thirteen. No more. In one swift movement he reached for the Glock he'd stuffed in the back of his belt. He brought the gun round and jammed it in Kadri's mouth. Kadri grabbed for the gun with both hands, the skin on his knuckles whitening as he gripped the barrel. Taher shook his head.

'Don't move,' he said. The girl looked up and Taher said to her gently: 'No one is going to hurt you.'

The girl wiped the back of her hand across her mouth and rose to her feet. She looked up at Kadri for a moment and then ran from the room.

'Mmmm,' Kadri mumbled as Taher forced the barrel deeper. 'You… can't…'

'I can.' Taher pulled the trigger and something on the far side of the room shattered as the bullet hit it. Kadri shuddered and slumped over. Taher wrenched the gun free and crossed to the back of the living area where a corridor led to several small rooms. He ran to the first one to find Kadri's brother staggering out in a daze, a pistol in his hand. Taher fired once and the man crumpled to the floor.

As Taher left the dwelling, Latif and Saabiq came out of the guest accommodation, woken by the gunshots.

'Get your stuff,' Taher said. He walked over to the brick building. There was a sliding metal door secured with two bolts. He slid the bolts and opened the door. In the darkness he could see nothing, but he could smell the urine and the shit and hear the low ululating.

'You're free to leave,' he said. '*Allez, allez.*'

Taher strode away. Latif had found the keys to the minibus and was in the driver's seat. Saabiq piled their kit into the rear. Taher climbed up and then turned back. The young girl stood a few steps away, a pale ghost under the starlight. For a moment, as she met his gaze, he wondered about her fate and what would become of her. A child could be changed by events, choose to take a certain path depending on circumstance. Left, right, straight ahead. Tomorrow is the first day of the rest of your life, little one, he whispered to himself. Choose wisely.

He faced forward and tapped Latif on the shoulder.

'Go,' he said.

Chapter Four

It had been three months since Silva had last seen her. A quarter of a year. A fraction of the lifespan left for Silva. All of that remaining for her mother.

A Saturday in Tunisia. Carthage International Airport crowded with people, a seemingly never-ending column of tourists disgorging into the arrivals hall. As Silva walked out, she scanned the waiting crowd. Francisca da Silva stood among the taxi drivers, holding up her own piece of paper, the word *BecBec* scrawled on in marker pen. The pet name was from Silva's childhood, from when she was just toddler and could only say her own name in a garbled approximation. Her mother smiled, her face framed by long dark hair just beginning to grey. Fine lines at the eyes and mouth. Lips adorned with a subtle shade of pink lipstick. As Silva approached she launched into French, matching the buzz of the language echoing all around.

'*Êtes-vous Mademoiselle BecBec?*'

'Mum.' Silva blushed. Somehow, whatever the situation, her mother had the ability to make Silva laugh. 'Stop it.'

'You're not BecBec or you're no longer a mademoiselle? If it's the latter then you might at least have invited me to the wedding.'

Silva dropped her bag and hugged her mother. They'd always been close, but the past couple of years had reinforced their bond, and Silva had come to depend on her mother throughout her court-martial and during her time in the military prison.

'I'm still single, Mum. With my prospects I will be for a while, I reckon.'

'Nonsense.' Francisca bent and hefted Silva's bag onto her shoulder. She turned and gestured towards the exits. 'What about that nice American boy you were seeing?'

'*Were seeing* is the operative phrase. He's past tense.'

'He dumped you?'

'No. It was the other way around.'

'Well.' Francisca led Silva across the concourse and they emerged into harsh sunlight. She raised a hand at the queue of taxis, and quipped as she did so. 'There'll be another one along soon.'

A battered yellow minicab took them into the centre of Tunis along palm-lined roads, Francisca pointing out various sights including the National Bardo Museum, infamous now for the terrorist attack that had taken place there rather than for its collection of wondrous mosaics.

Her mother had ensconced herself in a couple of rooms at a small hotel on the edge of the Medina souk. The hotel's colonial facade had seen better days but inside the place was clean and tidy, if a little spartan. Francisca apologised for the surroundings.

'Not like when I was with *The Times*.' She walked to the window and opened the shutters. The sounds of the busy street drifted in. 'In those days my expense account was bottomless.'

'It's better than I'm used to,' Silva said. 'Home or abroad.'

For a moment the street noise was all there was, Francisca standing by the window before turning.

'I'm sorry, Rebecca. About what happened. Sorry you're not over it.'

'I don't know if I'll ever be over it. I don't think it's something you can recover from. Perhaps it's something you're not *supposed* to recover from.'

Francisca slipped across the room and embraced her daughter. 'Hush. What sort of talk is that?'

Silva shrugged. Her mother held her for a moment and then went over to the bed. She sat and patted the mattress. Silva moved across and sat beside her.

'When you were little, when you were BecBec, you had a rabbit, remember?'

'Twitch,' Silva said. 'He escaped and you said he'd gone to find some bunny friends. Later, when I was older, you told me what really happened: Twitch had been killed by the dog next door.'

'I think you were eleven or twelve by then. Some of my friends said I was cruel, but I thought it was important to tell you the truth. I wanted you to understand that life could be unpalatable.'

'The boy in Afghanistan was a kid, Mum, not a rabbit. And it wasn't next door's dog that killed him, it was me.'

'I wasn't trying to draw a parallel, merely illustrating that shit happens. It happens to people it shouldn't happen to, people who've done nothing to deserve it. It even happens to pet rabbits. There's not much we can do but face up to reality.'

'It didn't just happen though, I pulled the trigger.'

'You pulled the trigger, but if al-Qaeda hadn't carried out the 9/11 attacks you wouldn't have been there in the first place. If the CIA hadn't funded the Mujahideen in their fight against the Soviet Union in the eighties then perhaps Bin Laden wouldn't have risen to prominence. And so on. How far back do you want to go?'

'I pulled the trigger.' Silva repeated the bare facts she'd mulled over so many times. Felt the tears coming yet again. 'In the end it was down to me.'

'Sweetheart.' Her mother raised a hand and stroked Silva's hair. It was as if Silva was a child once more. 'It hurts me to see you like this. At some point you have to move on.'

'I know.' Silva had told herself as much dozens of times, but the words refused to alter the reality of the situation. Still, her mother was correct, and invariably the advice she gave was the right course of action. 'I'll try to put it aside while I'm here.'

'There's no need to do that, we'll give it a good talking over, right?' Francisca smiled. 'But perhaps leave it at the airport with the unclaimed baggage when you return to the UK, yes?'

Silva nodded and changed the subject. 'What will we do?'

'See the museum, go to the beach, visit the souks, eat, drink, and – this most important of all – laugh!'

They'd done all of that and, for the week she'd been there, Silva had almost forgotten about Afghanistan. When they parted in the departure hall at the airport, she'd kissed her mother and waved as she passed through to airside. She'd turned back to see her mother fumbling with a piece of paper, unfolding it, and waving it above her head. It was the sign she'd held up when Silva had arrived: *BecBec*.

'*Au revoir*, BecBec,' her mother shouted. And then, in Portuguese, '*Até breve.*'

See you soon…

–

The document Holm had cobbled together on the day of the attack hadn't been received well, and Huxtable gave him two weeks to write a full report.

'Something I can show to Thomas Gillan,' she said. 'Something he can show to the prime minister. Pretty pictures and pie graphs. Lots of confusing figures. Plenty of footnotes and appendices. You know the kind of thing.'

When he strolled across Vauxhall Bridge and met Palmer for lunch in a pub round the corner from the SIS building, Palmer reached out a hand and patted Holm on the shoulder.

'Can't win them all, mate,' he said. 'Wouldn't be fair on the rest of us. We all like someone to blame. Makes us feel better.'

Brighter by the weekend. Finding a positive even when the chips were down. Palmer's generous and optimistic nature was the opposite of Holm's 'glass half empty' outlook on life.

'The Belgian lead you gave me was bogus,' Holm said as Palmer bought a couple of beers. 'Without it I wouldn't have advised Huxtable that an attack on UK soil was imminent.'

'The bogus Belgian, yes.' Palmer sipped his pint and made a face. 'Eighty per cent was as far as I was prepared to go, remember? It was your call.'

'Yes, but I expect an eighty per cent certainty to mean…' Holm paused and glanced down at the froth on his beer. Palmer was right. The other side of eighty per cent was twenty. It was his call. 'Didn't you lot have an inkling about Tunisia? I mean, you're head of the North Africa station, there must have been something?'

'Gossip, but nothing substantial, nothing we could act on. Nothing as good as eighty per cent.'

'No word on Mohid Latif?'

'We don't know where he is but according to the Border Force there's no record he travelled to Tunisia.'

'He's in the bloody picture at the cafe, Harry. Of course he travelled to Tunisia.'

'I know, but there's nothing from Tunisian immigration or our contacts on the ground. The only sliver of intelligence is that the Tunisian authorities have identified another one of the attackers as Adnan Kadri, a well-known people trafficker. The bad news is that he's dead.'

'The Tunisians killed him?'

'No. It appears he was taken out by rival traffickers.' Palmer raised his hands in apology. 'Sorry I can't be more helpful.'

Holm didn't really know what he'd been hoping for. Perhaps some reference to Latif which meant Six could take part of the blame. If not that then a miracle. At least the lunch had been good and Palmer had paid.

Holm slogged over the report for the next ten days and then attached the document to an email, pressed send, uttered a short prayer and waited for a response. It came the following afternoon as he was getting ready to leave for home. He trudged up the stairs to the fifth floor and slunk into Huxtable's office, head down. When she told him to take a seat he sank into a high-backed chair in a vain attempt to disappear.

'Right.' Huxtable tapped a long-nailed finger on the desk, her voice soft but ominous. Silk laced with acid. 'I thought we needed a talk about your performance. A review.'

'Ma'am?' Holm could see a copy of his report open on the desk. 'I thought this meeting was to discuss my document on the Tunis attack?'

'No.' Huxtable made a point of closing the report and pushing it to one side. 'I don't want to pre-empt the investigation into what went wrong. However it's obvious procedure was set aside for a period of – how shall I put this? – flying by the seat of your pants?'

Holm shrugged. 'Sometimes you have to go with your gut feeling. It was either that or forget the whole thing.'

'You were chasing paper planes.'

'What can I say? Everything had gone quiet. No chatter, nothing from the field. We weren't able to verify the original source for the intel so I came to you.' Holm leaned forward. It wasn't a great shot, but at least he'd managed to get the ball back across the net. 'You had my recommendation on raising the threat level and all the information.'

'And then you did a runner?'

'I didn't leave the situation room until close to six in the morning. We'd done all we could and in the end, as you know, a joint decision was made that the intel was wrong. We had no idea of the target or the location. All we knew was a threat had been made. It could have been anywhere from Tottenham to Timbuktu. We contacted every agent we had but nobody had any info. GCHQ had nothing but the original intercept. SIS gave us a lead from Belgium but it turned out to be false. The Americans either had nothing or weren't telling us anything.'

'What's that supposed to mean?'

'You know what it means. The Americans share intelligence with us when it suits them. If it doesn't suit them they play their cards close to their chests.'

'And the evidence for this?'

Holm shook his head. He had an old friend in the CIA who'd confirmed Holm's suspicions years ago. 'Strategy and tactics, old buddy,' his friend had said. 'Two separate things. Out in the field our countries play the game in very similar ways, but at the top of the tree the policy wonks are looking at it differently. Sometimes that means not telling our allies everything even if the end result is casualties on the ground.'

'Well?' Huxtable waited for a beat. 'I'll take your silence as an indication your allegation has no basis in fact. It's similar to your obsession with Taher. Your excuse for not finding him is he has to be receiving tip-offs from inside the security services, yes? That we have a mole?'

'Well, there's—'

'Absolutely no evidence to back up your claim.' Huxtable rapped the table like a judge using a gavel to bring silence to a courtroom. 'Now, let's move on to the real reason I called you here.'

Holm let himself slump farther down into the chair, as if in doing so he might avoid the hammer blow that was surely coming.

'As you know, JTAC has always recruited the brightest and best. We're lucky to be able to draw personnel from many different branches. You came across to Five from Special Branch originally, didn't you?'

'Yes.' Holm nodded. The way Huxtable phrased it made his transfer to MI5 sound like a cold war defection, but Holm had been an obvious recruit and he'd felt he was coming to the end of his days in the police. When the call had come he'd jumped at the chance.

'You had a lot to offer back then.'

Holm flinched. Huxtable was getting to the business end of the meeting.

'Although you've had personal issues recently, I see.' She indicated a printout on the desk in front of her. She looked up and gave a flat smile. 'Still, it happens to nearly all of us from time to time.'

The inference being that nothing personal would ever happen to Huxtable.

'My wife.' Holm shrugged. There was no point in hiding anything. Huxtable was all-knowing and all-seeing. 'She left me a couple of years ago. Demands of the job, I suppose.'

'There was nothing else we should have been informed about, was there? No indiscretion on your part?'

'No.' If only there had been, he thought. 'We broke up amicably.'

A straight-out lie. But then he was good at lying. To himself as much as anyone. The split had come out of the blue and the irony of that wasn't lost on him. He'd spent his life playing detective and uncovering secrets and there was his wife carrying on with the next-door neighbour right under his nose. They'd been at it for months and if he hadn't returned home from an overseas trip unexpectedly one day and caught them screwing on the living-room floor, they'd probably have continued to pull the wool over his eyes.

'I've been thinking,' Huxtable said. 'About a new role for you.'

'I'm happy where I am.'

'Sure, but your talents are wasted behind a desk. I'm looking for somebody to get out there and be proactive, to chase down leads.'

'Isn't that what the police are supposed to do?'

'They don't have time to develop anything these days. I'm talking about the bigger picture.'

Holm noted Huxtable's use of *the bigger picture*. Noted, too, the euphemisms aplenty in her statement: *wasted behind a desk* – useless at analysis. Doing things the police *don't have time to develop* meant investigating areas they didn't feel were worthwhile. While *get out there* suggested, quite simply, that Huxtable wanted him gone from under her feet.

'And this bigger picture? Where exactly am I to find it?'

'You're aware we get thousands of pieces of information a week, most of which are never followed up? Time and time again we have people who blip on our radar but are passed over because of lack of resources. Right-wingers, left-wingers, radicals of all types intent on getting their fifteen minutes of fame. There are snippets of intelligence which, as much as we try, we can't jigsaw together. Even with AI and a bunch of algorithms we're missing these at the moment. You might just get lucky.'

'You're kicking me out of JTAC.'

'We're supposed to be the Joint Terrorism *Analysis* Centre, Stephen. The problem is your recent analysis has been wide of the mark.' That flat smile again. 'And I'm not kicking you out. I prefer to think of it as moving you sideways, OK?'

'Sideways?'

'Yes. You'll remain under the JTAC umbrella, but you'll have an office of your own, a budget and a free hand to pursue whatever leads you want within reason.' Huxtable smiled, but the look wasn't a good one. 'Take some time off to think about it, OK?'

Huxtable reached for Holm's report. She glanced at the cover before sliding the document into her out-tray. He'd been dealt with. Rubber-stamped. Filed. Her gaze moved to Holm, a quizzical expression on her face as if she was surprised to see him still there.

He struggled out of the armchair and got to his feet.

'Yes, ma'am,' he said.

–

The funeral for Silva's mother took place fifteen days after the attack. Francisca da Silva had had a wide circle of friends and colleagues and, since she'd split with Silva's father, several lovers. She'd never remarried though, and it was Silva and her father who'd dealt with the arrangements. Silva had been an emotional wreck and near useless, but her father approached the situation much as he'd have tackled a military problem. He created checklists, delegated various tasks to friends and family, drew up contingency plans and imposed strict deadlines. Now though, as they sat in a car following the hearse, Silva could see the effort involved had worn away at him. His hair had greyed years ago, but there were other signs of ageing that seemed more recent.

'Friday,' he said, aware Silva was looking at him. 'Not a good day for a burial, but it was the only slot available. Fully booked, see? Damn good business to be in, funerals. There's an endless supply of clients and they don't answer back.'

Silva wasn't sure if the reference to Friday was religious. She didn't think so. Her father had never done God and she couldn't see him starting now.

'Are you OK?' she said. He hadn't asked her the same question. Not once in the past two weeks. 'I mean, I know you and Mum were—'

'Estranged is the word,' her father said. He didn't turn to face her. Rather he appeared to be studying the back of the chauffeur's head. As if there was something there that might explain everything. 'It was her choice, you know. That we separated all those years back. She wanted something more, someone else.'

'Do you blame her? She'd had enough of the worry, Dad.'

'That's a bit rich. I reckon she was always more concerned about you than she ever was about me.'

'That's different. Parents are always worried about their children.'

'She could never understand what drove you to sign up. She hated you being in the military. I think she felt by you choosing the army that somehow I'd won and she'd lost. She wanted something quite different for you, something more noble, as if fighting for what you believe in wasn't noble enough.'

'Dad, don't. This isn't the time.'

Her father fell silent, but what he'd said about her mother wanting something different for Silva was true. She'd wanted Silva to go to university, but Silva had struggled at school.

She was clever but not studious; she excelled at sports, but not in examinations. At the behest of her father she'd taken up shooting at an early age, and at sixteen she'd won a gold medal in a junior class at the world championships. As a child she'd never associated what she did on the range with the military, but looking back she could see there was an inevitability about her future linked to her prowess with her rifle. When, at a careers fair, she'd come across an armed forces stand, she'd tried to hurry on past, but the female recruiting officer had caught her eye. Almost unwillingly she found herself drawn to the displays. The officer explained about the opportunities which were opening up for women now the UK was finally allowing them to serve in combat roles. 'You could make a difference,' she'd said, pointing to a picture of British soldiers alongside smiling Afghan children. 'We're building schools, providing sanitation, protecting the local population from those who want to impose their barbaric ideologies on them.'

Back home the notion had festered. She knew her mother would be against it. Since her parents had divorced her mother's world view had changed. She'd emerged from the domineering influence of Silva's father like a butterfly breaking free of a cocoon. Her politics were increasingly left wing and she'd recently moved from a secure, well-paid job with *The Times*'s foreign desk to a position with a news agency that specialised in covering the Middle East and Africa. However when, after several weeks of considering the options, Silva told her mother she was thinking of a military career, she'd been surprised by the reaction. Rather than dismissing the idea out of hand, her mother encouraged her to do some research and make up her own mind. If Silva was happy, then she'd be happy, she said. Silva never kidded herself her mother had been wholeheart-edly in favour of her career choice, especially after all that had happened to her, but she never realised she'd *hated* it.

If that was the truth then her mother had hidden it well. Even after Afghanistan, when Silva had been in the military prison, her mother had been nothing but supportive and there'd never been a word of criticism. Perhaps, Silva thought, unconditional love and support was what being a parent was all about. What it was *supposed* to be about.

She turned to look at her father. He sat rigid, staring forward, unaware how much his words had hurt. It was precisely because she'd wanted to help people in the same way her mother had done that she'd joined up. Sure, she'd been a muddle-headed, idealistic teenager, but the sentiment had been genuine. To know the truth about her mother's feelings was a bittersweet agony. Bitter on account of the disapproval, sweet because it highlighted the unconditional love. And her mother had been wrong about who'd won: she'd joined up in spite of her father, not because of him.

Until the incident in Kabul, Silva had never regretted her career choice. The army had meant she could continue to shoot and they'd given her time off to compete. In return she became a poster girl for the recruiting officers, highlighting the very things that had attracted her when she herself had signed up. That effect was magnified when she won a bronze medal at the Olympics. Overnight she was transformed into a minor celebrity. Her picture appeared on the news, there were offers for product endorsements and speaking engagements, and she was shortlisted for awards. Of course the fact she'd been successful and in the public eye meant when the time came, the fall was much harder. Still, through all the chaos, the ups and downs, her mother had stood by her.

Silva remembered the day of her release from prison. Sharp words, a pile of civvy clothes, an officer handing her the letter announcing her formal dismissal from the army. She'd been marched to the gates and had stepped into another life. As she'd trudged away towards the main road, not really knowing what the hell to do next, she'd heard a familiar voice call out her name.

Rebecca!

She'd turned and there, a few paces away, stood her mother. Silva had collapsed in her arms, all the hardness and bravado of the past year gone, nothing but tears left.

'You know what?' Her father's words cut into her thoughts. He'd turned from his study of the chauffeur's head. 'The ironic thing is she's the one who's dead in a military conflict and we're still alive. You get how that works, because I'm afraid I don't.'

'I don't get anything much at the moment.'

'She was a journalist, for God's sake.' Her father shook his head. 'Bloody wrong place. Bloody wrong time. If it was down to me I'd bomb the fuck out of the bastards and be done with it.'

'We tried that. I was there, remember? And anyway, who exactly do you bomb?'

Her father said nothing for a few minutes. They drove through winding country lanes between hedges bloated with thick summer greenery. A church spire in the distance seemed to get no closer.

'Are you going to carry on working as a postie?'

'I'm on sick leave.'

'You mean on account of your mother's death? Compassionate leave?'

'No, Dad. Sick leave.' Silva tapped her head even though her father was now looking forwards again. 'Mental health. Any sign of stress and they sign you off. Like you might contaminate the letters or something.'

'And *are you* mental?'

'I don't know yet. I was pretty sure I was, but then I thought about what happened to me. Considering the circumstances I'm probably verging on being almost normal.'

'That's good to hear, Rebecca. Normal. Good to hear. Your grandmother was nutty, remember? Very difficult to deal with.'

'She had dementia, Dad.'

'Whatever you want to call it, she annoyed the hell out of me.'

They rounded a corner and the church was there. A thin spire touching a blue sky. A grassy bank surrounding an acre of graveyard. Cars parked on the verges. People waiting.

They climbed from the car and heads nodded and there were half smiles intended to show sympathy. Silva spotted a government minister, tried to put a name to the face but failed. There was a local MP and a large group of her mother's friends and co-workers from Third Eye News, the agency she worked for. Neil Milligan, the proprietor and chief editor of the agency, raised a hand. The poor man looked abject. Standing at a discreet distance were several photographers and a TV crew.

Silva began to greet some of the mourners before turning to see what had happened to her father. He stood by the limousine talking to the driver as if he had nothing better to do than pass the time in idle chit-chat. He shook the man's hand and came across to Silva.

'Colour Sergeant Wilkins. Gulf War,' he said. 'I knew I recognised him from somewhere. Top bloke.'

Chapter Five

A couple of weeks after the funeral, Silva's father called her. It was the only contact she'd had with him aside from a package he'd sent her containing the keys to her mother's place in Wiltshire and some documents relating to the will Silva had to sign and return.

'You need to come and visit, Rebecca,' he said. 'Asap. Think you can make it tomorrow?'

'Today was my first shift back at work, Dad,' Silva said. 'What is it, are you ill?'

'I'm fine, you're the one who needs to be ill. Tomorrow. Tell them you're mental again. That you might infect those letters. Get here before lunch. Shall we say eleven hundred hours, sharp?'

That evening she ran through the city. Followed the route she'd taken on her delivery round and pounded the same streets as she'd walked earlier. After the run she went to the seafront. A fleet of dinghies raced in the evening sun, and the ferry to Santander headed for the horizon. She returned to her boat and sat in the cockpit with a cup of cocoa. A swell caressed the hull and rocked her gently back and forth. Motion. Not staying still. It hadn't struck her until then that the constant movement was why she'd ended up living on a boat. Back when she'd bought the little yacht the intention was simply for it to be a place to go to when on leave from the army. Her mother's house was too small and her father's... well, there was no way she could have stayed there for more than a day or two.

The boat had turned out to be a godsend, providing a bolt-hole to retreat to after she'd completed her prison sentence. It was berthed in a marina that hugged the west bank of the river Plym. A collection of decaying pontoons and equally decaying yachts sat opposite an industrial quay where aggregate rumbled along conveyors from ship to shore pretty much 24/7. Freddie, the security guard who lived on the marina site in a Portakabin, was pushing seventy, but assured her he was more than a match for men half his age. He had two Dobermanns to help him but their natures could be deduced from their names: Beauty and Cinders. More often than not the dogs could be found curled up at Freddie's feet in the cabin, while he worked his way through an *ArrowWords* puzzle magazine, only occasionally glancing at the CCTV monitors. Still, the haphazard set-up suited Silva. Nobody came down the pontoon to chat to her; nobody, aside from Freddie, knew her name.

The last thing she wanted to do was visit her father. They weren't close and never had been. He was all stiff upper lip and polish your boots until you could see your face. What was on the surface was what the world saw and what was inside you kept private. Somewhere deep down there might have been some sort of love and affection for her, but if there was she'd never seen any sign of it. Her mother had been the polar opposite, wearing her heart on her sleeve, baring her soul, always telling Silva how much she loved her.

Silva sighed to herself. She owed it to her mother to go and see what her father wanted. Hard as it was to imagine, at some point her parents had cared for each other and Silva was a direct result of their union.

The next morning she called in sick. Said her first day back had been too stressful and she needed a little while longer to recover. She took her motorbike and rode hard up-country towards London. Her father lived an hour west of the city in a big old house inherited from his own father. Silva remembered the place from childhood visits to her grandparents, but she'd never lived there. Several acres of garden surrounded the house, a winding drive curling past a lake to an expanse of gravel. She followed the drive and parked up alongside a black Range Rover with smoked-glass windows. She got off her bike, removed her leather jacket, her helmet and gloves, and stood by the Range Rover for a while. She wondered if her father had all of a sudden given up his miserliness and decided to splash out on the smart new vehicle. Silva shrugged and went to the house.

Mrs Collins, her dad's long-suffering housekeeper, showed her in and through to the back where her father sat in a chair on the terrace. Next to him there was a glass-topped metal table on which stood a jug of cloudy lemonade and three glasses. The ice cubes in the jug had sharp edges and the surface of the jug was beginning to mist with condensation.

'Rebecca,' her father said as she walked over and bent to kiss him. He sat still while she did so and then brushed her away. 'You're late.'

Silva glanced at her watch. One minute past eleven. 'One hundred and fifty miles and I'm sixty seconds late. I'd say that was pretty good.'

'Pretty good, yes.' Her father watched her as she sat down. 'But not perfect.'

Silva wasn't surprised by her father's opprobrium. As a child she'd had to live up to his exacting standards, all too often failing to meet them. He'd treated her mother the same way until she'd grown tired of having the minutiae of her life controlled and micro-managed. When Silva was ten, her mother had upped and left, taking Silva with her. Looking back with the benefit of hindsight, Silva wondered if her father's nature could have been altered by his experiences in the Gulf. PTSD affected people in different ways, and his desire to control everything might have been a response to the stress he'd faced in the deserts of southern Iraq. Then again, it might not.

'You look fine,' Silva said, trying not to rise to the bait. 'I thought you might be poorly.'

'I told you I wasn't ill on the phone. Didn't you believe me?'

'There are times when people don't like to admit something's wrong with them.'

'Not me.' Her father paused and then knocked the table with his right fist. 'You got the keys and the documents I forwarded from the solicitor?'

'Yes.'

'You'll go there on your way back to Plymouth? Check the house is OK?'

'Sure,' Silva agreed without much enthusiasm. She changed the subject and gestured at the three glasses on the table. 'Are we expecting a guest? Or are you going ask your servant to join us?'

'Don't wind me up, Rebecca. Mrs Collins isn't my servant.'

'Lover?'

'Stop it.'

'Well, this is nice.' Silva leaned back in her chair. Below the terrace a large area of lawn led down to the lake. There was a boathouse at one end and a small island in the centre. 'Just think, I could have been delivering the mail to the good people of Plymouth instead of sitting here getting bored.'

'When were you last up?'

'Must be a year ago. You've repaired the boathouse, I see.'

'Repaired the boathouse, dredged and restocked the lake. A lot's been done in the house too. You'll see later.'

'Later?'

'You're staying over.'

'I am?' Silva turned to look at the house. 'You've hardly been in touch in the past few years and now you want to play happy families? I don't think so.'

'This isn't about me, this is about you.'

'I'm fine. I'm OK with where I live, OK with my job. I know you don't think being a postie is any kind of living, but it's risk free.'

'You were never one to be scared. You got a commendation for bravery on your first tour.'

'I'm not talking about what's out there.' Silva swept her arm and turned back to her father. She tapped her forehead. 'I'm talking about what's up here.'

'It was an accident. They tend to happen in war. Nobody was to blame.'

'Funny how you didn't come to my defence at the time. "No comment" was all they could get out of you.'

'I couldn't be seen to question the chain of command, but now I'm retired from the Ministry I can speak the truth. You weren't at fault.'

'What is this, "kiss and make up" time? Has Mum's death brought about a new sense of your own mortality? All of a sudden you feel responsible for your little baby?'

'Nothing like that.' Her father lowered his shoulders and shook his head.

Silva turned back to the lake. A rowing boat slipped into view from behind the island. A man sat in the boat, pulling slowly for a small jetty next to the boathouse. The boat slid across the lake and came alongside the jetty and the man climbed out. He was a similar age to her father, perhaps mid-sixties, with short grey hair. He wore a light-coloured suit at least one size too big. A floppy green hat which had seen better days sat on his head. He bent and lifted a fishing rod and a creel from the boat and walked across the lawn towards them.

He came up the steps to the terrace with a smile on his face. He dropped the fishing gear, removed the floppy hat, and made a small bow. The hat was adorned with a number of colourful feathers. Fishing flies.

'Matthew Fairchild,' he said, pulling a business card from a pocket and pressing it into her hand. 'I am so pleased to meet you, Ms da Silva.'

'You can call her Rebecca or Becky,' her father said. 'Plain Difficult once you've known her a while.' He reached for the jug and began to pour the lemonade. 'Any luck out there?'

'Oh yes, a nice brace.' Fairchild sat on a spare chair and bent and lifted the flap on the fishing creel. Two large rainbow trout lay inside. 'Do you fish, Rebecca?'

'No,' Silva said.

'You should learn. There's a certain satisfaction to it. Choosing the correct fly, finding the lie, executing the perfect cast. You have to be patient though. Cast and cast again until the fish bites. Then you have him. Or her.' Fairchild winked. 'Once the fish is hooked all you have to do is reel the beauty in.'

Silva looked at Fairchild. Wondered if he was the sort of older guy who would make a play for a woman less than half his age. If that was his game he could forget it.

'Who exactly are you, Mr Fairchild?' Silva said. 'More importantly, why has my father asked me here to meet you?'

'She's bright, Kenneth,' Fairchild said, almost as if Silva wasn't there. He closed the flap on the creel. 'Very bright.'

'No comment,' Silva's father said. 'But don't forget she was a minute late.'

'It was a two-and-a-half-hour journey. A minute is less than one per cent. Such a small margin of error. We can overlook that, I'm sure.'

'Who are "we"?' Silva said.

'Something has come up.' Her father hunched forward and tapped his nose. Lowered his voice again. 'Regarding your mother.'

'Mum?' Silva turned to Fairchild and back to her father. 'Is this to do with the probate?'

'Not exactly,' Fairchild said. 'I have a proposal for you, Rebecca.'

'I don't think so.'

'It's not what you think,' her father said. 'This is work.'

'If it's a job offer, you can forget it. I've got a job.'

'Not a real job. You're a postman, for God's sake.'

'I'm not a post*man*, actually.' Silva's patience was wearing thin. Visiting had been a bad idea. 'Although you'd probably be quite happy if I was. You'd have an heir then, wouldn't you? A proper heir. A male heir.'

'Should I leave you two for a while?' Fairchild shifted in his seat. He bent to pick up the fishing rod. 'You sound as if you need a few minutes to discuss things. Family matters. I quite understand, after all it's been a distressing time for both of you.'

'Nonsense.' Silva's father dismissed Fairchild's suggestion. 'Take her out on the boat, Matthew. Drop the mud weight overboard and don't come back until it's sorted.'

'Rebecca?' Fairchild shrugged. 'Shall we try that? Just so you can hear me out?'

Silva looked from Fairchild to her father and back again. Sighed.

'Whatever,' she said.

–

After taking his enforced break, Holm returned to work to find his new role meant a shift to a different office. The place was a tiny box room under a staircase. A couple of computers sat on what appeared to be desks from a school classroom, and a brown filing cabinet stood sandwiched between them. The two office chairs had seen better days and the single telephone was so ancient it looked like it was made of Bakelite and had come from the Cabinet War Rooms in Whitehall. There was, Holm noted with some dismay, no window.

He went over to the filing cabinet and pulled open one of the drawers. It was empty aside from a solitary typed index card that bore a reference to the IRA and Bobby Sands. Holm left the card where it was and slid the drawer shut. The events mentioned were from before his time in MI5, before his spell in Special Branch. He'd been a mere PC on the beat back when the Northern Ireland conflict had been at its height, but there was something appropriate about the card being in the drawer, him being in this room. Time had moved on and what was once relevant became nothing more than rubbish. Or, in these days of heightened concern for the environment, was slipped into the recycling bin. That was it, Holm thought. He was a product that had come to the end of its useful life and Huxtable had decided to send him off to the shredder to be pulped.

He moved across to one of the chairs and sat. To be fair to Huxtable, at least she hadn't pushed him out the door. He'd been given a chance to make amends, to work out the final couple of years he had left, to earn the right to leave without a cloud hanging over him. Holm adjusted the position of one of the computer monitors, and as he did so he thought about his new role. Basically she'd given him free rein, with the only instruction being to stay well clear of current operations. That meant he was to focus on areas other than Islamist extremism. Taher was strictly off-limits.

Which left what? Huxtable said she wanted weekly updates, but Holm knew he only had to fill a few sheets of paper with bullet points and wave them under her nose. The whole exercise was something of a charade, just a way to employ him until he could get his full pension, perhaps a means of keeping him sweet so he didn't make trouble. Yes, that had to be the truth of it. When you knew where the bodies were buried everybody was either your very best friend or your most hated sworn enemy. He'd worked for the intelligence services for long enough to realise nothing was ever quite as it seemed, but what Huxtable's ulterior motive might be didn't really concern him.

He was contemplating the fact there were *two* desks, *two* chairs and *two* computers when there was a rap on the door. Without waiting for an answer, Farakh Javed breezed in.

'Morning, boss.' Javed held a sheet of A4 paper in his right hand, in his left a cardboard tray with two coffees in disposable cups. He put the tray down on one of the desks and passed the piece of paper to Holm. 'A privilege to be involved.'

'You're not…?' Holm's mouth dropped open as Javed slipped into the spare chair and gave it an experimental swing back and forth. Any thought Holm had entertained about being able to sit in his office doing nothing except listen to a jazz CD or read a book had gone out the window. The non-existent window.

'This isn't funny though,' Javed said, gesturing at the piece of paper. 'It was stuck to the door. If I was the sensitive type I'd be taking it to my line manager and calling it harassment.'

Holm glanced down at the text written in felt tip: *The Top Top Top Secret Department*. Somebody's idea of a joke at his expense. Holm looked back at Javed. Another joke. This time, though, it could only have been played by Huxtable. He suppressed a groan.

'I know what you're thinking.' Javed lifted the lid of his coffee and slurped. He turned his head as if he was only just noticing the spartan conditions. 'What the heck did poor Farakh do to deserve this?'

'Something like that.'

'I guess I was guilty by association. Still, I seem to be the only one, huh?'

'There's isn't room for anyone else.'

'Right.' Javed took another slurp and then put the cup down, pulled out a pair of nail clippers and began to trim his nails. Holm could see he was going to have to set some ground rules. Javed smiled across at him. It was a smile that would have made the fairest maiden swoon into his arms. A trick played by Mother Nature because those fair maidens didn't stand a chance with the boy. 'So, what's the story? The only thing Spiderwoman told me was this was a special unit and we'd be operating with a wide brief. Sounds like a whole lot of fun, yes?'

'Fun?' Holm spat out the word. Farakh wasn't to blame, but Holm had the beginnings of a headache brought on by the lack of natural light and decent ventilation. 'Are you fucking joking?'

Chapter Six

'I've known your father a long time, Ms da Silva,' Fairchild said as they walked down towards the lake. 'We go back.'

'The army?'

'The army. He was a fine soldier. We were in some scrapes together in the first Gulf War.'

'You were special forces too?'

'I was. I understand the difficulties you've both faced.'

'My father has two problems with me. First, as you may have noticed, I'm a girl. Second, when I do what he would have wanted a son to do, I fuck up. Not only that, but the whole thing becomes public. I'm court-martialled and he's so embarrassed that in the end he takes early retirement from the Ministry.'

'I'm sure he's proud of your achievements. You've got an Olympic medal for shooting and were a world-class sniper, after all.'

'Class is easily lost. I should know.'

They reached the boat and Fairchild gestured for Silva to climb in. 'You might not fish, but do you row?' he said.

'Sure.' Silva clambered into the boat and sat. Fairchild took the aft seat. He pushed off from the jetty and Silva used one oar to turn them around. Once they were facing out into the lake, she dipped both oars and pulled.

The boat glided across the water and Silva pulled again. She was facing to the rear so she could see her father sitting at the table. Mrs Collins had come from the house with a newspaper and a pen. Her father was intent on doing *The Times* crossword.

'He loves you, of course,' Fairchild said. 'You do know that?'

'It's every parent's duty to love their offspring and my father would never fail to carry out his duty.'

'I'm sure it's more than duty.'

'I'm not. He loves me because it's in the rule book. Page one hundred and fifty, subsection six, paragraph two.'

Silva took several more strokes and then shipped the oars. The lake was only small and they were already nearing the centre.

'Forget about the mud weight, we'll just drift,' Fairchild said. 'See where we end up.'

'You like metaphors, don't you, Mr Fairchild?'

'I like intelligence. And, yes, wordplay. What about you?'

'I don't like waffle, so if you don't mind, could you please get to the point?'

'The point. Yes.' Fairchild looked across the lake to where a coot busied itself with a strand of green pondweed. 'She's after the snails.'

'Hello?' Silva waved an arm at Fairchild. 'I didn't think I was out here to learn about waterfowl.'

'No, of course not.' Fairchild turned back to Silva. The chit-chat was over and his face wore a serious expression. 'I was shocked when I heard about your mother's death. Very shocked. It was an appalling crime.'

'I'm done with condolences, Mr Fairchild. Sincere or not they don't help. I'm trying to forget what happened and concentrate on remembering my mother as she was.'

'Of course, that's understandable, even commendable. However, what if I told you the circumstances surrounding the attack in Tunisia aren't quite as simple as they first appeared?'

'I don't care. I can't change anything, I can't bring my mother back. Speculation is a waste of emotional energy and I don't have much of it to spare.'

'What do you know about what happened?'

'I told you, I don't want to go there.' Silva reached for the oars. She'd spent several weeks trying to banish the images she'd seen on TV and now here was Fairchild dredging it all up. 'I'll take us back to the shore. You can have a nice long chinwag with my dad about the good old days and I can get on my bike and go home and forget this conversation ever took place.'

'You haven't heard what I have to say yet.'

'I'm not interested.' Silva dipped the oars and began to turn the boat. She could feel a rising panic, emotion about to overcome her. She swallowed and gave a half smile. 'I'm sorry you've made a wasted journey, sorry you'll have to disappoint my dad. I guess he put you up to this. He can't help interfering. If I thought it was love, I'd be touched. Sadly, it's pride.'

'I think you misunderstand what's going on here. Your father came to me because we're old friends and he knew I'd be able to help. Well, I was only too happy to. The next logical step was to try and get you on board. He figured I'd be better at that than he would.'

'So this is about a job? Well, I'm grateful for the offer, but I'm going to pass.' Silva began to row. 'At least you caught some fish.'

'Perhaps I should elaborate.'

'Elaborate all you want,' Silva shrugged. 'But the answer will still be no.'

Fairchild ignored her. 'My work involves security. After I left the army I set up as a consultant of sorts. That's a loose description, anyway. I tend to work abroad, the Middle and Far East. Occasionally South America and Africa.'

'Let me guess, you run mercenaries, right?'

'I knew you were clever.'

'Not clever enough, apparently. And I doubt I'd be clever enough to work for you. I'm a risk. It wouldn't look so good for your company if I killed a swath of innocents on one of your protection jobs.'

'You shouldn't blame yourself for what happened in Afghanistan. Most people would have made the same call. The probability was the boy was a threat and you acted decisively to remove the threat and protect the patrol. To do any differently would have been negligent. In my mind you should have been given a commendation.'

'Funny, I don't remember the commendation. I do remember being court-martialled and thrown to the wolves.'

'Politics. It was important for the system to be seen to be working. You were a pawn in a game. Pawns are sacrificed so the queen can triumph. Ask yourself was it right for you to face sanction when a prime minister can give the order to kill tens of thousands and escape scot free?'

'I've done that many times. The only conclusion I've come to is the common people get stepped on while the big beasts get away.' Silva shipped the oars. They were a little way out from the jetty and the boat coasted in. 'Could you?'

Fairchild reached for the jetty as they slowed. 'They haven't caught the terrorists who killed your mother, have they?'

'No.' Silva pulled the painter from the front of the boat and tied it off. 'But I'm sure they will. It's just a matter of time.'

'You sound quite sanguine about it.'

'Look, if I was on a tour and I got the chance to slot the bastards, I would.' Silva lifted the oars from the rowlocks and stowed them in the boat. She stepped out onto the jetty. 'The problem is, I'm not, and if there's one thing my father taught me, it's don't sweat the stuff that isn't in your orders because there's nothing you can do about it. I've got to live with the way the world is.'

'Very noble.'

'Not at all, it's simply a matter of survival.' Silva bent and held the boat as Fairchild stepped out. When he had, she straightened. Tried to conceal her anger and appear gracious. 'Nice to meet you, Mr Fairchild. Give my regards to my father.'

Silva turned and walked down the jetty. She headed across the lawn and round the side of the house. As she walked she heard her father call her name. She ignored him. At the front of the house she took her helmet from the bike and pulled on her leather jacket. As she was putting her gloves on, Fairchild came out of the front door. He'd taken a shortcut through the house. Silva sat astride the motorbike and fired it up. Blipped the throttle.

'Rebecca!' Fairchild stood alongside. He shouted above the grunt of the engine. 'We need to talk!'

'We just did. Goodbye.'

'Your mother wasn't simply a journalist caught in the crossfire.' Fairchild placed a hand on Silva's shoulder. 'The news you've been fed isn't the whole truth.'

'What?' Silva shouted too, not able to fully understand Fairchild through the padding of her helmet.

'Your mother was killed deliberately. The fact the head of the women's charity was hit was a blind to throw the authorities. Your mother was the intended target and she was murdered because of a story she was working on. There are dark forces at work, Rebecca, but I know who was behind the attack and their motive. That's what I was, in a roundabout way, trying to tell you.'

'Who?'

'Turn the engine off.' Fairchild gestured at the key. Silva hesitated for a moment and then hit the kill switch and the engine died. 'That's better.'

'Who?'

'Sorry about earlier. I should have come clean instead of trying to approach the subject from a tangent. Let's go inside.' Fairchild turned to the house. 'I'll explain everything.'

'No!' Silva undid the chinstrap and removed her helmet. 'Don't play games. Who was behind the attack?'

Fairchild shrugged and nodded. He went across to the black Range Rover, opened the passenger door and retrieved a manila folder from the glovebox. He turned and walked back towards Silva, stopping a few paces away.

'This person, Rebecca.' Fairchild reached into the folder and pulled out a glossy photograph. He held it up. 'She was directly responsible for the death of your mother.'

Silva looked at the picture. It showed a woman standing at a podium. Long brown hair and catwalk-model features. Eyes like blue neon. Behind her dozens of placards held aloft by adoring supporters. To the front, flags waved by an enthusiastic crowd, their emotions whipped into a frenzy. The placards bore a single word: *Hope*.

'Karen Hope?' Silva had seen the woman many times on the news, read the approving commentaries in the papers. 'Is this some kind of sick joke?'

'I wish it was.' Fairchild pulled the picture back and looked at it himself. 'You're right about who she is though: US Congress-woman Karen Hope.'

'And how is she in any way connected to my mother's death?'

'You mother was investigating the Hope family and trod on too many toes. Quite simply she got in the way of Karen Hope's ambitions.'

'Her ambitions?'

'Hope is a virtual shoo-in for the Democratic nomina-tion. With the way the opinion polls are heading she's almost certainly going to be the next president of the United States of America.'

'And she killed my mother?'

'Correct.'

'Bullshit,' Silva said.

–

She nestled in behind a car transporter and rode along the motorway at a steady fifty-five, unable to trust herself to ride safely if she went any faster.

Fairchild had made her angry but she blamed her father for that. He'd asked her to come and visit and, if she knew him, he had to have been the one behind the crazy accusation Fairchild had made. What the purpose of such a story was, Silva had no idea. Then again she'd never been able to work out her father's motives and likely this was some kind of game or test. Pass and she'd be in his good books. Fail and his disapproval would follow. And walking out definitely fell under the *fail* heading.

Calmed by the monotony of the motorway, Silva played back everything Fairchild had said to see if she could work out exactly what was going on. Fairchild had claimed her mother was investigating Karen Hope, but that was plainly wrong. Her mother concentrated on the Middle East and North Africa, and she'd been killed while interviewing the head of a women's aid charity. When Silva had visited her in Tunisia a few months before her death, she'd been filing report after report on the people traffickers preying on the refugees prepared to risk everything to make the deadly sea crossing to Europe. Her work had nothing to do with US politics. Silva guessed there were plenty of journalists digging around looking for dirt on the congresswoman, but it was inconceivable her mother was one of them.

She tried to recall what she knew about Karen Hope to see if there was anything that might be a clue as to what her father was up to. Like the cryptic crosswords he did, his games often involved some measure of obfuscation. Peel away the obvious and perhaps the answer would reveal itself.

She knew Hope was a Democrat and was involved with the military in some way. If Silva remembered correctly the family business built up by her father was armaments. That and the fact Hope was on the right of the party gave her an 'in' with Republican voters, and broad cross-party appeal meant she was the front runner in the race to be president. Aside from the obvious military angle nothing suggested a connection to her father. Was there something there? Something from his time in the Ministry of Defence? She didn't know. If whatever he was up to was cryptic then she lacked the wherewithal to decode it.

She blipped the throttle and overtook the car transporter, noting a dark BMW with tinted windows behind her do the same. Now she thought of it, the car had been in her mirrors for several miles. Fairchild's Range Rover came to mind. It too had smoked-glass windows. Silva dismissed the coincidence and accelerated up to eighty. She rode in the fast lane for several miles, trying to clear the cobwebs and confusion from her mind. When she slowed for some congestion ahead she glanced in her mirrors again. The car was still there. For a moment a chill slipped inside her leather jacket, but then she threaded her way down between two lines of vehicles and left the BMW stuck in the stationary traffic.

When she reached Swindon she turned off the motorway and headed south to the town of Marlborough. Her mother's house lay a few miles outside the town on the banks of the young river Kennet. A lane led away from the main road and down to the river where a brick weir-keeper's cottage stood next to a foaming pool of white water. A picket fence surrounded the front garden, the grass within long and in need of a cut. Silva kicked down the stand on the bike, pulled off her helmet and listened to the rumble of the weir. As a child she'd grown used to the sound, the constant white noise so pervasive that when she'd moved away she'd found it difficult to sleep.

She slipped the keys into the lock and the door opened against a mound of letters, free newspapers and junk mail. She pushed the pile to one side and closed the door.

Silence. A waft of air filled with the scent of jasmine and coffee beans. Silva inhaled and stepped into the living room. Shelves crammed with books either side of a fireplace. A sofa with a throw and an abundance of cushions. A Turkish carpet on the floor. A plant in the window bay with leaves brown from lack of water. She dropped into the sofa and pulled a cushion to her body and hugged the softness. Remembered back to when she'd lived in this house as a teenager. Remembered the arguments and fights and the way she and her mother had rubbed each other up. Parent and child. Back then the place had seemed claustrophobic and they'd been under each other's feet with not enough space, Silva's unsuitable boyfriends matched against her mother's equally unworthy lovers. Later, when Silva was older and more world wise, the relationship had matured. Mother and daughter. Friends.

Silva wiped away tears, aware she was crying not solely for the loss of her mother. The visit to her father had crystallised the absence that had been there all along. She'd never really known him, and now her mother was dead she was alone.

She pushed herself up from the sofa. As she bent to pick up the mail she felt a breeze touch her cheek. Those smells again. Jasmine and coffee. She left the mail where it lay and turned and walked down the hall to the little kitchen. A broken jar of Java beans lay on the quarry-tiled floor. Behind the sink a window was half open. In the garden outside the white flowers of the jasmine tumbled down a wooden trellis.

Silva looked at the beans and the window. Somebody had forced the catch and knocked the beans onto the floor as they'd climbed in. She tensed and for a moment she thought of Fairchild and the 'dark forces' he'd talked of. Wondered about the black BMW with the tinted windows. She turned and looked back down the hall to where the narrow stairs led upwards. Was the intruder still here?

She moved along the hall to the stairs and stood and listened. Nothing. She went up slowly, easing her feet from step to step, trying not to make a sound. On the landing she peeked into her mother's bedroom. A jewellery box lay upturned on the bed and clothes had been pulled from a chest of drawers. The doors to a full-length cupboard stood open and several dresses lay on the floor. She moved across the landing to her mother's office. A bed, a Coldplay poster and a shelf full of shooting trophies testified to the fact this had once been Silva's room, but those were the only concessions to the past. A monitor sat on a table by the window while to one side several shelving units held an array of box files. Next to Chris Martin and his bandmates hung a huge map of the Mediterranean, North Africa and the Middle East. She reached down for the switch on the computer cabinet beneath the desk. After a few seconds a message flashed on the monitor screen.

Disc error. The internal volume is corrupted or missing. Boot from external drive? Y/N

Puzzled, she stepped back, feeling something beneath the sole of her foot. She moved her foot, bent down and picked up a tiny screw. She reached for the computer cabinet and dragged it from beneath the desk. At the back the rear panel was secured with five screws and there was a hole where the sixth should have been.

She looked at the screen again. The machine was an old one and Silva remembered her mother had used a laptop while she was in Tunisia. But where was it? All the personal possessions her mother had with her in Tunis had been sent to Silva's father; there'd been no laptop. Perhaps the device had gone to the agency her mother worked for.

Silva went back downstairs, uneasy. A local criminal wouldn't have removed the hard drive from the computer; this was something different dressed up to look like a simple burglary. She cleared up the mess on the kitchen floor and closed the window. She watered the plant in the front room and then went outside and stood by the weir. A torrent of water roared down the concrete apron and hissed into the pool below. She'd stood here many times. There was something about the way the water tumbled and churned in a froth of white. The constant motion and noise cleansed the mind of thoughts, and Silva had often found staring into the flow had the effect of putting the world to rights. This time, though, the noise was angry and more of a growl, as if her mother's death had conjured a malevolent spirit from the river.

The roar from the weir meant she didn't hear the near-silent footsteps of the man who crept across the grass behind her. But she felt his hands on her back. A hard shove and she was falling onto the slime-covered, sloping face of the weir. She crashed into the concrete sill and was swept into the churning pool below. She managed to splutter a mouthful of water before the undertow took her down into the turbulent fury of the weir. She tried to fight her way to the surface but found herself being dragged back by the force of the water and the weight of her wet clothes.

If you fall in, swim down and out.

The words had been drummed into her by her mother when Silva had been a young child. A life ring hung on a post to one side of the weir but was useless if you fell in when no one was around. It was useless if you were dragged below the surface.

Swim down and out.

Silva ignored her instinct to head up towards the light. That way was to fight the current and was always doomed to fail. Instead she kicked out and dived deep, feeling a surge of water grab her and carry her downstream away from the weir. Her knees grazed the stones on the riverbed and she pushed the bottom with her feet and shot herself towards the surface. She bobbed up twenty metres from the weir, coughed out a mouthful of water and swam towards the bank. As she pulled herself from the river she heard a squeal of tyres and a car revving, the engine sound fading into the distance as she hunched over on the soft grass and gasped for breath.

Chapter Seven

Silva spent a restless night in the cottage. She lay awake listening to every little sound: a creak on the landing, a fox screeching outside, the wind in the trees.

The previous evening she'd been on autopilot: escape from the water, get dry, find some spare clothes, treat the cuts, get some calories inside, try to rest. She realised her reaction had been a way of coping, the result of her army training. Push the emotion down and you survive, allow your feelings and fears to rise to the top and you end up making the wrong decisions. Now though, lying in the dark, the shock kicked in. Someone wanted her dead. If not that then at the very least they wanted to hurt her and scare her. But who? Fairchild's 'dark forces'? Whoever was in the black BMW?

Sometime in the predawn a car passed in the lane, the noise waking Silva from a fitful sleep. She jumped out of bed and went to the window. Headlights painted the hedgerows as the car drove away. The car was the final straw and she gave up trying to sleep and went downstairs.

She opened the back door and slipped outside into the pale light that preceded sunrise. The weir rumbled, the water churning in the pool below. She walked across to the sluice gate at the top of the weir and gripped the railings with both hands. The cold metal sent a sharp pain into the cuts on her palms. She flinched but continued to hold on, as if she needed to cling to some form of reality. She breathed in the sharp morning air, felt a mist on her face as spray rose from the frothing water, heard the sounds of birds starting their dawn chorus. All that *was* real. The other stuff, like Karen Hope, Fairchild's dark forces, the break-in and the mysterious assailant who'd pushed her into the water, was just the opposite. The realm of fiction. Things she didn't want to believe. Things she was frightened of.

Except it wasn't fiction. Somebody had attacked her.

She relaxed her grip on the railings and turned, almost expecting to see someone lunging for her, hands outstretched, intent on violence. She shivered, aware of how vulnerable she was, and hurried back into the cottage and locked the door.

Inside, she fished out a tin of rice pudding from a cupboard for breakfast and changed back into her own clothes. She spent another hour clearing up the mess the burglar had left behind and then fired up her bike and headed for north London and Third Eye News, the agency her mother had worked for.

She raced along the M4 but heavy traffic on the North Circular meant the eighty-mile journey took well over two hours, and by the time she got to Highgate it was mid-morning. The agency was located in a maisonette above a wholefood shop and consisted of half a dozen rooms filled with desks and screens and chatter. As Silva entered several journalists came over to greet her, and it wasn't until she'd spoken to them all that she was able to climb the stairs to the top floor where Neil Milligan, the editor, had his office. The room was a nook tucked in under the eaves and was crammed with piles of old newspapers and magazines. A desk sat beneath a skylight and a large TV hung on one wall showing rolling news. There'd been another terrorist atrocity, this one in Hamburg. A man had run amok with a knife and three people were dead. Not religious extremists this time: the attacker had been a white neo-Nazi, the victims young Turkish immigrants. Seeing Silva, Milligan rose from behind his desk and came over and hugged her. He was a thin man, his narrow face covered with a grey beard, his features sharp, his eyes keen.

'Where's it going to end?' he said. 'I'm getting tired of writing the same story over and over.'

Silva shrugged. Quite why Milligan expected she, of all people, would have an answer, she didn't know.

'Thanks for coming to the funeral, Neil,' she said. 'Thanks for setting up the fund too.'

Milligan had signalled his desire to create a scholarship in Silva's mother's name. The scholarship was intended to sponsor a journalism student through university. It was a nice touch and something her mother would have approved of.

'Not much good can come of this.' Milligan gestured at the screen. 'But it's important we try to cling onto some sort of hope.'

The final word of the sentence cut right through Silva. *Hope*. Karen Hope. 'Yes.'

The response was flat and Milligan picked up on it.

'You OK, Rebecca?' He tutted to himself. 'I mean, fuck, of course you're not OK. What I meant was—'

'Forget it, I know what you meant.' Silva dismissed Milligan's apology. 'My mother was working on a trafficking story when she was killed, right?'

Milligan recoiled, almost as if Silva was being disrespectful by getting straight to the point. 'Yes. She was trying to follow the migrant flows across the Mediterranean, talk to the victims, the perpetrators, the NGOs, the authorities. It was sheer bad luck she was interviewing the head of the charity when the attack happened.' Milligan moved round and sat behind his desk. Shuffled a sheaf of papers. He appeared distracted. 'I want you to know we're not dropping the story, and I fully intend to publish something with your mother's name on the byline.'

'What happened to her laptop?'

'It's probably downstairs somewhere. I know we had some equipment sent to us from Tunis.'

'Can I see it?'

'Why? There's nothing on the machine. The disk has been wiped, ready for a fresh install.'

'So how are you going to publish the people-trafficking story?'

'Your mother's files were backed up to cloud storage.' Milligan nodded at his own laptop. 'I can access them from here.'

'I was wondering if there was anything else she was working on. Something much bigger than people trafficking.'

'Bigger than trafficking? Not that I know of.' Milligan glanced up from the laptop. 'Look, I know what you're trying to do. You want to make sense of this and understand why your mother died.' He gestured at the screen on the wall. The chaos in the aftermath of a terrorist attack. 'But there *is* no sense to it. She was just doing her job and happened to be in the wrong place at the wrong time.'

'Are you sure about that?' Silva held Milligan's gaze, sensing he was being evasive. 'Because somebody broke into her cottage. They tried to make it look like a simple burglary but they removed the hard drive from her old computer.' Silva lifted her hands and turned them over. The grazing from her fall into the weir was evident. 'And when I was there yesterday someone attacked me and pushed me into the river. I nearly drowned.'

Milligan cocked his head. 'Are you all right?'

'I'm in one piece,' Silva said, lowering her hands and noticing the slight shake as she did so. 'Physically anyway.'

'Did you report it to the police? They could help. Victim support. That kind of thing.'

'No.' Silva wondered why she hadn't done just that. She'd been assaulted and the house had been burgled. At least the police would have been able to give her some reassurance. Unless… her train of thought was curtailed by an involuntary shudder. 'But it got me thinking if my mother might have stumbled across something, something which could have got her killed. I've an idea about what it might be and it has absolutely nothing to do with people trafficking.'

Milligan reached for a remote control and blipped the volume on the TV monitor up several notches. Sirens in the background. A reporter talking to camera. A blast of music as the channel went to an ad break. Milligan shook his head and mouthed the word *no*. He reached for his jacket on the back of his chair and stood.

'Let's take a walk,' he said.

—

Light chinked through the curtains and fell on Holm's face. He blinked awake, aware of traffic noise in the street outside, the growl of a heavy goods vehicle, the beep of a horn. Then somebody pounding on something. *Bang bang bang.* Holm screwed his eyes shut. He had a beast of a hangover for which Palmer was entirely to blame. As Holm was leaving work the previous evening, a text from his friend had bleeped into his phone.

'If you're going to drown your sorrows, best not to do it alone, eh?' Palmer signed off with a winking emoji, and half an hour later they were starting their second pint in the Morpeth Arms at the bottom of Millbank, ostensibly to celebrate Holm's new job.

The night had gone downhill from there, ending with a curry that Palmer insisted on paying for.

'The way you've been talking, it sounds like you could be taking early retirement soon,' he said. 'Best save your pennies.'

One Madras and several bottles of Cobra later, Palmer was bundling Holm into a taxi for the ride home. He could remember little else except the taxi driver's shake of the head when Holm had stepped out and vomited on his own front step. Drinking with Palmer tended to be like that.

'Bloody hell.' Holm heaved the words out and pulled a pillow over his head.

Bang bang bang.

The pounding came again. Then a pattering on the window. Stones or earth hitting the glass. Holm pushed off the pillow and cast the duvet aside. He staggered to the window, drew back the curtains and looked down into the street.

Farakh Javed grinned up at him before gesturing at the front door. Holm bent and lifted the sash window.

'Boss. Are you going to let me in or what?' The smile again. Like a bright sunbeam and about as welcome.

Holm groaned. This wasn't the sort of morning he'd been expecting. He'd hoped to phone in sick and lie in bed for a couple of hours. Later, when he eventually got up, to cook a hearty breakfast and veg out in front of some daytime TV.

'Well?'

Holm nodded and moved to the hallway. He buzzed the entry lock and a minute later the door to Holm's flat swung open and Javed stepped in.

'Some dirty wino's spewed on your front step,' he said. 'This neighbourhood's going to the dogs.'

'Tell me about it.' Holm crossed the room. He wondered about closing the curtains because the light was altogether too strong for his eyes. Instead he dropped onto the sofa. Javed was bouncing like a first-round featherweight who'd yet to land a punch. 'Sit down, you're making me nervous. Besides, what are you doing here?'

Javed stopped moving for a moment. 'You look like you could do with some fresh air.'

Holm shook his head and started to protest, but Javed was already moving back towards the hallway and heading for the front door.

–

Five minutes later Silva and Milligan were leaving the busy centre and strolling into Highgate Cemetery. Stillness. The peace of the dead. Milligan hadn't spoken since they'd left the agency and now he led the way in silence, following a path that wound beneath huge trees, the light from above filtered to a soft lime by a canopy of leaves.

'What's going on, Neil?' Silva said, trying to keep up. 'What exactly was it my mother was working on?'

'I told you, the trafficking story.' Milligan hunched over and shuffled along. 'She wanted to do a series, a piece on each country involved, she was interviewing the actors and—'

'You said.'

'I did?' Milligan stopped walking and shook his head. His eyes were wide open but his pupils tiny. He glanced back the way they'd come. 'Sorry. The past few weeks have been stressful. I've been under a lot of pressure.'

'I'm sure you have. It must be difficult when one of your journalists is deliberately targeted because of a story she was working on.'

'Yes, it...' Milligan's affirmative nodding stopped and changed to another shake of the head. He started to walk on. 'No, Rebecca, not deliberately. Your mother was killed by terrorists in league with the people traffickers. Their target was the head of a charity providing help to refugees, and your mother and the other victims were bystanders unwittingly caught up in the attack.'

'That's bullshit. If it was really true then why couldn't we have this conversation in your office? Why did somebody break into my mother's house? Why was I followed by a mysterious car on the motorway and then later pushed into the weir?'

'This isn't a discussion I want to have, OK?' Milligan increased his pace, striding away. Silva followed. 'You've had a warning, you might say a lucky escape. Take my advice and move on.'

'Move on? Are you fucking joking?' Silva caught up with Milligan. She was angry at the way he was being so dismissive. 'My mother was murdered and I'm beginning to suspect the facts aren't as simple as the authorities are making out.'

'Forget it, right? Forget whatever you think you know.'

'It's Hope, isn't it? Karen Hope?'

Milligan stopped and spun round. He shot a hand out and grabbed Silva by the wrist. 'For God's sake don't mention her name.'

'Why ever not?'

'Because I told you not to, OK?'

Silva paused and lowered her voice. 'How has it come to this, Neil?'

Milligan let go of Silva's arm. He stared down at the asphalt path. The surface was dotted with the white blotches of discarded chewing gum and he moved his right foot and scuffed at a piece. After a moment he looked up, his face drained of colour.

'I've got three children, Rebecca. They walk half a mile to school and back every day. Do you know how easy it would be for a car to mount the kerb and run them over? How easy it would be for someone to sweep past and throw acid at them? I'm not easily frightened, but I couldn't live with myself if...' Milligan's words trailed off as he looked across to an elaborate tomb where a cherub stood on a plinth. 'I've resisted pressure before but that's always come from big business or hapless politicians or tinpot dictators. This is different. This is much, much bigger. Global.'

'Global?' Silva was thrown. Milligan was opening up but now she was wondering if he was slipping into fantasy. 'Are you saying there's some kind of conspiracy?'

'Yes.' Milligan gulped and swallowed. Sweat beaded on his forehead as if he had a fever. 'Too many people have too much riding on this to contemplate the alternative. I've always believed in speaking truth to power, but the power in this case is too strong. I can't fight against them without losing everything.'

'Does anyone else have the story?'

'There is no story. I've told you nothing, Rebecca, *nothing*, understand?'

'At least tell me what happened to my mother's files so I can follow this up.'

Milligan glanced round, scanning the shadows under the trees. He stepped off the path, beckoned Silva to follow and darted away into a stand of thick laurel. Silva jogged after him and pushed under a tangle of branches into a little clearing. Milligan stood on the far side. He held his hands up.

'Stop.' He clenched his fists, fighting something internally before letting his hands fall to his sides. 'This is all I tell you, OK? You promise you won't try to contact me again? Promise you won't tell anybody we met?'

'I promise,' Silva said.

'The laptop was taken away by a couple of intelligence officers. They said it contained evidence that would help them track down the terrorists. When I logged on to our system and tried to discover what happened to the files your mother had backed up to the cloud, I found nothing. All the material had been deleted without trace.'

'But—'

'That's it. I don't want to hear another word.' Milligan stepped away. 'We can't meet again, not alone like this. It's too risky.'

'Neil, you've got to help me get to the truth!'

'I'm sorry about your mother, more sorry than you can know, but I'm done with this, understand?' Milligan turned around and started to go back the way they'd come. When Silva took a step after him he held up his hands. 'Let it go, Rebecca. For your own good. Your mother wouldn't have wanted you to pursue this at the cost of the lives of the people she loved.'

Milligan trotted off into the trees, dodged through a gap in a tall box hedge and was gone.

–

Outside the sun was brighter than ever and Holm squinted against the glare. His headache had subsided, but the last thing he wanted to be doing was chasing after Javed.

'What's this about?' Holm stepped across the pavement. Javed was indicating the park over the road, so they crossed and went in.

'You thought this was Taher, right?' Javed began to stroll up a path that curved round a kids' playground. 'Directly involved or behind the scenes, but ultimately responsible?'

'Yes.' Holm glanced over to where a toddler had tripped and taken a face plant. His dad was trying to console the little boy. 'Even if nobody believes me.'

'I didn't say that. I said nobody else believes you.'

'So you *do* think it was Taher?'

Javed turned his attention to a pair of pigeons crossing the path ahead. He stopped and watched as they squabbled over a discarded burger.

'Well?' Holm was running out of patience. He began to walk on. 'Do you?'

'Here.' Javed pulled out his phone and thrust it at Holm. 'I've got a Twitter account. Personal. I don't use it for much though. The occasional message to friends, plus I like to follow some footie stuff. Arsenal mostly.'

Holm raised an eyebrow. He couldn't imagine Javed as a football fan. 'So?'

'This was posted last night. It was to me and about half a dozen other Gunners fans, but when you read the message you'll see the other recipients were just a blind.'

Holm peered down at the phone. The tweet was in Arabic and he struggled to get beyond one or two words.

'A football fan who communicates in Arabic. So what?'

'I'll translate, shall I?' Javed smiled. '*The innocent one wakes. He seeks to avenge the wrongs which have been done. He shall punish the transgressors but others will fall as well. Women and children and babes in arms. Who can say if this is justice? Who will listen to my voice? Who will stop this madness?*'

Holm stopped in his tracks. 'Say the first bit again.'

'The innocent one. That's what the name Taher means, isn't it? Innocent, pure, clean, chaste.'

Holm pushed the phone away. 'I'm done with this, Farakh. Taher is strictly off-limits, remember? If you're worried home-grown extremism might have spread to football fans then you should have a word with Huxtable. She'll find somebody to look into it for you.'

'The Spider? No, I don't think you understand and she certainly wouldn't.' Javed shoved the phone back towards Holm. He was agitated, upset almost. 'Take a look at the username.'

Holm peered at the screen again, more to placate Javed than with any real interest. 'It's a bunch of letters and numbers. Makes no sense.'

'TCXGP1505. The digits. Do they mean anything to you?'

'1505?' Holm laughed. 'The fifteenth of May. Coincidentally, it's my birthday.'

'Now take the letters. It's a simple rotation cipher. Shifted by two. Child's play.'

'TCXGP.' Holm did the decoding in his head and as he did so a chill spread across the back of his hands. 'RAVEN.'

'Which is?'

'MI5's code name for Taher.' Despite the warm sun Holm shivered. A smidgeon of nausea began to rise from his stomach. 'Christ.'

'Your birthday and a code name supposedly known only to the security services sent in a social media message to me.' Javed took the phone back. 'Doesn't that strike you as just a little bit odd?'

Chapter Eight

Silva went to the Costa on the high street opposite the agency. She bought a cup of coffee and a muffin and sat at a window seat. Milligan was inside because she'd seen him come to a window and peer out nervously. This wasn't the Neil Milligan her mother had told her stories about. In his time as a front-line journalist he'd covered wars, famines and natural disasters. He'd been shot in the leg in the Balkans, captured by Angolan rebels in Africa and faced trial in Singapore for refusing to reveal a source. He'd won awards for his work. Silva concluded he'd either lost it or had a genuine reason to be frightened. Considering what had happened to her at the weir, she was inclined to think the latter and that wasn't comforting. She turned her head and scanned the cafe. Milligan's paranoia was infectious.

When she'd eaten the muffin and finished the coffee, she drummed her fingers on the table for a couple of minutes. She'd planned to wait for Milligan to emerge so she could try to talk to him again, but now, having seen him at the window, she came to the conclusion he wasn't going to open up to her.

She decided instead to return to her mother's place and take a good look through all the documents in the upstairs room. She dodged through the traffic and headed west, arriving at the cottage mid-afternoon. She sat astride the bike and removed her helmet. Listened. Nothing but the water tumbling through the weir. She kicked down the stand and dismounted. The attack had spooked her and she was angry it had changed her feelings about being here. After a minute's contemplation she went inside.

She spent several hours going through all the box files. There were documents relating to research her mother had done years ago as well as more recent material, but there was nothing that mentioned Karen Hope.

The sun had sunk by the time she'd finished. Down in the kitchen she found a tin of curry in a cupboard. There was dried rice in a jar on the side. Two saucepans went on the stove. In another cupboard a rack held several bottles of red wine. Silva smiled to herself; her mother enjoyed a drink and it wasn't hard to imagine her pouring a large glass and taking it outside to sit by the weir on a summer's evening such as this one. Silva opened a bottle and checked the rice and curry. While she was waiting for the rice to cook, she drifted through to the living room. Above the fireplace there was a corkboard with photographs and postcards. There were several pictures of Silva as a child, some of her with her shooting medals, one of her standing beside a Foxhound armoured vehicle in Afghanistan. Silva pulled off some of the postcards. These were from friends, and she recognised the names of various people who'd come to the funeral. Like her mother, the friends were well travelled. Peru. Japan. New Zealand. South Africa. Chichester Harbour. *Chichester Harbour?* Silva turned the picture over, interested to know which of her mother's friends would send a card from a little over fifty miles away. Presumably it was an attempt at ironic humour.

18 August

Dear Rebecca, remember the beach we used to go to here? West something or other, wasn't it? Those were happy times, good memories, a place with buried treasure and hidden secrets to be passed on from one generation to the next. I so enjoyed the many times we visited. I definitely Hope you did too. Love always and forever, Mum.

Silva stepped back from the mantelpiece and sat down heavily in an armchair. She'd never received this postcard. It was correctly addressed to Silva's boat at the boatyard, but there was no stamp. The card had never been posted. Had her mother meant to send the card and forgotten? All of a sudden Silva felt a wave of regret. If the card had been posted, if Silva had received it, things might have been different. She might have phoned her mother and perhaps the call could have changed events in some small way. A tiny ripple moving forward in time, disrupting the flow of atoms and altering history. The butterfly effect, but in this case not causing a storm but preventing it. Silva dropped the card into her lap. The cold shock at seeing the message had gone and now she found herself crying again, unable to reconcile the present with the past, reality with what might have been.

After a while she stood and went back to the kitchen. The rice was done and she drained it and served the curry. Poured herself some wine. She sat at the kitchen table, the postcard in front of her. She sobbed but as she read again she found herself unable to stifle a laugh. Nothing was right. For a start the card was post-dated. The eighteenth of August was several weeks off and yet her mother must have written it before she left for Tunisia months ago. Then the actual message on the postcard was all wrong. *Remember the beach we used to go to here? West something or other, wasn't it?* West something referred to West Wittering, a beach Silva had been to with her father, but certainly not with her mother. Her father had taught her to sail on the waters of Chichester Harbour and they'd beached their dinghy at West Wittering on occasion. Her mother had hated sailing and hadn't cared much for the sea. The message made no sense. *Hidden secrets to be passed on…* She turned the card over. The picture was of Chichester Harbour from the air and showed the vast expanse of water with all the little inlets. On a rising tide you could explore the creeks and, indeed, that was just what she'd done with her father.

Was that what her mother meant? That there was some kind of secret buried like pirate gold deep in a mudbank up a lonely creek? She turned the card back over and read the final line.

I so enjoyed the many times we visited. I definitely Hope
you did too. Love always and forever, Mum.

As a journalist, her mother was unfailingly accurate in matters of grammar and punctuation, but in this case it looked as if she'd written the card in a rush. *I definitely Hope you did too.* The words *definitely Hope* was not only bad English, *hope* had a capital H, an obvious error and one Silva was positive her mother wouldn't have made.

-

Holm was ensconced in his little office under the stairs by eight the next day. His head was clear and his body had recovered from the hammering he'd given it on the night out with Palmer.

After Javed had dropped the bombshell about the tweet, Holm had sent the lad away. He needed time to think, and Javed talked ten to the dozen. There was barely a gap between his words for a breath and he'd wanted Holm to act on the information immediately. They should go to Huxtable, make a request to Twitter for more information on the account that had sent the tweet, raise the terrorist threat level, possibly recommend cancelling the weekend's football fixtures. The latter suggestion had caused an ache to thump in Holm's forehead which had nothing to do with the copious amounts of alcohol he'd consumed.

'Enough,' he said. 'Go home and act normally. We'll talk tomorrow.'

Javed had slunk away like a scolded dog and Holm once again felt guilty for raising his voice. Still, it couldn't be helped. He needed space to himself.

Back in his flat he'd made himself a strong black coffee and sat at the kitchen table, a pencil and a pad of paper at the ready. Now, in the office, he pulled out the pad from his briefcase and looked at his scribblings. Holm didn't really understand Twitter or social media or why so many people lauded a medium that seemed to exist merely to allow the sharing of either pictures of cute animals or vile abuse. He did, however, understand the world of espionage, the world of covert communications. Except the tweet hadn't been covert. It was hidden in plain sight. An account directly referencing Taher and Holm. There were a couple of possibilities he considered and discounted. First, it was a stunt by Palmer or another of his colleagues. No, the security services didn't do pranks like that. It would be too easy for such a joke to backfire and endanger personnel in the field. The second possibility was the username was simply a coincidence. That seemed unlikely because the contents of the tweet mentioned *the innocent one* – which was what the name Taher meant, and the chance of random characters resolving to a cipher of RAVEN and the numbers of Holm's birthday was astronomical.

Which left the real possibility that somebody was trying to communicate with him and Javed. Somebody, Holm reckoned, who was prepared to betray Taher.

Who will listen to my voice? Who will stop this madness?

Holm felt a buzz of excitement each time he recalled the message. Was this the beginning of the end for Taher? Slowly it dawned on him that here was the solution to his problems. A way to make amends, get his mojo back and, quite possibly, finish his career on a high note.

Javed arrived at nine in his now customary manner, carrying two coffees on a cardboard tray. Holm nodded his thanks and reached for the piece of paper which had been stuck to the door of the office earlier in the week.

The Top Top Top Secret Department.

'See this?' Holm held up the note. 'This isn't wrong. Not the way I'm going to play it.'

'I don't understand.'

'This says it all. Tells you everything you need to know about what people think of us.' Holm flapped the piece of paper in the air again. 'We're a laughing stock. The has-been, washed-out time-server and the wet-behind-the-ears recruit. What relevance could we possibly have? Whatever we're investigating must be trivial and hardly worth a moment of anyone's time. We're going to be ignored down here in our broom cupboard. If anyone thinks of us at all it will be as an afterthought. We'll be mentioned in jokes over lunch, but the big boys will be concentrating on loftier matters.'

Javed looked disappointed. 'But Huxtable said we'd be working on something important.'

'Important?' Holm tapped himself on the chest. 'If that was the case, then what the hell am I doing here? No, Farakh, your career is at an end before it's even begun. You've fallen at the first fence, spun off at the end of the straight, blown your load before—'

'All right, I get it.'

Javed poked at the froth on his coffee with a wooden stirrer and Holm let the silence build. After a minute he spoke.

'What do you know about the animal rights lobby?'

'Hey?' Javed cocked his head on one side as if he'd misheard. 'You mean the people who break into laboratories and stuff?' He dumped the stirrer in his cup. 'Nothing, boss.'

'Well, I've decided that's our brief. No one cares about animal rights. It's not sexy like Islamic terrorism or espionage or threats to our national infrastructure from foreign governments, but there you go. Now, because we know nothing, we won't be accomplishing much in the first couple of months. We've got to do research and map out our strategy. Lay the groundwork, build from the base up. Actually producing any meaningful results is a long, long way in the future.'

'You're kidding me, boss? This isn't what I signed up to do. I speak fluent Arabic, I've got a degree in Middle Eastern Studies, my MA thesis was on the rise of ISIS, I know sod all about torturing bunnies.'

Holm smiled and gave a wink. 'Calm down, lad, I think you're missing the point here.'

'I…' Javed bit his lip. His gaze wandered to the computers and over to the filing cabinet. 'We're not really going to be investigating animal rights groups, are we?'

'Of course bloody not. It's a cover story.'

'So what are we going to be doing?'

'Keeping secrets. We don't have to report to anyone but the Spider, and that's down to me, right? You keep your lips sealed and if people ask you say nothing other than we're looking into the activities of various, potentially violent, animal liberation groups.'

'Sure, but you still haven't told me what this is all about.' Javed gestured at the sparse surroundings. 'I mean we're not exactly set up for a high-profile investigation.'

'Look, Huxtable has given me the freedom to do whatever I like. She either expects me to bimble along doing relatively little or she's hoping to give me enough rope to hang myself. Well, skiving isn't my cup of tea and I don't intend to get caught in her web.'

'You're mixing your metaphors, sir, and if I might say so, you're continuing to evade my questioning. You've also not mentioned the information I gave you yesterday.'

'Guilty on all counts.' Holm raised his hands. 'Time I came clean. The username was a cipher of RAVEN and my birthday, right? As you said, more than odd.'

'But the cipher was simple. I cracked it easily.'

'Just so. Which means whoever was behind the tweet wants *us* to know that *they* know the code name we use for Taher. What's more, by sending it to you and using my birthday as part of the username, it was plainly intended for us both.'

'That's what I thought.'

'However, if they know our code name they either have direct access to our systems or they're being fed information by somebody.'

'There's a leak then, a mole.'

'Or this is something different.' Holm paused. He glanced over to the filing cabinet where he'd found the index card relating to the troubles in Northern Ireland. 'Back in the day the IRA used code words to let the police know when they'd planted a bomb. It showed a threat was genuine and not a hoax. This could be similar. Somebody has passed my birthday and the code name of Taher – RAVEN – to an informant in the field. By using those two pieces of information in the username the informant has established they're genuine.'

'So, a benevolent mole?'

Holm shrugged. He didn't really have a clue what was going on but he wasn't going to let Javed know that.

'Anyway, in light of this latest twist, perhaps you can guess what I intend to do with our little two-person operation now?'

'I don't believe it.' A look of astonishment spread across Javed's face. 'We're going to go after Taher?'

'Precisely.'

Chapter Nine

Silva spent another restless night at her mother's house and the next morning rode cross-country from Marlborough to Matthew Fairchild's place which, according to his business card, was located south of London, a few miles from Gatwick airport. The weather had changed from the previous day and she hurtled along beneath dark clouds, heavy rain making the road surfaces treacherous. She turned off a main road, the headlight on her bike piercing the gloom as she drove into thick woodland. After a mile the trees gave way to manicured parkland surrounding a large mansion, the grounds protected by high fences. A light glared out from a stone gatehouse, a shadow in one window. Silva rolled the bike to a stop at the heavy iron gates and removed her helmet. The door to the gatehouse swung open and a security guard emerged. He nodded at Silva.

'You got a delivery?' he said. 'Only everything gets signed for down here. No need to go up to the house.'

'The delivery is me,' Silva said. 'Tell Mr Fairchild Rebecca is here. Rebecca da Silva.'

'Wait a moment.' The guard strode across to the gatehouse and disappeared inside.

Silva sat astride her motorbike, drumming her fingers on the petrol tank. The guard was taking an age. She was about to forget about the whole thing when he reappeared.

'You can go up there.' He pressed a little key fob and the gates began to swing open. 'Somebody will meet you at the front.'

Moments later she was gliding to a stop at the front of the house. At the top of a set of grand steps a door opened and Matthew Fairchild emerged.

'Rebecca!' Fairchild spread his arms wide and trotted down the steps as if he was making an entrance in some glitzy musical. 'Why on earth didn't you call ahead and let me know you were coming?'

'I was in the neighbourhood.' Silva removed her helmet. 'I thought we needed a chat about Karen Hope.'

'Right.' Fairchild's expression turned sombre. 'You'd better come in.'

Inside, dark oak panelling adorned the walls and Silva's feet moved silently across a thick carpet. Fairchild led her past a room where an open door showed a well-equipped office. There were several computer monitors and keyboards and a number of television screens showing rolling news channels. An array of newspapers lay spread across a large desk.

'The hub of my business,' Fairchild said, noticing Silva's interest. 'My game is security. Protecting business interests or charity projects, supporting governance through the provision of law and order. There are many places in the world where a little stability can go a long way. I seek to provide that stability.'

'And what about a terrorist attack in Tunisia? How does that fit in?'

'Through here.' Fairchild ignored her question and strode on until they reached a heavy wooden door. He pushed the handle down and went through. The room beyond was a cross between a library and a lounge. Tall bookcases towered over a set of armchairs that clustered round a huge fireplace. A window seat looked out onto a terrace. Fairchild gestured at the armchairs. 'Take a seat. I'll be back in a mo.'

He returned a minute later with a sheaf of papers under one arm. He put the papers on a low coffee table and settled into an armchair.

'Who killed my mother?' Silva said. 'I don't believe it was Karen Hope, but I'm prepared to accept she's mixed up in all this somewhere.'

'Mixed up?' Fairchild cocked his head to one side. 'Oh, I'm afraid "mixed up" is the least of it.'

'Show me.' Silva pointed at the fan of documents.

There was a pause before Fairchild spoke. 'What do you know about Hope?'

'Not much. She's a Democrat, but right wing. Her family are involved in the military in some way. She's the front runner in the race to be president. It seems as if she's a compromise candidate who can win over the centre ground.'

'For a young woman, you're remarkably well informed.'

'Don't patronise me.'

'I'm not.' Fairchild held up his hands. 'Most people these days, of all ages, can barely recognise any of our own politicians, let alone those from another country.'

'Get on with it.'

'Let's start with some background.' Fairchild extracted a sheet from the pile of documents. He slid it across the table. 'Everything you need to know is in here, but I'll summarise.'

Silva reached for the piece of paper. There was a picture of Hope at the top. Beneath the smiling face a couple of paragraphs listed Hope's biographical details and notable achievements.

'You are right about the military angle. Karen Hope's father founded what is now Allied American Armaments. By sales it's the fifth largest arms manufacturer in the US. The family connection helps Karen Hope appeal to a wide voter base, and many Republican voters are going to turn to her at the next election. Just think, recent presidents have been despised by roughly fifty per cent of the population. Karen Hope is different and offers exactly what her name suggests. A rare chance for unity in a divided country.'

'What is this? American Studies 101?' Silva shook her head. 'Can we get back to the point? About how Hope is responsible for the death of my mother?'

'Of course.' Fairchild reached for another piece of paper. A printout of a spreadsheet. Columns of figures. Dollar signs. Lots of zeros. 'How do you think Karen Hope funds her campaign?'

'Her father?'

'Right. American Armaments provide a good chunk of money, but here's the thing: until recently the business was fighting to be profitable and it looked as if the company would go under.'

'So?'

'Here.' Another photograph. A fifty-something man with a Panama hat over glossy blond hair. Perfect teeth bared in a grimace and white skin flushed red with the heat. Next to him a glamorous woman with a slim figure. 'Brandon Hope, Karen's brother. The woman beside him is his Italian wife, Pierra. Brandon used to be a diplomat and for several years he was the United States' top man in Saudi Arabia. He retired from the diplomatic corps a while ago and founded an aid charity which operates from a base in Italy. Of course at some point in the future Brandon or his sister will be expected to head American Armaments, but for now the father remains in charge.'

'I don't—'

'The arms industry has been notorious for kickbacks. Think British Aerospace, now BAE Systems. Remember the allegations concerning huge bribes the company paid to the Saudis?' Silva nodded and Fairchild continued. 'Well, Brandon Hope has been exploiting some of the personal connections he built up when he was a diplomat. As a kickback for arms contracts with the Saudi Arabian government worth hundreds of millions, he's been helping a wealthy Saudi backer distribute cash directly to terrorist groups across the Middle East and North Africa. This is done through his charitable operations in regions where accountability is close to zero. The effect the arms deals had on the bottom line of American Armaments was dramatic and occurred right around the time Karen threw her hat in the ring. Brandon's plan, I guess, was to ensure Karen would be president when it was time for the father to pass control of the company to his offspring.'

'Karen Hope can't have been aware of the link.'

'You know her, do you? Personally?' Fairchild reached for the picture of the congresswoman surrounded by cheering supporters. 'Appearance is everything in politics and Karen Hope has cultivated an image that shows her to be strong but fair, compassionate while at the same time willing to make tough choices. Don't be fooled though – behind the mask there's a woman determined to grab power by any means possible. Can you imagine her state of mind when she found out her brother had brokered an arms deal that involved funding terrorists? She'd have known if the information became public she would be swept aside, her political ambitions shattered.'

'I still don't believe she was involved.'

'Let's go on, then.' Fairchild paused and took a deep breath before continuing. 'Brandon Hope lives in Naples, but he owns a holiday villa close by on the Amalfi Coast in the town of Positano.' Fairchild reached for a photograph on the table and passed it over. There was a green wall and a metal bench. Brandon sat at one end of the bench staring out at the sea. Beside him was an Arab businessman wearing traditional Saudi clothes and with a white keffiyeh on his head, and two younger men of Middle Eastern origin who wore Western clothes. One was clean-cut with dusty black hair, an engaging smile and piercing brown eyes. He had clear skin and a wisp of hair on his chin. The other had a rich head of hair and a full beard. 'Brandon Hope and next to him the Saudi backer. His name is Jawad al Haddad and he's an extremely rich businessman with connections to the Saudi royal family. He owns an airline, a shipping company, a football club in the Netherlands and a large amount of commercial property. He's been involved in brokering a number of significant arms deals between the Saudi government and defence firms in the US and the UK, notably, of course, several eye-watering contracts involving American Armaments.'

'You said he had something to do with terrorism?'

'Just so. Haddad is on a US watch list of terrorist sympathisers. Allegedly he helped fund a training camp in Somalia and provided advice and contacts to ISIS commanders in Syria who were involved in selling oil on the black market to Turkey. Such overt activity had to stop a few years back when the Saudi government launched a crackdown on their nationals funding terrorists. In reality the crackdown was half-hearted and it was easy for Haddad to find another way of getting money out of the country.'

'Brandon Hope.'

'Correct.'

'And who are the other men?'

'The good looking one is unidentified, but the guy with the beard is a man by the name of Mohid Latif.'

'Should I know him?'

'Not yet, but the security services do.' Fairchild lifted another photograph from the table. 'This picture comes courtesy of the Tunisian police. It's taken from a CCTV camera on a building close to the cafe where your mother was killed.'

Silva took the picture and examined it. The still was monochrome and showed a street scene. A minibus sat across from the cafe, slewed in the road. Three men stood beside it, two of them holding assault rifles, the other a pistol. In the distance, distorted by the wide-angle lens of the camera, Silva could see the tables and chairs of the cafe. Anonymous people sitting at those tables, their faces too pixellated to recognise.

'My mother?' Silva's hand shook, the photograph flapping in her hand.

'The picture was taken at 2.31 p.m. exactly. Thirty seconds later the camera went offline when it was hit by a stray bullet.' Fairchild lowered his voice. 'Take a look at the man to the right of the minibus.'

Silva glanced down and tried to stop her hand from shaking. Like the other men, the figure to the right wore a chequered *shemagh*, but in this case it had slipped, revealing the face.

'Mohid Latif?'

'Yes. He was one of the attackers, and in the other picture there he is with Brandon Hope and a Saudi terrorist sympathiser. I don't think they were discussing aid budgets.'

Silva sighed. It was too much to take in. She looked at the picture of the villa again. The blue sea sparkled in the distance, white boats scattered on the surface of the water. Hope appeared hot and uncomfortable, the other men calm. It was like a scene from a movie set. Unreal.

'And Karen Hope?'

'Here.' Fairchild reached for yet another photograph. 'Tell me she isn't involved.'

Silva took the picture. The same metal bench, the same backdrop of sea and boats, the same green wall. Only this time Brandon and Haddad had gone and had been replaced by Karen Hope. Her head was turned towards Latif and the other man and was bowed slightly, as if she was listening intently.

A tingle slipped across the back of Silva's hand as she let the picture drop to the table. She lowered her voice to a whisper. 'If this is true – *if*, mind you – then you have all the information you need to expose Karen Hope and her brother. I don't see how I can add anything to what you've already discovered. Where do I fit in?'

'You haven't twigged?' Fairchild smiled. 'Where do you think these pictures came from?'

'I presume you've got sources. People who snoop for you.'

'These photographs were taken by your mother.'

'*What?*' Silva stared down, the photographs all of a sudden imbued with a heightened significance.

'Yes. Your mother was in Italy tracking Brandon Hope.'

'But what about the people-trafficking story?'

'The people-trafficking story led her to the Hopes. You see, the charity Brandon runs operates a rescue boat that scours the Med for refugees. Your mother suspected something dodgy was going on and discovered the Saudi connection and a much, much bigger story. A story that ultimately got her killed.'

'Because the Hopes wanted to cover up the links to Haddad?'

'Precisely. What she didn't realise as she took those photographs was that she was witnessing the Hopes signing her own death warrant. They were recruiting Latif and the other man to kill her. The attack on the head of the women's charity was just a front, a blind. She was the bystander, not your mother. You mother died because she was about to expose the Hopes and their dodgy dealings. Had the story come out, Karen Hope would have been toast.'

'How do you know all this? It can't be common knowledge.'

'Of course not. Your mother knew she was working on the scoop of a lifetime, a story that had the potential to bring down the most powerful person in the world. This was Watergate for the twenty-first century. Bigger, even. She knew that was dangerous so she took precautions. All her files were backed up to the agency's server, but she also kept a personal set in a virtual time vault.'

'A what?'

'They were stored in the cloud, and if your mother didn't log into the vault once every week, the files would be emailed to a trusted address.'

'My dad.'

'Yes. He hadn't a clue what he was dealing with when he received the files so he called me.'

Silva slumped in her chair. The vast sitting room somehow appeared to be getting smaller, the ceiling lowering, pushing her down, weighing on her. Even as the room shrank, Fairchild appeared to be fading into the distance while at the same time his voice was getting louder.

'Do you understand now, Rebecca? Why you, as the best in your particular field, need to be involved in this? What you need to do?'

The room had returned to normal but Silva had the sense she was floating above everything, looking down at herself in the armchair.

'No,' she saw herself say. 'I don't.'

'You need to travel to Italy. Once you're there, you'll make your way to the Amalfi Coast and the town of Positano. Every year Brandon and his sister spend a week there in the summer. It's a family tradition and could well be the last chance Karen gets for a relaxing holiday before she's elected president.'

'And when she turns up?'

'It's quite simple.' Fairchild tapped the photograph again, this time with more force. 'When Karen Hope turns up… you're going to kill her.'

Chapter Ten

London had been Taher's base for a number of years. The city was filled with people from a hundred different countries and they practised a dozen different religions. It offered instant anonymity. He owned a small flat high up in a grotty tower block far to the west of the centre where nobody bothered him, nobody asked what he was up to and nobody cared.

His journey back to the UK after the Tunisian mission had been a convoluted one. The trip took several days, but the route was well tested and allowed him to come and go without the risk of capture. On his return to the flat he prayed, unpacked, and ate a meal. That done, he stood at the window and looked out as the daylight faded. He caught sight of himself in the glass and moved closer to the window in order to banish his reflection. Lights blazed at the heart of the capital and he could imagine the night unfolding. It was a tableau that played out each evening, but he doubted the scenes were much different in Paris or New York or Sydney. The same type of people doing the same type of things. Alcohol and drugs leading to sex and violence. It was, he thought, a debasement of what it meant to be human. A dismal waste.

In front of his face the glass blurred and distorted as his breath misted the pane. He brushed the window with the tips of his fingers and wiped the mist clear. Peering out again, he saw not the bright lights of London, but a tiny settlement on the border between Saudi Arabia and Iraq. A small concrete dwelling surrounded by a number of billowing tents. A young boy running errands for his parents.

He is twelve years old. Not nearly twelve, not twelve and a bit, but twelve exactly. Nothing is planned for the day of his birth – his father explains to him the celebration of anniversaries and birthdays is the way of disbelievers. Still, his mother has given thanks to God and asked that Taher should live long and be humble. Taher has given thanks too and when, in the late afternoon, his mother asks him to tend to the goats in the paddock, instead of moaning he nods and goes out the back to collect some fodder.

It's hot outside and Taher sweats as he carries the food to the goats. He can hear laughter from inside the house. His little brothers and sisters playing happily, too young to lend a hand, too young to understand the hardship. After he's fed and watered the animals he kicks a rusty tin can round the yard. The sun is touching the horizon now, the heat slipping away as the stars rise in the east. A majestic spread of brilliance in the heavens over the desert. Taher imagines the stars are the glittering floodlights above a football stadium. It's the World Cup final and he's the best player on the pitch. He flicks the can up and over his shoulder and then boots it against a wall. 'Goal!' he shouts as his mother's voice floats out into the night air. It's dinner time. He looks over, seeing her silhouetted in the door to the house, his father behind carrying bread to the low table, his little sister Kaya on the floor at his mother's heels.

Then the world explodes, a fireball erupting from behind his mother, a heat hotter than a thousand suns searing through the air. Night turns to day and the scene imprints itself, scorching deep into his memories like a brand burned into the side of an ox.

His mother is torn into three pieces, her chest and head slamming against the wall, her legs and lower torso spiralling into the air, one arm flailing to the ground and rolling into the distance. He sees Kaya run out into the yard, for a moment thinking she might be saved but then realising her flesh is melting before him, peeling away in layers as she burns, her screams mercifully dying with her in a few seconds. From inside the house nothing but the roar of flame, his father and three other siblings in there somewhere. Dead or dying. Gone.

Taher runs towards the house but the heat is intense. He raises his arm to protect his face, the wash of flame scorching his skin. He staggers *forward one step, two, three, but it's no good. He can't get any closer and even if he could there's nothing he can do. Everyone he knows and loves is already in the hands of God. He falls to the floor and crawls away through the dirt, passing out among the goats, their frantic bleating the last thing he remembers from that awful day.*

The glass steamed again and he wiped it once more. The desert was gone, London back. London. The capital of Great Britain. So-called Great Britain. Taher had to prevent himself from thumping his fist on the window and obliterating the image. He hadn't known it all those years ago, but the devastation wrought that evening in the desert had come from a Tomahawk cruise missile launched from a Royal Navy destroyer stationed three hundred miles away in the Persian Gulf. The new way of waging war. The modern way. Just like a computer game. Type a few letters and numbers. Hit the *enter* key. Wipe away half a dozen innocent lives in a targeting error. For the few people that bother to read the news reports the lives lost are dismissed in a phrase that brought bile to Taher's throat: *collateral damage.*

He rubbed the area of old scar tissue on his right forearm and then looked through the dirty glass again, the city spread out before him. Cars spiralled along roads. People disappeared into a tube station. Aeroplanes hovered on the horizon on their final approach to Heathrow.

Well, there were other ways of fighting back, he thought. You didn't need a million-pound missile fired from a billion-pound ship, you didn't need to be a global military power. You just needed determination, a few trusted followers and the knowledge you were performing the will of God.

Yes, the day was surely coming when the good folk of London would experience *collateral damage* for themselves.

-

Silva was back in Plymouth. Walking the round. Delivering the letters. Thinking about the utter craziness of Fairchild's suggestion.

When Karen Hope turns up you're going to kill her.

She'd walked out on him after that, his voice echoing in her ears as she started her bike and rode away.

…you're going to kill her.

Fairchild was living in a world of make-believe and movies where snipers took potshots and escaped by jumping from buildings or hanging on to a rope lowered from a helicopter.

…kill her.

Assassinate the future president of the United States? Straight up madness.

And yet as she trudged the streets in the warm summer rain, the story Fairchild had spun snagged at her thoughts and refused to lie buried. What if her mother *had* discovered something about the Hopes that was incriminating enough for them to consider murdering her? Although her mother had no interest in American domestic politics, she'd certainly had many assignments related to US foreign policy. The relationship with Israel, the funding of the Taliban, the two wars in Iraq, the war on terror. Fairchild wasn't a back-room general either, and he'd served in several wars. Would such a man indulge in high fantasy? She didn't know, but if it hadn't been for the cryptic postcard her mother had written her she may well have dropped the whole thing.

…hidden secrets… definitely Hope…

There was something there but, try as she might, she couldn't fathom it, and by the end of the week her head was so muddled she decided to clear it by going for a run. She rode her motor-bike up onto the moor and ran under dark skies. She pushed through the pain barrier, her lungs bursting, her legs aching. After two hours of physical hell, she returned to the boat, exhausted. She took a shower in the toilet block and collapsed on her bunk, thinking her head was no clearer.

A while later, her mobile rang. She blinked and reached for the phone. Outside the sun was playing hide and seek with the rain clouds, the inside of the boat alternately a warm yellow or a cold grey. She peered at the screen. Didn't recognise the number.

'Hello?' She swivelled round and sat on the edge of the bunk.

'It's me, Becca. You OK?' Beneath the American accent there was a hint of Irish. Like an aftertaste in a whiskey. Wood smoke, coffee, peach. 'Because I just heard, sweetheart. About your mom.'

'You *just* heard?' Silva recognised the voice and felt her grip tighten on the phone. 'It's been weeks, Sean.'

'I've been in-country. Sudan. It's a long story, but the gist is I knew about the shooting but I didn't get the names. I didn't connect.'

'You didn't connect?' She remembered the space between them. Geographical and emotional. No one to blame, no one at fault, just circumstances.

'I'm so sorry, Becca. If only I could have been there with you. If only... well.'

She remembered the aftertaste. Burning and bitter and the warm glow seeping through to the tips of the fingers and making her whole body shiver. Her shadow stood black against the side of the cabin for a moment before fading as the sun disappeared once again. That was her and Sean. A warm glow fading to... to what?

Sean Connor, her sometime boyfriend, was thirty-three. An American of Irish descent out of Eastport, Maine. 'As north and east as is possible and as close to you Brits as that,' he'd said to her, holding up his thumb and finger an inch apart. 'Just the Atlantic Ocean between us.' The gesture had come with a wink and a raising of his glass as they'd sat in the bar on the base in Kabul. She'd first met him earlier in the day as the stars had twinkled in the predawn sky. Her patrol was making final preparations for an excursion into the mountains south of the city when the CO had turned up with Sean in tow. Plainly annoyed, the CO had introduced Sean and gruffly added 'out of Langley' as if that was all the explanation needed. Later, as they'd sat in the back of the Foxhound patrol vehicle taking them to their drop-off point, Sean had elaborated. He was a CIA intelligence officer, there to identify a particular terrorist leader believed to be in the area. Silva had spent the rest of the day with Sean, hunkered down in a makeshift bunker with only Itchy for company. Sean had watched as Silva had dispatched a fighter who'd made the mistake of venturing forth and then nearly crapped himself when the one man had turned into twenty and they'd had to do a rapid exfil down a steep gully.

Back in the Foxhound, speeding along the dirt road towards the base, Silva had ribbed him. 'I thought you were a spy. James Bond, Jason Bourne, derring-do and all.'

'Fuck that.' Sean had given her a grin and tapped his head. 'I'm an intelligence officer and my brain tells me to steer clear of bullets.'

'Right.'

'Forgive me for saying so, but force alone never wins the battle.' Sean nodded at Silva's rifle. 'Analysis of the situation leading to the formation of a specific strategy for victory will.'

'And what's your strategy for victory?'

Sean smiled, his intent now obvious from his flirtatious look. 'To ask you to have a drink with me tonight when we get back to the base.'

It had started there and ended, at Silva's behest, three years later. Their relationship had been conducted on Skype and WhatsApp and in the short periods of leave they could arrange to coincide. Silva had been in Afghanistan, then back to the UK, and then to Afghanistan again on what would be her final tour before she was court-martialled. Sean had flitted between Baghdad, Kabul, London and the US. He'd visited her once when she'd been in the glasshouse and she'd told him not to come again. When she'd been released she'd met him in London during one of his stopovers and that was the last time she'd seen him.

'Where are you, Sean?' Silva asked. From the delay and crackle on the line she suspected he was using a satellite phone and calling from somewhere remote. She felt her defences rise as if she needed to protect herself from something. Almost unconsciously she hardened the tone of her voice. 'And what do you want?'

'I'm in Plymouth, Becca. And I want to see you.'

–

The first week of Holm's pretend investigation panned out pretty much as he expected. Colleagues poked their heads round the door of the little office to see what he was up to, Huxtable nodded with approval when she saw the fake brief Holm had written on animal rights groups, and Javed continued to slurp his coffee, crunch his biscuits and clip his nails in a way that annoyed Holm immensely.

The two of them monitored the Twitter account of the mysterious user known as TCXGP1505, while Holm set up the dummy animal rights operation. He phoned his contacts and let them know what he was up to and made requests for information from various agencies. A policy book was created and a budget drawn up. Javed scoured the internet for extreme material and organised everything in a database.

The initial excitement Holm had felt when Javed had shown him the tweet slowly ebbed away though. TCXGP1505 remained silent. The account followed nobody and had no followers. The sole tweet was the one in Arabic that referenced the innocent one.

'I don't get it,' Holm said. 'I'm beginning to wonder if our source, if that's what it was, has been compromised.'

Javed looked up from his screen, horrified. 'You mean taken out?'

'It figures. What else can explain the lack of a follow-up?'

Javed shrugged. 'If it's somebody close to Taher then the risk must be enormous. Perhaps they got cold feet.'

'Perhaps.' But Holm didn't think so. They'd sent one message. The tease. The wake-up call. The bait. If the source was still alive there had to be another one along at some point.

And so it proved.

On Friday afternoon, as Holm was deciding whether to take up Palmer's offer of a couple of jars after work, Javed lurched back in his chair.

'We're on!' The chair rocked violently as Javed changed direction and hunched forward, his face inches from the screen. 'What the…?'

Holm stood and moved over. The tweet was a sequence of numbers, seventeen in all.

'18, 18, 14, 0, 21, 11…' Javed began to read them. He turned from the screen. 'Another code.'

'Makes sense, after all, it's what we spooks do, isn't it? Codes and dead-letter drops and listening to phone conversations. Least that's what I believed before I signed on. More fool me.'

Holm read the numbers back to himself and tried several simple substitution ciphers in his head. The first three tries were gobbledygook so he went across to his desk and grabbed a few sheets of paper and a couple of pencils. He handed a sheet and a pencil to Javed. 'Let's see what that brain of yours can do.'

Holm wrote the numbers out large. Then small. Then in a scrawl. Then neatly. He tried placing them in a clock face, moving round the dial in a random fashion. He multiplied the numbers together. Divided them. Added them.

'You got something, boss?' Javed said. He appeared to have a similar idea to Holm as he was using the calculator on his phone to perform some kind of complicated transformation. 'Because it's beyond me.'

'Nothing, and we can't very well give it to the bods at GCHQ. We have to work this out ourselves.'

'They want us to get this,' Javed said. 'Else why bother?'

Holm read through the numbers once more. There were, of course, certain codes that couldn't be deciphered. They were uncrackable and offered perfect secrecy even against the most powerful supercomputer.

'I've got it,' Holm said, realising what the cipher was. 'These numbers are from a one-time pad.'

Javed nodded, understanding immediately. 'So we're stuffed?'

'Unless we can find the key, yes.'

A code created with a one-time pad used a sequence of letters or numbers to encrypt the message. Without the source material, decryption was impossible.

Holm screwed up his piece of paper and lobbed it towards the filing cabinet where it bounced off the front and fell into the waste paper bin. He shook his head.

They want us to get this… Javed had said.

He stared at the filing cabinet for a few seconds and walked over and opened the top drawer. The drawer held various documents relating to the fake animal rights investigation, but Holm rummaged behind them and pulled out the index card he'd discovered when they'd first moved in to the office.

'Christ.' He read the name on the card. Robert Gerard Sands. The full name of Bobby Sands, the IRA hunger striker who'd died way back in the nineteen eighties. There were seventeen letters in the name and there were seventeen numbers in the tweet. He jabbed a finger at the name, not quite believing what he was seeing. 'This is the key. This is the one-time pad.'

'How the—?'

'I've no bloody idea.'

'A is zero, right?' Javed was at his shoulder now, the lad's face creased in concentration. 'At least that's what I was taught.'

'Yes, let's start with that.' Holm began to do the calculations himself. He wrote out the full code sequence, below that the name, and below that an A to Z scale numbered zero to twenty-five.

18, 18, 14, 0, 21, 11, 25, 8, 8, 13, 9, 23, 23, 5, 1, 14, 2

Robert Gerard Sands

A/0 B/1 C/2 D/3 E/4 F/5 G/6 H/7 I/8 J/9 K/10
L/11 M/12 N/13 O/14 P/15 Q/16 R/17 S/18
T/19 U/20 V/21 W/22 X/23 Y/24 Z/25

The first number in the code was 18, while the first letter in the one-time pad sequence was R. The position of R on Holm's scale was 17 so he took that from 18, which left 1. Letter 1 on the same scale was B, so B was the answer. He moved on to the second number, which was also 18. However, the second letter on the pad was O which was 14 on the scale. 18 minus 14 was 4 so that became E. The third number was 14 and the third letter B. 14 minus… before he got any further Javed had it.

'Ben Western Suffolk.' Javed smiled and moved back to his chair. 'Whoever the hell that is.'

'Search it.'

'I am.' Javed's fingers were already tapping his keyboard. He ran his eyes down a screen of search results. 'There's a number of newspaper reports from last week. A man called Ben Western went missing in Suffolk. Doesn't appear to be anything particularly interesting about the case.'

'A misper?' Holm used his old police shorthand. 'That's *it*?'

Javed peered at the screen again. 'Well it can't be a coincidence.'

Holm slumped back and tried to get his head round the information. How could it have anything to do with the master terrorist he'd been hunting for years?

'Do you want me to look him up?' Javed had closed the browser and opened MI5's internal database. It held huge amounts of information and cross-referenced the Police National Computer, material held at GCHQ and MI6, as well as international databases from foreign agencies and police forces. Javed began to type. 'Might be a chance—'

'No!' Holm swung his chair round. 'There could be a flag on the record.'

'You mean...?'

'Think about it. Whoever sent us the information on this Ben Western guy must be in MI5 or have some sort of access. That could have been any one of hundreds, even thousands, of people.' Holm glanced at the filing cabinet. 'Nobody else would have been able to get the index card in there.'

'But why the subterfuge?'

'I'm not sure, but whoever it is can't want Huxtable or anyone else to know what we're up to. They must realise Taher has a contact in the security services. It's what I've been saying for ages.' Holm held up a finger and thumb and squeezed them together. 'Every time I've been close to catching Taher he's slipped away. I'm not risking that again.'

'So what do we do?'

Holm thought for a moment. 'Animal rights. Start searching the PNC for crimes suspected of being committed by animal liberation groups. That will bring up dozens of records spread across the country. Pick a few from the Suffolk area we can use as decoys.'

'And then?'

'We follow the Yellow Brick Road to the Emerald City.' Holm waited for a quip back from Javed but there was nothing. He shook his head, wondering if the lad's cultural references bore any relation to his own. 'Don't tell me you've never heard of *The Wizard of Oz*?'

'Of course I've heard of it. I've dreamed of being Dorothy for half my life.' Javed pouted and laughed as Holm reddened. 'But you, I imagine, would be better suited to playing the scarecrow.'

Chapter Eleven

They arranged to rendezvous on Plymouth Hoe, close to the spot where Silva had sat in the rain on the day of her mother's death. She strolled across the expanse of grass towards the red and white lighthouse where a man stood looking out at the view. Hair the colour of desert sand and just as fine swirled in light curls. There was a hint of red in the hair and a dusting of freckles on the face. If he'd been standing at the bar in a pub in Galway he could have been mistaken for an Irish poet, the type of man who always had a smile for the teenage girls, a rhyming couplet for the women, a tall tale and a pint of Guinness for his mates.

As she approached, Sean turned as if something had alerted him to her presence. He didn't smile, simply made a shrugging motion and opened his arms and embraced her. She'd steeled herself not to get emotional, but the gesture overwhelmed her. With her mother gone, there was no one else she'd ever been as close to as Sean. She held him for a long time and neither of them said anything until she sniffed away the last of her tears.

'I wished you'd met her,' Silva said.

Sean nodded. 'So do I. From what you told me and what I read she was—'

'Stop.' Silva raised a finger to Sean's lips. 'It doesn't matter what she was or wasn't beyond the fact she was my mother. All the media coverage, the press stories, what do I care?'

'You must be proud of her work?'

'I'd prefer she was still alive.' Silva pushed free from Sean and they began to walk across the grass. 'I never thought this could happen.'

'There were risks in what she did.' Sean shook his head. 'But to be honest, these days there are risks for all of us.'

'And you?' Silva reached out and touched Sean's hand. 'Are you still in the field?'

'I try not to be.' That grin. A mirror of the one Silva had first seen in Afghanistan. 'You know me, I'm no hero, but on occasion, yes.'

'You mentioned Sudan?'

'Yup. North Africa is the new front. Three and a half thousand miles from Mauritania to the Red Sea, two thousand miles from the Med to Somalia. Makes what we were up to in Afghanistan look like a game of hide and seek in the park. Things are pretty bad out there right now.' Sean slumped his shoulders and looked apologetic. 'Well, you know all about that.'

Silva nodded. 'ISIS?'

'ISIS, ISIL, IS, Daesh, AQIM, al-Shabaab, whatever you want to call them. These groups are something akin to a hydra. Cut off one head somewhere and another one emerges. There's no stopping them. There seems to be an infinite number of young men deluded enough to believe the propaganda. We take out half a dozen and another six come forward. The hydra.'

'I wish you were desk-based.' Silva linked arms with Sean as they walked. 'I'd feel a lot happier.'

'What's this, a change of plan?'

'I still care about you, even if…' Silva made a funny face and wrinkled her nose. 'You know.'

'Look, if I was desk-based, my desk would be on the other side of the Atlantic and I'd be sitting behind it and staring at a computer monitor instead of staring at you.' Sean turned his head and looked her up and down. 'No comparison. On the other hand, I guess I could get a screensaver with a picture of you. That might do. Something nice to look at anyway. Something to remind me of the good times we once had.'

'Stop it, Sean. We've been through this before.'

'We have, Becca. I'm like a recorded message playing on an endless loop.'

'You said it.'

'I worry about you.'

'No need. I can take care of myself, remember?'

'I'm not talking about physical danger. I mean your well-being.'

'You sound like my dad. He's scared I might be going mental.' Silva turned and faced him. 'But I'm not. You can see that.'

'He said you're delivering letters. You're a mailman or something.'

'You spoke to him?'

'I didn't have your latest mobile number. He was very chatty. Wanted to know what I'd been doing in Africa. He seemed to be quite up on world events.'

'Not quite so up on events concerning his own daughter.'

'You're still at loggerheads, then?' Sean shook his head. 'I thought you'd have made your peace.'

'This is one conflict that will never end.'

'You're bitter at him for not backing you. I can understand, but you can't go on hating him for that. Not now.'

'He hasn't been around since I was ten years old. Years later he tries to make amends and we come to some sort of amicable understanding. Then, when I really need him, he abandons me again.'

'He was in a difficult position, Becca. He couldn't back you over the incident in Afghanistan, at least not professionally.'

'Well he didn't do so personally either. In fact with my father I'm not sure there's any difference. Strategy and tactics cover his whole life from his morning crap to his evening cocoa.

Everything has to be planned out in advance or timed to the second.'

Sean shook his head once more. 'You're as bad as him, you know? Stubborn, obstinate, and you think your way is the only way.'

'If I'm so awful, then why are you here?' As she asked the question the answer came to her. Silva stopped and let go of Sean's arm. 'Hang on, you didn't phone my father, did you? He phoned you.'

Sean shrugged. Didn't say anything. They resumed walking, heading down to the Barbican area of the waterfront. When they reached the quayside they sat down at a table outside a bar and ordered drinks.

'Look,' Sean said once the waiter had brought the drinks over. 'You're right, your dad called me a couple of days ago. I just happened to have a month here in London on embassy duties, but I'd have come from anywhere if I'd thought there was a chance we might get back together.'

'But not otherwise?'

'No.' Sean hung his head. He reached for his beer and took a sip. 'Why continue to beat myself up?'

'You're not my friend, then?'

'Not *just* your friend. I could never cope with that.'

As Sean put his beer down, Silva gave a resigned look and half smiled.

'Sorry,' she said.

–

Javed spent an hour conducting an extensive search for crimes associated with animal rights that had been committed in East Anglia. He printed out the results.

'Here you go,' he said, waving a dozen sheets of paper in the air, his voice tinged with triumph as if what he'd done was a major achievement. 'The animal libbers love it up there in Suffolk. Pig units, chicken units, Huntingdon Life Sciences just over the border in Cambridgeshire. By the number of incidents it seems to be a regular hotbed.'

'Great,' Holm said. 'But we're not really looking for animal rights activists, are we?'

'No, I guess not.' Javed lowered the crime reports and dumped them on the table. He swivelled his chair to face Holm. 'Pity.'

Holm reached across his desk for his old address book. The scrappy A5 booklet was full of contacts he'd made over the years, many from way back when he'd been a copper. Pre-smartphones, almost pre-mobiles, the pages were a mess of hurriedly jotted addresses and telephone numbers. Most, he realised, would be out of date, but he only needed a name or two. He flicked through the book, pausing every now and then as he tried to recall old colleagues and where they'd ended up. He was halfway through when he stopped and snapped the book closed.

'Suffolk Constabulary, of course,' he said. He smiled, a face coming to mind. And not just a face, a body too. Rounded and curvy and moving under the sheets like no one else ever had. 'Billie Cornish.'

'Who's he?'

'She. Billie was colleague of mine when I was on the Met. I'd completely forgotten she moved to East Anglia. If she's still there and in the job she might be able to help.'

'Are we talking work-related help?' Javed was digging, a grin on his face suggesting he'd worked out Holm's past relationship with Cornish wasn't solely on a professional level. 'Only we don't need any distractions.'

'It was a long time ago. I was younger and she was much younger.'

'I didn't know you had it in you, boss.'

'Fuck off.'

'Sounds like I might have to if you're planning to meet this woman. What are you going to tell her?'

'I'll tell her MI5 would appreciate some help.' Holm looked round for his phone. 'While I do that, you enter some of those crimes into our mock database so we have an excuse to go up to Suffolk and do some groundwork.'

'Right, boss.'

Holm wasn't surprised to find Billie Cornish had moved on and up. She'd been a Detective Constable fifteen years ago, wet behind the ears, wet... he felt a shiver go through him. He'd never met anyone as exciting before or since, and even though their affair had been short-lived, he still remembered every moment like yesterday. She wasn't much more than half his age back then, mid-twenties to his early forties, but she'd made all the running. She'd ended it too, three months down the line. She was going places, she said. Too many things to do, too many people she wanted to screw. He was sweet, he was a great lover, but it was never going to be a long-term thing between them – he could see that, couldn't he?

Yeah, he supposed he could. He'd had two kids under ten, a wife who'd made a nest without a word of complaint about the long hours he worked or the fact she'd had to sacrifice her own career to raise their children, a nice house in a decent part of London. And yet...

'You going to actually make that call?' Javed. The grin was now verging on subordination. 'Only we're supposed to be catching Taher before he retires and draws his pension.'

Holm dismissed Javed with a wave. He found a number for CID in Suffolk, but it took several calls before he was put through to Detective Chief Superintendent Billie Cornish at force HQ in Ipswich.

He found himself stumbling through a couple of minutes of casual chit-chat, embarrassed it had been so long since they'd been in touch. He congratulated Cornish on her rise through the ranks, played down his own position with JTAC and then he was on to the meat of the call.

'We've had some intelligence recently about a group of animal activists planning something big, something to rival the jihadis. The fox-hunting debate has been won, animal testing is on the way out and the public have lost interest. They need a marquee event to garner a little attention.'

'Other people taking their thunder, hey?' Cornish said.

'Something like that.' Holm paused. Even though he'd worked a long time in the security services, he still found the lying difficult, and he didn't like deceiving Cornish. 'The way the wind is blowing they need publicity to promote their cause.'

'We're not talking Huntingdon again, are we?'

'No, this is something different. It's right on your patch so I figured you'd be willing to get your hands a little dirty in order to help us.'

'Dirty?' Cornish sounded wary, unconvinced. She'd emphasised the word in such a way as to imply a degree of scepticism. 'What do you mean by that, Stephen?'

Holm sighed to himself. Cornish had always been keen on professional integrity, dead straight, and part of him was grateful her integrity hadn't been compromised on the scrabble up the ladder to the top. On the other hand a little bending of the rules would come in handy right now.

'Nothing dodgy.' Holm glanced across to Javed. The young man had raised his head and was listening intently. Holm turned and faced away. 'We just need to keep a lid on things and ensure nobody at your end gets too carried away.' Holm coughed. 'National security and all that.'

'Right.' Cornish still sounded hesitant. 'What do you want, then?'

'I'll tell you when we get there. If you could clear your diary from, say, elevenish on Monday morning?'

'Clear my diary? Stephen, that's going to be—'

'Lives are at stake, Billie.' If Taher was involved then there was no deception here, Holm thought. 'Many lives.'

There was silence for a moment before Cornish spoke again.

'See you at eleven Monday, then.'

Holm hung up.

'We're off up the Yellow Brick Road, then?' Javed said.

'Yes,' Holm said. 'But if we want to get to Ipswich the A12 would probably be a better bet.'

–

In the evening Silva and Sean met up with Itchy and his girl-friend, Caz. Caz's stomach bulged beneath her flimsy dress, a piece of news Itchy had been keeping from Silva. After a round of congratulations, Itchy began to open up on the joys of fatherhood.

'Man, in four months I'm going to be a dad,' Itchy said. 'How does that sound?'

'I'm not sure,' Silva said. 'Should I call Social Services to prewarn them?'

'You'll do fine,' Sean said. 'But kids are expensive – how's the money?'

'Tight.' Itchy grimaced and reached for his pint. He glanced at Silva. 'We were shafted, weren't we? Cast off. No demob money, no pension to look forward to. I've got bits and pieces here and there, but nothing permanent. Still, I couldn't be happier if I'd won the lottery.'

As Itchy turned to Caz and kissed her, Silva felt Sean's hand under the table, reaching for her own hand. Squeezing.

Later, back on Silva's boat and somewhat worse for drink, they kissed. For a few seconds Silva let herself go with the passion of the moment, but then she pulled away.

'You don't want this?' Sean said.

'I do and I don't.' Silva moved across to the galley area and filled the kettle. 'I don't want to go back to the way we were. A few days together and then weeks and months apart. It's not good for either of us.'

'Becca, you know how it is…'

'Yes, I do know how it is. That kind of life ruined my parents' marriage. Right now, considering all that's happened, I need stability or nothing.'

'Nothing?'

'You'll be gone tomorrow and I won't know where you are or what you're doing. I'll have no idea of when I might see you again.'

Sean came over and stood next to Silva as she scraped some instant coffee from the bottom of a jar. 'I wish things could be different.'

Silva leaned across and rested her head on Sean's shoulder.

'Me too,' she said.

–

She took him to the train station the next morning, weaving through the traffic on her motorbike with Sean clinging on for grim death.

'Jesus, woman,' he said when Silva pulled up. 'Dodging bullets in Afghanistan was preferable to that.' Sean dismounted and took his helmet off. He handed it to Silva who put it in the rear pannier. He stood for a moment. 'So is this goodbye or *au revoir*?'

'Neither.' Silva sighed. 'Where's the future in it, Sean? Being together wouldn't be being with you. Most of the time you'd be away and that's not what I want. Not at this point in my life at least.'

'There's hope, then.' Sean said. 'Years in the future. Decades. About the time when I'm in adult diapers and drooling.'

'Stop it.' Silva leaned across and hugged him. She hit the starter on the bike. 'You'll email this time? Phone, text, message. You know, like friends do?'

'I might,' Sean said. He looked as if he was about to make another quip. Then he reached out and touched Silva on the shoulder, all of a sudden serious. 'No, I will. Promise.'

'Good.'

She clicked the bike into gear and Sean stepped back. He turned towards the station and raised a hand as Silva rode away.

Chapter Twelve

Sean kept his promise to call much sooner than she expected when her mobile trilled out late the next afternoon.

'It was so good to see you yesterday, Becca,' he said. 'Better than good.'

'Hmmm.' Silva felt her defences slip but she tried to play it cool. It *had* been good to see him, but she didn't want to get his hopes up. 'I guess.'

'Do you want to do it again sometime?'

'Sure, Sean. Next time you're back in the UK give me a call.'

'So you wouldn't be on for tomorrow, then?'

'*Tomorrow?*'

'Something's come up. I've got tickets for a special event here in London on Monday evening. Once in a lifetime. History in the making.'

'Give me a hint. Theatre? Music? Sport?'

'Sort of all three. I need a partner on my arm and you're my first choice.'

'There are others?'

'Of course. They're falling over themselves but you've got the first refusal.'

She felt herself wavering. Seeing him again had made her realise how much she missed him, how much she craved the simple human interaction between two people who were more than friends. She'd shut herself away after her spell in prison. Sure, there was Itchy and a couple of others, but she wasn't close to them in the way she was close to Sean.

What the hell. 'OK, I'll—'

Sean hollered out something she didn't hear, and then he was filling her head with timings and where to meet and what to wear.

'What to wear?' It wasn't something Sean usually worried about. They'd spent the first three months they'd known each other in military fatigues.

'It's suited and booted. For me, at least. Just dress formal, I'm sure you'll look great whatever it is.'

Silva thought about the handful of fancy clothes she had. 'If you say so.'

–

They drove to Ipswich early Monday morning. On the way up Javed was a buzz of questions. One after the other. The incessant chatter began to annoy Holm. He was used to having space to think and had hoped the two-hour journey would allow his mind to drift round the subject of Taher and Tunisia and the mysterious informant who'd given them the tip-off.

No such luck.

Javed appeared to regard Holm as a fountain of all intelligence and policing knowledge he was determined to sup from. True, Holm did have several decades of experience while Javed looked as if he'd not even made the first repayment on his student loan. Still, the lad had to gain some respect before he earned the right to Holm's wisdom. In the end Holm slipped a Miles Davis CD into the player and turned the volume up. Javed at first winced, then sulked, and then dozed.

Like a baby, Holm thought as he pulled into the car park at Suffolk police HQ and somewhat cruelly applied the brakes a little too harshly.

'We're here,' Javed said, the sudden jerk waking him. He blinked and looked round. A large brick building encircled by a canal of green water stood in front of them. 'Looks like they're ready for anything. Perhaps we should dig up Millbank so we can have a moat too. MI6 have one, don't they?'

'I don't think this moat has got anything to do with terrorism,' Holm said. 'Probably just an architect's wet dream.'

'Wet dream, good.' Javed nodded in appreciation. 'What do we do now?'

'What *we* do is nothing. What *I* do is go in. Cornish is an old friend. I'd like to play on that a bit and you'll be a gooseberry.'

'Gooseberry?' Javed tilted his head. He made an obscene thrusting movement with his hips. 'So you're hoping to slide back into your old parking space are you?'

'No, of course not, I just meant…' Holm stopped. What did he mean? It had been a decade or more since he'd seen Billie. Fifteen since they'd rolled around in her bed. Cornish wasn't going to let their brief relationship from back then have any influence on her. Holm turned to Javed. Young, Asian, part-time Muslim, the lad's sexuality worn on his sleeve. He bit his lip. 'On second thoughts, you can come too. Billie Cornish always was one for ticking the boxes. You'll be right up her street.'

'Nice to know I'm wanted for something, even if it isn't my abilities.'

At the front desk, Holm was annoyed to learn Cornish wasn't on-site.

'She's out on a job,' the desk sergeant said. 'Dunwich Heath. She'll be gone a while so she left instructions you were to head up there.'

Back in the car, Javed plotted the destination into his phone. 'It's on the coast,' he said. 'Looks like a nice beach. Pity I didn't bring my Speedos.'

Half an hour later they were driving through heathland towards the sea. Yellow-tipped gorse and brown heather, a hint of the purple to come once that too was fully in flower. The road ended at a terrace of white cottages stuck out on their own. A grey sea churned in over a narrow strip of beach behind the cottages, and to the right stood several police vehicles. Two uniformed officers were preventing people in the nearby car park from venturing onto the heath and one of the officers waved down Holm as he drove up. Holm lowered the window and slipped out his identification.

'I'm looking for Detective Chief Superintendent Cornish,' Holm said. 'Is she here?'

'MI5?' The officer peered down at Holm's ID and raised his eyebrows at his colleague. He pointed across the heath to where several figures in white suits ghosted back and forth in a clump of stunted pines. 'She's over there.'

Holm thanked the officers and parked up.

They got out of the car, walked towards the trees and were met by an officer with a tablet which, when Holm flashed his ID once more, was thrust out for a signature.

'I don't think so,' Holm said. He tapped his nose. 'Not for Five, huh?'

For a moment the officer looked as if he was about to make a scene, but then he shrugged and let them pass.

'Sir?' Javed said.

'A trace,' Holm said. 'As in we don't want to leave one.'

Cornish stood over by the clump of pines conversing with a couple of white-suited CSIs. She had her back to them as Holm and Javed approached but was instantly recognisable from the long blonde hair which lay tightly plaited down to the small of her back. She had an inch or two on both the CSIs and a stature that suggested she could hold her own against anyone in a fight, male or female.

'Stephen,' Cornish said as she turned, offering her hand and smiling. 'Great to see you again.'

Holm reached forward and took her hand. It seemed ridiculously formal considering he'd made love with this woman, lain in a post-coital embrace, their sweat mingling as their heartbeats slowed.

'You too, Billie.' Holm smiled back. Cornish looked as good as ever. Better. He had trouble believing she was forty. 'It's been a long time.'

'Yes. The last case we worked on together was the girl we found in the Thames upstream of Teddington Lock. Three bin liners containing the body parts, the bags weighed down with bricks. If you remember, she was the wife of a right-wing nutcase who was planning to blow up a synagogue. She tried to do the right thing, but he killed her before she could report him. Of course in a strange way she still managed to put him behind bars. All's well that ends well, hey?'

'I wish you hadn't reminded me. The memory's cheered me up no end.'

'Sorry for dragging you out here, but needs must.' Cornish turned and gestured at the white terrace of cottages. 'We can grab a coffee over at the National Trust cafe in a bit and have a chat about what you want from me.'

'Sure, but one of your officers can help us. All we want to do is get the details for a crime that happened on your patch.'

'Sorry?' Cornish shook her head. 'I don't understand. You could have done that from London using the PNC. Why did you need to come all the way out here? Have MI5 not being paying their broadband bills or something?'

'Or something.' Holm stood with his hands in his pockets. Said nothing else.

'Is this what you meant by getting my hands dirty?'

'Look, if the case turns out to be of interest we'll want more information. A lot more information. This is the easiest way to investigate without arousing suspicion.'

'You could simply have phoned or emailed.'

Holm once more kept silent. Shrugged his shoulders.

'National security, right?' Cornish laughed and began to walk away. She gestured at the officer with the tablet. 'See Mike over there. He'll do it. If you need a printout or more info go back to HQ. I'll let them know you're coming. If you're still around in an hour or so we can have that coffee, otherwise it's been nice seeing you again, Stephen.'

'I thought she was an old buddy of yours?' Javed said once Cornish was out of earshot. 'Doesn't seem very friendly to me. Brushed you off like a speck of dandruff.'

'It's because we're spooks,' Holm said. 'Not much love for us in the police force. Sometimes I wonder whose side they think we're on.'

Was that it? Holm wondered, or was there something else. He thought they'd split amicably – after all she was the one who'd wanted to make the break – but perhaps there was a hint of regret layered in her brusqueness. Perhaps, unbelievably, there was still a spark of something between them, something that could be rekindled. On the other hand, perhaps he was just kidding himself.

They walked across to the officer Cornish had pointed out and made the request for the crime look-up.

'Some guy called Ben Western,' Holm said, trying to appear casual. 'A missing person case I think.'

'Did you say *Ben Western*?' The officer coughed out the name with a sneer. He glanced back in the direction of Cornish. 'Are you winding me up?'

'Sorry?' Holm tried to be polite. 'Is there a problem?'

'You might say so.' For a moment it looked as if the officer would snap at Holm again, but then he sighed. 'I think you'd better go and have another word with Detective Chief Superintendent Cornish. Tell her your crime is the Western misper case.'

'That's it?' Holm waited for some clarification but the officer managed barely a nod before he turned away.

'Helpful, this lot,' Javed said as the officer walked off.

–

Silva headed for London on Monday and, thanks to light traffic on the motorway, made the journey in a little under three and a half hours. Sean was staying in a large house bordering Wimbledon Common; with the security gates and cameras the place could have been the residence of a Russian oligarch. However, the man who let her in and showed her where to park in the subterranean garage spoke English with an American accent.

'Got a flat of my own here,' Sean said when he met her in the reception area and took her upstairs. He gave Silva a smile. 'Saves on expensive hotel rooms.'

Sean pushed open the door to his flat and showed her through to a luxuriously furnished living room. A balcony with French windows offered a fine view over Wimbledon Common, but the place felt like the serviced apartment it was: anodyne pictures of sandy beaches and sunsets, a few knick-knacks, plain linen. Nice enough, but impersonal.

'Don't you get tired of this?' Silva said. 'Not having anywhere to call home?'

'I've got a place back in Maine.'

'It's rented out.'

'And you live on an old boat.'

'The difference is it's *my* boat with *my* things.'

'Goes with the territory. I'll settle down eventually. Couple of kids. Little League. Barbecues. Wash the car on the weekend. Not ready for that just yet though.'

'Tonight,' Silva said. 'Why the secrecy?'

'I'm a secret agent, remember? Besides, don't you like surprises?'

Silva didn't respond. Surprises were nice when they came packaged in paper and wrapped in ribbons. Handed over with love. Not when they were buried in a muddy track and ripped someone's legs from their body. Not when they took away a loved one.

She dumped her panniers by the door and strolled over to where the French windows stood open. She looked out across the common, aware that just a few miles to the north east, Neil Milligan was probably sitting behind his desk at Third Eye News, while to the south of London, Matthew Fairchild was likely working in his office. She thought about Milligan's slippery evasiveness and contrasted that with Fairchild's steely resolve. Wondered what her next move should be.

'Tea?' Sean was across one side of the room by a small open-plan kitchen area. He'd made an effort, Silva could see. There was a plate of pastries, some fresh bread and a selection of cheeses. 'There's a buffet tonight, but I thought you might be hungry after the journey.'

'Great,' she said.

She moved from the window, determined to put Milligan, Fairchild, and Hope to the back of her mind for the rest of the day.

Chapter Thirteen

Cornish was standing near a white forensic shelter a good way across the heath, so Holm and Javed had to plough through the heather. As they approached, she looked up, her face quizzical.

'You're back,' she said.

'The Western missing person case,' Holm said. 'Our crime, apparently.'

'*What?*' Cornish scowled. 'Ben Western's got nothing to do with animal rights.'

'You look as surprised as your officer did.'

'What the hell's going on here, Stephen?' Cornish was spitting angry. Holm hadn't remembered her as having a temper, but perhaps that was what you needed to get on these days. Perhaps that was why he was stuck in a cupboard back at JTAC, pushing sixty, with nothing much to look forward to but a meagre pension and a cold empty flat.

'I don't know. Perhaps you'd better fill us in on who this Western fellow is.'

'*Was* – he's dead.' Cornish jabbed a finger at Holm, the anger back. 'And yet you don't know who the hell he is?'

'No, I don't.' Holm felt a tingle on the back of his right hand. He balled his fist to conceal his excitement. 'Maybe you could start at the beginning?'

'No, let's start in here.' Cornish lifted the flap on the forensic tent. 'I hope all that paper-pushing analysis work for JTAC hasn't weakened your stomach. Mind you, it's not as bad as the Teddington girl.'

Holm ducked at the entrance and followed Cornish inside.

'Shit.' He turned away for a moment and swallowed. 'What did you say about this being no worse than the Teddington girl?'

The man lay on his side, his face towards them. There was a large area of scorched heather surrounding the head and upper torso. The fire had consumed the hair, and the face was seared like a rasher of bacon left too long in the frying pan. The lips had burned back revealing white teeth and blackened bone, and the eye sockets were dark holes surrounded by carbonised flesh. Farther down, where the fire hadn't reached, the clothing hung loose. As Holm looked closer he could see a rippling as something moved beneath the material. Maggots, Holm thought, eating the parts of the body that hadn't been fried to a hard crust.

Outside, Javed had been trying to peer into the tent and the fact he'd disappeared a few seconds later suggested to Holm the boy had seen more than he wanted to. Lightweight.

'Is this Ben Western?'

'Yes.'

'Cause of death?'

'What does the expert from London think?'

'Very funny.' Holm shook his head but moved closer. He bent and examined the heather. He'd seen this before. 'There was an accelerant. He fell into the flames and burned alive.'

'Could be.' Cornish pulled something from her pocket. A phone. She flicked her fingers across the screen. 'Here. This was the scene before the CSIs started work.'

Holm peered down. A picture showed the man lying in the heather, only now, to the right of the body and clasped in one hand, was an empty bottle of Smirnoff vodka.

'Great.' Holm felt his earlier excitement fade. Had he been played by the person sending the tweets? Or perhaps there'd been an error, the wrong information sent. That never happened in spy novels but it wasn't hard to imagine a mistake being made, especially if the person sending the message had been in a hurry or at risk of being discovered. 'So Mr Western drowns his sorrows and wanders onto the heath, lights up a cigarette and accidentally sets fire to himself. How many of these types of losers do you get a year?'

'Not as many as in London, I'm sure, but all is not quite what it seems, Mr Expert.' Cornish reached out and pointed at the head of the corpse. 'Look closely at the base of the skull. There's an entry wound.'

'He was shot?'

'Seems likely. We'll know after the post-mortem.' Cornish stood beside Holm. She glanced at her watch. Pressure. Deadlines. Then the tension dissipated. 'Look, sorry I snapped earlier. It's good to see you again. Why don't I buy us something over at the National Trust cafe? Your colleague too.'

'He won't be hungry.' Holm gestured out through the flap of the tent. 'About to relieve himself of his breakfast by the looks of it.'

'You missed this.' A few paces away, Javed straightened. He hadn't been sick and didn't appear ill. He pointed at a canister lying on the ground. 'Down in the heather.'

'What is it?' Cornish said.

'A cigarette lighter refill. I guess there's your accelerant, not the vodka.'

Holm smiled. He was a little saddened Javed hadn't spewed his guts up, but on the other hand showing Cornish JTAC employed more than just paper-pushing analysts was worth the disappointment.

'I guess that's why we had to drive all the way from London,' Holm said. 'I don't know, Farakh, what would they do without us? Bloody country bumpkins.'

Cornish barked something out to one of the CSIs and directed him over to Javed. She shook her head.

'Thanks.' She nodded towards the sea. 'Let's get that coffee.'

Holm and Javed followed Cornish along a narrow path back to the car park. The little cafe was devoid of customers aside from a solitary police officer who was chatting to the woman behind the counter. When Cornish approached he nodded and made his excuses.

'That's what it's like these days,' Cornish said as they sat at a table. 'The loneliness of command.'

'I wouldn't know.' Holm said. He looked at Javed. 'Although sometimes a little peace and quiet would be welcome.'

'Believe me, there's never any of that.' Cornish stared out of the cafe window. The officer who'd left was talking to a colleague, and Holm had the sense Cornish wasn't exactly happy with her role.

'Ma'am?' Javed cut into the awkward silence. 'Who exactly was Ben Western?'

Cornish swung round. 'He worked as the operations manager at SeaPak, a container shipping company. They're based at Felixstowe and have a distribution centre there, as well as at Rotterdam in the Netherlands. Six months ago Western handed in his notice. Then, last week, he went missing. There was some evidence he might have been abducted, but it was sketchy. There was certainly no reason for him to run off and leave his wife and kids.'

'It happens.' Holm remembered walking into his living room to find his own wife straddling his next-door neighbour, his first thought – bizarrely – that he'd paid way over the odds for the deep-pile carpet the pair were fucking on. Perhaps he should have simply turned round and disappeared himself.

'Yes, but alarm bells started to ring.' Cornish paused. She took a sip of coffee, and when she spoke again the edge in her voice returned. Suspicion and a touch of aggression. 'Now, before I tell you anything else, I want to know what exactly your interest is in Ben Western.'

'Like I told you on the phone, animal rights.' Holm bent to his own coffee, trying to disguise the lie. 'Five are tracking a group out of Birmingham. We believe they may be planning something.'

'Crap,' Cornish said. 'One, as far as I know Ben Western has nothing to do with animal rights, and two, since when did

Stephen Holm concern himself with the antics of a few vegan loonies?'

'Since last month.' Holm didn't have to put on an act now. He lowered his head. 'Since the whole country went to a critical threat level on my advice. Since UK citizens died in Tunisia on my watch.'

Cornish looked abashed. She reached out a hand and touched Holm's arm. 'That was you?'

Holm nodded. 'Yes.'

'Those were a crazy few hours, even out here in the sticks. We had to lock down the port of Felixstowe and then there was...' Cornish let her words trail off and she turned her head once more. This time her gaze was directed up the coast to where a distant cluster of huge concrete buildings surrounded a brilliant white dome. Sizewell nuclear power station. 'You'd tell me if your investigation had anything to do with that, wouldn't you, Stephen? National security or not?'

Holm took another drink of coffee. Swallowed. He'd spotted the power station on the drive in, even pointed it out to Javed, but for some reason it hadn't even crossed his mind it could be connected.

'Of course I would,' he said.

–

'So,' Javed said as they watched Cornish drive off in a patrol car. 'What do you reckon?'

Holm wasn't listening. He was still considering Cornish's question about Sizewell. He'd refused to answer her probing directly, instead keeping up the animal rights charade, but if there'd been a real threat? Something which could have harmed her? National security or not, he pretty much knew he'd have told her the truth.

As it was, Cornish had let it lie. She'd given them some more information on Ben Western and SeaPak, but there wasn't much to go on and nothing to suggest a link to Taher. Pity, Holm thought. It would have been nice to spend a bit of time with Cornish. But that was stupid. A fine woman like her had to be married by now. There'd be kids, home life, a world away from work. Then again Holm had once known the same and it hadn't been enough. All of a sudden he was thinking of how old he felt, of how lucky Cornish's husband must be, of how his own marriage had ended in failure and recriminations.

'Hello?' Javed said as Cornish's car disappeared into the distance. 'Come in, number twenty-nine, your time is up.'

'Huh?' Holm flipped back to real life.

'I was asking about Ben Western and SeaPak.' Javed's gaze drifted seawards. On the horizon one tiny smudge after another lay strung out in a line. Cargo ships awaiting clearance into Felixstowe. 'What the hell can the murder of Western have to do with Taher?'

Holm moved towards their car. A breeze blew in off the sea, cold and damp. He'd neglected to put his jacket on when they arrived and now he felt chilled. 'I have no idea.'

–

The event started at six, and as they struggled through the rush-hour crowds, Silva felt ridiculously overdressed in her black cocktail dress. In his smart suit, Sean looked like an actor about to step onto the red carpet.

'The reception is at the National Gallery,' Sean said as they emerged from the tube at Charing Cross and walked across Trafalgar Square. 'It's a private function.'

They climbed the steps to the gallery and joined a small queue. A man was checking tickets and guiding people in past heavy security. Two guards were frisking every guest and leading them through a metal detector for good measure.

'You can't be too careful these days,' Sean said.

They strolled along a corridor and into a wing with restricted access. Another pair of suits, well muscled, a flash of a shoulder holster under one man's jacket.

'Howya doin', Sean?' one of the men said in a heavy American accent. He shook his head. 'Them Patriots not doing so well, right?'

'You got me there, Frank,' Sean said as they walked past. 'Maybe next season.'

'You didn't tell me this was *work*.' Silva understood now: she was eye candy for Sean at some embassy function. 'And to be honest I wouldn't have come if you had.'

'There you go, then. But I promise the experience will be worth it. Come on.' Sean took her arm and guided her across the room to where a rotund man was selecting nibbles from a table. He was eyeing a cocktail sausage with suspicion as they approached.

'Sean.' The man popped the sausage in his mouth and barely chewed before swallowing. Like the security detail he was American. He wore an expensive dark suit, but over his large frame the tailoring was wasted. Heavy jowls sagged with flesh and his neck was almost non-existent, while a bushy crop of curly brown hair added to the impression of size. 'Hell, where are my manners? And in front of a beautiful woman too. Who's your delightful partner, young man?'

'Mr Deputy Ambassador,' Sean said. 'This is my friend Rebecca.'

'Friend?' The deputy ambassador shook his head and extended his hand. 'Well, if you say so.'

'Hello, Mr Ambassador,' Rebecca said, feeling awkward.

'It's Greg. Greg Mavers. And I'm not the ambassador quite yet.' Mavers gave a wink to Sean. 'Now tell me, young lady, just what is it you do?'

'She's ex-military, sir,' Sean said. 'Served in Afghanistan.'

'A privilege, Rebecca,' Mavers said. 'You know, the way things have turned out, the vets just don't get the appreciation they deserve.'

'Tell me about it,' Silva said.

'Sorry?'

'Rebecca was hard done by, sir,' Sean said. 'Like a lot of soldiers were.'

'Beats me why anyone joins the army in the first place. The problem is...' Mavers shook his head and his voice trailed off as a smattering of applause echoed off the ceiling. 'Damn. My apologies, I've got to go or I'll miss my cue.'

He moved away through the crowd towards a small stage with a lectern. Silva craned her neck to see over the people in front of her. The crowd had surged forward like kids at a tweeny-pop gig, but she still couldn't understand what the fuss was about. Then there was another round of applause as Mavers stepped up to the lectern.

'Good evening, ladies and gentlemen.' Mavers's voice boomed out, the PA system totally redundant. 'The new American Room is a fitting symbol of the pan-Atlantic relationship. A gallery filled with portraits of notable Americans right here on British soil. I wonder if Thomas Paine could have envisaged such a thing when he set sail two and a half centuries ago.' Here Mavers paused for a burst of laughter. 'Anyway, without further ado, I'm pleased to introduce the benefactor who made the new gallery possible.' Mavers swung an arm out to one side where a tall brunette with striking features and iceberg-blue eyes stood waiting. 'Ladies and gentlemen, Karen Hope.'

Silva clutched at Sean, her legs almost buckling with the shock. Hope climbed the steps to the lectern and the room erupted in cheers and whoops. Silva felt Sean's hand take hers in a tight grip. If he noticed her reaction he appeared to think it was from excitement.

'Amazing, huh?' he said. 'I told you we'd be witnessing history. This is something you'll remember for the rest of your life.'

'Thank you, thank you.' Hope waved the audience quiet, but in the manner of an experienced politician she continued to milk the applause, not speaking until the clapping had faded to almost nothing. 'I'm honoured to be here today...'

The speech descended into a fuzz of noise. The woman's lips moved, mouthing words that made no sound. Sean stood next to Silva, staring in admiration. Nearly everyone was as beguiled as he was, but by the end of the speech, Silva felt physically sick. She excused herself, pushed through the throng and went to find a bathroom.

She sat in the cubicle for a few minutes and then emerged and splashed water on her face. She went back to the gallery to find Sean hovering near the entrance.

'Where have you been?' he said. 'Come on.'

He grabbed her hand and pulled her through the crowded room. There was an inevitability to what happened next, as if some unseen force was pulling her forward. Bodies parted and then Silva was face to face with Karen Hope.

'Sean Connor.' Mavers stood alongside Hope. Blustery, sweaty and, all of a sudden, quite obnoxious. 'Sean's a rising star in the Agency. One to watch. And Rebecca...' Mavers turned. 'Sorry, I didn't get your last name?'

Silva couldn't speak. Her mouth opened but there was nothing but a gasp of air.

'Da Silva,' Sean said. 'Rebecca da Silva.'

There was a momentary flash of something in Hope's eyes. A twitch from a muscle in her neck. 'That name sounds familiar. Do I know you?'

'Rebecca's mother was killed in the recent attack in Tunisia,' Sean said. 'The Islamists were targeting a women's charity if you remember?'

'The journalist.' Hope wore a mask of pure innocence and compassion. She reached out and grasped Silva's hands with both of hers. 'How awful. I'm so sorry for your loss, Rebecca. The world deserves to be a better place so we don't have to endure this type of tragedy.'

Silva muttered something and it was all she could do to restrain herself from wrenching her hands free. She tried to speak, but still nothing coherent came out. Hope gave a little nod towards Sean. Do something, it said. An executive order. Comfort on command.

Then Hope released Silva's hands and was wheeled away by Mavers to press more worthy flesh.

'Jeez, Becca, are you OK?' Sean had his arm round her. 'Do you want something to drink?'

'Air,' Silva said. 'I need air. I need to get out of this fucking place.'

An elderly man close by gave Silva a glance. Bad form, swearing, the look said. Especially from a lady.

Silva stumbled away, shrugging off Sean's attempts to come with her. She passed through security and ran outside. She walked across Trafalgar Square to one of the fountains and sat on the edge. She clenched her fists. Hope had *known*. What Sean and Mavers had taken for being well briefed was in fact evidence of her guilt. Silva had seen the fleeting look of horror cross Hope's face. The realisation this was the daughter of her nemesis. What else had she realised? Did she have an inkling that Silva knew the whole story?

The air was warm and the stone wall she sat on radiated the heat of the day but despite this she shivered. After a few minutes she walked back up the road to the gallery. She slipped inside and made for the toilets. Along the corridor a couple of guests waited by the cloakroom desk while an attendant retrieved their belongings. To one side there was an anteroom, and a sheet of paper with the words *Green Room* printed in bold type had been stuck to the door. A raised voice floated out. Instead of going into the toilets, Silva moved towards the door. She hung near the entrance and casually peered through the crack. Greg Mavers stood over near one wall, his bulbous face white, his eyes wide and staring. A disembodied finger jabbed at his face. Silva shifted her position, but she already knew who the finger belonged to because she could hear the near screech from Karen Hope echo round the room.

'An apology isn't enough, Greg. Not nearly *fucking* enough.'

'I'm sorry, ma'am, I didn't think it would be—'

'That's the problem, you didn't bloody think.' The finger jabbed again, this time the long fingernail grazing Mavers's pallid skin. He tottered backwards, the overbearing, buffoon-like character Silva had talked to earlier reduced to a cowering wreck. 'I'm beginning to wonder if you are ambassador material after all. I might have to reconsider my offer.'

'Please, ma'am, give me another chance, I—'

Silva eased away from the door. A security guard was coming down the corridor so she moved off towards the toilets. The guard disappeared inside the green room and moments later reappeared with Hope and Mavers. Mavers dabbed at his cheek with a tissue and scurried along a couple of paces behind Hope as she made for the gallery entrance. Silva followed.

Outside a limo had drawn up. The director of the gallery waited on the pavement and shook Hope's hand as a press photographer took pictures. Hope's demeanour had changed and she was all white teeth and smiles for the camera. Silva thought about Fairchild's words: *appearance is everything in politics.* He was right. Hope wasn't what she seemed. Silva had seen a chink of what lay beneath the surface when she'd come face to face with her at the reception, and in the green room the mask had slipped completely.

With the pictures done, Hope said goodbye to the director and sauntered towards her car. Mavers opened the door for her and she climbed in. More smiles and a wave, Hope exuding confidence, acting as if the election was in the bag. Slam dunk. Home run. Touchdown.

Silva stepped to the side of the pavement and leaned against a wall as the car pulled away. Her nausea had returned with the realisation that this woman, this murderer, this... *bitch*, would be the next US president.

Unless somebody could stop her.

Chapter Fourteen

The evening in London hadn't ended well. Eventually Sean emerged from the gallery, but he was on a high, unable to pick up on Silva's mood. When they got back to his apartment he wanted to talk about Hope.

'You saw her,' he said. 'Sensational. Just what the country needs – damn it, what the whole world needs.'

'Are you sure about that?' Silva said as she slipped out of the black dress. 'Sure she isn't just a little bit too good to be true?'

Sean eyed Silva as the dress fell to the floor, misreading her again. 'This is a little bit too good to be true.' He threw off his jacket. 'Do you want a drink?'

Silva reached for her jeans and motorbike leathers and began to pull them on. 'Never when I'm driving, thanks.'

'Rebecca? What's going on?'

'I'm leaving. I have to get back.'

'For what?'

Silva put on her jacket and reached for her helmet. She was cross at Sean for misleading her about the evening and angry with herself for allowing her guard to drop. 'For the rest of my life, Sean, that's what.'

'I don't…' Sean paused before raising a hand and making a dismissive gesture. 'Aw fuck it. Do what you want. I'm beyond caring any more.'

Silva nodded and headed towards the door. She clicked it open and stood for a moment. 'That's what I thought.'

She arrived home in the early hours and spent a good chunk of Tuesday asleep in her bunk. She tried not to think about Karen Hope and Matthew Fairchild and Neil Milligan and Sean. Tried not to think about her mother. On Wednesday she returned to work and walked the streets. Pushed letters through flaps. Nodded to colleagues in the sorting office at the end of her round. Hung up her bag and went home and fed herself and lay on her bunk and read until she fell asleep.

The next day she woke thinking this was it. Stuck on an endless wash cycle: soak, rinse, spin, repeat. Soak, rinse, spin, repeat. She remembered her mother's exhortation in Tunisia: *At some point you have to move on.* There was sense in what she'd said, but it was almost as if her death prevented the very thing she'd told Silva to do. She doubted anybody else could understand, not even Itchy. He seemed to have escaped the worst of the psychological trauma of what happened in Afghanistan. Was that because his life *was* moving on? He had a girlfriend, a baby on the way, something to look forward to. What did Silva have? Perhaps it went deeper than that though. Itchy was happy-go-lucky, fatalistic. Things always worked out all right in the end; for Silva, raised by two headstrong parents who believed in their own ability to make a difference in the world, the powerlessness she'd experienced after Afghanistan had been debilitating. And now, with her mother dead, the feeling was almost overwhelming.

She went off to work, collected the mail for the round and filled her postbag. She was keen to get moving, keen to stop thinking. Halfway through her shift she was shoving a bunch of mail into the letterbox of a little terraced house when she noticed the front door wasn't quite closed. Whatever, she thought. Not her problem. But as she turned to go she remembered the old woman who lived there. She walked with a frame and always had a smile for Silva. Once, a cup of tea and a chocolate biscuit had appeared. 'Because, you know, you look like you could do with something sweet in your life,' the woman had said.

Now there was no tea, no smile, just the door ajar. Silva pushed and shouted 'Hello.' There was no reply. She walked into the hallway and peered into the living room. The old woman lay stretched out on the floor, her head crocked towards Silva, her eyes blinking.

The ambulance came within ten minutes and Silva held the woman's hand as they waited.

'She's fractured her hip, the old dear,' the paramedic said as he closed the doors of the ambulance. 'Nothing to worry about, but if you hadn't found her…' The paramedic pinched his nose and shook his head. 'In this weather the smell doesn't bear thinking about.'

The ambulance drove away and Silva sat on the low wall outside the house. She pulled out her phone and called her father. Within ten seconds of him answering she was chiding herself for being concerned with his welfare.

'You disappoint me, Rebecca,' he said. 'That woman murdered your mother to further her political ambitions, and yet you walked out on Matthew Fairchild. Ignorant and down-right rude.'

'Rude?' Silva clenched the phone in her hand. 'Dad, he wanted me to kill Karen Hope.'

'Of course. What else are we supposed to do?'

'Well, duh, phone the police like most normal people would?'

'There's no need to be flippant.'

'I'm being sensible. This is something for the authorities. If the police aren't good enough then look up a mate from your old boys' network and speak to someone in the intelligence services.'

'I'm not sure you understand the complexity of this. If it was that simple we'd have already called the spooks. You need to reconsider your decision, Rebecca. Matthew knows what he's doing. He showed me the details of the operation and the plan is foolproof.'

'Please tell me you haven't bought into this mad scheme, Dad.'

'Your mother trusted me with those files, Rebecca. I'm doing it for her. She was a decent woman and she deserved more. I let her down, I owe her, and this is my way of paying her back.'

There it was, Silva thought. The sentence was as close to an admission as she was ever likely to hear that her father had never stopped loving her mother. In all the years they'd been separated he hadn't once admitted the responsibility for the failure of their relationship might lie with him. Now he was saying he'd let her down. It was as if her death had softened him in some way, as if it had cracked open his hard exterior shell and revealed that he was, after all, human.

'She wasn't a pacifist, you know.' He was talking again. 'She abhorred war, but understood there was sometimes a need for action. This is one of those times. The Hopes killed your mother because of a lust for power and money. She would have understood the need to eliminate them.'

Silva sighed. 'Dad, I know you're trying to do the right thing, but surely this isn't the way. Please tell me you're not getting involved. Please tell me you'll drop this.'

'I'll do what I want. It was good to see you the other day, Rebecca. We must do it again sometime.'

Her father hung up and Silva remained sitting on the wall for a long time. When a neighbour came out from the next-door property and asked if she was OK, she stood, shrugged and walked off down the street to deliver the rest of the mail.

–

They were back in the office. Pension Man and the Boy Wonder. Two superheroes fighting a global terrorist network with Taher at its centre and the world on the brink of disaster. Something like that anyway.

Over the past couple of days Holm had put a lot of thought into their next steps. Did they ignore the mysterious Twitter account and the clue that led to Ben Western? Holm was minded to do so. It was possible the information was bogus or the whole thing was a set-up designed to push him in the wrong direction. On the other hand the execution-style murder of Western – which it appeared to be – was rare enough to warrant another look. On a hunch Holm called a friend he'd once worked with in Special Branch. Special Branch was now renamed and reconfigured as Counter Terrorism Command, but his friend was still hanging in there.

Bob Longworth and Holm went way back, even further than Holm and Palmer. They'd graduated from Hendon Police College at the same time and risen through the ranks. A few years ago, Holm had tried to persuade Longworth to move to JTAC, but he'd declined.

'You know me, Stephen,' he'd said. 'Paperwork makes my head hurt. Pointless and expensive paperwork doubly so. I try and do as little of it as possible.'

'Bob,' Holm said when Longworth picked up. 'A favour. Off the record, at least off my record. Can you do that for me?'

'Depends entirely on what it is,' Longworth answered.

An hour later Holm hand-delivered a note to Longworth at Scotland Yard and promised him payback in the form of a lunch. Longworth glanced down at the note.

'Why can't you route this through official channels?' he said.

'I've been sidelined,' Holm said. 'After what happened in Tunisia I'm supposed to stay well clear of anything in this area.'

'I'd heard something on the grapevine but didn't believe it.' Longworth looked pained. 'Stephen Holm investigating bunny huggers?'

'Now you can see why I don't want Huxtable to know about this.' Holm pointed at the piece of paper. 'She'll have my bollocks in a glass jar on her desk if she finds out.'

'If she finds out I helped you go behind her back then mine'll probably be floating in there too.'

'So she'd better not find out, right?' Holm patted Longworth on the shoulder. 'For both our sakes.'

Back in his office Holm made a call to Billie Cornish. The request was similar to the one he'd made to Longworth.

'What do you want those for?' Cornish asked. 'You're not keeping something from me, are you?'

Holm said he wasn't and that he'd let her know if anything came of it.

A few hours later both requests had been granted and Holm had two sheets of paper on his desk. He skimmed through the information on both, not quite believing what he was reading.

'OK,' Javed said. 'Are you going to enlighten me?'

'Ballistic reports.' Holm weighed the two pieces of paper. 'One from the Met's trip to Tunisia to investigate the cafe killings, the other from Cornish's man-on-the-heath murder case. The bullet used to kill two of the victims in Tunisia was a nine millimetre hollow point fired from a Glock 19. Care to have a guess as to the weapon and ammunition in the Suffolk case?'

'You're fucking joking.' Javed lunged for the two pieces of paper. He snatched them from Holm and peered down. 'You're telling me Taher killed Ben Western?'

'To be precise I'm saying it is likely one of the guns used in the attack in Tunis was also used to kill Western, probably by Taher or an accomplice of his. Whatever, it looks like our mysterious Twitter account was on to something after all.'

The evidence was so shocking that Holm suggested they adjourn for lunch. They grabbed a couple of baguettes from a sandwich bar and walked down Millbank to find a bench. They ate by the side of the Thames.

'People will be talking, sir,' Javed said, gesturing at a woman who walked past. 'That's Julie from Cyber Security. Once she gets back inside the gossip will be spreading like wildfire. You and me sharing a quiet moment by the river.' Javed smiled. 'If you like, I could put my hand on your knee to stir things a little more.'

'Fuck off.' Holm looked pointedly at his leg. If Javed so much as brushed a hand near it he'd floor him. 'Let's concentrate on Western.'

'If you say so.'

'Boats.' Holm nodded at the river where a tourist cruise boat was passing. No doubt the guide was pointing out the MI5 building because heads were craned to the side. 'Ships, to be precise.'

'SeaPak?'

'Of course.' Holm took a bite of his baguette. 'SeaPak are a container shipping company. According to Cornish they bring goods in and out of the UK via Rotterdam. It seems obvious to me that Western, as a manager at SeaPak, must have been killed because he stumbled across some kind of smuggling operation. Throw Taher into the mix and what do you think was being smuggled?'

'I don't know, guns?'

'Guns, weapons, bombs, chemicals. Something else too: people.'

'People? You mean trafficking?'

'No, I mean terrorists. Either UK citizens trying to return surreptitiously or foreign nationals ducking in under the radar.' Holm took another bite, wiped some cream cheese from his chin. 'Either way it means another trip to Suffolk.'

'To see Billie Cornish?'

'No, to visit Felixstowe and get the lowdown on SeaPak Containers.' And, Holm thought, if they needed to liaise with Cornish while they were in Suffolk then there was no harm in that, was there?

–

Silva returned from work to find a black Range Rover standing at the gates to the marina. As she walked across, Fairchild got out.

'What are you doing here?' she said before shaking her head. 'I spoke with my father earlier. I guess that's why you've come.'

'He suggested I have another try.' Fairchild raised an eyebrow. 'He said you had a stubborn streak.'

'I'd need half a brain to do what you're suggesting. You're crazy to think I'd kill Karen Hope.'

'Crazy? Possibly, but the circumstances dictate the response and in this case there is only one option.' Fairchild watched a white motor boat speed upriver. 'Let me try to persuade you again.'

'Mr Fairchild, I told you before I don't like games. I was up early and it's been a long day. I want to have a shower and grab something to eat and veg out.'

'Let's make a deal, then. I'll wait in my car while you have your shower, then I'll take you for an early dinner. We'll go over everything again and I'll give you some additional material to examine at your leisure. If, after further reflection, you want to know more, then all well and good. If the answer is still no, I'll accept it and you won't hear from me again. Does that sound like a plan?'

'It sounds crap.'

'Rebecca. Do this for your father, OK? And if not him then your mother.'

Silva sighed. One of Freddie's dogs had slipped out through the gate. Fairchild bent to scratch the animal on the head.

'OK,' she said.

-

They drove up late that afternoon, Holm having booked a room at a Travelodge outside Ipswich so they could get an early start the next day. When he'd called Cornish and told her they were coming he'd been surprised when she suggested he and Javed come round for dinner.

'It would be good to catch up,' she said. Holm's heart skipped a beat but any hopes he had were immediately dashed as Cornish added: 'We'd be delighted to have you over.'

After the call, Holm thought about the *we'd be delighted* bit. Cornish and her husband. Happy families. For a moment he was insanely jealous.

Having dumped their kit at the hotel they headed for Cornish's place. The single-storey modern house sat in the middle of nowhere surrounded by the flat Suffolk countryside. Glass and steel and crisp white walls converged on a central tower that rose out of an atrium. To one side there was a paddock with several horses, to the other a large garden with a tennis court.

'She's done well,' Javed said. 'Or perhaps her husband has.'

Holm grunted. He was beginning to regret having accepted Cornish's invitation. The idea of sitting across the table from an ex-lover as Cornish made eyes at a man who was presumably younger than Holm, better looking, and with better prospects, was grating.

A ring of the bell at the side of the porch brought a shout from inside and seconds later the door was swinging open. Cornish stood there with an open bottle of red in one hand and a smile on her face.

'Come in, Stephen, Farakh.' She made a sweeping gesture. Her mood had changed from the other day as if she'd cast aside a mask. 'Great you could make it.'

They stepped into a huge open-plan room, to one side a gleaming kitchen, to the other a dining area, beyond that several sofas arranged in a semicircle facing a floor-to-ceiling window that overlooked fields.

'Pleased to be here,' Holm said. He took in the tasteful décor, the art prints on the walls, the high-end music system. Compared to his measly flat the place was unbridled luxury. 'This is nice.'

'Nice, boss?' Javed said as Cornish stepped forward to greet them. 'It's amazing.'

'Glad someone likes it.' Cornish shot Holm a look but smiled as well.

They moved in and Holm glanced across to where a dining table had been set for four. Any notion that Cornish was single vanished. In a moment or two Mr Right would be striding out. Steely handshake. Beach-ready body. Blue eyes. Holm felt completely inadequate. From somewhere behind him a door clicked open. Footsteps on the tiled floor. He gritted his teeth and breathed in, determined to be magnanimous. Turned.

'This is Emma,' Cornish said. 'My wife.'

'Hi.' Emma was blonde like Cornish, mid-thirties, good figure. 'You must be Stephen. I've heard a lot about you.'

Holm opened his mouth but then closed it again. He realised he'd probably say something inappropriate. Behind him Javed sniggered.

'What a turn-up, boss,' Javed said. 'You're outnumbered three to one.'

Cornish looked at Javed and turned to Holm. 'He's not, is he?'

'Yes,' Holm said. He shook his head. 'Bloody hell.'

Chapter Fifteen

An hour later Silva and Fairchild were seated at an outside table in a restaurant down in the Barbican. Fairchild pondered the menu briefly and selected a seafood platter. Silva chose bass served with couscous. The waiter brought over a carafe of house white and, after Fairchild had tasted it, poured two glasses.

'Cheers,' Fairchild said, raising his glass to Silva. 'Here's to success.'

'In what?' Silva couldn't believe the arrogance of the man. 'I haven't agreed to anything and it's unlikely I will.'

'Right. Here's to you, then.'

She reluctantly picked up her glass and chinked it against Fairchild's. He smiled and glanced round.

'Well?' Silva said.

'You see that guy at the cafe next to us?' Fairchild jerked his head to the right. 'Gavin. He's one of mine.'

Silva looked across to where a thickset man sipped from a lager glass, an open paperback in his other hand. The man turned for a second and met Silva's gaze.

'And the girl leaning against those railings talking on the phone?' Fairchild made a small hand gesture towards an attractive woman in a short skirt. She looked like a secretary who'd just popped out of the office to call a friend, but she too rotated her head slightly in their direction. 'Lona. She's with me too.'

'Fantastic.' Silva said. 'Are you trying to intimidate me?'

'I very much doubt that would be possible, Ms da Silva. Anyway, scaring you isn't the intention. Gavin and Lona are aides.'

'You mean protection?'

'If you want to put it like that, yes.'

'What I want is for you to get to the point.'

'OK.' Fairchild took another sip from his glass and made a face. 'This is one of those wines that actually gets worse with each mouthful. I really shouldn't have accepted it.'

'Mr Fairchild?'

'You're perhaps wondering why I'm involved in all this.' Fairchild put his wine glass down. He contemplated the pale liquid, wistful. 'Back in the Gulf War your father saved my life. He didn't get a medal for it, but he has my eternal thanks nonetheless.' Fairchild glanced up. 'Life, Rebecca, is what you make of it. I like to think I've made something of my time on earth, but I wouldn't have had the chance had your father not risked his own skin to save mine.'

'He never said.'

'True heroes tend to keep quiet and they don't ask for anything in return for their deeds.' Fairchild turned his hands palms up. 'But when your father came to me with your mother's files I knew I had to help.'

'Help I can understand, but this plan of yours is madness.'

'Killing Karen Hope is the only way to avenge the death of your mother.'

'I don't buy that. Why not just release all the material to the press?'

'If it was so easy why hasn't Neil Milligan published the information? He's the only other person who's seen your mother's files. The story would be the biggest he'd ever covered. Fame and fortune. The scoop of the century.'

'He told me his family was threatened, but that doesn't scare me. We should simply hand all the material to the newspapers.'

'Brave words, but futile. You see I wouldn't mind betting the authorities know some, if not all, of this already. No media outlet will touch the story, firstly because the government will issue D notices to prevent publication, secondly because the forces that threatened Milligan will threaten anybody who tries to disseminate the information.'

'I told you, that doesn't worry me.'

'Well it should.' Fairchild held his wine glass and swirled the contents, gazing down into the pale alcohol. He appeared distracted, disturbed perhaps. He took another sip and put the glass down. 'Your father wants Hope dead and he thinks you're the right person to kill her.'

'Great. Nice he has faith in me for a change.'

'Rebecca, there are dozens of stories floating around the US media about Karen Hope. Everything from dodgy arms deals to devil worship. One I read says she had a baby and killed it and ate the child's heart as part of a witch's spell. Depending where you choose to get your news, she is either a white supremacist or a communist. She's secretly a Muslim. A Jew. A Scientologist. A radical pro-lifer. A vegan who lives on spinach smoothies. An alien.'

'Fake news.'

'Exactly. Day and night the public are bludgeoned with these stories – why do you think they'll believe your mother's?'

'Because there's proof. The photograph with Haddad and Latif.'

'I saw an image the other day that showed Hope having sex with a horse. Is that proof she's into bestiality?'

'Of course not.' Silva stayed silent for a beat. She turned her head in the direction of the man with the lager. 'If you and my father are convinced killing her is the only option why don't you use your own people? You must have dozens of mercenaries you can call on.'

'You've overestimated my set-up. I have people on the ground in various countries, but most are freelancers and none as capable as you. This is a job for a specialist, for somebody at the top of their field.' Fairchild looked at Silva and sighed. 'Here.'

Fairchild unzipped a leather document folder and pulled out a large envelope. He reached in and carefully extracted a couple of pictures. One was an aerial photograph, the other a similar image to the one of the villa Fairchild had shown her before; this time the little terrace was empty aside from a table with a parasol.

'I think I mentioned that Brandon Hope's holiday house is in Italy on the Amalfi Coast,' Fairchild said. He pointed at the aerial photograph. 'This is the town of Positano and the villa sits on the cliffs on the west side. I've rented a house on the east side. It's a little over one kilometre across the water to the villa. The fifteenth of August marks the end of the festival of the town's patron saint. In the evening there will be a spectacular firework display with a lot of very loud bangs. For the past five years Karen Hope has spent the week of the festival at the villa. Brandon always holds a small party on the night of the fifteenth. The guests watch the display from the terrace, food and drinks first of course and then the fireworks. There'll be plenty of time to set up and no rush to get away. With the confusion in the town it will take the police ten or fifteen minutes to arrive and they'll have absolutely no idea where Hope was shot from. Even if they were to bring in ballistics experts, it will be weeks before they conclude it was an extreme long-range shot from a sniper. Pinning down the shooter's position will be impossible so whoever does this will be able to escape scot free.'

Silva looked at the pictures. Fairchild had it all worked out. Did he really believe he could convince her? 'You're mad.'

'No, you're the one who's mad, remember? Cracking up because of the mistake you made in Afghanistan. Angry you can do nothing about your mother's death.' Fairchild reached for his napkin and dabbed his mouth. 'I can understand. We all make mistakes and frequently we're powerless to do anything to effect a change. Well now's your chance to put things right.'

'If what you told me is true, I still don't understand your reluctance to go to the media. Somebody will get the story out there. The conspiracy can't be that big.'

'Hope springs eternal. A new Hope. However bad things get, there's always Hope. Love and Hope conquer fear and hate.' Fairchild crossed his arms. 'Campaign slogans from the primaries, Rebecca. The US is waiting, but the bigger picture is the globe is waiting. There's an overwhelming imperative that Karen Hope becomes the next leader of the Western world. We are living in dangerous times. A steady hand on the tiller is what's required. Straight ahead. Not left, not right, but down the middle. Nobody is going to believe this crap.' Fairchild gestured at the envelopes. 'On the other hand, those who know it's true will do anything to prevent it coming out. Anything, understand?'

Silva glanced over at the blonde woman. 'You mean…?'

'That's why they're here. Not to say they'll do much good if my card is marked. Much as I want to stop Karen Hope, I value my life too. It's why evil people are able to do evil things, Rebecca. Because most of us are too scared to stop them.'

'What about the terrorists who carried out the attack?'

'We'll deal with them separately.' Fairchild put his napkin down on the table, pushed back his chair and stood. He slid the envelope across the table. 'There's more information in here and the evidence you want too. When you've read through everything, call me. If you're still not interested then our relationship is at an end. I'll respect your decision either way, but I'm not sure your father will.'

'You're leaving?' Silva glanced to where the waiter was carrying two plates of food over. 'Without eating?'

'Tell him I was called away.' Fairchild pulled out his wallet and laid two fifty-pound notes on the table. 'Urgent business.'

'But…?'

'My time is precious. You'll make your decision based on the evidence. I don't think anything else I say will sway you.' Fairchild gestured at the envelope. He'd done arguing and there was an air of resignation about his manner. 'Forgive me for saying so, but you're more than this, more than passing time here, delivering letters, marking the days. You've done some remarkable things in your life so far, Ms da Silva, and I fully expect you to carry on in that vein. If we don't meet again, then I wish you luck.'

Fairchild stepped away from the table and whirled round. He headed along the quayside, his aides moving from their positions and following at a discreet distance. The waiter laid the two plates on the table and glanced at the rapidly disappearing figure of Fairchild.

'Change of plan,' Silva said. She pointed at the seafood platter. 'It's just me, but you can leave that and I'll see what I can do.'

—

Six a.m. the next morning and the bleeping of the alarm on his phone came all too early. Holm rose, showered and dressed. He'd slept badly and was still suffering from a thumping headache as he met Javed in the car park. There'd been four empty bottles of red wine on the table when the night had finally ended and Javed hadn't moved beyond fizzy water.

'You drive,' Holm said, chucking the keys to Javed. 'Be a bit rich if I got pulled over for drunk driving.'

Javed nodded and wisely chose not to make a joke.

Felixstowe lay a few miles to the south-east of Ipswich but the journey was quite long enough for Holm. Every turn of the steering wheel or dab of the brakes had him feeling nauseous.

The port was bordered by an industrial area with dozens of warehouses housing companies, all of which appeared to have something to do with shipping. SeaPak occupied a site adjacent to the railway. Hundreds of containers sat in stacks and a large building had a loading bay on each side. They cruised past and swung into the port proper. At the gate they were met by one of the port police, given visitor badges and shown where to park. They waited in the car for Cornish.

'Not much security,' Javed said, pointing at the fence. 'The place is wide open. Can you remember anything being flagged up recently?'

'No.' Holm grunted a reply. He turned his head as a little Mazda sports car pulled alongside. Cornish. She lowered the window.

'Well, one of you looks like they had a good night's sleep at least,' she said.

'That'll be Farakh.' Holm wondered how Cornish could appear so radiant. Perhaps it was the fifteen years she had on him. 'Me? I'm looking forward to my own bed.'

'I try to avoid mine if possible,' Javed said. 'Makes for more fun.'

'You, Emma and I should go out clubbing sometime,' Cornish said. 'Could be quite a night.'

'That's a date. I just need to think about what to wear and—'

'Stop!' Holm scrunched his eyes shut. He needed a coffee and a couple of painkillers. Something to eat too. 'Let's get on with it.'

'Stephen,' Cornish said smiling. 'You sound like the proverbial bear. Can't take your booze any more, is that it?'

'We didn't get breakfast.' Javed placed his hand over his mouth and said in a stage whisper. 'Proceed with caution.'

'Once we're done here, I'll buy you breakfast. There's this great truckers' place just along the road that does—'

Holm held up his hand. 'For God's sake! The port. SeaPak. What we came for.'

'OK.' Cornish nodded. Last night she'd tentatively put forward her idea there was some kind of smuggling operation going on. As she'd elaborated, Holm listened and pretended he was hearing the theory for the first time. This wasn't about drugs or cigarettes or any other low-grade contraband, she said. This was something far more valuable and explained why a professional hit – and that's what the ammunition and weapon suggested – had been carried out. The conversation hadn't gone further because Emma had said talk about the job was off-limits. Now Cornish elaborated.

'People,' she said, waving at a stack of containers in the distance. 'Into the UK by the back door. I don't know what the hell that has to do with animal rights, but there you go.'

Beside Holm, Javed coughed. 'That's a gotcha,' Holm said. 'The animal rights thing is bogus.'

'A ruse?'

'Just so.' Holm clicked open his door and got out. Javed and Cornish got out too and the three of them stood in front of the cars. A giant blue crane straddled a line of containers and plucked one from the ground. Like some sort of monstrous insect it scurried away down the dockside to its lair, a huge ship already laden with hundreds of containers. The crane plopped the container onto the boat.

Cornish gestured and they began to walk across to a large warehouse. 'This is a BIP, or border inspection post. Containers can be pulled in here for examination. There's a refrigerated section for cargoes for human consumption and an ambient section.'

'So it's mainly health and safety?'

'Yes. The Border Force have an X-ray scanning unit though. Any container can be passed through so it can be inspected without unloading the contents.'

'So what has SeaPak and the murder of Ben Western got to do with this?'

'I'm not sure, but as a manager at SeaPak Western had unrestricted access to shipping manifests and logs. Container shipping is a complicated business and each container has a number which identifies it. The number determines where the container goes. For instance that ship in the harbour.' Cornish pointed to the boat at the end of the quay. 'It could have come from the Baltic. Some containers might be offloaded and others might be loaded. Some may stay on the boat because they're heading for an onward destination. The boat could then go to Rotterdam where a similar thing happens. And so it goes on, containers loaded on and off at every stop.'

Holm reached up and placed his palm against his forehead. The pain behind his eyes was, if anything, growing. 'Your point?'

'If you've got control of the manifests you can decide where each container goes. You can also falsify the records of what's in each container.'

'But you just said the Border Force can open and inspect any container they want.'

'Yes.'

'Well, there you are. Your theory breaks down.'

Cornish was silent for a moment. 'Have you heard of the *CSCL Globe*?'

'No, what is it? Sounds like some kind of movie award.'

'Not quite. The *China Shipping Container Lines Globe* is one of the largest ships in the world. It's four hundred metres long and can carry over nineteen thousand containers. And that's just one ship. Each year this port handles over four million TEUs.'

'TEUs?' Holm thought again about a strong coffee and something sweet to eat.

'Twenty-foot equivalent units,' Cornish said. 'No matter about the terminology, you get my point. Ten thousand containers a day. Up to four thousand lorry movements too. Then there are the trains.'

'Bloody hell.' Holm turned towards the quayside. Rows and rows of containers stretched into the distance, stacked three or four high.

'I think "needle" and "haystack" are the words you're looking for, boss,' Javed said. 'If ten K containers go through here each day the chance of finding something must be minuscule.'

'That's true,' Cornish said. 'But intelligence from various sources allows the Border Force to target individual cargoes. Even so, when one of the big vessels comes in it really is needles in haystacks.' Cornish halted at the vast doorway to the warehouse. 'I think it's about time you came clean with me, don't you think?'

Chapter Sixteen

Silva left Fairchild's envelope untouched until the next day. It sat on the saloon table along with a letter from her bank and a postcard from Sean. The picture on the front of the card was of a cute kitten and the caption said: *You are Purrfect*. On the other side Sean had scribbled a brief note: *Sorry. Can we talk? Love, Sean*.

No, they couldn't talk. At least not about the most pressing issue in Silva's life. She realised she'd been petulant walking out on him, but the situation around Karen Hope had to be resolved before she could even begin to consider if she had any kind of future with Sean.

She left the postcard on the table, picked up the envelope and ripped it open. It contained the photographs of Positano she'd already seen as well as various other images: Brandon Hope with Jawad al Haddad and high-ranking Saudis at some trade conference; Karen Hope on the election trail; other members of the Hope family; some blurred pictures of Mohid Latif. There were a number of other pieces of paper including a map and an itinerary. Everything to do with Fairchild's mad plan. That wasn't what she was interested in, so she delved inside again. This time she pulled out some kind of dossier. Printed but with additions and amendments scribbled across it in red pen. Pieces of shorthand, editing marks, a few short sentences. The handwriting was her mother's.

A rush of emotion overcame her and, for a moment, with the dossier in her hand, Silva could sense her mother's presence.

Move on, Rebecca. Live your life.

But she couldn't. She knew too that in a similar situation her mother wouldn't have been able to either. She began to read.

–

An hour later she'd finished. Little in the dossier was new – essentially it contained the same information Fairchild had told her – but seeing the amendments and comments in her mother's own hand lent a certain veracity to the evidence. Whereas she'd been convinced Fairchild had been spinning the story, now she read the same information as the plain, unadorned truth. There was more though.

Several pages detailed arms exports. These were above board and legal, the arrangements brokered between governments and signed off at official visits by US and UK diplomats. On one page there was a copy of a handwritten memo purportedly from a US State Department official to somebody in British intelligence. The memo was a masterful piece of obfuscation, skirting round the subject of what Brandon Hope might or might not be up to and gleefully ignoring the evidence that Jawad al Haddad could be funding various terror groups. The official advised that, all things considered, British and American interests were best served by continuing the policy of reviewing Hope's file on an annual basis, but of taking no further action for now.

Passing the buck, Silva thought. Both governments suspected Brandon Hope could well be a conduit between Haddad and the terrorists, but they weren't prepared to risk the loss of the lucrative arms trade. The death of innocent civilians didn't appear to have weighed on their consciences at all.

Silva knew that kind of moral myopia would have incensed her mother, and she could well imagine the memo being the catalyst that had triggered the investigation into the Hopes. The problem was that her mother had miscalculated the lengths the family would go to in order to fulfil their political ambitions.

In short, Francisca da Silva had been murdered so Karen Hope could become president.

–

They finished their tour of the port after speaking to Border Force officials and the port police but without telling anyone the purpose of their visit. As good as her word, Cornish took them to a truckers' cafe just up the road. A huge mug of dark tea and a plate of sausages, eggs, hash browns and baked beans put Holm in a much better mood. He mopped up the last of his egg with a piece of bread and pushed his plate away.

'This doesn't go any further,' he said. 'We need to keep a lid on it to prevent anybody getting tipped off. So nothing up the ranks or down, OK?'

Cornish nodded. 'Sure.'

'You suspected people smuggling, right?' Holm couldn't help but glance to his left where two truckers conversed in a language he couldn't place. Cornish nodded again. 'Well I think you're bang on.'

'Right. My preliminary hunch is this is something to do with Eastern European women sold into sex slavery.'

'We're MI5, remember? As unpleasant as your hunch sounds, that wouldn't interest us.' Holm turned his head to look out the window. Next door was yet another haulier's. Dozens of containers. Truck cabs parked in a line. 'Imagine if a couple of terrorists were hiding in the depths of a container. Their chance of being discovered would be minimal.'

'Aren't there easier ways of getting into the UK?'

'Not if these people don't have the right passport, not if they're on a watch list, not if they want to pass undetected, not if they're taking equipment with them. And by equipment I mean weapons and explosives. There could be people arriving at this port tonight who are on Europol's most wanted list. They could have travelled from anywhere. All they have to do is board a cargo ship and slip into the UK unnoticed. Then...' Holm clenched both his hands into fists and placed them together before pulling them apart and spreading his fingers. '*Boom!*'

'Bloody hell, Stephen, do you have proof of this?'

'Until a few days ago we had nothing.'

'But this is a priority with the security services, I guess. I imagine you'll be in contact with my chief constable so we can pool resources?'

'Not exactly.' Holm glanced at Javed. The young man gave an almost imperceptible shake of his head as if to confirm Holm's words. 'You see…'

'*What?*' Cornish looked from Holm to Javed and back again. 'Tell me!'

'Nothing,' Holm said. He leaned forward. 'I'd like to know more about the new operations manager of SeaPak.'

For a moment Cornish appeared perturbed, but then she gave a half smile.

'Spooks,' she said, shaking her head. 'The word trust simply isn't in your vocabulary, right?'

'Well…'

'Come on, then, rather than tell you, I'll show you. Let's go.'

Outside, they piled into Cornish's car and went on a twenty-mile drive through the quiet Suffolk countryside. They left the main road and negotiated a tangle of tiny lanes which ran through prime agricultural land. Fields of corn rolled gently into the distance, bisected by occasional pockets of woodland. Heat haze rose at every crest of the road and they barely saw another vehicle. Then they rounded a corner and Cornish slowed. On one side of the lane stood a newish dwelling. There was a separate garage and out front a blue Mercedes glowed with a fresh wax sheen.

Cornish stopped their car well before the house. She gestured through the windscreen.

'The current SeaPak operations manager lives here. Paul Henderson. A couple of my lads have spent the best part of two days dissecting his life. Apparently the Merc is his wife's new car. He's had major work done on the house in the last couple of months – a new bathroom and kitchen for a start. There's a paddock to the side of the house and a stable block has been erected. He's bought his daughter a pony and—'

'I get the picture. Ben Western wouldn't cooperate or discovered something he shouldn't have. He was threatened and left his job. Perhaps he then tried blackmail or said he'd go to the police. The ultimate result of which led to his murder. Henderson, on the other hand, was happy to take a bung.'

'Yes, if the containers hold what you say they do, then all of a sudden Mr Henderson has some questions to answer.'

'I told you, we don't know for sure what's coming in yet.' Holm turned to the back. 'Farakh, anything to add?'

'I'm wondering how this works,' Javed said. 'How altering the shipping manifests helps the smugglers out. I mean it doesn't stop the Border Force from picking out individual containers.'

'You think Border Force officers could have been paid off too?'

'No,' Cornish said. 'That's unlikely because they're on constant rotation. You'd have to nobble more than one of them. Plus their bank accounts and lifestyles are monitored.'

'Port security?' Javed wasn't giving up.

'We're talking about a twenty- or forty-foot container weighing several tonnes. You can't just pop it through a gap in the fence. Each container going in and out is recorded and there are number-plate recognition cameras to check each vehicle. Only registered truckers can get access to the port area.'

'There has to be some reason this bloke is all of a sudden flush with cash.'

'Yes.' Cornish put the car back into gear and they cruised past the property. 'And that's where you come in. I need to access the manifests without causing suspicion. I need surveillance, logistical support, a way of tracking the containers. I need to get into Henderson's bank account and I need a tap on his phone.' Cornish shrugged. 'I could get all that, but we're a small force and it will take time. MI5 could do it with a simple click of the fingers.'

'Sure, but we need to keep a lid on this.' Holm turned to Cornish. He sighed, knowing his next words weren't going to go down well. 'And, for now at least, you need to steer the investigation in another direction. Western's death was nothing to do with what goes on here at the port. Perhaps he had gambling debts, perhaps he had an affair and the relationship turned sour. Whatever, SeaPak is to be allowed to continue operating. Henderson needs to be left alone.'

'No way!' Cornish looked horrified. 'I'm not letting go of this now.'

'I'm not asking you to let go of it. I'll get the manifests, the bank account details, surveillance, all that, but not a word of what we've discussed goes beyond your lips until this is in the bag.'

'National bloody security again, right?' There was anger all of a sudden. Sarcasm. Cornish's easy-going manner of the past few hours gone. 'You've got no jurisdiction here, no power to command me to do anything. I'm answerable to my chief constable and him alone.'

'Of course, Billie,' Holm said softly. 'But my boss happens to be Thomas Gillan, the Director General of MI5, and he has the ears of both the home secretary and the prime minister. I think your chief constable is answerable to them, don't you?'

–

Later, after she'd finished work, Silva wandered over to the Barbican and sat in a bar at the quayside. The shadows grew long and the sun hovered low and weak in the west. She made a bottle of Corona last an hour, sucking on the lime wedge when she'd finished. The envelope was back on the saloon table alongside Sean's card. In terms of gravity the contents of the envelope should have been uppermost in Silva's mind, but it was Sean's words she kept coming back to: *Sorry. Can we talk? Love,*

Sean. He deserved better, and before long he'd undoubtedly luck out. She had a vision of him in a garden surrounded by a white picket fence. Smoke from a barbecue. Bottles of beer in a bucket of ice. Kids running amok. A woman on a veranda with a plate of cookies. She wasn't sure if that was her. Not yet. Perhaps not ever.

She bought a cappuccino and shivered as she sipped the foam from the top. She fended off a polite offer from a hopeful young man to buy her another drink with a 'no thank you' and a smile and pushed herself up and walked to the Hoe.

As she stood at the top of Madeira Drive and looked down at the sea, a car pulled alongside her. A BMW. Black. Tinted windows. The same car that had followed her on the motorway. A door clicked open and a man got out.

'Ms da Silva,' the man said. He wore a dark suit with a white shirt and a sober tie. He was mid-forties and his brown hair was short and neat. A pair of rectangular, rimless glasses completed the outfit and made him look like a bank manager or an accountant. 'Might I possibly have a word?'

The accent was impeccable, with the pure vowels and precise consonants. She wondered if he was an associate of Fairchild's.

Silva bounced on the balls of her feet. 'What is it?'

'We can walk, if you'd like,' the man said. He indicated the route up to Plymouth Hoe. 'Or we can stop here.'

Silva shook her head. Wondered what the heck was going on in her life to make strange middle-aged men hit on her.

'I don't know what the hell you want, but you've got one minute and then I'm off.'

'Right.' The man nodded back into the open door of the car. There were two others in there. A man in the driver's seat and a woman in the rear. The woman had an overcoat on her lap and her right hand lay under the coat in an odd way. 'One minute is quite enough.'

'Well?' Silva faced the man, aware her back was to a low wall. Beyond, the sea frothed on rocks far below.

'We're with the government.'

'Good for you. Can I see some identification?'

'My name is Simeon Weiss. There's no need to be alarmed, Ms da Silva, we're just here to help you.'

'Sure you are.'

'I've come to warn you that Matthew Fairchild is mentally ill and his schemes are ill-thought out and dangerous. He snatches at threads and constructs elaborate scenarios, dreams up stories, lives in a world of make-believe.'

'Make-believe?'

'Yes.' Weiss paused and smiled. 'And that brings me on to your mother. She stumbled on a minor discrepancy to do with a multimillion-dollar arms deal. The story might have made the business pages, but your mother wanted more. She elaborated the facts, embellished the story to the point where it was unpublishable garbage. Fairchild went one better and twisted the whole thing into a tale of dark forces spreading across the globe. He's quite mad and, for the safety of you and your family and friends, you'd really be better off not having anything to do with him.'

'Is that a threat?'

'It's advice. Good advice.' Weiss sidled closer. 'And people who ignore our advice usually come to regret doing so.'

In a blink the distance between them vanished and Weiss was up close, his hand at Silva's neck. As Silva's arm went up in a block, something jabbed into her stomach. She looked down to where Weiss's other hand held a small pistol.

'Steady,' Weiss said. 'We wouldn't want a silly accident.'

Silva choked as Weiss forced her onto tiptoes, his fingers tightening round her throat. The stone wall pressed into the back of her thighs. One push and she'd tumble over and fall.

'It's a long way down.' Weiss made a play of glancing behind her. 'What do you reckon? Fifteen metres? Twenty? And nobody would ever suspect a thing. You'd be just another sad statistic.'

She tried to speak as Weiss pushed her backwards. For a moment she was weightless, the horizon spinning as her vision blurred. In a desperate attempt to free herself she kicked out, but her foot met with nothing but air as Weiss released his grip and stepped sideways. She fell and grasped the wall, slumping down on the pavement as he walked away.

'I hope you've got the message,' Weiss said as he opened the car door and climbed in. He shut the door and the window slid down. 'Because there's more where that came from if you didn't, understand?'

The car slipped off almost silently as Silva pushed herself up from the ground. She walked up to the Hoe and sat on the bench in the exact same spot as before. In the fading light she looked out across the water to where a warship lay in Plymouth Sound, anchored to a huge buoy. At this distance the figures milling on the bow were the size of ants. Men and women just like herself, Silva thought. Willing to put their lives on the line for their country, to risk everything while doing their duty. Not like the politicians and the shadowy figures in London. Not like the people in the black car. They were playing with people, squishing them underfoot as if they *were* ants. She remembered back to Afghanistan and all the soldiers who'd been lost out there. For what? Like each and every one of them she'd signed up willingly, obeyed orders, but when the shit hit the fan she'd been dropped quicker than a live grenade.

A long, low horn echoed across the water. The warship had cast off from the buoy and was easing round, heading for the open sea and whatever dangers lay at its destination. Silva took a few moments to get her breath back and then she stood. The threat from Weiss had backfired. Rather than dissuade her, it had instead confirmed her mother's story as true and flipped her intentions one hundred and eighty degrees. Her mind was made up. Tomorrow she'd phone Fairchild and tell him she would travel to Italy. And on the fifteenth of August she was going to kill Karen Hope.

Chapter Seventeen

Taher was at the window again. Morning. A rush of humanity struggling through gridlock to slave at jobs nobody wanted doing, to earn money to spend on things nobody needed. Except there was nothing human about the rush. These people were animals, never meeting each other's gaze, living in a bubble. When their government bombed civilians, they chose to read headlines about celebrities dancing or eating slugs. While their government paid for hundreds of thousands of refugees to be corralled in vast camps where they had to fetch water from a standpipe, they complained about the cost of a cup of substandard coffee.

If only they knew true hardship.

After his family had been wiped out in the missile strike, Taher's uncle had rescued him and taken him in. Cared for him. And each year on the day of Taher's birth they'd prayed together. Asked that Taher could have a long life so that he might fully avenge the deaths of his parents and his siblings.

Taher's family was Bedouin, and while many of the tribe had moved to the cities, his father had preferred the simple life.

'Hard, but honest,' Taher remembered him saying. 'We scrape in the earth and are rewarded with bounty.'

So it proved. The barren acres his family owned turned out to have rich deposits of monazite, a mineral containing rare-earth metals. The deposits had only come to light after the missile strike, when the cliff behind the house had collapsed and the ore had been exposed. At first the ore had been near worthless, but the rise and ubiquity of the smartphone sent the prices of the rare-earth metals soaring. His uncle might, Taher supposed, have claimed the land for his own. Nobody would have cared: after all Taher had been only twelve years old when his parents had died. But his uncle wasn't like that. Greed didn't motivate him. Even now, when Taher had a tidy sum in the bank, his uncle still lived out in the desert with his wife and a few goats. Life, he said, was about worshipping Allah, serving Allah, doing Allah's will. The fire from the sky had taken Taher's family, but the fire from the sky had also revealed the treasure that would help Taher avenge their deaths. Infinite wisdom. Infinite justice.

When Taher turned eighteen the money his uncle had put in trust had been released. By Saudi standards it wasn't a fortune, but it was enough to pay for Taher to go to university in London. When he finished his studies he was offered a post in the Saudi civil service, but he turned it down. He also turned down a lucrative position in Saudi Aramco, the country's state-owned oil company. There were other things he wanted to do and they didn't involve sitting behind a desk.

When he asked his uncle's opinion, the old man said the pursuit of justice was not to be rushed. There was plenty of time.

Plenty of time.

Taher spent a year learning to fight with the Taliban in Afghanistan and another in Iraq causing havoc alongside insurgents in Baghdad, but his talents were underused. He wasn't a guerrilla soldier. It wasn't that he lacked the bravery or skills, more he didn't believe he was making much difference. As long as the war remained distant, the infidels could ignore it. Twenty-five dead on a Kabul street? Nobody cared. Fifty dead in a Baghdad market? The casualties barely registered. But half a dozen killed in Paris, or London, or Berlin? Such attacks resulted in front-page headlines, rolling news coverage and days of analysis. And yet, with a few notable exceptions, the attacks seemed to be low level, amateurish and carried out with little planning. Plus, the perpetrators were caught or chose martyrdom. Taher wasn't afraid to die for a cause, but it seemed to him a waste of resources. In the desert they'd wasted nothing. Even an empty can of Coke could be used as a football.

Plenty of time.

'There are people,' his uncle said on one of Taher's visits to the desert. 'People who are sympathetic.' His uncle indicated the patch of ground where Taher's family home had stood. 'You should know there are those who would be willing to provide you with the means to succeed. Not just to avenge the deaths of my brother – your father – but to ensure a different future. It has been done before and it can be done again.'

Taher nodded. 9/11. Hundreds of thousands of dollars had funded the operation and that sum was peanuts compared to the millions al-Qaeda had received in funding from benefactors across the Middle East.

'Do you know these people?' Taher wasn't sure how his uncle, who lived a subsistence existence miles from anywhere, could possibly be acquainted with men who might have sufficient wealth to support an ongoing campaign. 'And can I meet them?'

'If you so wish.'

He did so wish.

Silva's call to Fairchild had consisted of precisely three words: 'I'll do it,' she'd said before hanging up and instantly wondering what the hell she was doing. Despite her reservations, she allowed Fairchild to set his plan in motion, and early on the tenth of August she found herself at Heathrow boarding a plane for Italy.

Three hours later the sparkling blue of the Adriatic filled the window to Silva's left as the aircraft banked on its final approach to Brindisi. A hum came from the plane's hydraulics as the pilot tightened the turn and then the blue sea turned to brown earth and grey concrete. Ground rush. The skid of wheels. A steward making an announcement. Local time is ten thirty. The temperature is twenty-eight degrees. Please remain seated until the aircraft has come to a complete standstill.

Itchy woke as the plane rolled to a stop and people stood and reached for the lockers.

'We're here?' He blinked and looked around. 'Italy?'

Silva had been feeling tense, but she laughed. 'Where else? Afghanistan?'

'Might as well be,' Itchy said, as the aircraft rolled past flat terrain and old warehouses.

For a moment Silva regretted involving him, but then she shrugged off the feeling. Itchy was an adult. She'd presented him with the facts and he'd made up his own mind. There was also the small matter of the twenty-five thousand pounds Fairchild had reluctantly stumped up when Silva said she needed her spotter and wanted him well paid.

'I'm in,' he said, as they sat in a noisy pub in Plymouth city centre. 'How could I not be for twenty-five big ones?'

'Don't let the money blind you to what we're doing,' Silva said.

'I'm not. If what you told me is true, the cow killed your mother.' Itchy lifted his pint and supped. 'That being the case, I'd whack her for fifty quid and expenses.'

'Right. What kit do we need?'

'Beyond the shooter?' Itchy put his pint down as Silva nodded. 'The obvious, like a scope, binos, et cetera. Then we need a couple of accurate maps, large scale. A high-resolution satellite image. A quality camera with good optics, a video cam with a long lens so we can watch on a screen without having to put ourselves on view. A GPS so we can measure an accurate distance for practice shots.' Itchy lifted his glass again and gave a small nod with his head. 'Finally, a bottle of champers we can crack open when it's all over.'

'I won't be celebrating.'

'I thought you said this Hope woman was instrumental in the deaths of civilians, that she was connected with some Arab scum who's supplying weapons and cash to terrorists? If topping her isn't a reason to celebrate, I don't know what is.'

'I guess.'

'Come on, this'll be fun.'

'Fun?'

'You don't miss it, Silvi? Sure, we were shit scared half the time out there, but this…' Itchy looked at the people crowding the bar. There was a darts match taking place on one side of the room. Little arrows thrown at a target. One hundred and eighty. Bullseye. Not much at stake other than pride, maybe a round of drinks. Itchy shook his head. 'Fuck this, right?'

He had a point, Silva conceded. She'd been a lot of things in the army – frightened, exhilarated, downright bored – but she'd never felt as isolated as she did now in the hubbub of the surrounding conversations.

See the Pilgrims lost last night. Crap, hey?

My landlord's kicking up a fuss about the rent again. Much more and I'll thump the Paki bastard.

Look at the arse on her, mate. Bent over the table you wouldn't mind her piggy face, would you?

'You're right.' Silva turned away, gave a thin smile and reached for her glass. 'Fuck this.'

They waited in baggage claim for what seemed like an age until their luggage appeared on the carousel. There was little security and only a cursory check of their passports. Still, Silva was nervous since her passport was one Fairchild had procured for her. It had a false name that matched a credit card and a medical insurance certificate. Itchy had a similar set, and they both had new mobile phones. Fairchild assured her everything would stand up to scrutiny but it didn't stop her feeling a wave of relief as they left the arrivals hall and strolled through the airport terminal.

She texted a number she'd been given and five minutes later a large Fiat van rolled into the pick-up area. A bulky man Silva recognised as Gavin – one of the two people Fairchild had pointed out to her back in Plymouth – was at the wheel. Gavin was built like a wrestler. Broad shoulders and huge biceps. A hand the size of a dinner plate when he thrust it out in a greeting.

'Gav,' he said, as they got into the van. 'Porter, bodyguard, personal shopper, dogsbody.'

'Right,' Silva said, trying to be friendly as she shifted across and sat in the middle seat.

'The journey will take about three hours,' Gavin said as he nudged the van out into the traffic. 'But Mr Fairchild thought it would be better to transit via Brindisi rather than Naples. Especially afterwards.'

Afterwards was when Karen Hope would be lying in the basement of an Italian hospital with a hole in her head. The world's media would be camped outside. There'd be an international outcry, messages of sympathy from world leaders, meaningless virtue-signalling hashtags on social media. The mobilisation of a kill team to hunt down the assassin.

Fairchild had told her not to worry about the aftermath. There'd be uproar at first, but the information about the Hope family's involvement with terrorism would trickle out. Within a month Karen Hope's name would be mud.

Gavin was talking again.

'The place we're going is up in the mountains. The Monti Picentini. Be cooler there.'

'Thank fuck,' Itchy said. 'Hope it's not too basic.'

'The opposite. It's a luxury retreat. You'll be very comfortable and it has the bonus of being in the middle of nowhere. We can prepare without being disturbed.'

Soon they were heading away from the airport and the coast along an arrow-straight road across the flat countryside. Silva hadn't been to Italy before, but so far she wasn't impressed. Gavin turned his head.

'It gets better,' he said. 'Once we cross to the west coast and begin heading up. The mountains where we're staying are something else, and you should see Positano. Picture postcard is an understatement.'

Silva couldn't help but think of the card her mother had left for her. She tensed. If only the message could have been a simple *wish you were here… see you soon… love, Mum.*

'Picture postcard,' she said. 'Great.'

–

It was two weeks since their visit to Suffolk and they were back in Thames House in the little office under the stairs. Holm had written a long report for Huxtable detailing the trip to Ipswich and claiming it as a resounding success. He told her they'd liaised with Suffolk Constabulary and set up channels of communication to ensure any re-emergence of extreme animal rights groups in the area would be effectively monitored.

There hadn't been any more tweets from TCXGP1505 and it seemed as if the reference to the dead SeaPak operations manager was all the help the mysterious informant was going to provide. Still, it was enough. Holm pulled a sheaf of printouts towards him. Paul Henderson's bank details. The new manager was clearing ten thousand dollars into the account each month. Only this wasn't his normal account, not the one his salary was paid into, not the one he paid his bills from. This account was registered in the Channel Islands.

It had taken Holm a while to get the information but that was because he hadn't wanted Huxtable to know what he'd been up to. Eventually the account details had pinged into his inbox, but while the financial details were interesting there was little else to help them.

'The money's coming from a numbered account in Singapore,' Holm said. 'So we're buggered.'

'Oh,' Javed said.

'Yes, oh.' Holm jerked his arm and cleverly floated the piece of paper across the room and into a waste bin. He sighed. A numbered account had no name attached to it, or rather the name was known only to high-ranking bank officials. The information would only be revealed in a criminal investigation, and in Singapore that was unlikely to happen without some sort of international pressure. 'It's a dead end unless we can get the shipping manifests, and that isn't going to happen without spilling the beans to the Spider.'

'But if you have an ordinary job like Paul Henderson you don't set up an offshore account and you don't receive a secret gift of ten thousand dollars a month for doing nothing.'

'Of course you don't. The trouble is, unless we can get some sort of intelligence on Henderson or the manifests we're not going to get any further.'

'So what do we do?'

'You go and fetch some coffees while I think on it, right?'

Javed muttered his disapproval, but he got up and left the room. By the time he'd returned with two coffees and a plate of blueberry muffins, Holm had worked out a solution.

'Nazi memorabilia,' he said.

'You what?' Javed crunched his face. 'Have you lost the plot?'

'A twist in the plot, more like.' Holm reached for a muffin. 'It's like this: during our investigations we've come across Henderson. We've discovered he's importing Nazi artefacts and they're like gold dust to fascist groups. Bits of the Führer's bunker. Tatty old SS uniforms. Propaganda material from the thirties. The right-wing nutters worship this sort of stuff, make shrines of it. Henderson is creaming off a cool ten K a month simply by getting the stuff through customs. Once it's here he auctions it to the highest bidder. To combat the trade we're going to need the shipping manifests for SeaPak. We'll need to obtain them surreptitiously so as not to alert Henderson but I reckon we can do that through the Border Force by telling them we need the manifests for every vessel for the past three months.'

'Fascists? I thought we were investigating animal rights groups? Do you think the sudden change of strategy will wash with Huxtable?'

'Remember the attack in Hamburg a few weeks ago? A right-wing terror group targeting immigrants? Perhaps I can weave that into the story. Anyway, as long as we're bumbling along on our stupid little investigation, Huxtable doesn't care.' Holm took a bite of his muffin and then tapped the document in front of him. 'I told her we were successful in disrupting an extreme animal rights group so who's to say we can't do the same with the fascists? She'll sanction a request for the manifests to the Border Force. They'll get them and pass them to us.'

'And if the act of getting the manifests flags us up to somebody?'

'That's a risk we'll have to take, right?'

Javed didn't look convinced, but he nodded. 'Right.'

–

An hour later the van was edging into low hills, following a winding route towards Naples. Before they hit the coast again they headed north, and at the town of Calabritto they left the main roads behind and forged up into the foothills of the Monti Picentini. Dense forests clung to steep terrain, with lush grassy valleys below, and as they pushed deeper, high stony crags towered above them, angular and bare. The tiny road they were on hairpinned back and forth, and just as Silva was tiring of the constant weaving, they turned off the lane onto a small track. The track skirted a steep valley and at the far end, nestled under a mass of near-vertical forest, stood a wooden lodge. Something like a large ski chalet, with a steep pitched roof and a balcony running across the front of the building.

'È qui,' Gavin said as they rumbled towards the house. 'Own water and power, satellite internet. The only thing you can't get is a mobile phone signal.'

'Our stuff?' Itchy said, leaning forward.

'In the outbuildings. I drove overland from the UK with everything except the weapons. For obvious reasons they had to come via a different route. You don't need to know about that.'

'This terrain doesn't look good. Too many trees. We'll never be able to get a clear line of sight to set up a range.'

'On the contrary.' Gavin stopped the van. He gestured to the side of the lodge where a path disappeared into the forest. 'A twenty-minute walk takes you to the top of the ridge. There's another ridge running almost parallel around a kilometre away. You can hike over and set up some targets. Will that do?'

'What do you think, Silvi?'

'Sounds good,' Silva said. 'LNs?'

'LNs?' Gavin switched the ignition off and turned to Silva. 'What does that mean?'

'Local natives. Is anybody going to be around to see this?'

'Oh! No, we're on our own up here. There are a few walkers to look out for, but I don't think there are any trails near. Anyway, this isn't the UK. The Italians like hunting and guns.'

Inside the place was as luxurious as Gavin had promised. Downstairs was open plan with a huge living area centred round a fireplace with a teetering stone chimney that rose through the house. Gallery bedrooms sat to either side, accessed by a balcony which ran round the entire upper level.

'Nice,' Silva said. 'This Fairchild's?'

'Mr Fairchild told me information should be on a need-to-know basis.'

'And we don't need to know, right?'

'Correct. If the operation is compromised the fewer details each member has the better.'

'I can tell you've done this before.'

'No comment.' Gavin pointed to the gallery above. 'Pick yourself a room and I'll fix us a late lunch.'

'You're a cook too?'

'Usually there are staff, but in the circumstances Mr Fairchild thought it best we self-cater. And I'm afraid that includes clearing up afterwards.'

'Blimey,' Itchy said. 'Just like being back in the army and messing together.'

'But better paid.' Gavin smiled flatly and headed for the rear of the lodge and a kitchen area.

Silva and Itchy did nothing for the rest of the afternoon except chill out, and in the evening Silva retired early. Her room had an antique four-poster bed and a large en suite bathroom. A glazed door led to a small balcony. She stepped out. The heat of the day had subsided now the sun was behind the mountains. She breathed in the scent of the hillsides: pine needles, earth, wild flowers. Sean, she thought, would have loved to come to Italy. He'd often talked about how they should take a tour of Europe. She wondered whether she'd ever see him again. The ways things were she doubted it, but then she couldn't see beyond the fifteenth of August. How life was going to pan out afterwards was anyone's guess. Sean, as a CIA agent, was almost certainly going to be involved in the hunt for Karen Hope's killer, and that wasn't going to be conducive to whatever was left of their relationship.

Silva shivered. A breeze had sprung up, cool air flowing down from the mountains. The sky above the distant peaks now wore a corona of burnt ochre, while way down the valley the street lights of a distant town started to flicker on. One by one, dots of white in the dark shadows of the night. She turned and went back into her room.

Chapter Eighteen

The next morning they carted a dozen cardboard boxes in from one of the outbuildings and set about unpacking and checklisting everything. Itchy gawped at the quality of some of the pieces.

'Swarovski, nice,' he said examining the pair of spotting scopes. 'Easily a couple of grand each.'

'Any good though?' Silva said.

'Are you kidding me? You could make out the hairs on my backside at five hundred metres if you wanted to.'

'I'll pass, thanks.' Silva nodded at the rest of the kit Itchy had requested. 'What about the other stuff?'

'Top notch. Your Mr Fairchild doesn't mind splashing the cash, does he? Three grand for the video camera and lens, a survey-quality GPS, Zeiss binos. All I can say is me likey verily muchly.' Itchy replaced the scope in its case and glanced at Silva. 'Is this legit, Silvi? You said Fairchild owed your father but this is a hell of a way to pay him back.'

The thought had crossed Silva's mind too. Fairchild had plenty of money but that wasn't the point. He was risking much more than his bank balance by sponsoring the operation.

'If it's not because he owes my dad then I guess it must be ideological,' Silva said. It was the truth and Itchy appeared to accept her answer. She pointed to the far side of the room where a long aluminium flight case sat apart from everything else. 'We'd better take a look at that. The rifle.'

'Oooh yes, let's!' Itchy rubbed his hands and moved across. He stopped next to the case, made a bowing gesture, and swept his arm to one side. 'I mean, after you, of course.'

They shifted the case to the low coffee table and Silva clicked open the catches and opened the lid.

'Perfect!' Itchy peered in at the weapon encased in foam. 'Our trusty old L115A3.'

The weapon was identical to the rifle Silva had used in the army. Bolt action with a five-shot magazine firing .338 rounds. Also in the case was a telescopic sight and a suppressor to minimise sound and muzzle flash.

'There are better, but I'm used to it. No point trying something new.'

'This is a one-shot mission, right?' Itchy said as Silva ran her fingers over the gun's stock. 'No second chances.'

'There's going to be a firework display, so a miss might not be noticed. But if I hit her with a non-killing shot it's unlikely I'll get another one in.' Even as she spoke there was a small part of her that recoiled at the clinical way she'd said the words.

'We'd better make sure you don't miss, then.' Itchy walked over to the dining table where he'd laid out maps and satellite imagery. 'Do some practice at the exact distance and get some information into the DOPE book. You ready for that, Silvi?'

'Yes, I guess.' She turned to Itchy. He was head down over the documents, working on the numbers. She knew this was black and white for him. Hope had been complicit in the deaths of innocent people and was guilty as charged. All that remained was to carry out the sentence.

The DOPE book was the data of previous engagements, a data reference specific to each individual weapon. Since Silva had never fired this particular rifle, the book was empty. Only by firing the weapon multiple times in different conditions could they work out how to set up the rifle and scope.

Itchy continued to pore over the maps and the pictures, and within a few minutes he had the distance and elevation figures for Positano.

'Fairchild chose good,' Itchy said, pointing down at the map. 'One thousand, two hundred and twenty-nine metres is my best guess until we get in on the ground. I don't know if he knew what he was doing but there's a height difference of just twenty metres and perfect line of sight, albeit it at an acute angle. Should make doing the ballistic calcs a doddle. We've just got to hope a sirocco doesn't blow up from the south. Pushing against the cliffs it would cause one hell of an updraught. Accuracy would go out the window.'

'What would I do without you?'

'Miss.' Itchy laughed. 'Then again, I've got to do something for the money, right?'

'Aside from the wind, what will the weather be like?'

'You know forecasts, but probably warm. Low to mid-twenties in the evening. Humidity around sixty-five per cent. Air pressure something like one thousand and fifteen millibars.'

'Sounds perfect.'

'It needs to be.' Itchy shook his head and looked at the satellite image. He traced his finger from one side of the bay to the other. 'It's one hell of a shot. The bullet's going to be arcing down like the end of a rainbow by the time it reaches Hope. Be a drop of something like ten metres. And if you've only got one chance...'

'We'd best get out and practise, then,' Silva said. 'Come on.'

They hiked up to the trail Gavin had pointed out, leaving the rifle behind but taking stakes, a steel target board and the GPS. They set up a firing position on top of the ridge and selected a suitable target location across a small valley. Navigating their way down through the thick *macchia* and up the other side was almost impossible, and by the time they got to the top Silva was scratched all over. She pulled out a water bottle from her sack and took a long draught while Itchy wandered around taking GPS readings.

'Here,' he said, scuffing the ground with his foot. 'One-two-two-nine with a twenty-metre difference in elevation. We should be able to simulate the shot perfectly aside from the barometrics. We can adjust for that later.'

'I'd half forgotten all this stuff. Didn't think I'd ever be using it again.'

They rigged the steel plate, stuck a paper target to it and headed off back down the valley and up the other side. Itchy took some more GPS readings to double check and they returned to the lodge for lunch.

After they'd eaten, Itchy cleared away the plates.

'You ready?' he said. 'For the serious business?'

Silva nodded, but in truth she felt far from ready. The last time she'd fired a weapon it had ended in tragedy and now all of a sudden the reality of the situation struck her. She was planning to kill Karen Hope, but Hope wasn't a soldier belonging to an opposing force. She was a civilian. She was guilty of a horrendous crime, but shouldn't any punishment be legally sanctioned by a court of law?

'Silvi?' Itchy stood beside her. 'She killed your mother.'

'Yes.' Silva nodded. 'You're right. Let's do it.'

She gave the rifle a final check and grabbed a box of cartridges. They spent the next few minutes loading several magazines and firing a few close-range shots in the field at the front of the lodge in order to zero the sights. Then they hiked back up the side of the mountain. Itchy set up his spotting scope and pulled out his phone. He opened his ballistics app and shielded the screen from the glare as he began to input various figures. Silva eased herself down and tried to get comfortable with the rifle as she lay on the rough ground. She bent to the scope and tried to acquire the target.

'It's a long way,' she said. 'I can't see much.'

'Follow the treeline until you get to the vertical rock face. Go up a little and you're there.'

'Got it.' The target didn't exactly spring into view – the circles were tiny – but at least she could see the thing. 'I hope this is going to be a lot easier when we get to Positano.'

Itchy didn't say anything for a moment. Then he began to give her some figures to dial into the scope. She clicked the dials round.

'All good,' Itchy said, bending to the spotting scope. 'Send when ready.'

Silva took several deep breaths and held steady. Did no more than caress the trigger.

A crack came from the rifle and Itchy was speaking long before the retort echoed back at them off the facing ridge. Silva noted the puff of dust fly out from the rocks above the target.

'You're two metres up and around thirty centimetres right.'

Silva made another adjustment to the scope and settled again.

Crack. A puff of dust.

Itchy gave her more instructions.

Crack. Dust. Crack. Dust.

Silva let off another shot and changed the magazine. Several more shots followed until a ping came back at them from the ridge.

'Shot. You hit the plate.'

Another adjustment.

Crack. Ping.

And another.

Crack. Ping.

Finally, after a dozen more rounds, Itchy peered through his spotting scope. 'Nice. That last one was almost dead centre. Let's try some groupings now.'

With the scope adjusted, Silva shot through the rest of the magazines until they were out of ammunition.

'You haven't lost it, Silvi,' Itchy said. 'Those groupings. Tight as ever you were. The army must have been crazy to get rid of you.'

'Tell me about it.'

'I just did.' Itchy grinned. 'Come on. If we hike across to the target now, I can stick a new one up ready for tomorrow. Means I can have a lie-in.'

Silva pushed herself up from the ground and dusted herself off. She picked up the rifle and stared across to the far ridge. Positano at night was going to be a very different proposition.

'We shoot tomorrow, but the day after we don't come up here until sunset,' Silva said. 'We'll take a couple of torches over to the targets to illuminate the area and shoot once it's fully dark. We need to simulate the conditions.'

'You're right. Different atmospherics and temperature at night. We'll have to account for the variation in humidity at the coast too.' Itchy reached for the spotting scope and began to detach it from the tripod. 'I didn't factor that in. Stupid.'

Silva watched as Itchy packed away the kit. She wondered what else they hadn't factored in.

–

The Border Force didn't hang around and the next morning an email with several attachments dropped into Holm's inbox. Javed stood by his shoulder as he opened one of the spreadsheets.

'Jesus,' Holm said as myriad lines of data scrolled on his screen. 'Cornish was spot on. Needle in a haystack. I don't see how we can find anything.'

'Three months' worth of container movements,' Javed said. 'Ten thousand containers a day, so that's close to a million separate entries across all the spreadsheets.'

'This is a nightmare.' Holm took in the top few rows. Toys from China. Car parts from Hungary. Textiles from Vietnam. 'We'll be here until my retirement before we can make sense of this.'

'Not at all. We'll pull all the records into one file. Remove the ones unrelated to SeaPak and use a bit of programming to identify any anomalies. Write a formula or a macro or something.'

'Hey?'

'Do you mind, sir?' Javed gestured at Holm's seat. 'If I could sit down and have a look. Perhaps this time you could get the coffees?'

For a moment Holm thought about saying he wasn't anyone's dogsbody, but then he looked at the rows and rows of figures on the screen. Clicking a mouse button was at the top end of his technical ability; formulas and macros were a foreign language. A coffee and a cake might be just the thing.

He went to the canteen where he bought two coffees and a couple of pastries and returned to his office to find Javed leaning back in the chair, working on his nails with his clippers.

'We've hit gold, sir,' Javed said, looking overly smug with himself as he gestured at the screen. 'Took me all of five minutes.'

Holm sighed. He didn't know if he was pleased or disappointed. 'Show me.'

'First, I extracted the SeaPak data. Then I de-duped the port destinations and the ship names, then—'

'You *what*?'

'Removed duplicates so there were only unique port and ship names as the end points and carriers for the containers.'

'Right.'

'Then I began to write a formula intending to pull out data for use in a graph. However, I pretty soon found an error.' Javed pointed to the screen. 'Look at this container. SPKZ300176. The SPK is the owner identifier – in this case SeaPak. The Z specifies the container type product code, the six-figure number is the container identifier. This particular container pops up in May, June and July. It produces the same error in my formula too.'

Holm shook his head. 'Which is?'

'The start point and the end point are identical. Look, the container was loaded onto the boat in Felixstowe. The boat is the *Excelsior* and she makes regular trips between Rotterdam and Felixstowe. However, according to the records the container wasn't offloaded in Rotterdam, but rather came back to Felixstowe. It never left the ship.'

'What the hell does that mean?'

'In short, it means the container went from the UK and travelled to the Netherlands, but because it wasn't disembarked, to all intents and purposes it never left English soil. Which means it was never checked when it came back to the UK. The records show the container had a domestic origin, hence it wasn't flagged for inspection.'

'So there could have been anything inside?'

'Precisely. The set-up Cornish showed us at Felixstowe was redundant, because the container would have been let through with no checks.'

'But I don't understand. If it originated from the UK then there's no smuggling going on.'

'Right, that's what I thought until I looked through some more records and found a sister container which was loaded at Rotterdam. That container returned to Rotterdam without leaving the ship. Start and end port were the same.'

'Perhaps there's an error in the document.'

'Not at all. Now, when they load the cargo I'm guessing there's some kind of algorithm so they position containers according to weight and destination. You don't want to have to unload cargo if it's going to an onward destination.'

'You're losing me, Farakh.'

'Hang in there, we're almost finished.' Javed pointed at the screen, his finger hovering over one of the cells on the spreadsheet. 'That's the location on the boat where the container is stored. Take a look at our original container from Felixstowe and the second container from Rotterdam.'

Javed flicked between locations on the spreadsheet. Figures swirled and changed and the beginnings of a headache began to throb right between Holm's eyes.

'I…' He felt enfeebled, left behind. He knew he should have gone on more courses, but it was too late now. He closed his eyes for a moment and then blinked them open. 'For God's sake put me out of my misery.'

'There. The loading locations on board the *Excelsior*. Container Alpha and container Zulu have location IDs which differ by only one digit.' Javed turned from the screen. 'I'm guessing that means they were slap bang next to each other on the boat.'

–

Late the next afternoon a swirl of dust at the end of the track signalled they had visitors. Silva got up from where she was sitting on the veranda and called into the house for Gavin.

'Trouble,' she said when he emerged. She pointed down the valley to where a red sports car was dodging the potholes. 'What shall we do?'

'Nothing,' Gavin said. 'That's Mr Fairchild.'

Fairchild swung the car round in front of the house and clambered out. Lona, the woman Silva had seen with Gavin in Plymouth, was with him. She wore jeans and a tight top which emphasised her breasts. Her lipstick matched the colour of the car to a shade.

'Who is she?' Itchy whispered, awestruck.

'Your wife's got a kid on the way, Itch.'

'Oh, yeah. My bad.'

'Rebecca!' Fairchild bounded up the steps. He turned to Itchy. 'And you must be Richard. Heard all about you. Top bloke, from what Rebecca told me.'

'Um…'

'This is Lona.' Fairchild gestured at the woman and she climbed the steps and moved forward to kiss them, Italian style, each in turn. Itchy's eyes grew in size as she bent close. 'Lona's here to coordinate everything. She'll be your CO on the op – right, Lona?'

'Sure thing, Matthew.'

'In my absence, what she says, goes.'

'Mr Fairchild?' Gavin had come across. He glared at Lona. 'But we're all set. Equipment in order. Everything ready. Good to go.'

'I don't doubt it, Gavin.' Fairchild gave a half wave, dismissing any argument. He moved across to a wicker sofa and sat. 'Now, drinks. A toast to the success of the operation.'

For a moment Gavin stood, impassive. Then he turned and went inside.

'Don't you think celebrating is a bit premature?' Silva said. 'Sort of counting your chickens?'

'Oh, I have no doubt as to the outcome. On the morning of the sixteenth the news will be about Karen Hope. Stories will·begin to emerge about her background. Questions will be asked. It will cascade onwards from there over the next few days, becoming an avalanche within a week.'

'You'll leak the material?'

'Just so. Then all of a sudden the imperative will be to flip the situation. The death of Hope will be spun not as a tragedy but as a lucky escape. A staid but reliable candidate will step into the breach and be elected.' Fairchild turned his head as Gavin emerged with a tray which held an ice bucket with a bottle in and several glasses. 'Great. Richard, you'll do the honours? You look like a man who knows how to handle a fine champagne.'

Itchy shifted uncomfortably. As far as Silva knew the closest he'd come to opening a fine champagne was twisting the top off a bottle of cheap Prosecco.

Gavin put the tray down on the low table and Itchy reached for the bottle and began to remove the foil covering. He loosened the wire and eased out the cork. There was a loud pop and the cork shot from his hand, skimming Fairchild's shoulder and disappearing into the meadow.

'Well, I hope Rebecca's a better shot than you.' Fairchild said. He pointed at the bottle where the froth was beginning to bubble out. 'Well, pour it, man. I don't like to see good fizz going to waste.'

Itchy sloshed champagne into the glasses and Fairchild reached for one and raised it to the light.

'To a steady hand and a good, clean kill,' he said. 'Cheers.'

–

'When are we going to tell Huxtable?' Javed asked.

Holm shrugged. They'd worked on the info and had come up with a theory. The container put on the ship in Rotterdam had made the cross-channel journey six times, twice each month in May, June and July. It had joined the *Excelsior* at Rotterdam and gone to Felixstowe and back to Rotterdam. According to the manifests it never left the ship. The other container had done the same journey except it had joined at Felixstowe. The ship took the route weekly and every second week the two containers were on board. They were, without fail, next to each other on the boat.

'This is how it goes, yes?' Holm said. He'd just about got the gist of it now. 'At Felixstowe container Alpha is loaded onto the *Excelsior*. The boat departs for Rotterdam. Meanwhile, somewhere in mainland Europe, container Zulu is loaded with whatever it is that's being smuggled. It goes by road to Rotterdam. No border checks, nothing. It's loaded onto the *Excelsior* alongside container Alpha. At some point on the journey from Rotterdam to Felixstowe the containers are opened and whatever's inside is shifted from one to the other. In Felixstowe, container Alpha is unloaded. The port of origin is listed as Felixstowe. Since that's in the UK no checks are needed. For some reason the Border Force's systems aren't set up to spot the anomaly and the container leaves Felixstowe without even a chance of being examined.'

'Yes, but what's in the containers?'

'Whatever Taher wants. Terrorists and weapons, I suspect.'

'Every two weeks?'

'Not necessarily. Could be they continue to move the containers whatever. Perhaps there are usually legitimate goods inside, so if there did happen to be an inspection the Border Force would have to be very lucky to strike gold.'

'So what do we do next?'

'According to the schedule the container will be on board the *Excelsior* bound for Rotterdam the day after tomorrow. If we're going to meet its twin on the other side of the North Sea then I'm afraid we have to tell Huxtable something.'

'Not the truth?'

'No. I'll use the Nazi memorabilia story. We've discovered that Henderson has links with far-right groups in the Netherlands. We make the case for going over to Rotterdam and liaising with our Dutch counterparts. Take it from there.' Holm shrugged. 'To be honest, as long as we keep a low profile, she's not bothered what we do.'

The Spider was a little more prickly than Holm expected when he put forward his plan. First the budget wouldn't stretch, then she said it was out of their jurisdiction, finally – and rather insultingly – she proposed sending an away team comprised of operatives better able to function under demanding conditions. By which she meant younger in the case of Holm, more experienced in the case of Javed.

In the end, though, she caught herself in her own web: the budget wouldn't extend to a full-scale operation and with the heightened levels of threat in the UK and abroad, the best agents couldn't be spared.

'We're going on a trip,' Holm said when he returned to the office. 'To the Netherlands.'

'Us?' Javed said. 'You mean you and me?'

'Yes. Don't sound so surprised. You seem to have caught a whiff of the Spider's scepticism. You don't think we're up to it?'

'No. I mean, yes.' Javed bit his lip for a second. 'I mean—'

'You mean you're up to it but I'm not, right?' Holm glared at Javed. 'How many countries have you visited?'

'Loads. Last year I went to the Seychelles.'

'I'm not talking about holidays, I mean on service business.'

'None.'

'How many live operations have you been on?'

'None.'

'How many arrests have been made as a result of your research or actions?'

'None.'

Holm shook his head and tutted. He gestured at Javed's monitor. 'You're good with computers though, right?'

'You know I am.'

'Well get on that thing and get us flights to Amsterdam and car hire once we're there. And make the car a decent one. I don't fancy driving God knows how many kilometres in some jalopy.'

'Driving?'

'Don't look so surprised. How else are we going to track the container back to its origin?'

'I thought…' Javed turned and stared at his screen. 'You know. Helicopters. Satellites.'

'You've been watching too many movies. This is you and me, lad. The Spider might scrape to a few tankfuls of petrol and some cash for a snack or two on the way, but helicopters and satellites are out of the question.'

'But if we tell her we're after Taher, wouldn't that help?'

'If we tell her we're after Taher then I'll be drawing my pension next week and you'll be issuing parking tickets around Westminster.' Holm put a finger to his lips. 'No, we keep this quiet. Hush-hush. Stick to the guff about old Nazi uniforms and moth-eaten swastikas. That's what we're after. I can see our colleagues in the canteen coming up with a few jokes at our expense, but the last laugh will be on us.'

Javed turned back to his screen without saying anything and Holm wondered if the young man believed a word of it. He wasn't too sure himself.

Chapter Nineteen

Fairchild and Lona left the next morning. Lona was taking Fairchild to the airport before going to Positano to make preparations. Silva and Itchy continued to practise for the rest of the week, and late on the afternoon of the fourteenth of August they piled the equipment into the van. Gavin drove and they wound their way out of the mountains and headed for the town of Salerno. From there they followed the road along the Amalfi Coast. The route hugged the coastline, winding back and forth along steep hillsides which plunged to the sea. Houses clung to cliffs or sat on rocky outcrops, and hotels loomed precipitously above stone walls and wire netting that held back crumbling buttresses. The effect was haphazard, but the vista was undeniably beautiful.

'Beats rainy Plymouth,' Itchy said as they crawled along in a queue of tourist traffic. 'Just about the only thing the same are the boats.'

Itchy was right. Yachts and motor boats dotted the sea along with numerous sightseeing craft. Huge gin palaces cruised past, tanned beauties of both sexes splayed out on the foredecks. Silva thought of the Hope family and their wealth. She glanced at her watch. By her reckoning, Karen Hope had less than thirty hours left to live.

She closed her eyes. Swallowed back a feeling of nausea. Thought, oddly, of Sean. She remembered him being in awe of Hope, beguiled, enchanted. What would he say if he knew what Silva was about to do? She doubted he'd understand her motivation or be in any way sympathetic. Perhaps that lay at the root of the problems between them. Extraordinary circumstances had thrown them together but were they really suited? She wasn't sure and now, with what was about to happen, she wondered if she'd ever get to find out.

–

A little while later they came to the outskirts of Positano. The view was breathtaking. A succession of white buildings cascaded down to the sea where several superyachts lay at anchor. Beyond, individual dwellings sat on slopes that looked inaccessible to anything but a goat.

Gavin pulled to the right and stopped. There was no room for following cars to pass and almost immediately a horn blared.

'Let's go,' he said. 'Everything up there.'

He got out, opened the rear doors of the van and gestured to a small passage where stone steps led up to a gate of iron bars. A woman was unlocking the gate. Lona.

'*Buona sera*,' Lona said. 'Welcome to Positano!'

Silva nodded. She understood what was going on here. No point in trying to be clandestine in a tiny seaside town packed with tourists. Best to hide in plain sight. She smiled and moved forward to greet Lona, hugging her and hoping her mannerisms didn't seem too awkward. Lona acted like a welcoming hostess, dropping little phrases for any neighbours who might be eavesdropping, and then they all mucked in to carry the luggage up the steps and inside to a small courtyard.

Once they'd unloaded, Gavin disappeared to park the van while Lona showed them into the house. The interior was a succession of little rooms jigsawed into three storeys. The only room of decent size was on the top floor, a large living area with a balcony that looked out across the bay.

'You'll set up here,' Lona said. The friendly facade had gone, replaced by a cold professionalism. 'Perfect, right?'

Silva strode across the room. The doors to the balcony were open and she stepped out. Their position was on the east side of

Positano and the town was a maze of little streets off to the right, houses jumbled everywhere. She tried to recall the location of Brandon Hope's villa, but she couldn't make it out.

'It's there.' Lona was beside her. She pointed. 'The far side of the town, the third house down from where the road curves away from the bay. You'll need optics to see it properly.'

Silva shielded her eyes from the glare of the low evening sun. The distance didn't seem any less now she was looking for real and not merely at a map. In fact, all of a sudden, the shot appeared almost impossible to pull off.

'Easy.' A hand rested on her shoulder. Itchy. He gestured back into the room. 'We'll set up well inside. In the dark, nobody will be able to see in.'

'It's the dark I'm worried about,' Silva said. 'We'll have trouble picking out the villa.'

'Nonsense. I'll spot it up with the scope while it's light and get the exact bearing and elevation using the range finder and GPS. We just dial that in and bingo!'

Bingo.

Silva liked Itchy's confidence. In Afghanistan he'd been the same. Nothing was impossible, no problem couldn't be broken down into its basic elements, each then approached and dealt with.

'It's cos I'm not clever,' he'd once said to her. 'Not like you. I need to work at stuff. One and one is two. Two and two is five.'

One and one…

'You're not having second thoughts?' Lona had picked up on Silva's misgivings. 'About killing Hope?'

'She murdered my mother.' Silva could see the villa now. The house clung to the cliffs on the far side of town, facing the sea. The angle was acute and at this distance – around three quarters of a mile – there was only a speck of green wall and a smudge of terracotta roof. 'I just want to make sure we do this right.'

'Good.' Lona turned and left the room.

'I'm thinking ditto,' Itchy said. 'About the second thoughts. You still good to go?'

'Yes. Like I said to Lona, she killed my mother. It's just…'

'It's not like picking off random Taliban fighters? They're nameless, brutal killers. If we don't slot them they slot one of our mates or plant an IED and a British soldier goes back home to his wife and kiddies with no arms and legs. You want to take it to its logical conclusion, Hope's no different. Worse, in fact. The people she had killed were innocent non-combatants.'

'You're right.' Silva turned away from the vista and smiled at Itchy. 'We've gone over this before. I'll shut up before you think I've gone soft in the head.'

'I'll admit for a minute I was worried about my twenty-five K.'

'Well, then,' Silva gestured back outside. 'We'd better start doing some two plus twos while we can still see.'

–

On Thursday Holm and Javed took a flight to Schiphol, touching down a little after four p.m. local time. The inside of the airport was cavernous and sterile and the Avis desk could have been anywhere in the world. The assistant spoke impeccable English and had impeccable make-up, teeth and manners. The car was an equally perfect Audi A4 in bright red with virtually nothing on the clock. Holm had to concede Javed had done well with the model, but he wasn't so keen on the colour.

'If we're following a lorry, don't you think the driver's going to spot us in the mirrors?'

Javed shrugged. He'd had a word with the woman at the desk and it was the A4 or a white, bottom-of-the-range Micra.

'Never mind. Let's get going.'

They headed south for Rotterdam, but there wasn't much to look at. The countryside was flat and boring and half of it seemed to be covered with tarmac. Despite the highway system, or perhaps because of it, the traffic was appalling and they arrived at the port one and a half hours after they'd left the airport.

They drove in beside a railway line, beyond which lay stacks of containers. The quayside was over a mile and a half long and several huge ships were berthed against it, cranes moving back and forth, loading and unloading containers.

'This is…' Holm's voice trailed off. He'd thought Felixstowe was big, but Rotterdam was another order of magnitude larger.

'Twelve million containers a year,' Javed said. 'Three times the throughput of Felixstowe.'

As with Felixstowe, security appeared lax, a chain-link fence was all that protected the port area. They pulled up at a set of sliding gates and Javed spoke into a grille. Once he'd established they were expected, the gates slid open and Holm drove through and parked the car outside a large office complex.

'We're early,' Holm said. According to the manifest the *Excelsior* was due to arrive from Felixstowe at ten p.m. 'Let's hope there's a canteen or something here. Mind you, we'd better be careful not to miss the boat.'

'No chance of that.' Javed pulled out his phone and showed Holm an image. Holm squinted at the screen. There was a map of the coast of the Netherlands.

'What's this?'

'A marine traffic website. There's the *Excelsior*.' Javed jabbed at the phone. 'She's about twenty-five miles away. Allowing for unloading, the container should be coming down this road in about three or four hours. We can monitor everything from here.'

Holm groaned. At a stroke, Javed had taken all the fun out of the night. They'd arranged to visit the port control room where they could watch the ship dock and unload. Now the visit was unnecessary. Holm pushed the phone away. He knew he was being left behind by technology, but he didn't care. He'd see out his time with his notepad and a pencil.

'Shoe leather,' Holm said. 'In my day you had to earn your stripes by wearing your soles out. Now there seems to be an app for everything. Won't be long before I'm replaced by a kid sitting in a room with a touchscreen.'

'Talking of which…' Javed smiled and reached into the back of the car where he'd parked his bag. He rummaged in a side pocket and handed something to Holm. 'Here.'

Another phone. This time in a clear plastic pouch and bound with gaffer tape to some sort of battery pack. The whole package was encircled with a length of bungee cord.

'What the hell is this?' Holm tried to work out what the contraption was but was distracted by Javed grinning. 'OK. Tell me.'

'It's a tracker. I found one of my old phones and cobbled it together with this charging pack. One of us can attach it to the truck the container is loaded onto. Then we can follow the progress of the vehicle through Europe. You see the old phone updates its location via a server every few minutes and my current phone displays the result on a map.'

'How…?'

'An app.' Javed grinned again as Holm shook his head. 'Thought you'd like that.'

Holm turned the package over in his hands. 'And who's going to attach it to the truck?'

'Perhaps that should be your job, sir?' Javed was laughing now. 'What with your experience of live operations and all.'

–

A couple of hours later they were inside the port control room. Holm had got tired of waiting and anyway they needed to introduce themselves to their Dutch counterparts. The day had filtered into a grey twilight, and huge sodium lamps glowed orange over the lanes of vehicles awaiting clearance to leave. Drizzle wafted beneath the lights, swirled by a chill wind blowing in off the North Sea. The warmth and darkness of the control room was soporific and Holm tried to stay alert as they monitored the *Excelsior* as she docked. Within minutes of coming alongside, the cranes got to work, and as each container was plucked from the ship, its consignment number flashed up on a screen. Holm began to get bleary-eyed trying to spot the one they were interested in but eventually Javed gave him a nudge.

'There it is.' He pointed at the screen and then out through the control room window. Far down the quay a container was being lowered onto a truck. 'Blue cab, Christmas tree lights on the grille. Got it?'

Holm nodded and they went outside into the light rain, dragging a reluctant port police officer with them. They began to work their way down a line of vehicles. Holm had made sure their visit was flagged as a familiarisation exercise rather than anything specific, but the man wanted to know more.

'What exactly are you looking for?' he asked. 'We don't get much of interest coming from the UK.'

'It's just routine,' Holm said. 'To check our systems more than anything. Highlighting areas of concern. Possible improvements we can make. Learning from what you do here. After all, Rotterdam has three times the throughput of Felixstowe.'

Javed stifled a laugh as the officer pointed at the main office building.

'You've seen how it's all logged. Cameras, number-plate recognition, driver identification.' The officer grimaced. 'Why do we have to stand out in the wet?'

'Shoe leather,' Javed said.

'Hey?' The officer turned to Javed. 'I don't understand.'

'Never mind.' Holm casually gestured at the next truck. 'This one looks interesting. The one with the Christmas tree lights. Let's have a word with the driver.'

'Sure.'

The officer waved up at the cab and the driver opened the door. 'Consignment papers, please.'

The driver, a burly guy with little English, reached onto his dashboard for a clipboard. He handed it down.

'I just pick up,' he said. 'Why you need to check already? Only marine parts for some ship.'

'Marine parts?' Holm scanned the documents, noting the container number at the top right, the driver's name – Ivan Kowlowski – top left. He peered at the side of the container and checked the numbers matched; they did. 'Good, good. All OK.'

Javed slipped towards the rear of the vehicle and disappeared. Ahead, the line of trucks had moved on and a space had opened up.

'Come on. I got to get moving. Long way I drive.' The driver glanced in his mirror. 'What your man doing back there? He mustn't get me into trouble.' The driver was rising from his seat, swinging himself down from the cab. 'I need to see.'

Holm followed the man towards the rear of the vehicle and turned at the end.

'Where he go?'

'Um…' Holm tried to think of something to distract the driver, but he was already moving on round to the nearside. The driver cursed in his own tongue and then laughed.

Holm rounded the end of the truck. Steam billowed up around Javed as he stood urinating against the rear set of tyres.

He shook himself and zipped up his fly. 'Sorry, boss. Had to go. You know how it is.'

The driver continued to laugh as he walked back round to the cab and hauled himself up. The port police officer waved him on and the lorry slipped forward, then stopped at a barrier where a number of vehicles were waiting at a set of traffic lights.

'The toilets are one hundred metres away.' The police officer frowned. 'Are you finished?'

'We're done, thanks,' Holm said while glaring at Javed. 'You run a very efficient operation. I'll be putting in a favourable report to my superiors. I think there's a lot we can take from the way you structure things here.'

The officer turned and walked off. At the control building entrance he spoke to another officer, jerking his thumb back in the direction of Holm and Javed.

'What the hell were you doing?' Holm said. 'You're a disgrace. Pissing on that man's truck.'

'Boss?' Javed looked hurt. 'It was a diversion. He won't remember me poking around the back of the vehicle, only the stupid little British guy with the weak bladder.' Javed pulled out his phone, the screen a beacon of light in the darkness. Holm peered across. There was a map of the port of Rotterdam, a little icon in the dead centre of the screen. As the lorry moved through the traffic control and edged round towards the main road, the icon slid across the map. 'And look, I've attached the phone so we can follow our truck wherever it goes, day or night, rain or shine, hell or high water.'

Chapter Twenty

They drove through the Dutch countryside, the darkness punctuated by an orange glow from dozens of greenhouses. Up ahead the truck rumbled on at a steady fifty. After a couple of hours they passed into Germany and Kowlowski took the opportunity to stop, pulling off the autobahn and into a rest halt set amid a forest of trees. The interior light flicked on and they had a clear view of the Pole as he clambered into the rear of the cab. A curtain slipped across and the light went out.

'You're kidding me.' Holm looked round. There were several other lorries parked up, a gentle hum of an engine on a refrigerated trailer on one of them. Away from the lorries the halt was deserted, lines of empty car-parking spaces washed by the light from above. This wasn't like a UK motorway stop. There was nothing. No restaurant, no petrol station, nowhere to grab a snack or buy a newspaper.

'It's going to be a long night, boss,' Javed said. 'A very long night.'

-

The clock on the dash crawled through the hours. Twelve, one, two, three. Holm contorted himself into various positions but couldn't get comfortable. He rested his head against the side window and gazed up at the cloudless night sky where thousands of pinpricks of white light inched across the heavens. Javed lay across the back seat, sleeping as if he was in a luxury hotel bed. Another one of life's paradoxes, Holm thought: the young slept easy, whereas when you were old and tired and your head was full of worry, sleep wouldn't come.

At five, the morning light began to filter across the eastern horizon, and half an hour later Kowlowski was up and checking the truck. A cursory kick of the tyres and a more sustained examination of the rear doors of the container and then he was back in the cab, the engine firing up and the Pole easing the lorry down the slip road and back onto the autobahn.

Holm started the car and followed. Javed continued to sleep until Kowlowski pulled into an *Autohof* for breakfast.

'I'm starving,' Javed said, sitting up and gazing across to the service station building. 'Do you think…?'

They could see Kowlowski loading a plate with food before finding a seat in the cafeteria. He'd bought a newspaper and was thumbing through the sports section.

'Yes,' Holm said. As much as he needed food, he was desperate for the loo. 'You grab some snacks while I powder my nose. Then we swap. If Kowlowski heads off we've always got your app, right?'

'You've changed your tune.' Javed slipped out his phone and checked the screen. 'But yes, it's working fine.'

'Good, let's go.'

An hour later they were back on the motorway with a load of food and several bottles of water. The girl on the till had looked at Holm with some suspicion as he'd piled up a huge selection of snacks on a tray. 'English,' Holm said, and the girl had nodded as if that provided an explanation for just about any kind of deviant behaviour.

They travelled south, the Swiss mountains looming ahead. Holm began to feel uneasy. Where the hell was Kowlowski going? Javed sat with a European road atlas open on his lap. His forefinger ranged the page as he studied the map intently.

'Italy,' he said.

Silva woke to the smell of fresh bread and coffee and the sound of a rap on the door.

'*Colazione.*' Gavin's voice floated in. 'Breakfast.'

Silva blinked. A harsh light sliced through the window shutters and painted bands of gold on the wooden floor. She rose from the bed and walked across and opened the shutters. The view was incredible. Below, a turquoise sea shimmered in a breeze, dozens of boats bobbing on a gentle swell. To her right, cliffs soared above the town, layers of houses beneath stepping down to the beach like some sort of lopsided wedding cake. Away from the dense cluster of apartments and hotels, individual villas dotted precipitous slopes that climbed to a blue sky, a wisp of cloud caressing the clifftops. Then she blinked and her eyes were drawn across to the far side of the town and the green house with the terrace, and she remembered the reason she'd come to Positano. Her heart sank and she trudged back into the room.

Breakfast was leisurely and Gavin chatted about his time with Fairchild. He, like Silva and Itchy, was ex-military, but navy rather than army.

'Logistics,' he said. 'That's why Mr Fairchild took me on.'

'What about Lona?' Silva said.

Lona had eaten quickly and disappeared into town on what she said was a reconnaissance mission; even so, Gavin lowered his voice.

'She's new. I only met her a few weeks ago. She's cool, very assured, but I have no idea what her background is.'

'Do you trust her?'

Gavin reached for his cup of coffee. He took a sip. 'Not really, but I trust Fairchild.'

After breakfast Gavin left them to it while they got to work. Silva set the rifle up in the centre of the room a couple of strides in from the balcony. The barrel rested on a small bipod, while the stock sat nestled in a gel bag. A camping mat provided some cushioning from the hardwood floor. Out on the balcony,

Itchy rigged the video camera. Ostensibly he'd be filming the fireworks, but in reality the camera was zoomed in on the Hopes' villa. A feed from the camera was displayed on a monitor inside the room. A pair of drapes hung over the doors to the balcony, a narrow slit giving Silva enough field of view so she could see the villa. Itchy poked his spotting scopes beneath the drapes. They loaded cartridges into spare magazines and placed them within easy reach. There was a water bottle, a towel for drying Silva's hands, a foil strip of painkillers, some snacks, tools for making adjustments to the rifle, a first aid kit, binoculars, lens wipes for the optics.

'We're done,' Itchy said. He walked across to Silva and gave her a fist bump. 'If this doesn't work out it's not for lack of planning, right?'

Silva nodded. Itchy hadn't meant it that way, but his words implied that if it didn't work out it was down to her.

They packed all the other kit away and stowed the bags near the front door; when they left it would be in a hurry. Gavin prepared a cold meal for dinner that evening. He began to wipe down the surfaces in the bedrooms to remove any fingerprints.

'There's a family of five arriving the day after tomorrow. Beforehand a cleaner will be coming in. If the police ever do manage to work out this place was where the shot originated from, any traces will be obscured by the holidaymakers who stay here in the next few weeks.'

'Logistics?' Silva said. 'I can see why Fairchild employed you.'

The rest of the day ticked away with a slow inevitability and eventually the sun disappeared behind the cliffs leaving a shifting sea of orange behind. The orange faded and white light flared from the boats lying offshore. During the day they'd arrived one after the other, each finding their own little spot to anchor. Now it was dusk the parties on board were in full swing.

'It's another world out there, Silvi,' Itchy said as he panned his binoculars from boat to boat. 'Where do these folk get all their money and why haven't we got any of it?'

Once it was dusk, Silva lay prone and checked the rifle. Itchy stared through his spotting scope, looked at the DOPE book and calculated the numbers for the umpteenth time. He suggested some adjustments, but the time for any last-minute changes was slipping away.

Lona had slipped away too. After her morning reconnaissance she'd returned and announced she had business elsewhere. Gavin muttered something under his breath, but whatever his complaint was it was silenced by a stare from Lona. When she'd gone, he was more vocal.

'We're the ones taking the risk,' he said. 'If it goes pear-shaped, we'll be the ones in the *penitenziario*. Lona will be miles away.'

Silva ignored Gavin. Grunts always complained about their superiors and that's what Gavin was, a grunt. Itchy and her too. Soldiers in the line of fire. Obeying orders, taking the shilling, generally getting shat on. Still, with zero hour nearly upon them, she wondered if she'd been foolish in following Fairchild's plan. Given the information, she could have tracked down Karen Hope and taken her out herself. That way she'd have been in control of the situation.

'Silvi?' Itchy. Moving. Beginning to fidget. 'You OK?'

'Yeah.' She'd spent countless hours with Itchy, sometimes in the most uncomfortable or dangerous situations. Confined in a makeshift hide with the enemy all round, the pair had developed a sixth sense about the other person and now was no different.

'Good, because the party's starting.' Itchy gestured at the screen to one side of the room. The brightness had been turned way down so as not to dazzle them in the darkness, but the picture was clear enough. A man had emerged onto the terrace. He had a cigarette in one hand and a glass of wine in the other. He put the glass down on a small table and raised his hand and ruffled his glossy blond hair.

Silva bent to one of the spotting scopes. The image was framed by a myriad of white flowers and greenery which spiralled round an iron trellis. Low lighting on the terrace illuminated the figure in the centre: Brandon Hope. Hope moved towards the edge of the terrace and looked out to sea. He took a drag on his cigarette and a sip of his wine. Then he turned to his left and stared across towards Silva.

Silva flinched, for a moment uneasy, but then she calmed. There was no way Hope could see her. Not at a distance of over a kilometre and into the shadows of a darkened room.

She peered through the spotting scope once more. Brandon had been joined by an elegant and well-dressed Italian woman Silva recognised as his wife, Pierra, and an older man with little hair and round glasses. There was no sign of Karen Hope.

'Well?' Silva said to Gavin. Fairchild's aide was pacing the room, every so often making a whispered telephone call. 'Where's our target, Gavin? We haven't seen sight nor sound of her since we arrived yesterday.'

Gavin stopped pacing. 'She's supposed to be at the party. I can't tell you any more than that.'

'Great.'

A few minutes later there was movement on the terrace and Silva looked through the scope again. A tall woman wearing a pale dress breezed into view. High cheekbones, glossy brown hair, nods to the other guests as they parted to let her through.

'Panic over,' Gavin said. 'She's here.'

Chapter Twenty-One

They drove through Switzerland and into Italy. Long periods of mind-numbing tedium spent tailing the lorry were interspersed with brief moments of anxiety whenever Kowlowski stopped for a break; Holm and Javed had to do their own ablutions in those breaks, aware Kowlowski could move on at any moment.

They passed Florence, still headed south, and as night fell they were on the outskirts of Naples.

'It figures,' Holm said. 'This is the perfect place to pick up a couple of terrorists who've made the crossing from North Africa. There are ISIS training camps aplenty over there.'

'Yes, but why don't they rendezvous with the container in the Netherlands?' Javed shook his head. 'All Kowlowski has to do is stop in a lay-by somewhere outside Rotterdam and meet them there. They don't need all this subterfuge.'

Holm took his eyes off the road for a moment and looked at Javed. He hoped the lad wasn't right because if he was they'd just driven over a thousand miles for nothing.

'Look, boss.' Javed pointed ahead. 'We're here.'

The indicator lights on the truck flashed yellow and a sign above the motorway showed the route to the port off to the right. Holm merged onto the exit slip, keeping a few vehicles between their own and the truck.

Twenty minutes later the truck rolled into the port. Kowlowski stopped at a barrier, produced his papers and was let through.

'We could show them our ID,' Javed said. 'Stress the need to cooperate across borders.'

'We could,' Holm said. 'But we won't. I don't trust the Italians.'

'*Cosa Nostra* and all that?'

'Whether or not the Mafia have their dirty fingers round the neck of the port authorities or not is irrelevant. I simply I don't want anyone to know we're here.' Holm pointed at Javed's phone. 'Now stop wittering and make sure we don't lose him.'

After half an hour of negotiating some ill-lit and very dodgy backstreets, they managed to park outside the port but alongside a fence close to a quay. The truck had pulled up on the quayside beneath a set of floodlights and they watched as a forklift unloaded a number of crates from the container.

'Volvo Penta,' Javed said, lowering a pair of binoculars from his eyes. 'Marine engine parts, like the guy said.'

'A cover story, you'll see.'

'You mean there's something else in those crates?'

'No. They probably do contain engine spares. It's what's coming back to the UK we're interested in, remember?'

'There's something else written on the crates.' Javed shifted his position and refocused. 'It says *MV Angelo.*'

'Motor vessel *Angelo*. Right.' Holm climbed out of the car. This part of the port was away from the container ships and the general cargo. The quayside was clean and tidy and a number of expensive-looking white fenders were stacked in a pile near an empty berth. He took out his phone and held it up. 'Stay in touch.'

'Where are you going?'

'For a wander. Sit tight.'

Holm walked along the fence, trying to appear as if he was simply a lost tourist wandering in the dark. A hundred metres farther on a little cafe sat sandwiched between two derelict warehouses. A table and a couple of chairs had been arranged outside on the narrow pavement and an A-board sign was adorned with a scrawl of chalk and the name of the cafe at the top: *Luigi's*. Light shone from inside where there were three more tables and a long counter. The wall behind the counter was adorned with football posters and press cuttings, some of the posters going back decades. Holm strolled in. There was a little handbell by a plate of pastries. He picked up the bell and gave it a shake. Moments later a man entered through a back door. He wore an apron, the white material curving over a substantial stomach. A round face mirrored the stomach, while the top of the man's head wore a dusting of grey hair shaved razor close. Luigi, Holm assumed.

'Could I have a coffee?' Holm spoke slowly in English. 'A cappuccino?'

'*Si, si. Un momento.*' Luigi turned to an ancient-looking machine and began to prepare the drink. 'English, right?'

'Yes.'

'Manchester?'

'No, London.'

'Ah, Arsenal, Chelsea, Tottenham Hotspur.'

Holm wasn't much interested in football, but his father had taken him along to Millwall when he'd been a kid. He doubted the owner would have heard of the team.

'Napoli,' Holm said. He spotted the front page of an old newspaper stuck on the back wall. 'The UEFA Cup in '89, yes?'

Luigi turned, a broad smile on his face. 'You know about that? All the way up there in England?'

'Of course.' Holm nodded. He took another glance at the headlines on the paper. 'You beat Stuttgart. Maradona scored a penalty.' He paused for a moment and pulled out some euros. He spread the coins on the counter. 'How much?'

Luigi shook his head, his expression almost dreamlike. 'For you, my friend, it is gratis.'

'Thank you.' Holm glanced round the cafe. The place was empty. 'Quiet, yes?'

'Not always like this. It's busy in the day, but I like to keep open all hours. Gives me something to do.'

'I'm glad.' Holm paused. 'I was wondering about the boat.'

'The boat?'

'This *Angelo*.' Holm turned and gestured outside towards the dock. 'Where is she?'

'Not good.' Luigi scowled and shook his head. 'It is not right.'

'I don't understand. What isn't right?'

'You don't know about this boat, this so-called *Angelo del Mediterraneo*?'

'No.'

'Pah.' For a moment it looked as if Luigi might spit on the floor. His mood had changed. 'She's a rich man's plaything. A superyacht. But I can tell you she's no angel, she brings immigrants. Hundreds of them.'

'From where?'

'From out there on the sea. They set out in little boats and wait to be rescued. The *Angelo* comes along, picks them up and brings them here. I don't like it. *We* don't like it. There are too many. They're leeches. They're coming to steal our jobs and to rape our women.'

'I see.' Holm peered down into his coffee cup. All of a sudden the drink tasted bitter. 'Where is she now, the *Angelo*?'

'Out there somewhere. She came in last week. You should have seen them. The women with their heads covered, the men with that look in their eyes. They're not clean, I can smell them from here, I wish—'

Holm didn't wait to hear what Luigi wished for. He took out the coins again and threw several onto the counter. As he reached the door Luigi had switched to Italian and Holm didn't have to hear any more.

As he walked back to the car he recalled the stories he'd read about refugees crossing the Med. They attempted the journey in small rubber boats that were entirely unsuited to an open sea voyage. With fifty or a hundred people in each craft they were often found in a pitiless state. If, that is, they were found at all.

The boats easily capsized and over the last few years thousands of refugees had drowned.

He reached the car and leaned in the passenger window. Javed had reclined the front seat and lay dozing.

'Wake up,' Holm said. 'Get out that app of yours that tracks nautical traffic and see where our missing vessel is. She's called the *Angelo del Mediterraneo*.'

'Huh?' Javed blinked and screwed his eyes up for a second. He put the seat back upright and looked past Holm and pointed to the dock. 'No need, boss.'

Holm turned round. A huge white motor boat loomed at the end of the slip, deck lights ablaze, crew members at the rails. She eased forward, water churning around her. On the dockside several port workers appeared and ropes were thrown from the boat and made fast. A gangway was towed into position and crew members began to come ashore. As they did there was a splash of blue light as three police cars approached along the dock. The vehicles stopped and police officers and customs officials got out. To one side there was a small temporary building and the customs officers disappeared inside. Then the passengers began to disembark, some helped because they could barely walk, one carried on a stretcher, a woman with a baby which Holm reckoned could only be a couple of days old.

'Look at the state of them,' Javed said. 'They're half dead.'

Aside from the medical emergency on the stretcher, the others were shepherded into a long line and, one by one, taken into the makeshift customs checkpoint.

'Your theory's pretty much out the window,' Javed said. 'There's no smuggling going on here, is there?'

'No.' Holm wondered how he would explain the situation to the Spider. He'd intended to tell her their search for Nazi memorabilia had chanced on a terrorist smuggling operation. To come back with absolutely nothing was asking for trouble, and to say she wouldn't be happy was a vast underestimation of her probable mood when she discovered they'd been on a wild goose chase.

'You can't win them all, boss.' Javed smiled. 'And at least we get to have a decent Italian meal tonight.'

'Bollocks,' Holm said.

–

The clock on the wall ticked slowly towards ten. Each minute dragged and yet the time slipped away all too quickly. On the terrace the party guests conversed as if they were in a silent movie, but there were no subtitles and Silva could only imagine the words as she hunched over one of the spotting scopes.

I haven't seen you for ages, Karen. How's life?

Good but hectic. So much to do before the end of the year.

Like killing journalists so they don't ruin your chances of getting elected?

Oh, gosh! That was nothing, a minor hiccup, soon dealt with. Another drink?

'Rebecca?' Itchy nodded at the clock. 'Five to. We should get ready.'

Silva nodded and moved to the rifle and eased herself down to the floor. She flexed her fingers and wrapped her hands round the weapon. She began breathing in and out slowly, relaxing herself, and making a rhythm she could work between. She would fire just after an exhale, when her chest had stopped moving and her body still had high oxygen levels.

'No rush,' Itchy said. 'Once the display starts you'll have ten minutes, so take your time getting comfortable.'

Silva lowered her head to the sight and peered through. Karen Hope stood to one side of the terrace with her brother slightly in front of her. The old man with the glasses hovered near a stone wall at the edge, while a teenage girl filmed the action on the water with a phone. Then a man stepped over to Karen. He wore a red and white checked headcloth and had a thick moustache. Alongside him stood a woman in her mid-thirties and a young girl of nineteen or twenty. Both wore loose hijabs, but the younger woman kept her eyes down, demure, subservient.

'It's Jawad al Haddad.' Gavin strode across to the monitor and peered at the screen. 'We weren't expecting him.'

'Does it change anything?' Silva said.

'No.'

'Who are the women?'

'His wives, Lashirah and Deema.'

'*Wives?*'

'Lashirah is a minor member of the royal family, a real princess. Deema – the young girl – is Haddad's brother's wife. The brother died and, as is the custom, Haddad stepped in.'

'I bet he did.'

'Here we go,' Itchy said as a whoosh came from out on the water. A firework climbed into the sky, a solitary missile leaving behind a white trail and bursting into a succession of stars, each of the stars themselves exploding until the sky was filled with glittering flame. The display had begun.

Other people moved out onto the terrace. More of the Hope family's friends and acquaintances. Silva recognised the actress she'd seen at the gallery opening in London and there was a man she thought might have been an Italian politician. Their faces were lit up as the sky above turned red, blue and green. Bang after bang. Fizz after fizz. Rockets soared into the sky and cascades of fire poured down.

The crowd of people shifted to the edge of the terrace for a better view, but in doing so they obscured Silva's own view of Karen Hope. She was now only visible intermittently behind the heads and shoulders of the guests.

'You seeing this, Itchy?' Silva said.

'Patience. Plenty of time.'

Silva blinked. She kept the rifle steady. No point in chasing Hope back and forth until there was a chance of a clean shot.

A cough came from behind her. Gavin. 'Don't worry, these people get bored easily. In a couple of minutes they'll drift back inside looking for another drink. They're more interested in networking and gossip than a few fireworks.'

'Right. But what about Hope?'

'The Hopes will stay out and watch to the end. It's a tradition. You'll see.'

Gavin was correct; after a minute or two several of the guests turned and slipped away. And then there was Karen Hope, her face lifted to the sky as she followed each wave of fireworks with an 'ooh' or an 'aah'. Silva shifted slightly and allowed her finger to hover near the trigger. Brandon was slightly off to the left of centre, the crosshairs of the scope pointing at thin air, Karen Hope to the right. Silva waited. She would let Karen Hope walk into the line of fire. Hope moved a little to the left, the crosshairs now brushing her shoulder.

'Oh fuck!' Itchy moved beside her. 'Hold your fire.'

'What's up?' Gavin said.

'Do you see him, Silva? The boy?'

'What…?' Silva pulled her head back for a moment. Itchy had his eyes to the spotting scope, his arm flailing in the air. She bent to the rifle again and saw him. A boy of two or three. Karen Hope had picked the young lad up so the kid could get a better view of the firework display. 'I thought Karen didn't have children?'

'She doesn't, it's Bandon's son, Karen's nephew!' Gavin shouted. 'Just take the fucking shot. You're running out of time.'

The way Hope held the boy meant a chest shot was now impossible. And the boy had pressed his cheek against his aunt's face, staring with her out over the water at the fireworks. Silva shifted a fraction, moving the reticle up to target Hope's head. Her finger slipped onto the trigger as the crosshairs jumped, the boy's face now right in the centre. Her body tensed at the same time as a muscle in her right hand twitched.

'Steady.' Itchy's voice came soft and low. 'The bullet will take well over a second to get to the terrace. If Hope moves in that second, you'll hit the boy.'

'Damn it.' Silva made a tiny adjustment and centred Hope's face once more. She drew in a breath and held it. She just needed to concentrate.

'The display will be over in the next couple of minutes.' Gavin loomed behind her. 'You have to take the shot now.'

'Not a good time to talk, mate,' Itchy said. 'Keep schtum.'

Silva focused again. Blinked. Her finger curled towards the trigger but didn't touch it. She could hear a pulse of blood in her ears, realised she needed to breathe, realised she was shaking.

'The boy,' she said, letting out a puff of air. 'I can't.'

She moved her right hand from the stock. She kept her eye to the scope, but the situation was now hopeless. Lashirah – Haddad's wife – had moved up close to Hope and she reached out and stroked the boy's cheek. The three of them occupied the centre of the scope.

'Shit.' Itchy shifted. Uncomfortable. Fidgeting. 'It gets worse.'

Itchy was correct. Two men in suits emerged onto the terrace. Silva could see one wore a black earpiece, a slender wire curling down inside the man's jacket.

'Secret Service,' Itchy said. 'Bodyguards for the future president.'

'We're out of here,' Silva said. She pushed herself back from the rifle. 'This is way too risky now.'

'Well if you won't take the shot, I fucking will.'

A *click* came from behind her.

'Easy, Gav, easy.' Itchy's voice was low and steady. 'Let's not do anything hasty, hey?'

Silva rolled on her side. Gavin stood with his right arm outstretched, his hand wrapped round a small automatic pistol, the gunmetal glinting with every flash of the pyrotechnics.

'Move away from the rifle.' Gavin waved the gun. 'You and Itchy get out on the balcony and stand to one side. If you try to stop me I'll shoot you.'

Itchy looked at Silva. Their only weapon was the rifle but there was no way that could be used in a confined space. Silva pushed herself to her feet, stepped through the curtains and walked out onto the balcony. Itchy followed.

'Good.' Gavin moved forward and lowered his bulk to the floor behind the rifle. 'Now, then…'

'You're crazy, mate,' Itchy said. 'Silva's got an Olympic medal, years of experience, is one of the best shots in the world, and yet this is an extremely tough one, even for her. You haven't got a fucking chance.'

'Itchy's right,' Silva said. 'I'd say the odds of hitting Karen Hope with my first shot were no better than fifty-fifty.'

'We'll see, I'm not a bad shot myself.' Gavin lowered his head to the optics. He was breathing heavily, his posture tensed, and he was simply the wrong build to lie comfortably behind the rifle. 'And if I don't hit first time, I'll take another, right?'

Wrong, Silva thought. The L115A3 had a five-shot magazine and she'd placed a spare mag close by. However, the rifle had a bolt action. After each shot the chamber had to be manually reset. Doing that and maintaining any sort of accuracy over a distance of over a thousand metres was difficult, even for her. For Gavin it would be impossible.

For a moment she considered rushing Gavin. She could see by Itchy's stance he had the same idea. But Gavin had placed his handgun within easy reach and he'd be able to shoot one or both of them before they got anywhere near him.

'Bingo! Lashirah's taken the lad. She's moving away.' Gavin's hands tightened on the rifle and a deafening *crack* came a moment after.

'Christ!' Itchy said, swinging the binoculars up to his eyes.

'I got Hope, I'm sure I got her!'

'Itchy?' Silva strained her eyes to see across the water. The terrace was just a tiny blur of light. 'Sit rep?'

'I can't tell. Hope's down, but…'

'I fucking told you!' Gavin was pushing himself up from the rifle. 'She's wasted.'

'…it doesn't look like she's hurt. She's crawling across to… oh fuck!'

Silva dashed in from the balcony. She moved to the video monitor. The dim image showed Karen Hope on her hands and knees. One Secret Service agent crouched with a weapon drawn covering the water, while the second was bending over Lashirah Haddad, first placing a hand on her neck, then moving to her chest.

A succession of rockets climbed higher and higher into the sky, each exploding brighter and louder than the last. Once more a shimmering rain cascaded down and it looked for a moment as if both the sky and the sea were on fire. There was a final tremendous *bang* and the last firework poured golden sparks down on the still black water.

Silence. A brief smattering of cheering and applause from around the bay. And then, from far, far across the water, the sound of a young child screaming.

Chapter Twenty-Two

Itchy came in from the balcony. He shut the doors, closed the shutters and pulled the curtains across. Then he crossed the room and reached for the light switch.

'You fucking idiot.' He strode over to where Gavin stood next to Silva staring at the monitor. 'What are you going to tell Mr Fairchild now?'

'He told me it was important to take the shot.' Gavin shrugged. 'Whatever the consequences.'

Silva was trying to make sense of the image on the monitor. Lashirah Haddad lay unmoving on her back with an agent hunched over her. The Hopes and the other guests had retreated inside the villa.

'Is she dead?' Itchy said.

'I don't know,' Silva said. 'Looks as if she was hit somewhere in the chest. The bullet would have passed through her body. I guess it depends if it missed her heart or not.'

'They think the shot came from the water.' Itchy jabbed a finger at the screen. 'Look at the way the other agent is hunkered down.'

The second man had a weapon drawn and was keeping low behind the terrace wall. The wall provided cover from somebody shooting from the sea, but their own position was at an angle to the side and higher up.

'Small mercies.' Gavin shook his head. 'I'm sorry. I just wanted to get the job done.'

'Well you've done the job now, mate.' Itchy bent and picked up the pistol. 'Name me one reason why I shouldn't pop you?'

'Put the gun away, Itchy,' Silva said. 'We need to work together to get out of this, OK?'

'She's right.' Gavin gestured at the sniper rifle and boxes of kit. 'We need to stick to the plan and make our getaway before the cops decide on a house-to-house.'

'Well, we'd better hurry, then.' Itchy moved to the balcony door and cracked it an inch. There was a percussive *chop chop chop*. 'They've already got a helicopter up.'

'How the—?' Silva said.

'Naples,' Gavin said. 'It's just over the ridge. Probably no less than five minutes' flight time.'

For a second nobody moved. Then, as one, they jumped into action. Silva began to disassemble the rifle, removing the bipod and putting the weapon in its case. Itchy was dealing with the AV equipment and other items, while Gavin sorted out the rest of the kit. Within ten minutes they had everything down in the courtyard.

'If the police come knocking now, we're stuffed,' Silva said. 'Red-handed is the word.'

'Fingers crossed, then,' Gavin said. He disappeared down the steps and five minutes later he had the van idling outside. 'Come on!'

Silva and Itchy didn't need any encouragement. They grabbed their stuff and piled it into the back of the van. The helicopter was still out there, hovering high above the sea, a searchlight picking out the motor boats and yachts. On the water a police patrol craft sped between the boats while an ever-increasing cacophony of sirens echoed through the town.

They climbed up into the van and Gavin pulled away.

'We'll take the back way out of here,' he said as he turned a sharp right and then left, zigzagging up and away from the main road. 'You've seen the coastal route. Even if the police don't put a roadblock in, it'll be gridlock as the news of the shooting spreads.'

The lane narrowed to barely the width of the van as it cut under the huge cliffs that loomed over the town. Gavin flicked the lights off so they were driving on sidelights only. To the right the terrain fell away precipitously. Somewhere down there was the main road and below that the sea. The van bounced as it hit a small bolder and for a second the steering wheel was spinning freely. Then Gavin grabbed hold and wrenched it round. Silva closed her eyes.

When she opened them the horizon lurched one way and the other before they crested a rise and were on a flat road high above the town and the sea.

'Thank God,' Itchy said as Gavin turned the lights back on. 'That was worse than being in the lead vehicle on a patrol in Helmand Province.'

'Back to the lodge?' Silva said.

'No.' Gavin stared through the windscreen into the darkness. 'I've got specific instructions. We're to rendezvous with Lona near Salerno. Then we'll drive north to Florence where there's a private airfield.'

'What about Brindisi?'

'It's way too risky coming back into the UK on a scheduled flight. This way you'll be pre-cleared. It's unlikely there will be anyone to check you when you land. Here.' Gavin took one hand off the wheel and reached into a pocket and pulled out a business card. 'This is the place. If anything should happen, get to the airfield.'

'If anything should happen?' Silva took the card. 'I don't like the sound of that.'

'Standard procedure, isn't it? A backup plan?'

'Mate,' Itchy said, 'we wouldn't have needed a backup plan if you'd stayed calm.'

For a moment Gavin concentrated on the road ahead. Then he shook his head. 'I'm sorry. I guess I got carried away with the operation.'

Silva said nothing. When someone got carried away things went wrong. That's how it worked in the army. That's why you obeyed orders, did your bit, but no more.

It took them an hour of tortuous driving along tiny roads and tracks to get to the rendezvous point, and it was close to midnight when Gavin pulled into a lay-by behind a red sports car. He dimmed the lights on the van.

'Lona,' he said.

–

Javed expressed his disappointment when Holm said there'd be no Italian meal.

'We're going to sit here and watch the boat,' Holm said. 'After driving all this way I'm not going to give up so easily. We'll stay all night if necessary. If Kowlowski leaves with the container, we'll follow him.'

The refugees were processed and taken away in a couple of coaches. The police and customs officers left and several of the *Angelo*'s crew disembarked. An array of sodium lights bathed the empty dockside in orange.

'This is a waste of time, boss,' Javed said. 'We could have been on our second bottle of Chianti by now, bellies nicely full with pasta, the prospect of some delicious gelato ahead.'

'This isn't a culinary tour,' Holm said.

'More's the pity. Do you think old Huxtable would let us take a couple of days off? See Naples and die?'

'If Huxtable finds out you've been gallivanting on taxpayers' money, you *will* see Naples and die.'

'Whatever. It would be better than going straight back to—'

'Stop.' Holm held up his hand and pointed at the ship. 'Look, some more people are leaving the boat.'

The captain of the *Angelo* – a tall figure in a smart uniform, a cap on his head – led two men down the gangway. In the dark it was hard to make out their faces, but Holm was sure one had a full beard. They stood on the quayside and raised voices drifted in the night air. Broken English from the captain. He gestured first to one side and then the other. A shrug which said there was nothing he could do. Holm caught snippets of the conversation.

There'd been a change of plan, the captain announced. Many police. Helicopters. Way too risky. The meeting was off. They'd proceed directly to the UK.

The two men stepped away from the captain and conferred for a moment before following him along the dock to where a shadow stood beneath one of the floodlights, a cigarette in his hand.

'That's Kowlowski,' Javed said. 'The truck driver.'

'Just so,' Holm said.

As they approached Kowlowski, the truck driver stuck out a hand and greeted the captain. He nodded towards the two men. As one of the men turned, the light from overhead swept his face.

'Christ,' Holm said. 'That's Latif. The guy from the cafe attack in Tunisia.'

'Mohid Latif? Are you sure?'

'Yes, of course I'm bloody sure.'

Kowlowski gestured to his lorry. The vehicle sat by a vast warehouse and it was hard to discern what was going on, but Holm heard the scrape of metal on metal.

'They getting into the container,' Javed said. 'You were right. How did you know?'

'A hunch, lad.' Holm turned to Javed and winked. 'And if we'd been in a restaurant eating gelato we've never have seen this.'

'Are we going to stop them?'

'On what grounds and by what authority? We have no jurisdiction here and no evidence either.'

'So what the hell are we going to do?'

Holm nodded at the dashboard and tapped the steering wheel. 'Drive,' he said.

–

In the shadows the door of the car clicked open and a figure got out. No glamour this time, no friendly greeting. Just jeans and a jogging top and an angry glare. Lona walked across and stood by the passenger door to the van.

'What the fuck happened?' Lona said. 'You're supposed to be one of the best shots in the world.'

'Is the woman badly hurt?'

'Yes. As I understand it she's in a hospital in Naples. Haddad is sending a team of doctors from Saudi. The bullet hit her in the chest close to her heart. It's touch and go.'

'And the boy? Is he all right?'

'What boy?'

'Brandon's son.'

'Oh, him. He's fine,' Lona said dismissively. 'You, on the other hand, you're in some serious—'

'It wasn't Rebecca's fault,' Gavin said. Despite his size and muscles he tensed as Lona turned to him. 'I pulled the trigger. I shot Lashirah.'

'*You?*' Lona was open mouthed for a moment. 'How this can be any more fucked up, I don't know.'

'Ms da Silva wouldn't take the shot because Karen Hope was holding the boy in his arms.'

'She wouldn't—?'

'No, I wouldn't,' Silva said. 'Got a problem with that?'

'I haven't got a problem with anything, but Hope's still alive and that *is* a problem.'

'Tactically it was wrong to take the shot. The risk was too high. If I'd hit the boy then I'd have missed my chance for good.'

'Fuck tactics, strategically we're stuffed. How easy do you think it will be to set up another operation now Hope's been forewarned? She'll be whisked away from here and her security will be tightened. We won't stand a chance of getting close again.'

'It doesn't matter. We're done.'

'I'll need to speak with my boss and see what he says.'

'He can say what he likes, I said we're done.'

'Sure.' Lona appeared not to have heard. She pulled out a phone. 'I'm going to call him now. Don't go anywhere.'

Silva looked across at Itchy as Lona walked away. He shrugged and lay back in the seat and closed his eyes. Which was exactly what she felt like doing. The adrenalin from before had gone and now there was only an emptiness in her stomach. She wanted to sleep it off and go home. Fill her postbag, walk the round and deliver some mail. Forget about Hope.

'You two, out.' Lona had returned. She gestured at Silva and Itchy. 'Take my car and drive to the airfield. Gavin and I will dump the gear in the van and make our own way back to the UK. Mr Fairchild will contact you when you get there.'

Silva nodded and she and Itchy retrieved their bags from the back of the van.

'The weapons and ammo?' Silva said. 'My fingerprints are all over the rifle.'

'Don't worry, we'll make sure there's no evidence left behind.' Lona pointed at the car. 'Now go.'

And that was it. Silva glanced back at Gavin but he could only offer a shrug. Then they were in the car, Silva climbing behind the wheel and starting up, the headlights sweeping the sky as they pulled away.

'Fuck,' Itchy said, punching the dash. 'Fuck, fuck, fuck, fuck.'

Chapter Twenty-Three

They drove through the night, stopping every couple of hours to swap over. As the sky lightened in the east, they were on a motorway an hour from Florence.

'We need to eat,' Silva said, taking an exit to a small service station. 'And other things.'

'You're growing soft.' Itchy laughed. 'You used to carry a funnel and a bottle in Afghanistan.'

'Well I haven't got either and this isn't Afghanistan.'

The services sold coffee and a few pastries and not much else. They ordered using the smattering of Italian they'd picked up from Gavin and returned to the car where they found a police motorcyclist had parked alongside and was now peering in the driver's window. After a short debate as to whether they should run for it, they approached the car.

'Hello?' Silva said.

The police officer looked up. 'American?'

'English. Is there a problem?'

'Identification, please.' The officer stepped back. His eyes flicked sideways to the cafe.

Silva tried not to panic. This was a routine stop. The officer was more interested in getting his breakfast than making an arrest.

She unlocked the car and found her fake passport. Itchy did the same. There was a folder containing driving documents in the glove compartment. The only issue was a driving licence. Silva hadn't expected to be driving, and anyway her own genuine licence would have been useless alongside the fake passport.

The officer took a cursory look at the passports and then turned his attention to the other documents. There was a wad of material from the hire car company. Insurance, warranty, breakdown cover. He leafed through several pages and nodded before handing it all back.

'*Si*. Good. Now your licence, please.'

Shit. She considered the options. Fight or flight. Either meant they would become fugitives in a foreign country. There was another alternative. Bluff.

'Yes.' Silva bent to the car again before recoiling and raising her hands to her face. 'Oh no! My handbag! I must have left it at the last place we stopped.'

'Your driving licence.' The officer appeared not to have understood.

'It's in my bag.' Silva tapped herself on the head and turned and pointed down the road. 'It's back there. How stupid.'

'Where did you stop, please?'

'Miles down the motorway. Ages ago.' Silva scrunched her eyes up and willed tears. 'Oh God, what are we going to do?'

'Are you hungry?' Itchy. He had his passport in his hand and sandwiched in the pages were several fifty-euro notes. He held the passport out to the policeman. 'Perhaps you could just check my documents again. We can be on our way and you can get yourself a nice breakfast.'

Silva held her breath. Time seemed to stop for several seconds before the officer turned and a smile washed onto his face as his gaze alighted on the passport. He reached out and a finger and thumb closed on the notes. He pulled his hand back and the notes disappeared into a pocket.

'*Si, si*. All good.' He began to walk away but then turned and looked back. 'Drive safe.'

The officer strolled off towards the services and Silva let out a low whistle.

'Jesus, Itchy,' she said. 'That was risking it.'

'Nah, easy.'

'Let's get out of here before he changes his mind.'

Silva tried to keep her speed down as they drove up the motorway and half an hour later she took a turning signposted towards the airfield. They drove across flat countryside populated with vineyards. They passed through a village with nothing more than a garage and a cafe. Several old men sat drinking their morning espressos, faces like walnuts, heads turning to follow the car as if they'd never seen one before.

The airfield appeared on their right. A small terminal building was all glass and steel and a runway stretched into the distance, the concrete surface shimmering in the heat. To one side a succession of light aircraft were parked on a huge apron, while a number of maintenance hangers sat up against the boundary fence.

They slotted the car into a space in the car park, pulled out their bags and walked to the terminal.

Inside there was a single desk in the entrance foyer. Flowers and cool air. A woman with a smile walking from behind a desk to greet them.

'Rachel and Steve, right?' The woman was using the names on their false passports. She continued in perfect English. 'Your aircraft arrived half an hour ago and is being prepped. If you'd like to come through to the lounge I can serve you refreshments.'

'How—?' Silva tried to prevent her jaw from hitting the floor.

'Mr Fairchild informed us you would be arriving this morning. The flight plan was short notice, but we are well used to dealing with VIP customers here.'

'VIP...?' Itchy appeared to be equally gobsmacked as they followed the woman through to the lounge.

Several sofas faced a huge window which looked out across the runway. A small jet stood to one side, a fuel hose snaking to one wing from a bowser. Before Silva had a chance to admire the jet, a waiter approached and asked them if they would like coffee and something to eat. Silva nodded dumbly and slipped over to the sofas.

If either the waiter or the receptionist were surprised at Silva and Itchy's somewhat dishevelled appearance, they didn't show it.

'The other half, hey?' Itchy dropped into an armchair. 'Only it isn't the other half, is it? More like the one per cent.'

'Your passports, please?' The receptionist seemed to be doubling as security. 'Only a formality.'

Silva produced her passport, Itchy the same. The inspection was cursory at best and the receptionist gave them another big smile and wished them an enjoyable onward journey.

Two coffees appeared but they'd barely started them when a steward came in through a door which led airside.

'Rachel and Steve?' he said, making a small bowing motion as he approached. 'We're ready to depart, but you can finish your coffees if you'd like.'

'No, we're keen to be off,' Silva said. 'What do you say Itch— er, Steve?'

'Yeah, let's go,' Itchy said.

The steward picked up their bags. 'If you'd come this way, please.'

They went through the door and out onto the concrete. The steward took them across to the jet. Boarding steps led up to the cabin door and, as they climbed the steps, the pilot appeared from within.

'Mr Fairchild sends his compliments.' The pilot ushered them into the cabin, Itchy having to stoop slightly. 'It you take your seats we're cleared to take off in a couple of minutes.'

The interior was tiny. Just eight seats in total arranged four either side of a narrow aisle. As Silva buckled herself in, she could see up front to the flight deck. The pilot was flicking some switches while the co-pilot read from a checklist. The steward stepped aboard and pulled the cabin door closed. He settled into a seat at one end as the engines whirred into life. Silva felt a burst of acceleration, and the plane zipped down the runway and soared into the air. The countryside fell away, vineyards and cornfields and the sparkling blue of a huge lake. The aircraft banked to the right and headed north-west. Half an hour or so later they were passing over the Alps and Silva allowed herself a small sigh of relief. The next possible issue would arise when they landed.

She needn't have worried. The steward explained that flight and passenger details had already being filed and it was unlikely there would be any sort of check. He was right, and when they landed at Biggin Hill two hours later a car was waiting for them as they left the aircraft and they were whisked away, headed for Heathrow and the car park where they'd left their motorbikes. By mid-afternoon they were on their bikes and bound for the West Country.

–

They stopped for fuel at a motorway service station a little way past Bristol and bought food and drinks. They sat at a table by a window and Silva gazed out, waiting for her coffee to cool. The annual late-summer exodus to Devon and Cornwall was in full swing and the car park was rammed with tourists. Vehicles packed with luggage and jaded children. Surfboards and canoes strapped to roof racks. Everything seemed so mundane and ordinary after the turmoil of the last few days. Everything except an unusual black BMW with smoked windows that was parked alongside their motorbikes.

'Ms da Silva!' Simeon Weiss eased himself down into a seat alongside Itchy. He adjusted his glasses. 'And Mr Richard Smith. This is a nice surprise.'

'Is it?' Silva turned. The female lackey who she'd seen before hovered close by. 'Or is this harassment?'

'Not at all. We were just passing.' Weiss turned to the woman and she nodded at him. 'But you might say this is a fortuitous meeting. You see, things have happened, Rebecca. Events, you might say. I think it would be a good idea if we had a little chat.'

'About what?'

'What you've been up to.' Weiss cocked his head towards Itchy. 'What you've both been up to.'

'Riddles don't do it for me, Mr Weiss.' Silva bent to her coffee. Tried to catch Itchy's attention. 'Perhaps you could be more specific?'

'*The Italian Job*. You know the movie? Turns out real life is similar. The crooks almost get away with the crime, but not quite.'

'No idea what you're on about, mate.' Itchy coughed out the denial. 'We've been on holiday in Wales.'

'Wales?' Weiss looked incredulous. 'What sort of holiday destination is that?'

'Snowdonia.' Itchy was continuing with the alibi they'd come up with but the words were coming out as if he was reading from a script. 'Camping.'

'Camping?' Weiss raised an eyebrow. 'What, you mean tea in plastic mugs, corned beef hash and ten quid a night for one dodgy shower and a stinking toilet block?'

'No, not on a site. Up high. Wild camping.' Itchy was warming to the task but Silva wanted him to stop. 'We did the Carnedds and Tryfan and—'

'You and Ms da Silva cosying up together in little tent?' Weiss smiled. 'Only I thought you were married, Richard. Playing away, were you?'

'We were practising,' Silva said, taking over. 'For a race.'

'I see.' Weiss bit his lip as if weighing the truth was a challenge. Finally he nodded. 'So you wouldn't happen to know anything about the Amalfi sanction?'

'The *what*?'

'There was a shooting in Italy yesterday. The wife of a businessman who was attending a party in the town of Positano.'

224

'I'm sorry to hear that.'

'I'm sure you are. The businessman was a high-ranking Saudi national. As you can imagine, the Saudis are not best pleased. The diplomatic fuss is considerable.'

Silva shrugged.

Weiss raised his right hand and used his forefinger to scratch the corner of his eye. 'One interesting fact to emerge is that the bullet used was a .338 lapua magnum. I'm sure you're familiar with that type of ammunition since it is precisely the calibre you would have fired hundreds of times yourself.'

Once more Silva kept silent. Itchy shifted his position, nervous. He tapped his fingers on the table.

'The sniper must have been a crack shock because he... or she... was out on a boat off the coast. Hitting the target at that range while on a moving platform was quite an achievement.' Weiss looked pointedly at Itchy's fingers as the nails drummed out a rhythm. 'The Italian authorities believe the attack was some sort of internal dispute among Saudi factions.'

'There you go, then. Case closed.'

'Not really, Ms da Silva. You see there was somebody else at the party last night. A VIP. It's been kept out of the news for security reasons, so you won't read about it in the papers or online.'

'I'm not interested in celebrities. Not really my thing.'

'Oh, this isn't a celebrity, Ms da Silva. This person is a friend of yours.'

'I don't think so.'

'But I haven't told you who it is yet, so how can you be so sure?'

'Because I don't have many friends.'

'I guess I can understand that.' Weiss curled his lip. 'Bearing in mind what happened in Afghanistan.'

Silva tensed but kept still. Weiss was trying to gall her, to provoke some sort of response. She wouldn't give him the satisfaction.

'Well, I'm going to cut to the chase. The VIP was Karen Hope. Congresswoman Karen Hope. This wasn't an internal Saudi matter at all, this was an attempt to assassinate the next US president. What do you say to that?'

'What is there to say? I met Karen Hope once for about thirty seconds. She isn't a friend and I can't see what this has to do with me.'

'Let's stop this charade, Rebecca.' Weiss banged the table with the flat of his hand. 'Matthew Fairchild persuaded you that your mother had uncovered some vast conspiracy involving Karen Hope. Despite my warning you fell for his patter and agreed to go on his little mission to Italy. Unfortunately the operation went wrong and, instead of killing Karen Hope, you shot an innocent Saudi woman. I tried to tell you about Fairchild, but you wouldn't listen. Now you'll have to suffer the consequences.'

'I didn't shoot anyone.'

'I think you did.'

'As Richard said, we were on holiday in north Wales.'

'Camping,' Itchy added helpfully.

'Yes, so you claim.' Weiss pointed out the window in the direction of the BMW and the motorbikes. 'Where's your tent?'

'We didn't use a tent, we bivvied,' Silva said.

'What about food? Where did you buy it?'

'Local shops, here and there.'

'Card payment or cash?'

'Cash.'

'What about restaurants?'

Silva shook her head. She knew Weiss was trying to pin her down to something he would be able to verify.

'We didn't eat out, our budget wouldn't stretch to it.'

'It's all so, so convenient, Rebecca.' Weiss cocked his head on one side. A smile became a grimace. 'But it won't wash. You're lying, and one way or another I intend to find out the truth.' Weiss pushed back his chair and stood. 'You'd better come up with a more believable story because we'll be questioning you again. Next time I can't promise the surroundings will be quite so friendly.'

Weiss turned and walked away, his aide following. Itchy bent to his coffee and took a sip.

'You reckon he bought it?' he said. 'The Wales stuff?'

'No.' Silva stared after Weiss as he pushed through the doors to the outside. 'I don't think he did.'

–

They pulled up outside Itchy's place mid-afternoon. Itchy hefted his panniers from his bike.

'Thanks,' Silva said. 'And I'm sorry for getting you involved in this.'

'I'm a grown up, Silvi,' Itchy said. 'I knew the score before we set out. My only regret is we didn't get Hope.' Itchy moved towards the front door. 'What are you going to do now?'

'Go home and sleep. After that I have no idea.'

'I'll see you though, right? Around?'

'Of course.'

Silva flipped her visor down and fired up the bike.

When she got back to the boatyard, Fairchild's black Range Rover was parked up by Freddie's office. Inside Fairchild was chatting with Freddie and the two Dobermanns lay curled at his feet.

'Rebecca!' Fairchild nodded to Freddie and came bounding out. He took her arm and walked down to the pontoons with her. 'Look happy. I told Freddie I had some good news for you.'

'You don't though,' Silva said.

'Not really.' Fairchild patted a newspaper he'd tucked under his arm. He pulled it out. *Princess Dies* punned the tabloid headline. 'Lashirah Haddad is dead.'

'Shit.' They'd reached the pontoon and Silva had to stop and steady herself. She wondered why Weiss hadn't told her. Perhaps he reasoned that she already knew and he could trick her, or else she'd be more likely to confess if the crime wasn't murder. 'This is a nightmare.'

'The worst kind.' Fairchild waited until Silva began to walk again. 'The general consensus appears to be this was an attempt to take out Haddad. There's nothing about Karen Hope and no reference to the fact the villa is owned by her brother.'

'And where are they, the Hopes?'

'They've gone to ground. No sign of them anywhere. I'm sure a few journalists' palms have been crossed with gold so as to downplay the connections between Haddad and the Hopes. They'll spin some story about this being a terrorist plot against the Saudis, neatly turning the tables. I wouldn't be surprised if the regime use Lashirah's death as an excuse to crack down on opposition groups at home.'

'This is so wrong.'

'Yes.' They'd reached Silva's little boat and Fairchild gawped at the yacht as if he couldn't believe anyone could live on such a craft, let alone go to sea in it. 'Your home?'

'It suits me.'

'I can see why it would.'

'What's that supposed to mean?'

'In a house you're attached to the earth by concrete and bricks and mortar. Here you're only tied on with the dock lines. You could flick them free and sail away.'

'This isn't the time for pap psychoanalysis.' Silva stepped over the lifelines and moved to the cockpit. She slid open the hatch and descended the companionway steps, shouted back over her shoulder for Fairchild to come aboard. The boat rocked as he stepped onto the deck. He poked his head in the hatch and turned round to descend the steps.

'I'm sorry,' he said. 'About Gavin.'

'It's a bit late for that now.'

'Yes.' Fairchild seemed to shrink. He looked longingly at the seats in the saloon and moved across and slumped down at the table. There was a large circular burn mark where Silva had accidentally placed a hot pan on the surface. He reached out and touched the blackened circle. 'Do you know what would happen if Haddad found out who did this?'

'I can only imagine.'

'I don't want to sound racist, but they regard life differently out there. People are stoned to death. They have their hands chopped off. They're beheaded. Haddad will want more though. He'll want to see somebody suffer. He'll track down everybody connected with this and kill them. At least he'll kill them after he's done torturing them.'

'It's a bit late to be having regrets now. I'm sorry the job went wrong but it wasn't my fault.'

'You misunderstand. I came here to warn you. You should take precautions, perhaps go away for a while.'

'You're kidding me.'

'No.'

'But nothing that happened in Italy can lead Haddad back here, can it?'

Fairchild didn't answer. He touched the burn mark on the table again.

'Hello?'

'There's a possibility the location of the training base might have been compromised.'

'The lodge?'

'Yes. I heard there were people up there yesterday. Not police, nor were they Italian.'

'Is there a link back to you?'

'The lodge is owned by a holding company based in Bermuda, so not directly, no. With a lot of digging Haddad might be able to find out, but that's not the issue.'

'So what is?'

'Apparently there were a couple of cars and a van. They didn't go inside the lodge but they took away bags of rubbish, among other stuff.'

'And?' Silva was having trouble comprehending. 'We made sure all the military gear was kept separate. Nothing incriminating went in the bins.'

'It's not the rubbish they were interested in, it's what was on the rubbish. What was on the cans of beer, the bottles of water.' Fairchild rubbed at the burn mark as if trying to erase it. 'I'm talking about fingerprints belonging to you and Itchy. You've both got convictions. I don't think it would be too hard for Haddad to run a check, and when he does your name will come up. Rebecca da Silva. Olympic shooter. Sniper. Now that's incriminating enough, but when Haddad mentions your name to Karen Hope the motive for the shooting will be obvious.'

'Fuck. Do you think he'll take this to the authorities?'

'Put yourself in his position. Would you?'

'No,' Silva said quietly.

'And, given what your mother knew, Haddad and Hope won't want to either.' Fairchild turned and peered through a porthole. A fishing boat was passing close by and Silva's yacht began to bob as the wake washed against the hull. 'They're going to come after you, Rebecca. You have to get away from here. You are, quite literally, a sitting duck.'

Chapter Twenty-Four

Taher received a call.

'There are some loose ends,' the voice on the end of the phone said in Arabic. 'Rebecca da Silva and her spotter, her father, Matthew Fairchild, the journalist at the news agency.'

'That's a lot of loose ends,' Taher said. 'Sounds as if somebody has been a bit careless.'

'Nobody has been careless, it's simply a matter of good housekeeping. Don't the Bedouin take their shoes off at the threshold to prevent dirt entering the tent?'

'We do, but we also try not to step in shit in the first place.' As soon as he'd spoken Taher wondered if he'd gone too far. He was annoyed at the way things were panning out, but he needed to keep his paymasters sweet for just a little longer. 'What do you want me to do?'

'Milligan. The journalist. We warned him but he obviously didn't take the threat seriously. We need to deal with him as soon as possible.'

'Neil Milligan and Francisca da Silva? People will put two and two together.'

'If you do this right they'll come up with nothing more than an unfortunate coincidence.'

Taher sighed. It was no good arguing. Milligan should have kept his blabber mouth closed. He knew what would happen if he told anybody about the story Francisca da Silva had been working on. Now it looked as if he hadn't paid heed to the warnings. Was journalistic integrity really more important to the man than the safety of his wife and children?

'And the others?'

'For now you just worry about Milligan.' Silence for a moment. 'An unfortunate coincidence, OK?'

The phone went dead and Taher moved to the window and considered the problem he'd just been handed. Looking out over the city was always his first action when it came to making decisions. Up here above everything there was a clarity missing at ground level. The hustle and bustle and anarchy were replaced by silence. Chaos turned into serenity.

He thought of the violence he'd committed or helped orchestrate. Explosions, bullets ripping into flesh, vehicles ploughing into crowds. He understood the damage he'd caused and the scars he'd left behind – both physical and emotional – but that was the idea. Only by giving these people something they couldn't forget would they begin to remember they only had themselves to blame.

Neil Milligan. Case in point. The journalist only had himself to blame for what was going to happen to him. He was a niggle in the grand scheme of things, but at the moment he'd become the most important item on Taher's busy agenda.

He turned from the window, turned from the peace and quiet.

An unfortunate coincidence.

He nodded to himself. Yes, that's exactly what people would say.

–

Kowlowski didn't appear to be in a rush to get back to Rotterdam and the journey took a couple of days. Holm and Javed at first followed behind the truck, stopping whenever the Pole stopped, but after the destination seemed obvious they overtook the lorry and headed north as fast as possible, Holm reasoning they needed to get to Rotterdam first.

'What if you're wrong?' Javed said. 'What if they stop off en route?'

'They won't.' Holm turned his head. The truck was somewhere back there, miles behind them. 'The captain of the *Angelo* mentioned the UK, didn't he? Plus we know the container keeps appearing on the manifests, and if Latif and his mate wanted to go somewhere in mainland Europe they could have done it in a car.'

They reached Rotterdam early on the second morning. The app on Javed's phone showed the truck hadn't reached Germany so Holm took an executive decision.

'We'll get a room somewhere.' He ran his fingers through his hair. It was greasy and he could smell his own body odour. Always a bad sign. 'We need a wash and a bed and some proper sleep.'

'A room? A bed?' Javed smirked. 'Didn't know you cared, boss.'

'Two single beds. We'll clean ourselves up and get our heads down. We should be able to manage a few hours' kip before the lorry turns up.'

They found a cheap hotel on the outskirts of Rotterdam. The receptionist looked at them a little oddly. Two men wanting a room on the spur of the moment at nine in the morning. Holm mentioned they were British police officers on a case.

'What was that about?' Javed said.

'She thought we were… well… you know? I think I put her straight.'

'Straight? I doubt it, boss.'

Holm ignored Javed. He was too tired to care what the hell the receptionist thought. He needed to sleep.

In the room Holm was pleased to see the single beds were a good distance apart. He dumped his bag in the corner, kicked off his shoes and lay down on one of the beds. The last thing he remembered was asking Javed to set an alarm and the first thing he saw when he woke was the young man leaning close.

'What the fuck?' Holm put up his hands. 'Get off!'

'It's five p.m., boss.' Javed stood. 'I've showered and had something to eat at the cafe next door.'

'The truck…?' Holm sat up and rubbed his eyes. 'We haven't missed it?'

'Kowlowski's just crossed the border into the Netherlands. He'll be a couple of hours yet.'

'When does the *Excelsior* depart?'

'It's sails this evening. They'll start loading shortly.'

'Good.' Holm swung his legs off the bed but paused before standing. 'We need flights to the UK. We need to be there before the ship arrives back in Felixstowe.'

Holm had a shower, grabbed something to eat at the cafe and then they made for the port.

Kowlowski arrived about an hour later. The Pole swung the truck in and coasted down to where containers were already being plucked from the dockside by huge cranes. Holm got out of their car and went across to the customs building.

'You again.' It was the same officer as before. He nodded over to a small Portakabin. 'The toilets are over there. If you can be bothered.'

As they left the officer was speaking to a colleague and laughing, an accusing finger pointing at Javed. The story of the urinating Englishman had obviously done the rounds.

'God knows what kind of reputation British intelligence is getting thanks to you.' Holm shook his head. 'Come on.'

They sauntered along the dockside down a narrow corridor of containers, trying to look like a couple of jobsworths.

'We're not really interested, right?' Holm pulled the collar of his coat up against a wind that was funnelling between the stacks of containers. 'The last thing we want to do is make ourselves any more work. We just want to tick the boxes and get on home to a cool beer and a warm woman.'

'I might remind you that I don't like either of those things.'

'There. Kowlowski's done.' Holm glanced sideways while pretending to inspect the doors of a nearby container. At the end of the row the crane grabber had positioned itself over Kowlowski's truck. The arms lowered and clamped themselves in place. The container soared upwards and outwards in a manoeuvre Holm found strangely balletic. 'The stowaways are on board. Let's go back to the hotel and book some flights from Schiphol for early tomorrow morning. With luck we'll be in Felixstowe for breakfast.'

Javed gave Holm a smirk. 'Not much on the menu there, boss, right?'

Thanks for reminding me, Holm thought.

Chapter Twenty-Five

Silva rose early. She climbed from her bunk, dragged the kettle onto the hob and lit the gas. Flipped the radio on as a presenter read a news summary. Train drivers were on strike and there was countrywide commuter chaos. Overseas, the Pope had condemned the killing of a foreign dignitary on Italian soil, pleading for all religions to work together for peace and under-standing. Back in the UK a fifty-seven-year-old man had been stabbed in north London. Another murder in the capital. The victim was one Neil Milligan, the owner and editor of the well-regarded Third Eye News agency. Police enquiries were continuing but so far no arrests had been made. The end of the piece noted the agency had, coincidentally, been struck by tragedy earlier in the year when noted foreign correspondent Francisca da Silva had been killed in a terrorist attack in Tunisia.

The kettle whistled out a warning and Silva turned off the hob before slumping down at the saloon table in shock. Milligan was dead, taken out by either Weiss or, more likely, Jawad al Haddad. Her mother had been close friends with Milligan. Not lovers – at least Silva didn't think so – but confidantes. His death meant another part of her mother's life was erased for good, another link to the past broken.

She sat for a few minutes and then got up and peered out of the companionway; she thought about Fairchild and his warning. The estuary was grey and almost still, just a slight movement as the tide began to ebb. Three boats up from hers a rope frapped against the mast and across the water there was a low rumble as a conveyor belt carried aggregate from a large cargo ship to the shore. All of a sudden she felt exposed. The little marina had a high fence and twenty-four-hour security with a guard, but the fence was old and rickety and Freddie likewise.

She ducked below and slid the hatch shut. She drew the curtains and hunkered down at the table. Fairchild had left her a burner phone, a pay-as-you-go mobile that was untraceable. Silva pulled it out. She was tempted to ring him but then wondered about Itchy. Was he a target? She didn't want to phone him either in case Weiss was somehow listening in, but she felt responsible and he deserved a warning. She hadn't unpacked the day before, but now she pulled the pannier bags open and took out all the clothing she'd taken to Italy. She rummaged in a locker for some fresh items and stuffed them in the bags. Then she clambered up through the companionway, slid the hatch shut and locked it, and made for her motorbike.

Ten minutes later she pulled up outside Itchy's terraced house. A knock brought him to the door and he hustled Silva inside.

'You hear about the money?' he said. His mouth widened into a smile. 'Twenty-five K. Not bad, considering.'

'What?'

'I've been paid. Twenty-five thousand pounds. It appeared in my bank account overnight.'

'Never mind the money,' Silva said. She followed Itchy through into the living room and closed the door behind her. 'Neil Milligan is dead.'

'Who?'

'The journalist my mum used to work for. He knew about the story, knew about the Hopes. He's been murdered.'

'Murdered?'

'He was stabbed and it was made to look like a mugging, but that's just a cover.' Silva shrugged and let her arms hang loose. She was at a loss. She stared past Itchy. The wall behind him had been stripped of wallpaper but little pieces of the gold-flecked covering remained. Itchy's house was a refurbishment job and for a moment Silva thought about the ridiculousness of the situation. Here she was worrying about his renovation project when just two days ago she'd been attempting to kill the next president of the United States. 'My guess is we're next.'

'Caz.' Itchy tilted his head and looked at the ceiling. 'She's upstairs.'

'Did you tell her anything about the Italy trip?'

'Only that I was going on a security job. Protection. That sort of thing. She doesn't know where we went, who we met, or any of the details.'

'Good. Is there anywhere she can go for a few days? Not family – they're too easy to trace – a friend perhaps?'

'She's got a mate in Edinburgh.'

'Perfect. Tell her something's come up. She shouldn't be worried but it might be safer if she went away on a little holiday. Say it's a treat. Spend some of that money.'

'Shit, Silvi. I hate lying to her.'

'Don't lie, then. Just don't tell her the whole truth, right?'

'OK.' Itchy nodded. 'And us? I guess we could just bugger off in your boat.' Itchy made a wavy movement with his hand. 'Head out to sea?'

'She can do about five knots with a good wind. That's a hundred and twenty miles a day. I don't think we'd get far before they caught up with us, do you?'

'We're not going to just sit here and wait for them, are we?'

'No. Remember Afghanistan? What we did there? If there was an enemy sniper pinning down our unit we didn't wait to be picked off, did we?'

'No.' Itchy was moving to the doorway. He'd got the message. 'We went out into the field and hunted them down.'

'Exactly.'

–

Hunting the enemy down was all well and good, but Silva had something else to do first.

'We need to visit my dad,' she said into her helmet microphone as they cruised up the motorway. 'I want to persuade him to go somewhere safe for a bit.'

'Good luck with that.' Itchy's voice crackled back through the earpiece. He'd met Silva's father. 'A tenner says he refuses to budge.'

Silva didn't reply. Itchy was almost certainly right.

They arrived at her father's place a couple of hours later. Silva told Itchy to wait by the bikes and she went up to the front door. Mrs Collins answered with the look of somebody not best pleased to receive visitors.

'You,' she said. Behind the housekeeper the parquet flooring in the hallway shone like a mirror.

'Yes, me.' Silva was afraid to step in from the porch. She nodded at the floor. 'Would you like me to remove my boots?'

'You could go round the house.' Mrs Collins gestured at the gravel drive. 'He's down by the lake, fishing.'

'Fishing?'

'Don't ask.'

'Right. Thank you.'

Silva retreated down the steps and walked round to the back. She found her father sitting on an old director's chair perched precariously at the end of the wooden jetty. He held a fishing rod in his right hand, and every now and then he swished the rod back and forth, the thick fly line curling behind him before he sent it shooting out over the water. Silva stepped onto the jetty with a deliberately heavy footfall.

'Dad? What are you up to?'

'What does it look like I'm bloody up to? I'm trying to catch something for dinner.' The response came without any note of surprise, as if her father had been expecting her all along.

'Any luck?'

'Not even a nibble.' Her father wound in the line and placed the rod down on the jetty. 'I see Karen Hope's still alive.'

'Yup. Snafu. That's me. Failed again. Only this time I don't think any of it was my fault.' Silva noted the fishing rod and the green canvas bag. 'That's Fairchild's, isn't it?'

'He sent it to me.'

'No he didn't. He's been here again, hasn't he?'

'Well, yes, he came by yesterday.'

'I guess he told you what happened?'

'Yes.'

'And warned you about Haddad?'

'Yes.'

'And you heard about Neil Milligan?'

'Yes.'

'So what the hell are you doing here, Dad?' Silva stood with her hands on her hips. Her father was fiddling with the fishing line. Untying the fly and placing the hook back in a small tackle box. 'You obviously didn't take Fairchild's warning seriously, but the news about Milligan should have made you realise that Haddad doesn't mess around.'

'I'm not running away, Rebecca. I'm no coward. If Haddad shows up here we can have it out mano-a-mano.'

'Dad, Haddad's not going to turn up in person. He *is* a coward. He'll send his henchmen and they don't play by Queensberry Rules.'

'I was in the SAS, remember.' He snapped the lid of the tackle box shut and put it in the canvas bag, picked up the bag and the rod, and stood. 'I can take care of myself.'

'I don't doubt it, but what if there's three of them? Five? Ten?'

'Did Matthew Fairchild ever tell you how I saved his life in Iraq?'

'This isn't the time for—'

'Rebecca! Listen, will you? This is important!' The temper was characteristic of her father, but there was a waver to his voice that Silva hadn't heard before. She paused and nodded. He continued. 'We were deep in the southern desert, exfilling from a vantage point where we'd been calling in air strikes on Iraqi Scud positions. Our hide had been compromised so we had to make a swift getaway. Fairchild was bringing up the rear when he was hit. I told the rest of the guys to head on and create a diversion while I went back for him. When I got to Fairchild it was obvious he wasn't going anywhere fast. He'd taken a round in the knee. He told me to leave him a pistol and go, but I wasn't having it. I got him to play dead and I scrambled up a nearby hill and hid in a gulley. About five minutes later the first of the Iraqis came round the corner. Fairchild stayed still and I allowed the soldiers to get up close. Then I opened fire. There were nine of them and I took out seven, while Fairchild got two. When I got back down to him I realised three of the Iraqis were still alive. According to the Geneva Convention they were now off-limits, but that was utter crap. If we'd left them they might have been able to attract the attention of other nearby patrols. They'd have been able to point out the direction we went.' Her father paused and there was only the sound of a light wind brushing the rushes, a gentle lapping of little wavelets against the side of the jetty. 'I shot them, Rebecca, one by one, and that still haunts me to this day.'

'Dad.' Silva moved forward. She couldn't remember the last time she'd shown her father anything other than cursory affection, but now she wanted to tell him she loved him and cared for him.

'No!' Her father held up a hand. He had tears in his eyes. 'The point is we do what is necessary to help those we care about. Right and wrong don't come into it.'

Silva stood a pace away. Was her father saying he loved her, cared about her? 'I don't understand.'

'The best chance for you is if I remain put. When they discover you're not in Plymouth they'll come looking here. Let's see what kind of state they're in after that.'

Silva nodded but she wondered if her father had slipped over into fantasy, if this wasn't some attempt to return to a time when he was younger and fitter and a world of possibilities still lay before him.

'Itchy's here, Dad.' Silva changed the subject. Her father had always liked Itchy. 'We'll stay over if that's OK? Be off in the morning.'

'Itchy?' There was a flicker of annoyance, as if he was cross she hadn't told him this important news straight away. The emotion of a moment ago was gone. 'Why ever didn't you say so, Rebecca?'

With that her father was off down the pontoon and heading for the house, shouting for Mrs Collins to bring cold beers and some of those dry-roasted peanuts they'd stocked up on at Christmas. It was all Silva could do to trot after him and wonder what it was with father–daughter relationships.

Chapter Twenty-Six

After a boozy dinner where her father and Itchy vied to tell the tallest army stories, Silva retired to one of the attic guest rooms. She lay on the bed and thought about her promise to Itchy that they'd go on the offensive. Quite how they were going to do so she had no idea. Their only chance of escaping from Haddad's wrath would be to expose him and his dealings with the Hopes. If she could get the information her mother had discovered out into the media, then public pressure would force governments – UK, US and Saudi – to act.

She tried to sleep, but the problem wouldn't go away and her mind was a maelstrom of competing ideas, none of which offered a solution. She wondered how her mother might have approached the problem. As a journalist she'd have gathered evidence and collated it, each piece adding to the case she would make in the story. But did Silva have all the evidence yet?

Hidden secrets.

It came to her then. The postcard of Chichester Harbour her mother had left for her.

She climbed out of bed. Her leather jacket lay over the back of a chair and the postcard was still inside one of the zip pockets. She pulled it out.

18 August

Dear Rebecca, remember the beach we used to go to here? West something or other wasn't it? Those were happy times, good memories, a place with buried treasure and

hidden secrets to be passed on from one generation to the
next. I so enjoyed the many times we visited. I definitely
Hope you did too. Love always and forever, Mum.

She realised with a start that the eighteenth of August was tomorrow. She reached for her phone and pulled up a map of Chichester Harbour. A satellite image showed a series of deep-water channels penetrating inland, vast mudflats exposed at low tide. She zoomed in. There was an odd spit of sand which curled back from the open sea. Scattered white dots of small boats moored behind the spit. On the main sea-facing beach, a regular line of something Silva reckoned were beach huts.

Nothing on the screen sprung out at her so she put the phone down and returned to bed where the problem continued to nag her until eventually she drifted off to sleep.

When she woke it was still dark. She climbed out of bed and went over to the window. In the garden a crescent moon rippled in the waters of the lake. Closer, a shadow moved across the lawn, while to the right another approached the house.

Silva eased back from the window. In thirty seconds she'd dressed and was inching down the corridor to Itchy's room. She tapped the door gently and entered.

'Itchy!' she whispered.

'Huh?' Itchy stirred beneath the duvet. 'Wassup?'

'Don't put the light on. We've got company. Two. Outside.'

'Shit.' Itchy slipped from the bed. There was a rustle as he dressed. 'They armed?'

'No idea, but wouldn't you be?'

'Yes, but we're not.'

'No.' Silva considered the situation. There were two men about to break into the house. If they'd been sent by Haddad then likely they were highly trained, had weapons and were prepared to kill. 'Go and wake Mrs Collins and tell her to stay in her room. We don't want her wandering around.'

'And you?'

'I'll see to my father. Try and get him up here. Perhaps we can barricade the stairs.'

As she spoke a tinkling of glass came from the hallway, the creak of a door.

'They're in,' Silva said. 'Go!'

She ran out into the corridor and moved towards the stairwell. A grand staircase spiralled round to the first floor and then on down to the ground floor. Moonlight shone through the front door and reflected on the polished flooring. The sheen was disturbed as two figures passed along the hallway. They disappeared out of sight, heading, Silva suspected, for the stairs.

She was about to go back and find Itchy when there was an explosion of noise. A loud bang followed by the *phut phut phut* of a silenced pistol. Then another bang.

'Dad!' Silva screamed. She reached the lower floor and ran along the corridor to her father's room. There was a smell of cordite, and as she entered the room she tripped on someone lying prone in the doorway. She stumbled, turned and knelt. 'Oh my God! Are you hurt?'

'I expect he's dead.' Her father's voice came from the far side of the room at the same time as Itchy bounded in and flicked on the light switch. 'I went for a killing shot and I'd be surprised if I missed.'

Silva looked at the body. She put a hand out to feel for a pulse at the man's neck then realised it would be a wasted effort. His jacket lay open and blood inked out in a circle across his shirt. She raised her head. Her father sat on the floor half hidden behind an armchair. There was a pistol in his lap.

'Dad,' Silva said.

'Browning HP,' her father said. 'Nice to see it still does the job. Better than the German crap he's using.'

Silva turned back to the man on the floor. His right hand clutched a Glock pistol. 'Austrian, Dad, not German.'

'Same difference.'

245

'Silvi!' Itchy tapped her on the shoulder. He made a jabbing motion into the corridor at the same time as there was a clatter from the far end. 'The other one's out there.'

She reached for the Glock and then spun into the corridor. At the end, on the right, a door stood open. She nodded at Itchy and then crept down towards the door, both hands holding the weapon. Itchy kept to the right and when he reached the door he looked back at Silva. Then he reached in for the light switch.

The room was her father's study. A leather-topped desk with a high-backed chair. Bookcases. At the floor-to-ceiling window, heavy velvet curtains that rippled in the non-existent breeze.

Silva fired at the same time as something cracked into the wall beside her head. She threw herself across the corridor and fired through the opening again. After the sharp retorts came the smashing of glass, and she moved forward and into the room, covering the window. As she edged in she felt a waft of cold air from outside. She inched towards the window. The glass was gone and the window had been opened onto the small balcony. She took another step and then Itchy shoved her to one side as a shot echoed from the garden below.

'The light,' Itchy said. 'You're silhouetted like a cut-out on the range.'

He moved back across the room and turned the switch off. Silva peered through the window again. A swathe of white illuminated the lawn for a moment and then there was the sound of wheels spitting gravel and an engine revving hard before fading into the still night.

'They're gone,' Silva said.

'Whoever *they* are.'

'Right.' She handed the Glock to Itchy and walked back to her father's room, Itchy following. She looked down at the body on the floor. The man's face seemed familiar, and he certainly wasn't a Saudi. She cocked her head and moved round the body to view the face from a different angle.

'Bloody hell,' she said.

'You know him?' Itchy said.

'This is so crazy. I can't believe it.'

'Silvi! Who is it?'

'I only know his first name is Frank. He was at a reception in London where Karen Hope gave a speech. He's an agent. Sean knew him.'

'Sean? You mean he's…? Oh great. We're really fucked, then.'

'Better fucked than dead.' Silva's father pushed himself up from where he'd been hiding behind the chair. He walked over. 'That little shit would have killed me if I hadn't shot first.'

'It's self-defence, then,' Silva said. She reached out and gently took the Browning from her father. She engaged the safety and uncocked the weapon. 'But this is definitely not legal.'

'It was perfectly legal when I was in Iraq. Defending the realm. Putting my life on the line for others.'

'Dirty work, Dad. You don't get the credit, only the blame.'

'Well I'll face the consequences when the police get here. There'll be an outcry if they lock me up simply because I shot a burglar.'

'I don't think he was a burglar.' Silva cast a glance at Itchy. 'And I don't think we should call the police either.'

'Why not?'

'I told you this man is a US agent.' Silva moved her foot and prodded the man's arm. Blood was pooling on the carpet. 'He and his mate were sent here to kill me.'

'Rebecca?' Her father looked at her as if she was a child again and had performed badly in a school test. 'What on earth have you got yourself into?'

'What have…?' Silva wondered if her grandmother's dementia was hereditary. 'This guy is working for the US government, Dad. Do you understand what that means?'

'I told you this wasn't simple. I told you the only way was to kill Karen Hope. Now it's all gone fubar.'

Her father was right about one thing, she thought. This was fubar. Fucked up beyond all repair.

'Folks.' Itchy. 'We haven't got time for this. We've got to split.'

'What about the body?' Silva stepped back. The pool of blood had grown. 'We can't just leave it here.'

'You go. Kenneth and I will deal with that.' Mrs Collins stood in the hallway looking at the stain on the carpet with some concern. 'After all, cleaning's what I'm good for, right?'

–

'What the hell was that all about?' Itchy's voice buzzed with static in Silva's helmet as they rode into a brightening sky. 'Did Mrs Collins just reinvent herself as some kind of fixer?'

'I've no idea.' Silva grimaced to herself. There was something going on between Mrs Collins and her father, but what it was, aside from possibly fulfilling each other's sexual needs, she didn't know.

They put a couple of dozen miles between themselves and her father's place before Silva suggested they pull over and take a break. They headed down a lane and bumped the bikes through a gate and into a field. She pulled her helmet off. Talking on the bike-to-bike headsets was one thing, but she couldn't think straight while she was riding and they needed some sort of plan.

Itchy kicked down the stand on his bike and waited for orders. As if Silva knew what the hell she was doing.

'Well?' he said after a minute.

'I don't know, Itch.' She looked at the dawn sunlight filtering through a nearby hedgerow. 'I always thought Fairchild was bullshitting about a global conspiracy. It seemed straight out of a Dan Brown novel. But those two men back at Dad's place suggest he's not far short of the mark.'

'If we're up against the US government – hell, any government – we might as well turn ourselves in now.'

'Perhaps I'm wrong. Perhaps Karen Hope has a few people on her dodgy payroll. If she's happy to pay for somebody to kill my mother then bribing a few agents would be par for the course.'

'Sean.' Itchy fiddled with his helmet. Stared at the ground. 'Could he…?'

Itchy didn't finish the sentence but he didn't need to; Silva had already played out the chilling possibility in her head that Sean could somehow be involved with Hope. He'd certainly been enamoured with her. Was it pushing the bounds of possibility to think she'd recruited Sean to her side? Silva knew it wasn't. Sean was a patriot, and if Hope had appealed to that part of him he'd have been with her.

'Silvi?' Itchy had his head up now and he met gaze. 'He wouldn't, would he?'

'I don't know.'

And she didn't. All Sean's words, all his declarations of love, all his talk of a future together, was that a charade? She remembered when he'd called her after her mother's death. It was the first time they'd been in contact for months. Was the call out of genuine concern or had Karen Hope initiated it? Perhaps Hope had a notion her mother might have a backup plan which involved passing the files to somebody else. The obvious person would be Silva. *Get close to her, Sean. Find out what she knows.* Silva could imagine Hope intense and passionate, her hand on Sean's arm. *This isn't about me, it's about our country's future. God bless America.*

'Silvi?'

'I'm going to call him,' Silva said. 'I'll use Fairchild's burner phone.'

Itchy nodded. They'd both turned their own phones off and removed the batteries so there was no chance of anybody tracking them, but the burner phone was clean. Once she'd made the call she'd ditch it.

Sean answered after a couple of rings, a tentative 'hello' to an unrecognised number.

'It's me,' Silva said. 'Rebecca.'

'Rebecca!' Sean's voice jumped an octave. 'Where are you?'

'I'm out and about.' Silva was already on the defensive. Why would his first words be a question about her location? 'Just pottering around.'

'I heard about Neil Milligan. I understand he worked with your mother.'

'He was murdered, Sean.'

'I know. Tragic. Wrong place, wrong time.'

Wrong place, wrong time. The same phrase she heard so often about her mother's death.

There was a pause before Sean continued. 'You sound like you're having a hard time. Can we meet up?'

There. The bait. The hook.

'Sure. I'd like to see you.' Silva played along. 'When and where?'

'Well that depends where you are. I'm in London at the moment but I have to go to Cambridge later today for a trilateral US/UK/Saudi trade summit. After this evening I'm free for a couple of days. Perhaps we could explore Cambridge together.'

'Cambridge?'

'Yes. I'll be at a British military base close by. RAF Wittering. Do you know it?'

'RAF…?' Silva nearly dropped the phone. She swallowed. 'No.'

'Well, we could meet in Cambridge tomorrow sometime. I'll book a hotel. Do you want to text me your ETA?'

'I'll do that. Got to go. Bye.' Silva hung up and then took the phone and shoved it into the hedge. 'Fuck.'

'Silvi?' Itchy was standing a little way off. 'What is it?'

She unzipped her leather jacket. The postcard was in an inner pocket. She pulled it out and passed it to Itchy.

'This.' Silva told Itchy what Sean had said and let him read the postcard. 'Mum said Wittering had hidden secrets to be passed on from one generation to the next. I thought it had something to do with the beach in Chichester Harbour, but I was wrong. Sean is going to a trade summit at RAF Wittering for some Saudi trade deal.' Silva pointed to the date at the top of the postcard. 'My mother post-dated the card for the eighteenth of August. That's today. It can't be a coincidence.'

'A military base and Saudi involvement? Sounds like a pie the Hopes might have their fingers in.'

'It does.'

'And Sean, do you think he's mixed up in all this?'

'I don't know. Would he have told me about RAF Wittering if he was trying to keep it hush-hush?'

'He might have.' Itchy lowered his shoulders in a sign of resignation, as if he was apologising before he spoke. 'If it's a trap.'

Chapter Twenty-Seven

The descent into Heathrow was bumpy, nothing but cloud swirling outside the cabin window until all of a sudden the aircraft lurched lower and west London appeared below as they lined up for the final approach.

An hour later they were on the M25 heading round the top of London in stop–start traffic.

'No worries,' Javed said, his fingers on the screen of his phone. 'The *Excelsior* is still a good few hours out. Plenty of time.'

Holm gripped the wheel and willed the traffic to clear. Did they have plenty of time? The issue, he thought, was Huxtable. At some point he'd have to inform her, but if there really was a mole in any branch of the intelligence services then as soon as they began to formulate a plan Taher would be alerted. Holm wanted Latif, but he wanted Taher more. For now he had to keep quiet.

They'd arranged to meet Cornish at Felixstowe and she was waiting in the port car park as they pulled in some time after twelve.

'I want you to know I'm not happy,' she said as Holm and Javed got out of their car. 'You just breeze in and compromise a case we've been working on without a moment's thought and now this.'

'Sorry, Billie.' Holm held up his hands. The need to keep things under wraps just a little longer meant getting on the wrong side of Cornish once again. 'You know how it—'

'Yeah, right. National fucking security. Well I can tell you if anything goes down here in Suffolk, I'm holding you personally responsible.'

'Sure.' Holm was no longer interested in arguing. He wanted the old Cornish back. The one who had, despite being married to somebody else – a woman indeed – ignited a tiny spark in his belly, made him feel something. 'Shall we just get on with it?'

They walked across to a four-storey office building. The top floor doubled as an observation post and comprised one large room with a three-hundred-and-sixty-degree outlook.

'We can watch from up here.' Cornish had calmed. She indicated a number of desks. There were several pairs of binoculars and a number of workstations. On one screen was a map showing marine traffic data. Another flicked between security cameras. A third had a feed from the main gate, one side showing CCTV of the barrier and the other detailing the trucks and their drivers as they were cleared to enter or leave. 'I'll get some food and drink sent up.'

'Thanks,' Holm said.

'She's in the fairway.' Javed stood over by the screen showing marine traffic. He touched the screen and a pop-up appeared next to the symbol for the boat. 'ETA thirty minutes, it says here.'

'You saw the container loaded in Rotterdam?' Cornish said.

'Yes.' Holm walked over to Javed. The screen was awash with little symbols and at intervals of thirty seconds or so there was a flicker and each symbol moved a fraction. 'We're guessing at some point during the crossing the cargo was transferred to the second container. The second container was loaded here, hence when it arrives it won't be subject to a customs check.'

'We could flag it for inspection anyway. Run it through the X-ray scanner.'

'No. We need to let the container go so we can track it to its end point.'

'And what if the terrorists escape?'

Holm saw Javed look away from the screen for a moment.

'There are no terrorists,' Holm said flatly and without much conviction. 'We were barking up the wrong tree. The container is full of Nazi memorabilia. The stuff fuels the right-wing nutters and might well turn a few of them into terrorists. Which is why we need to get on top of it.'

'Crap. We both know that's rubbish. Stephen Holm wouldn't be chasing artefacts from the Third Reich as if this was some twisted edition of the *Antiques Roadshow*.'

'I told you, I'm out of favour. Destined to do the petty little jobs nobody else wants to do until the day I draw my pension. When we were here before I thought we'd cracked something big, but it turned out to be a minor case of nasty Nazis.'

'Right, and I'm head of the Met.' Cornish walked across to Holm and her hand brushed his forearm. 'Look, I don't know what's going on, but I want you to promise me if you need help you'll ask for it, OK?'

Holm gave a small nod of his head. Point conceded. Offer accepted.

Cornish whirled about and headed back down the stairs.

'We should tell her the truth,' Javed said. 'We're out on our own with no backup. She could come in handy.'

'Perhaps.' Holm moved his attention from the screen to the quayside. A huge container ship was easing away from the dock. The water frothed and boiled as the bow thrusters and the rear screw worked the vessel sideways. A series of Chinese characters were painted at the bow and Holm wondered if the ship's destination was the Far East. All of a sudden he had a weird notion it might be rather nice to be on the proverbial slow boat. Weeks at sea, the route mapped out, no decisions to make.

Cornish returned a few minutes later with a tray laden with cups of coffee and a plate of sausage rolls. As she and Javed tucked in, Holm went over to the window.

'You're right, Billie,' he said. To hell with it, he couldn't bring himself to deceive her any longer. 'We're talking terrorists, but it is vitally important the information stays secret.'

'Christ.' Crumbs fell from Cornish's lips and she reached for a paper napkin. 'How many?'

'Two, we think. One of them at least was part of the group that carried out the Tunisian attack. The one I fucked up on.'

'But JTAC and the security services are all over this, right?' Cornish put down her plate and joined Holm at the window. She gestured across the estuary towards the town of Harwich on the opposite bank. 'I mean, you've got agents out there ready to track these people. To take them down at the appropriate time.'

Holm continued to stare out of the window. He didn't speak. The Chinese boat had left the port and was steaming towards the open sea.

'Stephen, it's just you? Can you tell me why?'

'Walls and ears, Billie. That's why. We'll be going to my boss as soon as we know what we've got. Until then I'd be grateful if you'd keep to our original story about the Nazis.' Holm turned and smiled. 'And yes, I'd be grateful for your help too.'

Cornish smiled back but before she could speak Javed was on his feet, binoculars raised to his eyes.

'She's here,' he said. A small container ship was passing to starboard of the Chinese vessel and a pilot boat was waiting to guide her to a berth. 'The *Excelsior*.'

–

Trap or not, they headed east, skirted London and took the motorway to Cambridge. A succession of smaller roads followed until they eventually coasted along a country lane that ended at a small copse overlooking RAF Wittering.

'Nice one,' Silva said, patting Itchy on the back as they parked their bikes. Itchy had worked out the route before they'd set off, finding a circuitous way in and a place to watch the airfield which wouldn't bring them to the attention of personnel on the base. As an observation point it was near perfect. The copse sat halfway down a hill overlooking the runway. A muddy car park looked well used and a board with a map on showed a number of public footpaths criss-crossing a nature reserve. In the late afternoon the place was deserted.

Itchy took a pair of binoculars from his pannier and handed them to Silva.

'Badger watching,' he said. 'Right?'

Silva nodded. She had no idea if there were any badgers about but it was a decent cover story.

They walked through the woodland until they neared the edge. They dropped to the ground and began a slow crawl. Silva pushed through a patch of brambles, the thorns scratching her face. Itchy followed.

'I feel like a badger,' he said. 'I just hope I don't come across one down here.'

No chance of that, Silva thought, as Itchy's curses soured the still air.

At the edge of the wood they crouched behind a clump of bracken. Silva broke off a few fronds and wove them round her binoculars, but she hardly needed the optics; the runway was only a couple of hundred metres from their position and the main part of the base lay beyond that. There was an industrial estate at the top end of the runway and various military buildings sat behind a control tower. Farther away lay a small village of near-identical brick houses – accommodation for the base staff. Silva remembered similar houses from her childhood. Far from the outward appearance of sterility and blandness, the places she'd grown up in had felt welcoming and safe. A sanctuary away from what lay beyond the fences and the barriers. Nobody could hurt you while the base was patrolled by soldiers with guns. The danger came when you ventured outside into the real world.

'Something's going on.' Itchy was head down, peering through the bracken. 'Several police cars and four trucks have just driven out to one side of the runway. There's a limo there too.'

Silva raised the binoculars. Itchy was right. The convoy had taken up a position near the base of the control tower. The day had turned gloomy, with heavy clouds overhead, and the strobing lights on the police cars swept the tower with a blue flash every second. To one side of the tower was an area of raised decking and a red carpet ran from a series of steps towards the runway. A number of soldiers in dress uniform stood near the decking.

'What the hell is this?' Silva said. 'It looks like a presentation or a ceremony of some kind.'

'The trucks,' Itchy said. 'Look at the trucks and the logo on those banners at the back of the stage.'

She swung the binoculars and adjusted the zoom. White letters on a background strip of red and blue, the red colour matching the carpet. *Allied American Armaments*. 'The Hope family's company.'

'The trucks must have come from the factory in Birmingham. There's an advanced avionics research centre there. They build surface-to-air missiles and guidance systems among other stuff.'

Birmingham was forty miles to the west so Itchy's guess was probably right.

'The limo.' Silva refocused. The chauffeur had opened the door to the car and a man ducked out and straightened his jacket. 'That's Jonathon Walker, Secretary of State for Defence.'

'Wouldn't know him from Adam, but if you say so.' Itchy tapped Silva's shoulder. 'I do know him though.'

A man in a pale suit had followed the minister out of the car. A pasty face, glowing blond hair, a roman nose like his sister's.

'Brandon Hope.'

Brandon was an awkward figure, a shambling man hardly in control of his own body. He had nothing like the presence of his sister Karen. Walker placed his arm at Brandon's back and guided him along the red carpet to greet a couple of military personnel. A photographer was walking backwards taking pictures; beside him a woman with a video camera on her shoulder swung round to keep the men in shot as they passed.

'This is all wrong,' Silva said. 'This isn't clandestine.'

Her mother had mentioned something about secrets at RAF Wittering, but there was nothing dodgy going on here, not with all the soldiers and the truck drivers, not to mention the photographer and the camerawoman.

'What the hell was the postcard on about, then?'

'I don't know.' Silva pulled away from the binoculars and returned Itchy's tap on the shoulder. 'But we'll find out soon enough. There.'

She pointed to the east where a star hung incongruously in the late afternoon sky. There was a low hum and the brightness moved lower. Now they could hear a roar and make out the silhouette of a large aircraft.

'You're right. Not clandestine at all,' Itchy said. 'Not in a jet of that size.'

The aircraft glided in. The body of the plane was windowless and a logo of a golden palm with crossed swords adorned the tail fin. A screech of rubber on tarmac came as the jet touched down and the aeroplane rolled along the runway. It turned onto a taxiway and slowed to a stop.

'Saudia,' Silva said. 'The national airline of Saudi Arabia.'

Ground crew were busy moving a set of steps into position at the front of the plane and then the door opened and a man in Arab dress descended the steps.

Walker moved forward to shake the man's hand, Brandon Hope close behind. Walker gestured to his left where there was a woman in a Royal Air Force uniform. Silva had her as the base commander. Next came an American general. An angular face and a severe haircut. Stars on his shoulders, a host of colours on his left breast. After him, a man and a woman in suits. As Walker introduced them, each received a handshake from the Saudi.

'Who's he?' Itchy said.

'No idea.' Silva tried to remember the photos Fairchild had shown her of Haddad. In some there had been other Saudis, but she didn't recognise the man from the plane.

As the introductions were going on, a pair of forklift trucks appeared and the tailgates of the lorries came down. Each lorry now disgorged pallets of equipment which were picked up by the forklifts and ferried across to the aircraft and lined up. A single pallet was taken to a point a few metres in front of the stage and somebody draped a Saudi flag in the centre, while a Union Jack was placed on one side and the Stars and Stripes on the other.

'Exports,' Silva said. 'This is nothing more than a ceremony to mark a trade deal between American Armaments and the Saudi government. In this case the weapons have been manufactured in the UK at the factory in Birmingham, hence the trilateral nature.'

At the end of the line of dignitaries there were two more men in suits. For a moment the binocular lenses were full of the backs of Walker, Hope and the Saudi. Silva pulled right and the pudgy face of Greg Mavers slipped into view. Standing next to Mavers was a very sober-looking Sean Connor.

Chapter Twenty-Eight

By the time the *Excelsior* had docked and the container had been unloaded it was early evening. Straddle carriers roved up and down the rows of containers and moved them onto waiting lorries. Holm and Javed sat in their car on the ring road and waited. At eight o'clock Holm's phone buzzed. It was Cornish.

'The container's on a lorry and it's leaving now,' she said. 'Index Tango Alpha three, four Lima X-ray. White cab.'

'Thanks, Billie,' Holm said. 'I owe you.'

'Forget it, Stephen. Just stay out of trouble and keep us safe, OK?'

'Will do.'

Javed flicked the sun visor down and peered into the little vanity mirror on the back.

'Here we go,' he said a couple of minutes later. 'Tango Alpha three.'

There was a grunt of diesel engine and a rumble as the truck drove past. Holm waited a couple of moments and pulled out. Before long they were rounding Ipswich and heading west.

'Where do you think?' Javed said.

Holm shrugged. To be honest, he had no idea. The truck could stop anywhere. All it took was a couple of minutes to open the back doors and Mohid Latif and his companion could scramble out and be off.

After an hour the lorry was at Cambridge, and as the road bent to the right Holm settled in for a long drive. They were closing on the A1, the main trunk route to the north, the destination surely either northern England or Scotland. However, twenty miles up the A1 Holm was surprised when the lorry abruptly turned off the main road into a small industrial estate. Dim lights on low poles glowed in the dusk. Beyond the estate there was a succession of identical buildings and a tall chain-link fence.

'What the hell is this place?' Holm said. The lorry had stopped at a barrier next to a security box. Beyond was an area of hard standing and a large warehouse. Inside the box a solitary figure stood in a blaze of yellow light. To the right of the box a number of shipping containers were stacked two high. After a moment or two the barrier hinged upwards and the lorry drove in.

Javed was head down over his phone. 'RAF Wittering.' He looked up. 'At least the bit behind that fence. This looks like some kind of business park attached to the base. Probably aerospace industries related to the airfield.'

'This is crap. We're going to get spotted here.' Holm turned his head. A few car lengths back they'd passed a gate to a field full of head-high maize. He reversed the car, relieved to see the gate was open. He drove in and parked behind a hedge. 'Have to do. Come on.'

Holm was out of the car and making for the warehouse on the field side of the hedge.

'Boss.' Javed was right behind, stumbling in the now near darkness. 'We've got to be careful. We could get shot if we venture onto the base.'

'Forget the base.' They'd reached the corner of the field. Through the hedge they could see the truck backing up to the warehouse. Huge double doors stood open, blackness within. The truck inched inside, its reversing lights illuminating pallets and wooden crates and some sort of racking system. In the security box the guard had returned to reading a magazine. 'This has nothing to do with the military. Now give me a bunk up.'

The fence was a couple of metres high but there was no barbed wire. The barrier was a deterrent rather than an impediment. Javed cupped his hands and Holm stepped onto the makeshift step. He grasped the top of the fence and hoisted himself up. The edge of the fence dug into his stomach and ripped his shirt, but he swung over awkwardly and dropped down the other side. Javed pulled himself up and over in one smooth movement.

'Show-off,' Holm said. A strip from his white shirt hung down towards his knees and when he put his hand to his stomach his fingers found a warm sticky liquid.

'Man down?' Javed said.

'I'm fine. It's just a graze.' Holm pulled the strip of linen free and dabbed the cut. He tucked the remains of his shirt back in. 'Come on, we need to get closer.'

The security was minimal. There didn't seem to be any cameras, and shrubs dotted the grassy area round the warehouse, providing plenty of cover. They reached the edge of the building and moved along until they came to a door set into the metal cladding. From inside came the revving and idling of the truck's diesel engine. Holm tried the door but it was locked. He gestured back towards the front of the building and as he did so he heard the engine rev again. Seconds later the truck cab rolled out from the warehouse and drove to the gate. The guard raised the barrier and the truck drove off.

'He's dumped the container,' Javed said. 'Should we try and get inside?'

Holm considered the terrain. A multitude of shrubs would allow them to make their way to the front of the building undetected, but they'd have to cross the open tarmac to get to the doors. It was now dark and floodlights illuminated the whole area. If the guard turned, he'd spot them.

He tapped Javed on the shoulder, made a circling motion and set off along the wall of the warehouse. At the rear there was a small strip of land and beyond that a fence which marked the edge of RAF Wittering. The runway was lit up and a series of lights dotted off into the darkness. A large jet waited on an apron of concrete, a door near the cabin open and a set of steps in place. A glow shone from a cargo hatch and a fuel bowser stood near the aircraft.

Holm turned to the building. There was a set of double doors, a mirror to the ones at the front. He moved across. There was a standard-sized door set into one and he was surprised to find it was unlocked. He eased the door open and stepped into the dark of the warehouse.

'Fuck.' Holm smashed his ankle on something low down. 'We should have brought a torch.'

'Here.' Javed's face lit up in the glow from his phone. A bright light on the back blinked on and Javed moved the phone to illuminate the area in front of them. Dozens of lengths of scaffolding lay in a metal rack; it was the corner of the rack that had connected with Holm's ankle.

Holm bent and rubbed his foot and moved forward. The cavernous space appeared almost empty, but in the centre was the container on its trailer.

'There,' Holm said. The rear doors were closed, but there was no seal. 'Let's open it up.'

Holm winced at the noise as Javed shifted an empty pallet box over to the container. Holm clambered up on top of the box and worked at the handle. Metal squeaked on metal as the rods top and bottom sprung from their holes and Javed helped Holm pull the door open. Inside were a number of wooden crates, each labelled with the words 'Genuine Volvo Penta Marine Parts'.

'These are similar to the ones we saw in Naples,' Javed said. He began to undo the metal ties holding one of the crates closed and then lifted the lid. 'Looks legit to me.'

'Right.' Holm moved his attention to the rear of the container where there was something odd about the back wall. He tapped the metal and glanced down the side to the open doors. 'Too short,' he said.

'What is?'

'The inside of the container. There's something beyond this.' He tapped the metal again. 'With these boxes loaded you wouldn't notice if you glanced in from the rear.'

'But anyone taking their time would realise.'

'Yes, but remember this container never left UK jurisdiction. If it was ever checked the inspection would be cursory at best.' Holm moved to one side where the seam of a weld looked rough and badly made. He grasped at a couple of bolt heads. 'Here, help me.'

Javed came across. He flashed the light of his phone at the corner, placed it on a crate, and moved to lend a hand. By gripping the bolt heads they were able to lift a section of the wall. Something clicked and the wall swung open on invisible hinges. Behind was a small compartment the width of the container and a pace deep.

'They're not here.' Holm looked round, trying to conjure something from the bare metal. 'The men. They should have transferred over from the container Kowlowski loaded onto the boat.'

'I told you, boss. They got off somewhere in mainland Europe, or else they switched to another container. Some kind of trick.' Javed picked up his phone and shone it round. 'You know we could work in here. It's not much smaller than our office.'

Holm wasn't listening. He'd fucked up. Latif was home free. Somewhere in the UK. Before long he'd begin to prepare for the next attack. People would die and it was all Holm's fault. Stephen Holm, no longer a name that would be associated with the capture of Taher, but rather one that would go down in the training manuals under the heading of how not to do it.

'A trick. Right.' Holm tapped the side of the container. 'Damn.'

He bit his lip. Something didn't make sense. If this was a clever ploy then what exactly was the container doing here empty? It could simply have been left at the SeaPak depot at Felixstowe or even outside the warehouse with the other containers. Why bring it inside?

'Take a couple of pictures,' Holm said, backing out to allow Javed more space. He moved past the crates and clambered down from the container. A glow now came from the door they'd come through and there was the noise of a vehicle heading their way. He walked across the warehouse, careful to avoid smashing his ankle again, and approached the door. He edged closer and peered out.

--

The ceremony had only lasted fifteen minutes. There had been a speech from the stage, a folding and exchanging of flags, and the cutting of a ribbon which had been stretched across the aircraft's cargo doors. As soon as it was over the dignitaries disappeared onto the air base, presumably to a reception of some kind. A group of soldiers dismantled the stage and rolled up the red carpet. The forklifts began to load the pallets onto the plane, an air maintenance crew appeared and a fuel bowser was brought alongside. Loading and preparing the aircraft seemed to take forever, but eventually the last pallet was hoisted up and disappeared inside the cargo hold.

By then dusk had fallen and the plane stood in darkness, only the lights from its cockpit bright against the flat grey of the airfield.

'That's that, then,' Itchy said. 'Whatever's going on here is totally legit. Your mother might not have liked the fact the Hopes were selling arms to the Saudis, but there's nothing illegal about it.'

He began to rise from the undergrowth, convinced their surveillance operation was over.

'We wait,' Silva said. 'For the plane to take off.'

'For fuck's sake, Silvi, how do we even know it's going to leave tonight?'

'The cockpit light is still on. If the crew were going to go to stay over they'd have shut the plane down.' Silva turned to Itchy. 'Look, we might as well see this through. When the plane's gone we can scarper. Tomorrow I'll meet up with Sean in Cambridge and try to find out what this is all about.'

Itchy sighed and lowered himself down.

Half an hour later it was fully dark. Lights on the runway stretched into the distance while over on the base arc lamps lit up the roads and buildings. The plane was but a shadow.

'There,' Silva said. A couple of ground crew had appeared. They were walking beneath the plane, making a visual inspection. Chocks were removed from the wheels.

'They're off,' Itchy said.

'Not with the side cargo door still open they're not.'

Just aft of the flight deck a whole section of the fuselage had been hinged up so the crates of equipment could be loaded. Earlier a high-reach forklift had raised the crates to the door; they'd been manoeuvred inside and slid into the depths of the plane one after another. Now there seemed to be a last-minute alteration to the cargo manifest because the forklift was back. It approached the aircraft and picked up a pallet from inside. Down the pallet came and the forklift wheeled round and headed for the industrial estate which bordered the airfield. There was somebody down there waving a torch near where a set of gates stood open. The forklift crossed a taxiway and went through the gates and into a large warehouse. Within a few seconds it was back out again without the pallet. The figure with the torch swung the gates closed and the forklift drove back towards the main airport buildings.

'Bloody hell,' Itchy said.

'Yes, bloody hell.'

Silva could feel her heart beating fast. All the build-up, the ceremony, the preparation of the aircraft, the loading of the cargo, the long wait, had taken several hours. In less than a couple of minutes the forklift had pulled a pallet of weapons from the plane, deposited it in the warehouse, and whizzed off. If anyone was watching then they'd either been paid off or been given an excuse as to why a single pallet had to be unloaded. Perhaps it was too heavy, perhaps it was the wrong pallet, perhaps the cargo was damaged and was too dangerous to transit.

Now the jet was preparing to leave. The cargo hatch was shut and the engines started and throttled up. The aircraft taxied round, paused for a minute at the end of the runway, and then was accelerating away and lifting off, the lights on the wingtips flashing as it roared into the distance.

'Glass the warehouse.' Itchy motioned at Silva's binoculars. 'Fifty metres to the left at the intersection of the fence and the cornfield.'

Silva raised the binoculars. That part of the airfield was unlit but there was enough ambient light so she could trace the line of the fence until it reached the field.

'Do you see them?'

She did. Two figures hunched down in a hedgerow watching the proceedings just as Silva and Itchy were. She zoomed the binos. A solitary lamp at the corner of the fence cast a pale glow illuminating the two men. One with a youthful face, jet-black hair, brown skin, the other with much older features, balding and white.

–

Holm had grabbed Javed and they'd legged it back to the fence as the forklift zoomed towards the building. No sooner had it disappeared inside than it was out again, sans pallet. The guard they'd seen round the front swung the gates to the airfield shut, and closed and locked the warehouse doors. They crouched behind some shrubs until the guard drove off in a small white van and then they climbed the fence and hid in the dense maize. After they'd watched the aircraft take off, Holm pushed up from the ground, brushing mud from his trousers.

'That's it.' He stared to the west where a few minutes earlier the Saudi plane had disappeared into the night. 'Weapons.'

'In that crate?' Javed stood. 'How do you know?'

'A guess based on where we are and the nationality of that aircraft. Worse, it looks as if it's officially sanctioned.' Holm started to trudge along the side of the field and back towards the car. He felt deflated. If he took any of this to Huxtable she'd close him down. 'Certainly somebody turned a blind eye or two. A nod and a wink. An agreement to brush a little dirt under the carpet.'

'Even if you're right, it was only one pallet.'

'One pallet of what, and how often?' They reached the car and Holm scraped the bottom of his shoes on the sidewall of the front tyre, trying to shift the mud. 'Whatever, the pallet is going to Felixstowe. Next stop Naples via Rotterdam. We need to get to the port and liaise with the Border Force so they can open up the container.' Holm got in the car and started up. Javed slipped in the passenger side. Holm slid the car from the field and drove to the main road. He filtered into the traffic. 'Otherwise the crate is going to Italy where the *Angelo* will ship it across the Med.'

'To where?'

'I don't know.' Holm paused as he overtook a coach. 'Can you get that shipping app up and take a look at past routes the boat has sailed?'

'Yeah, one mo.' Javed pulled out his phone. His fingers slid across the screen and he whistled. 'It's like a slug's trail, criss-crossing the Med and looping back on itself, but since the *Angelo* has been rescuing people in distress, that figures.'

'But there's one place the boat's gone to multiple times, right?'

'Yes.' Javed turned his head, keeping the screen hidden from view. 'Care to guess?'

'I don't need to guess, I know,' Holm said. 'Tunisia.'

'The tourist resort of al Hammamet to be precise.' Javed tapped his phone. 'Huxtable. We have to tell her what we've discovered.'

'On the contrary.' Holm hunched forward. There was a junction ahead and he needed to take the exit if they were going to Felixstowe to alert the Border Force. For a moment his hand hovered over the indicator stalk, but he didn't flick it. He'd changed his mind. 'We're telling nobody, Farakh.'

'You just told me they're smuggling weapons, right? Well they're sitting in the warehouse right now just waiting to be picked up. We've got to stop them.'

'Remember the mole? If it becomes common knowledge we've discovered the smuggling operation then Taher will vanish into thin air just as he's done numerous times before. The most important thing we can do is find out the ultimate destination for the weapons and hope Taher is involved at the other end.'

'And how the hell are we going to do that?'

Holm shrugged. 'At the moment I haven't a bloody clue.'

Chapter Twenty-Nine

Silva and Itchy took two rooms at a Travelodge a dozen miles up the A1 from RAF Wittering. There was a pub attached to the hotel, and after a meal they sat and drank a couple of beers and discussed what they'd seen. Silva put the battery back in her phone. Several texts pinged in from Sean. He'd be in Cambridge overnight. Did she want to meet tomorrow? She replied that she did and would arrive in time for lunch.

'And what are you going to tell him?' Itchy asked. 'If he's involved in this you'll have shown our hand.'

'I know,' Silva said. 'But I can't believe he is. I think he was there on genuine US State Department business. You saw Greg Mavers? He's the deputy ambassador. Then there was that American general and the UK defence secretary. I don't think any of them would be aware of what happened later on.'

'Do you think he'll believe you?'

'No idea.' Silva took a sip from her beer. 'But I want you to visit Fairchild and tell him what we saw. Stay there until I turn up or call you.'

'And if you don't?'

'Then you'll know Sean is part of the conspiracy, won't you?'

Itchy's eyes widened and he picked up his pint glass, taking a long draw before clunking the glass down on the table.

'Yes,' he said. 'I guess I will.'

–

The next day she met Sean in the centre of Cambridge and they wandered through the city before having a meal in an old inn. Dark panelled walls, low ceilings, and a lack of natural light gave the place a conspiratorial atmosphere. The palpable tension between them when they'd parted in London had gone and Sean was back to his old self.

'I love England,' Sean said as they tucked into their food. 'So much history. Did you know Isaac Newton supposedly drank in this pub?'

'Let me guess, he liked to get smashed on cider, right?' Silva said, trying to be her old self too, trying to behave as if the madness of the past few days hadn't happened.

'Cider?' Sean cocked his head. 'Oh, I see.'

Silva bent to her food and took a few mouthfuls. 'I'm sorry about storming out.'

'No.' Sean put a hand across the table. 'I'm the one who should be sorry. I was a bit blinded by Karen Hope and the whole occasion and I didn't read your mood. Getting over your mother's death is not something that happens overnight.'

Silva nodded. 'Thanks.'

They finished their main course and ordered dessert and coffees, Silva all the time trying to appear casual and relaxed. As Sean shovelled up a spoonful of sticky toffee pudding, she asked about the trade summit. He paused for a moment and then shook his head.

'I suppose I can tell you. It's no secret. I'm sure it's going to be widely reported.'

'And?'

'The US and UK governments have done a massive trade deal with Saudi Arabia. The deal's worth billions and secures thousands of jobs.'

'Are we talking arms?'

'Yes.' Sean put his spoon down. Tilted his head. 'How did you know?'

'An educated guess,' Silva said. 'On the phone you mentioned you were at RAF Wittering. I doubt the military would have been involved had the deal been about mere widgets.'

'Right.' Sean picked up his spoon again but then stopped. 'Is there a problem?'

'Just that you were helping facilitate the export of weapons to Saudi Arabia, weapons which will be used to kill innocent—'

'Hang on.' Sean raised both hands. 'We're not going down that route. I know your mother was critical of UK and US policy in the Middle East, but you can't pin the blame for her death on me. Besides, the Saudis are allies. They provide stability in the region.'

'They fund militants.' Silva plucked a fact from something she'd read in her mother's dossier. 'For instance, fifteen of the nineteen 9/11 hijackers were Saudis.'

'That's ancient history. We're fully aware of everything Saudi Arabia does these days.'

'Really?' Silva let the question hang. She sat back in her chair. Folded her arms.

'What is this, Becca?' Sean pushed his unfinished pudding to one side and leaned forward, closing the distance. 'Why the sudden interest? You've never been much bothered before.'

'Before was when my mother hadn't been killed by terrorists.'

'This deal's got nothing to do with that. This is all perfectly legal, with an audit trail and full accountability.'

'If so then why were you, as a CIA operative, there?'

'Greg Mavers needed an analyst he could call on in case something came up in the reception and he needed quick answers. Knowing I could probably wangle a couple of days off afterwards I volunteered. It was as simple as that.'

'Are you sure?'

'Jeez, Rebecca, I don't have to answer to you.'

'Even if what was happening at Wittering in some way involved my mother?'

'How in the hell could it?'

'Karen Hope.' Silva held Sean's gaze as he stared across the table. She felt as if he was trying to see what she was thinking, what she knew.

'Karen Hope.' Sean reached for his drink. Took a draught. 'You're talking American Armaments, right?'

Silva nodded, realising the question was tentative. A probe to discover something deeper. So far nothing she'd said gave anything away, but without a hook Sean wasn't likely to open up. 'Shortly before she was killed, my mother uncovered unsavoury details about the Hope family business. The substance of it was serious enough to threaten Karen Hope's presidential chances.'

'I see.' A beat. No more. But just enough. Sean continued. 'What, exactly?'

'She found Karen Hope has links to a Saudi associated with funding terror groups. The Hopes, realising the information could never be allowed to get out, had my mother killed. Next came Neil Milligan, the head of the news agency my mother worked for. I spoke to him about my mother's research, but he told me to forget the whole thing. He was scared – rightly so, it proved.'

Sean opened his mouth to speak.

'No,' Silva said. 'I'm not finished.'

She moved on. There was a picture, she said, that showed Karen Hope with Haddad, a man who was a known terrorist sympathiser. Hope, fearing exposure, had paid to have Francisca da Silva eliminated. Neil Milligan had been at first threatened and then he too had been murdered.

'That's it,' Silva said.

Sean gave a nervous laugh. He raised his head and blew out a long breath. 'Let's just say, in some other crazy life, I believe you. What on earth did your mother discover that threatened Hope's election? Just being seen with Haddad wouldn't be enough.'

'Something to do with arms dealing.'

'So?' Sean shook his head. 'There's nothing illegal in arms dealing. In fact Karen Hope's major selling point is she's not a wishy-washy liberal. Her base are going to vote for her anyway, so attracting those to the right of that is part of her plan. She's got nothing to hide.'

'But suppose she *has* got something to hide. Suppose the Hope family have been supplying money and weapons to terrorists. This isn't some dodgy news story, Sean. It's part of the arrangement the Hope family have with Jawad al Haddad. He brokered the arms deal with the Saudi government, and Brandon Hope, as a kickback, makes sure certain shipments are delivered to Islamic extremists. Haddad's hands appear to be clean but his objectives are still fulfilled. What's more, in a few months' time, he's going to have a receptive ear in the White House.'

'It sounds like a bad conspiracy theory.' Sean shook his head. 'I'm sorry, Rebecca, I don't believe it. I think your mother was sold a dummy in order to try and discredit Karen Hope.'

Sean looked at her but said nothing. The sounds of the pub intruded. Cutlery chinking on plates. The hubbub of conversation. A chorus of laughter from a nearby table.

'I think,' Sean said eventually, 'that it would be best if you passed all the information to me. I'll see to it that it gets to the right places. Not only has your mother been duped, but this looks like an attempt to subvert democracy.' Sean shrugged. 'Sorry.'

'Fine.' Silva eased back into her chair. She needed to get out of here. It had been a mistake to talk to Sean and now she worried what he might do. She pointed at her empty glass. 'Could you get me another drink? I'm going to the loo.'

For a second Sean looked bemused but then he nodded. 'Sure.'

Silva stood and weaved between the tables, heading for the toilets. She glanced over her shoulder. Sean was at the bar, trying to attract the attention of the barman. Silva changed direction and made for the exit. To one side of the door there was an array of coat hooks, empty in this warm weather aside from Silva's leather jacket and helmet. She grabbed them and slipped outside, sprinting across the road to where she'd left her motorbike. A few seconds later she was riding away, dodging cyclists and pedestrians, and trying not to look back.

Chapter Thirty

She headed south, intending to rendezvous with Itchy at Fairchild's place. First though, she wanted to check on her father.

It was a little after nine thirty in the evening when she coaxed the bike up the gravel drive. The house loomed dark against a red sky, clouds piling in from the west. The windows stood black and empty, as if the place had been abandoned long ago.

She pulled up at the steps and turned the engine off. The headlight dimmed and she was left sitting astride the bike in a pale gloom. When she removed her helmet she could hear nothing except the distant rumble of a tractor and, closer, a pheasant clucking out a call as it flew up to a roost in the branches of a nearby tree.

Silva dismounted and moved towards the front door. She climbed the steps and turned the big brass doorknob. The door opened.

'Dad?' she said. 'Are you here?'

Nothing.

She walked in and carefully closed the door behind her. She fumbled at the wall until she found a switch. She flicked it and lights came on in the hall and stairwell.

'Dad? Mrs Collins?'

A wash of embarrassment came over her as she pictured her dad and Mrs Collins upstairs, going at it like teenagers. She moved to the foot of the stairs. Listened again. Still nothing. No bed creaking, no sound of Mrs Collins crying out. She shook off the vision and turned and went across the hallway to the kitchen-diner. The table was set for two and a large Le Creuset casserole pot sat on a cast-iron trivet in the centre. Silva walked over and touched the pot. Latent heat, a faint warmth. She lifted the lid. Meat, potatoes, veg. Her father liked to eat at six prompt, retire early. The casserole had been on the table for over three hours.

She lowered the lid with a clink and returned to the hallway. At the far end was an under-the-stairs toilet and the door stood open a crack. A vertical bar of white suggested somebody had left the light on inside. She crossed to the door and pushed it open.

Mrs Collins. Sprawled on the floor, her body contorted, her head twisted to the side as if she had reacted in surprise to something. Her left ear and part of her jaw had gone, blown away by a bullet that had carried on to hit a small mirror above the washbasin. Crazed glass reflected Silva's face in segments of emotion. Shock. Horror. Fear.

Silva knelt. The head wound hadn't killed Mrs Collins. There'd been a second shot. Upper left side of the chest. A *coup de grâce* direct to the heart. The pale-blue apron she'd been wearing bore a smudge of red blood and, farther down, a brown gravy stain.

They'd come shortly before six, then. Mrs Collins had either run to the toilet to hide or she was already inside, perhaps washing her hands before calling Silva's father to eat.

Dinner's ready!

Words she never got to say.

Silva stood and eased out of the little room and back into the hall. Where was her father? She shivered, thinking of his bedroom once more, but now the image was of him in a heap like Mrs Collins. If he'd had a chance he'd have defended himself, but this time the attackers would have been forewarned that he was armed.

She ran over to the stairs and bounded up two at a time. On the landing an occasional chair which usually stood by one wall lay on its side and the carpet runner had been scuffed up. She paused outside her father's room, her hand on the door handle. Despite everything, she loved him. Perhaps because of everything. She pushed the door and, more in hope than in any real expectation, she called out.

'Dad?'

'Rebecca.' The voice came flat and low, and with an undertone of sadness that only came to her too late.

'Dad!' Silva flung open the door and rushed in.

'Rebecca.' Her father sat in an armchair on the far side of the room. An anglepoise lamp on an occasional table cast yellow light on his face. His head hung low and there was a crimson bruise on his right cheek. His hands lay on his lap, bound together with a cable tie. The sadness had gone from his voice and now there was resignation. Defeat. 'I'm sorry. I let you down.'

'Dad, I—'

'Ms da Silva. So nice to see you again.' The bulky figure of Greg Mavers emerged from the shadows; beside him stood a grunt holding a pistol. Mavers chomped his jaws together. 'I'm only sorry it couldn't have been in more auspicious circumstances.'

'You.'

'Well, yes.'

'He's an old man.' Silva gestured at her father. 'Is that your idea of a fair fight?'

'Self-defence,' Mavers said. 'He's dangerous. We had to disarm him.'

'And Mrs Collins? Was that self-defence?'

'Brenda?' Silva's father looked up. 'Is she…?' His words tailed off and he shrank into the armchair.

Mavers shrugged. 'We can throw accusations about collateral damage back and forth. For instance, Lashirah Haddad. What did she do to deserve her fate? Perhaps you put it down to sheer bad luck she happened to step into the path of your bullet?'

'I didn't shoot her.'

'And I didn't personally shoot Mrs Danvers or whatever her name is.' Mavers nodded sideways at the man with the gun. 'So I guess we'll call it even, shall we?'

'You won't get away with this.'

'It's you who are not getting away with trying to pervert the democratic process and meddle in the sovereign affairs of another country.'

'Karen Hope killed my mother.'

'Forget it, Rebecca.' Silva's father raised his head for a moment. 'The Yanks will justify anything. Always have, always will.'

'He doesn't speak for them all, Dad. He's gone rogue.'

'You think so?' Mavers was smiling. 'You're as misguided as you are naive. I'd have thought with a boyfriend in the Agency you'd have understood just how the world works, but then again perhaps his pillow talk kept to the script.'

'What the fuck are you talking about?'

'You've been played, Rebecca.' Silva's father was shaking his head. 'Sean must be in on it. He's sold you out.'

Her father spoke softly, but she felt the fury in his words. It was as if he was the one who'd been betrayed. She felt light-headed, giddy. 'Sean, he wouldn't—'

'Enough!' Mavers raised a hand. 'We're leaving.' He motioned at the man with the gun and then pointed at Silva's father. 'Make sure he can't get free. You're with me, Rebecca.'

Mavers gestured at the door and for one moment Silva wondered if, alone with Mavers, she could escape. Her hopes were dashed when they encountered another man in the corridor. Like the first grunt, he had a gun.

'After you,' Mavers said. 'And no tricks, no funny stuff.'

They went downstairs and outside. Parked round the side of the house there was a silver Ford van with diplomatic plates. Mavers slid the rear door open and the grunt pushed Silva in. Mavers stood by the door and glanced at his watch. Minutes ticked by.

'What's going on?' Silva said. 'What are we waiting for?'

'That.' Mavers turned his head and peered back at the house. The second grunt ran from the front door and down the steps. A high pitched repetitive beeping pierced the air. 'Now we go.'

The grunt jumped into the van and started the engine. Silva strained to see what was going on. There was a glow from one of the downstairs windows. Yellow and orange light flickering. The shrillness of the smoke alarm over the crackle of flame.

'No!' Silva shouted. She leapt forward, trying to make for the door before Mavers could slam it shut.

The man in the back raised his gun, turning the weapon so he could bring the handle down on Silva's head. Once. Twice. Three times.

Then nothing.

–

She woke to a moving light. A single bulb hanging from a piece of wire in the ceiling. A draught from somewhere moved the bulb and the arc of its shadow crept over the walls and swept her face. Silva rolled over, aware of a throbbing at the side of her head and a sensation of stickiness round her left eye. She raised a hand and a scab of dried blood fell away. The light bulb swung and flickered and she was remembering the fire.

They'd left her father tied to the chair in his room and torched the place. She imagined him sitting there as the flames rose around him, imagined the fear he must have felt. She closed her eyes and almost inevitably thought of her mother too. What evil could have conspired to take both her parents from her in a handful of months? And the only other person she loved, Sean, had given her up to the enemy.

That thought caused the throbbing in her head to pulse faster. Had he really done that? Put his loyalty to his country above her? She held back a sob. Perhaps he'd never really loved her at all, perhaps everything had been a sham. She remembered the times they'd spent together, the quiet, tender moments, the laughs… no he *had* loved her.

Had or did?

A wave of emotion hit her and it was as if she was falling into the weir at her mother's house all over again. Sliding down the weed-covered sill and plunging underwater. No air. No light. Slipping down into the depths. She tried to take a breath but could do nothing but wheeze. She gagged against a constriction in her throat, fighting asphyxia.

Sean?

His face was distorted in a blur of tears and then she was biting her lip in anger, feeling pain, tasting blood.

She blinked, the copper tang of the blood snapping her back to reality. She was lying on a piece of sacking stuffed with straw. The light bulb illuminated four walls of crumbling bricks and mortar rising to a roof of asbestos sheeting. In one corner there was some kind of trough, and water dripped from a join in the galvanised pipe that ran from the trough to a stopcock halfway up the wall. Scattered in one corner were several piles of dried faecal matter. Silva looked closer, but couldn't distinguish if the crap was animal or human. The latter would suggest she wasn't the first to be brought here. Not the first to wait in trepidation of what was to come.

Did Sean know where she was or what fate awaited her? Would he really have turned her over to the American authorities? Then again, this was nowhere official. Not a prison or a police station or a military base. She thought of Afghanistan. There'd been places where al-Qaeda militants had been taken. Black sites. Deniable. Places where the Geneva Convention didn't apply. American operatives had waterboarded suspects and worse. Not that the British were without guilt. Silva knew UK intelligence officers had been present when militants had been interrogated. Silva hadn't much cared back then. The militants had to be stopped by any means necessary. Now, though, the tables had been turned.

Thanks to Sean.

He must have called Greg Mavers, told him Silva knew about Karen Hope and Haddad. She didn't think he had any knowledge of what Mavers intended to do, but his loyalties were divided. When pressed, had he come down on the side of his country? Like Hope, Mavers would have appealed to his patriotism for sure. He'd have told Sean the very future of democracy was at stake, that there was only one option.

She pushed herself up from the ground, sat upright and looked round. At the roof eaves there was a small gap where the rafters met the wall. A patch of blue sky and a smudge of cloud.

How long had she been here? She rubbed her head. Just a few hours, or had she been unconscious for longer? It didn't really matter. Nobody knew where she was and nobody was coming to rescue her. Sean had always been an unlikely knight in shining armour, and now his armour was tarnished.

Silva stood, feeling dizziness and a sharp pain in her forehead. She took a moment to recover and then walked round the room, examining every inch. The door was of heavy boards, bolted through. There was no handle on her side, nor did there seem to be any sign of a lock or hinges. She figured the door must open inwards, which if the room was for animals made sense. She gave the door a tentative push, but it was solid and immovable.

The only other thing of interest was the water pipe. The piping looked substantial, but the fixings holding it to the wall had corroded. Silva reckoned she could pull the pipe free and use a length of it as a weapon.

She was about to test the strength of the wall fixings when bolts clattered on the door. Silva stepped back into the corner of the room as the door swung open.

'You're awake.' Greg Mavers stepped into the room. Close behind came the two men who'd been with Mavers at her father's house. One held a pistol while the other carried an iron bar and a length of rope. Mavers waved a hand at the room. 'I'm sorry the surroundings aren't up to much, but there you go.'

'This can't work. There's too much of a trail. Too many people know.'

'Oh but they don't, Rebecca. Not the damaging stuff. They know about a few arms deals and some money which may or may not have come from various unsavoury sources. They don't know about the rest of it.' Mavers moved a finger to his right eye. Scratched something. 'The problem is, you do know everything.'

'And I've told others. If I disappear it will all come out.'

'Then I'll need to know the names of the people you've told.'

'I won't talk.'

'You will. You must have had enough training to know that not talking isn't an option. It doesn't take much for people to spill the beans. I should know, I'm ex-CIA. Been there, done that. So if you thought you were dealing with some pen-pushing diplomat, then I'm afraid you're mistaken.'

'You won't know if I'm lying or not.'

'Let me explain.' Mavers tilted his head at the man with the iron bar and rope. 'We'll need to investigate everyone you say you've told. So lie if you wish, but it's not going to be pleasant for those you finger because we'll have to interrogate each and every one of them.'

'Well, I haven't told anyone.'

'You've changed your tune, but if that's true then good. The problem is we need to be sure. The iron bar will help. We can beat you with it. We can break your fingers or smash your kneecaps. We can do other things. Think what it would feel like with that piece of metal inside you. Especially if we heat it up. At the end, we'll know if you're telling the truth or not.'

'You're going to kill me.'

'You're an assassin, Rebecca. You killed Lashirah al Haddad. Sure, you denied it earlier, but I don't believe you.' Mavers moved forward. 'Our friends in Saudi Arabia would like you turned over to them, but I won't hear of it. Their methods make ours look positively benign. To be honest I'd like nothing better than for you to be taken to the US to face trial, but the issue with that is your mouth. Far better you simply disappear.'

'Don't you think there'll be questions asked? First my mother, then Neil Milligan, then me? Too much of a coincidence.'

'There are questions asked about the moon landings, about Elvis Presley, about 9/11. Compared to those world events your death will be but a footnote. I really don't think anyone will be interested.' Mavers stepped back towards the door, careful not to turn his back. 'Now, think very carefully about what you are going to tell us when we return, OK?'

Mavers slipped out the door and the two men followed. The door swung shut, the bolts clunked across and the light swung gently in the draught.

Chapter Thirty-One

Holm slept in his own bed for the first time in days, but the following morning he was back in the office with Javed. The lad fired up his computer and his fingers hovered over the keys.

'If I do a search it will be logged,' Javed said. 'The Spider probably has a screen on her wall showing what each of us is googling. Cheap flights, gnocchi recipes, ripped abs, that sort of thing.'

Holm eased himself into his chair. He wasn't sure how much longer they could keep this quiet anyway. 'Just do it,' he said. 'RAF Wittering.'

Within in a few seconds Javed had found a *Financial Times* article detailing a trade summit that had taken place at the airbase. A huge arms deal had been signed off by the secretary of state for defence, and a top Saudi diplomat had attended along with the US deputy ambassador and several senior military figures from the UK and American military. There'd been a ceremonial handover of the first tranche of arms and the shipment included surface-to-air missiles and other air defence equipment. Afterwards there'd been a reception hosted by Allied American Armaments.

'Surface-to-air missiles,' Javed said. 'The thought of Taher getting his hands on a couple of those is chilling.'

'American Armaments.' Holm looked at the article. 'That's the Hope family, right? *The* Hope family, as in Karen Hope.'

'Yes.' Javed rapped the keyboard and did a fresh search.

Holm leaned in and read more. The Hope family were of Italian origin and Brandon Hope had returned to his roots.

He'd married an Italian and settled in Italy. This after several years as a diplomat in Riyadh. His experience in the Middle East had come in handy when he'd begun to get involved in the family business, and according to the *Financial Times* he'd been instrumental in brokering the recent deal thanks to his relationship with Jawad al Haddad, a billionaire Saudi with connections to the royal family.

'Haddad. Shit.' Holm remembered something he'd overheard in the situation room earlier. 'There was an attempt on his life a few days ago. Dissident Saudis apparently, but whoever it was, his wife was killed in the attack. Have a guess where?'

'Saudi Arabia, I assume?'

'Wrong. Positano. A stone's throw from Naples. It only stuck in my mind because we were there at the time. Now the location appears to be more than a coincidence.'

'Definitely, boss. Look at this.' Javed had clicked open another page. 'Several years ago Brandon Hope set up an aid charity that operates across the Middle East and North Africa. Among other things it runs a boat that rescues migrants who are attempting to cross the Mediterranean.' Javed looked up. 'That was the boat we saw Mohid Latif disembark from. The *Angelo*.'

'A rich man's plaything. That's what Luigi the cafe owner said. And remember the captain of the *Angelo* explaining to Mohid Latif that a meeting had been called off? Something about helicopters and police and it being too risky? Latif could have been going to meet Haddad in Positano. We should have been on to this before. We were too blinkered in going after Taher. *I* was too blinkered. Shoe leather rather than research.'

'Do you think Brandon Hope is directly involved with Taher?'

'Possibly.' Holm sat for a minute and spun the facts round in his head, tried to jigsaw them into place. 'But more likely he's simply turned a blind eye to help out Haddad. Anything on our system on him?'

'You mean internally?' Javed moved his hands from the keyboard as if he was scared he might accidentally type something incriminating. 'Isn't that a bit risky, sir?'

'We have to know.'

'Right.' Javed paused, still nervous, then he punched the keys and stared at the screen. 'Haddad's on a CIA watch list. He's believed to have orchestrated funding to various extremist factions.'

'I'm getting a feeling in my water, Farakh. What about American Armaments and the Hopes?'

Javed typed some more. Clicked. Sat back in his chair. 'Nothing.'

'Nothing?'

'Nothing on American Armaments, just a biographical entry on the Hopes.'

'There can't be *nothing*? What about the arms dealing and Brandon Hope's relationship with Haddad?' Holm peered across, sure there must be some mistake. Javed shrugged. 'Nothing is highly suspicious.'

'Perhaps, in the light of Karen Hope's next job, the material has been moved to a higher security-clearance level. You could always ask Huxtable.'

'Pah.' Holm dismissed the suggestion and instead reached for his phone. 'I've got a better idea.'

–

The blue under the eaves slipped away to be replaced by near black, the occasional twinkle from a star. Silva knew Mavers would be making her wait, as time passing was one of the most effective ways of arousing fear. When he came back she'd have to try and play him. If she could make him believe there was something else she knew perhaps she could do a deal. Then again Mavers didn't seem like the kind of person to haggle with.

She took a drink from the galvanised trough. The water tasted of rust and earth, but it quenched her thirst. She examined the pipe again and was convinced she could pull off a length. With the element of surprise, she fancied her chances against Mavers and one guard; with Mavers and two guards, not so much.

She lay on the makeshift bed of straw and tried to conserve her strength. Mavers was right, resisting torture was impossible. She'd have to tell him something. She was working out exactly what when the door rattled open again.

'Ms da Silva.' Mavers entered first, the two grunts behind him. One held a pistol and the other had swapped the iron bar for something that looked alarmingly like an electric cattle prod. 'Are you ready?'

'Yes.' Silva sprang to her feet. 'And you should know my mother hid some papers to do with Karen Hope.'

'Clever Mommy.' Mavers shook his head. 'But it doesn't work like that, Rebecca. If the documents do exist – and I very much doubt they do – then I'm not going to ask you to take us to them, you're simply going to tell us where they are.'

Mavers made a small gesture with his hand but Silva didn't wait for his henchmen to react. She flung herself at the water trough and grabbed the pipe. It broke away from the wall and she was left with a metre-long section of metal in her hands. Water sprayed out in a jet, momentarily disorientating the nearest grunt. Silva stepped forward and swung the pipe at the man holding the gun. He dodged and moved away. She lunged at him again, but as she did so she felt a sharp pain in her midriff followed by a spasm that rushed down her leg. She stumbled to the ground to see the man with the cattle prod standing over her.

'Shoot her in one knee to start with,' Mavers said. 'That will stop her misbehaving. Then get her clothes off and we'll move on to the next step.'

The man with the gun walked across the room. He raised the weapon and pointed it at Silva. She flinched as a sharp report echoed in the room and a spray of blood flicked across her face.

The man with the gun fell forward, his mouth half open in pain or surprise. He slumped to the floor, fluid pumping from a hole in the side of his head. For a moment Silva thought the gun had suffered some kind of catastrophic failure and exploded in his face. Then she saw the masked figure at the doorway. Dark-blue combat fatigues. A Heckler & Koch machine gun. Special forces. *British* special forces.

'Don't move!' The figure brandished the gun and came into the room followed by another masked soldier.

'I don't know who the fuck you are,' Mavers said. 'But I'm with the US government and you're interfering with an important operation. You're also trespassing.'

'Shut up.' The figure in blue gave an almost imperceptible nod and the second soldier let off a round. The man with the cattle prod reeled back, crumpled and went down. The soldier bent and picked up the gun. He checked the clip and then calmly walked over to Mavers.

'You won't get away with this,' Mavers said. 'There'll be serious repercussions.'

He raised an arm but the soldier thrust the weapon into his face and fired. Mavers keeled over, his substantial body shuddering as it hit the floor.

'What the—?' Silva said as she recoiled from the shots.

'No questions.' The soldier held out a hand and hauled Silva to her feet. 'Let's go.'

The soldiers thrust her out of the room and led her into a large cow barn. Dim light came from overhead fluorescent tubes; on the ground was a mass of straw, fresh manure and a row of troughs with the remains of a feed. They jogged through the barn and out one end. A security floodlight on a pole hung over a green tractor. Parked beside it sat a black Range Rover. As they approached, the door clunked open and a man climbed out. Dusty hair and a colonial tan suit.

'Rebecca.' Matthew Fairchild nodded. 'Good to see you're OK.'

'I don't...?' Silva stood still, for a moment utterly confused. She pointed towards the cowshed. 'You realise your men just killed the US ambassador?'

'The deputy ambassador to be precise.'

Fairchild gestured at the Range Rover but Silva didn't move. Then she turned, intending to thank the two special forces guys, but they'd vanished.

'What is this place?' she asked.

'A black site run by the US. Totally deniable and off the books, unless they all of a sudden decide to admit to its existence, which they won't.'

'But the tractor, the cows...?'

'It's a working farm with an American expat owner. Isolated, plenty of outbuildings, a surprising array of useful equipment, and the potential for lots of unexplained noises. Just the place for working over enemies of the state.'

'Which state?'

'That depends.'

'On British soil? Bloody hell.'

'Come on, Rebecca. You can't get squeamish now simply because the tables were turned.' Fairchild got back into the Range Rover. 'Let's go.'

'How's this going to work?' she said as she went round and climbed in the passenger side. 'I mean three dead men, one of them the US deputy ambassador?'

'I've no idea.' Fairchild started the Range Rover and eased off. 'To be frank, the fact Mavers went rogue is not my problem. It's an American mess and they'll have to sort it out for themselves.'

They passed a collection of farm buildings and threaded through a dense forest, black against the Range Rover's headlights. For half an hour she saw nothing she recognised, then there was a sign for London and the M40. Fairchild hadn't spoken again and every question she asked had been answered with a shake of his head. Now, as they joined the motorway, he appeared to relax.

'How did you find me?' Silva said.

'Later. When we get home.'

'Home?'

'My home. It's obviously not safe for you to go anywhere near your own place.'

'Oh my God, you don't know about my dad, he's—'

'He's alive, Rebecca. Bruised but in fine fettle. He'd have come with me if I'd let him.'

'He's *alive*?' Silva choked, tears filling her eyes. 'I thought… God!'

Fairchild put a hand out and touched her on the knee. 'He's in a safe house being watched over by a couple of mates from the regiment.'

She slumped back in her seat. The thought that he'd died had wracked her with guilt. They'd never properly made up but now there was a second chance for her to do that. She made a silent promise to herself she wouldn't let the chance slip by.

The past few hours had been overwhelming and tiredness swept in. She closed her eyes for one moment and the next there was a hand on her shoulder.

'We're here.'

The night was gone, the darkness replaced by golden sunbeams shining through lush woodland, Fairchild's mansion standing bathed in the morning light. Fairchild showed her in and took her through to a huge dining room; within seconds a pot of tea and a cooked breakfast had arrived.

'Tuck in,' Fairchild said. 'You must be hungry.'

Silva nodded as the tray of food was placed on the table. She went across and sat down. 'Where's Itchy?'

'He's upstairs chilling out. Don't worry, he told us everything. It's all under control.' Fairchild took a chair opposite her as she began to eat. 'You'll be wanting answers, but I'm not the person to give them to you.'

'Who is, then?' Silva muttered through a mouthful of bacon.

'He'll be here in a minute.'

'Right.' Silva carried on eating. Took a drink of tea. When she'd finished, Fairchild asked if she wanted some more. 'No,' she said.

Ten minutes later there was the sound of the front door opening and one of Fairchild's aides appeared.

'He's here, sir.'

'Show him through.'

Silva turned her head to see a man in a dark suit walk into the room. Rectangular frameless glasses. Short brown hair. A hand moving up to touch his glasses. The bank manager-cum-wolf in sheep's clothing.

Simeon Weiss.

–

'What the hell is he doing here?' Silva pushed back her chair from the table and glared at Fairchild. 'You've sold me out, you bastard!'

'Nobody's sold anyone out, Ms da Silva,' Weiss said. 'Least-ways not yet.'

'Please, Rebecca.' Fairchild gestured at the table. 'Sit down and listen to what Simeon has to say.'

'He threatened me and he killed Neil Milligan.'

'We did not kill Mr Milligan,' Weiss said.

'Who did, then?'

'Hope's people.'

'Mavers? The CIA?'

'She paid off Mavers and a few others, but the CIA? Good God, no, she hasn't got control of them. At least not yet.'

'That's what this is all about, Rebecca.' Fairchild approached the table and drew out a chair. 'Stopping Karen Hope before it gets to a point where she can't be stopped.'

Silva turned to Weiss. 'I thought that's what you were trying to prevent me doing? Stopping Karen Hope.'

'Well—'

'I think,' Fairchild said, 'it's about time we came clean.'

Silva snorted. 'Right. As if I'd believe anything you said after all that's happened.'

'Let's start at the beginning.' Weiss was at the end of the table. He sat down and laid both hands flat before clasping them together. 'Karen Hope is not what people think she is. Not the saviour come to lead us out of the wilderness. Not a Kennedy-type figure. Not even a moderately competent politician. But she is power hungry, corrupt, and will stop at nothing to achieve her ambition of becoming president.'

'I know that.' Silva gestured towards Fairchild. 'Matthew briefed me on the whole thing. Hope killed my mother in an attempt to cover up her brother's dealings with Jawad al Haddad.'

'Yes.' Weiss's hands went flat on the table again. He leaned forward. 'Although it will never become public, your mother was something of a hero. We knew of Hope's relationship with the Saudis, of course, but we only discovered the true extent of it through your mother's research.'

'We?'

'The security services.'

'You were keeping tabs on her?'

'We keep tabs on a lot of people, Rebecca, and every now and then all the watching and listening and hacking pays off. That was the case with your mother. We intercepted some of her file uploads and discovered the information about Hope. We followed up various leads and checked the veracity of your mother's work. We came to the shocking conclusion it was not only true, but there was even more dirt buried.'

'And that is?'

'You don't need to know.' Weiss shook his head. 'Suffice it to say it confirmed our plan of action had to be put into place immediately. We needed to prevent Hope from becoming president – not, I'm afraid, because of a moral imperative, rather because of the risk of massive global destabilisation if the information came out at a later date. Imagine the scandal. There'd be an impeachment, her removal from office, a totally unsuitable vice-president stepping into the job, questions about America's role in the world. If, on the other hand, she wasn't exposed, think of the leverage the Saudis and Haddad in particular would have over her. Policy in the Middle East would be in hock to them for the next four to eight years.' Weiss paused and took a breath. 'However, getting rid of Hope was easier said than done. We could allow your mother to continue her work and cross our fingers that when the story came out it would result in Hope having to withdraw her candidacy. There were several risks though. One, would your mother be able to get the story out in time? Two, would she be believed? Three, the revelations would do untold damage to the UK's relationship with the Saudis. Our defence contracts are worth billions and support thousands of jobs. And think about the other ways the Gulf states invest in this country. They own football teams, property, huge chunks of well-known companies. In short, we are dependent on the whole region for our financial security and stability. There had to be another way to stop Hope; the question was, how?'

'Yes, how,' Fairchild said. He smiled across the table at Silva. 'Were it to be discovered the British government had interfered in the democratic process of another country there'd be UN sanctions, a trade war, perhaps even, in the worst case, military conflict.'

'Although,' Weiss said, 'I was hearing snippets of information from my colleagues in various agencies Stateside that they were looking for a way out of the situation themselves. They saw the danger of Hope becoming president too. However, they didn't have the information we did, and even if they had it's debatable whether there'd have been anybody brave enough to release the material.' Weiss bowed his head for a moment. 'And then something happened, something both serendipitous and tragic, and I realised the argument for more extreme measures had swung heavily in our favour.'

'My mother's murder,' Silva said.

'Yes,' Weiss said. 'Once that happened and we joined the dots the time for diplomatic pressure and subterfuge were over. Hope had proved herself to be beyond the pale. She'd sanctioned a terrorist attack, which left many people dead, to further her ambitions. In ordinary circumstances we'd have been seeking extradition and a trial. However, these are far from ordinary circumstances. I was summoned to a meeting with my boss, Thomas Gillan – the head of MI5 – and he agreed with my analysis. The problem was that when he went to Downing Street and made subtle hints that for the sake of British national security Hope had to be stopped, the prime minister wouldn't hear of it. Risk the special relationship? Act against our closest ally? Inconceivable! After the meeting the cabinet secretary and the national security adviser spoke privately with Gillan, expressing their dismay at the prime minister's stance. I'm afraid our politicians lack bravery and are more inclined to think short term and of their own political futures than for the good of the country. Despite the prime minister's attitude, there was an understanding between Gillan and the two civil servants. Gillan came back to me and authorised an operation to stop Hope whatever it took. I explored several options, options that didn't involve the death of Hope, but in the end I concluded there was only one with minimal risk and maximal chance of success. The secrecy involved was such that myself, Gillan and Matthew are the only people who know the whole truth. You can imagine the consequences if this ever got out.'

'Simeon knew my area of expertise,' Fairchild said. 'He came to me seeking a third party, a rogue operator, who could kill Karen Hope. Because I knew of you through your father, I told him we didn't have to look very far to find the perfect assassin with all the motivation we needed. We prepared the files and sent them to your father, making out they'd come from a time-controlled online vault. All I had to do was call him, and with a little prompting he asked for my help. At first he was sceptical when I made the proposal to kill Hope. To be honest he was concerned for your safety. I told him the operation was foolproof, and with a little persuasion he came round to my way of thinking. To *our* way of thinking.'

'So the whole thing was a set-up.' Silva bristled. 'All you had to do was approach me with a plan and show me the evidence.'

'It wasn't quite that simple,' Weiss said. 'The intelligence services as a whole know nothing of this. Hence my little performances at the service station and on the Hoe in Plymouth. They were staged so I could say you'd been investigated. I wanted to make sure your name was in the system, but the reports I submitted were tagged with the label *no further action*. Spooks watch spooks, and anyone observing either incident would have concluded there was absolutely nothing friendly about our meetings.'

'And the break-in at my mother's house?'

'Yes, a ruse. The break-in sowed the seeds of a conspiracy in your mind. As did the act of pushing you into the water.'

'You could have killed me.'

'Time was short and we needed to spur you on. By then we'd already identified Positano as possibly the last chance to carry out some kind of attack, at least on non-US soil. The problem was, we needed deniability. A bomb or a close-quarters assault was much more likely to go wrong or be traceable. A sniper attack, on the other hand, could see Hope killed with a single shot, carried a low risk of other casualties and stood little chance of detection. It just so happened you appeared on the scene. Not only one of the world's best shots, but somebody with the motivation to carry out the attack.'

'And if I'd succeeded you'd have given me up afterwards, right?'

'That might have seemed a good option, but it would have been much too risky. At some point connections would be made. Matthew is a freelancer, but he's been in the intelligence services earlier in his career. Far better for us to ensure you killed Hope and made your escape.'

'But I didn't.'

'No.' Weiss sighed. 'And that brings us to the here and now and our little problem.'

'Which is?'

Weiss scraped his chair away from the table and stood. He glanced across at Fairchild before walking across the room. He stopped at the door and turned.

'Karen Hope.' He reached out and hit the door frame with a clenched fist. *Tap, tap, tap.* 'And how we're going to make sure you get another chance to kill her.'

Chapter Thirty-Two

Taher stood and looked through the window. This time the vista was not of the crowded streets of London, but of rows of olive trees on a vast plain that stretched to the border with Algeria. Sand dunes rippled the horizon, reminding him of home, reminding him of why he was here in Tunisia waiting for the weapons.

He'd fulfilled his side of the deal. He'd set up the route and arranged all the details. They'd carried out a dozen trial journeys with the containers and not once had there been any sign the authorities knew what was going on. On the last trip Latif and Saabiq had ridden in the container from Naples to Rotterdam. Once on board the *Excelsior* they'd emerged from their hiding place and retired to an empty cabin, courtesy of the captain. Later, when the ship had unloaded, they'd left the ship along with the crew. There'd been no checks on either of the containers.

That had been the final test and now Taher was confident the operation could succeed. Every month or so a large delivery of armaments would arrive at the airfield near Cambridge. The Saudis would send an aircraft to collect them, but a single pallet would go missing from the consignment and end up on the *Excelsior* bound for Rotterdam and beyond. And these were no ordinary weapons. Not cast off Russian goods from decades ago. Not cheap Chinese copies. There were the latest in hi-tech rocket launchers. Laser guided. Massive destructive power. In the coming months the weapons would be distributed, ready for an offensive early next year. The plan was to disrupt tourism in

Morocco, Tunisia and Egypt, from West to East Saharan Africa, and the rockets would help to accomplish that aim.

For Taher it wasn't enough. Africa was a long way from northern Europe where the previous attacks had done little to bend the minds of the sanctimonious British, the arrogant French or the smug Germans. They needed to be reminded of what it was to be afraid, of what it was like to have death call at their own front doors. When he'd informed Haddad he was ready for the big one, the Saudi had smiled.

'Of course you are,' he'd said. 'Once all this is over I promise you will have what you desire.'

So Taher had done everything asked of him. As well as setting up the smuggling route, he'd eliminated Francisca da Silva and dealt with Ben Western and Neil Milligan. The reward was continued support from Haddad and something else too. A present from the Saudi that Taher had stored in the roof space of a lock-up garage he rented in west London. Long and sleek things they were. Massive destructive power. He smiled to himself. When the deal was done and the first tranche of weapons had been handed over, he'd head back to the UK. Latif was waiting for him, and together they would avenge the deaths of Taher's family.

He took a second to whisper two words, clenching his fists as he did so.

'Collateral damage,' he said.

–

Harry Palmer wasn't free at short notice, so Holm had arranged to meet for lunch the following day.

'Next door to yours?' Palmer said, referencing the Pizza Express across the street from Thames House.

'No, too close to home,' Holm said. 'Do you know the place we used to go years ago? Twelve thirty.'

'Curiouser and curiouser,' Palmer said before confirming he'd be there and hanging up.

The place they used to go years ago was the Pear Tree Cafe in Battersea Park. Holm liked it for a clandestine meet because there were numerous entrances to the park and, once inside, dozens of paths to follow.

Holm and Javed found a rare parking spot close by and entered the park at twelve. They approached the cafe in a circuitous manner and Holm had Javed stand off and keep watch while he went in and awaited Palmer's arrival. An expanse of glass curved round one side of the cafe and Holm sat at a table near the entrance. At twelve twenty-five Palmer slipped into a seat opposite Holm, appearing to materialise out of thin air, but likely coming in through the kitchens.

'Very good,' Holm said. 'You got me.'

'What is this, Stephen?' Palmer winked. 'Are we playing at lovers or co-conspirators?'

Holm grimaced. 'Not the former, please.'

'I thought you'd gone over to the other side.' Palmer gestured through the window. 'He's a good-looking lad, I'll give you that.'

'You spotted him?'

'He's down at the lake pretending to feed the ducks.' Palmer raised a hand and made a little pecking motion with his thumb and fingers. 'Only, what sort of twenty-something male would be doing that? Plus he hasn't got any bread.'

They ordered food, Palmer going for soup and a roll, which allowed him to make a joke about giving some to Javed for the birds.

'Enough,' Holm said. 'This isn't funny, Harry.'

'It's deadly serious if you're relying on that kid.' Palmer couldn't help another smile but the expression quickly turned solemn. 'Is this about your little project to round up Nazi fanboys? I heard about it on the grapevine.'

'No.' Holm lowered his voice. 'This is about Taher.'

'For Christ's sake, Stephen, are you *asking* to be sacked?'

'I'm on to him, but I need your help. One more push and I've got him.'

'Really?' A look of surprise crossed Palmer's face. 'Are you sure you're not delusional?'

'No. What's more, Taher is somehow linked to the Hope family. *The* Hope family, as in Karen Hope.'

'Now I know you're delusional.' Palmer frowned and the surprise turned to concern. 'You need to back off before the Spider gets a tug on one of her threads. If she discovers what you're up to she'll come for you. The resulting mess won't be pretty.'

'I'm not backing off and I'm quite sane, thank you.' Holm lowered his voice. 'There's some dodgy arms dealing going on between Allied American Armaments and the Saudis, the net result of which is Taher getting his hands on a bunch of weapons. What's strange is there's nothing on the system about Brandon Hope or the company. Nothing, do you hear?'

'Nothing. I see.' Palmer nodded. Holm had his attention. 'You want to know if I've heard something?'

'Hope is involved in a charity that works in North Africa. If there's anything going on in the region you'd be aware of it, right?'

'One would hope – sorry – so.' Palmer tapped the table. 'But no, there's not been a whisper.'

'This could be big, Harry. I think Brandon is shipping the arms across the Med in a boat he owns. The weapons are going to Taher who is then distributing them to the jihadis: AQIM, al-Shabaab, ISIS, whatever. I can't believe your people on the ground haven't got even an inkling.'

'Well, quite. Very worrying.' Palmer scratched his chin. 'You have proof of Brandon's involvement?'

'Not directly. It's just me and the lad at the moment, so we're struggling to keep on top of it all.' Holm turned his head. Javed was down by the lake. 'But if I can land Taher I'll be back in favour, and if you help me you'll be in line for some credit too. A lot of credit.'

'We'll need to proceed carefully, Stephen. You know how things are.'

'Are you talking about Karen Hope and her presidential ambitions?'

'There is that, of course, but I was thinking of the Saudi link too. We don't want to embarrass our allies.' Palmer glanced at the window. 'Who knows about this?'

'Only me and Farakh. Huxtable doesn't have a clue.'

'Are you sure?'

'Yes. I've been keeping a lid on the information. Too many times I've been close to Taher and he's disappeared in a puff of smoke.'

'Are you suggesting…?' Palmer let the sentence hang.

'You know I am. Hell, we've talked often enough about it before. You even admitted yourself you were worried.'

'Yes, but the Spider?'

'Not Huxtable, but the people around her. Somebody with high-level access. Perhaps even in one of the foreign agencies we share information with. I've long suspected the Americans haven't being playing by the rules.'

'The CIA?'

'Yes. It makes sense now we know Allied Armaments and the Hopes are linked to Taher. The Agency could be running interference to safeguard their national interests.'

Palmer narrowed his eyes, his brow creasing. 'That's extremely concerning.'

Holm nodded. Although Palmer was obviously troubled, Holm felt a weight lifting from his own shoulders. The SIS officer was more used to dealing with this sort of thing than Holm was. He'd know what to do.

'OK.' Palmer steepled his hands. 'So we need to keep this to ourselves. I understand.'

'It's the only way to be sure Taher isn't forewarned.'

'Right.' Palmer looked both excited and nervous. 'We can do this. First you give me the full details, second we formulate a plan of attack. I'm glad you came to me, Stephen. If we work together on this then Taher is history.'

An hour later and they were done. Palmer slipped away while Holm went across to where Javed was sitting at an outside table nursing an empty latte glass.

'Well?' Javed said. 'What did he say?'

'He said you're crap at field craft,' Holm said. 'You might as well have hung a sign round your neck.'

Javed shook his head, annoyed. 'I meant about Taher.'

'I know.' Holm patted Javed on the back. 'Go home and pack some fresh clothes. And think *hot*. We're going to Tunisia.'

–

Silva sat at an outside table on one of the terraces. A stone-columned balustrade ran in an ellipse above an oval pond. White flowers and green lily pads and giant orange fish lurking in the depths. There was tea in a silver pot and bone china cups and saucers. A selection of biscuits on a plate.

She'd jumped up when Weiss had dropped the bombshell about a new mission to kill Karen Hope, but his footsteps were already echoing down the corridor. A door closed and a car crunched away down the gravel driveway. Fairchild told her not to be too hasty. There were things, he said, that she needed to know. Weiss worked for a small department within MI5 known as the Special Accounts Unit. Ostensibly the department dealt with allocating funds to freelance operatives and non-governmental groups, but in reality its purpose was to carry out highly secretive missions that needed to be deniable. Even within the security services, few people knew of the true nature of the SAU.

Now Fairchild sat across the table from her. He reached for the teapot and poured the tea.

'Despite being called the Special Accounts Unit,' he said, 'there is absolutely no accountability. Simeon Weiss can do almost anything he likes and get away with it.' Fairchild slid a cup and saucer across the table to Silva. 'You might be wondering how I got involved with Simeon. I'd like to tell you it was altruism, a sense I should do something for my country, but I'm ashamed to say it's more related to certain indiscretions from my past. These days some may call them crimes and who am I – a white, privileged, male – to disagree?'

'What on earth are you talking about?'

'Mr Weiss has a file on me. A few sheets, no more, but enough information to have my wife packing a suitcase and hiring a lawyer. Enough to have the police knocking at my front door. Enough, in short, to ruin me.'

'He blackmailed you?'

'Yes. This was years back now, but I'm merely using it as an illustration of the way the man thinks, the way all of his ilk think. They *use* people, Rebecca. In a way, Weiss is just like Hope. He'll do anything to get what he wants.'

'Are you saying he'll give me up if I don't go along with this?' Silva shook her head. 'But he said himself that was too risky.'

'What is risky is trying to second-guess him. He'll do whatever he thinks needs to be done.'

'For the country?'

Fairchild laughed. 'For Simeon Weiss.'

'Who else knows about this?'

'The operation to kill Karen Hope?' Fairchild turned his head and gazed out across the manicured lawns towards the gatehouse. 'You heard what Simeon said. I've no idea if that's the truth or not.'

'Somebody in the government?'

'I doubt it. Most politicians understand very little of what really goes on. Their outlook is too short-term: a parliament, a second term in office. The future of this country depends on events that take decades to seed and grow fruit. There are people who are working on scenarios involving who the next president but one might be. Friendships are being cultivated in Chinese universities right now that will serve this country well into the second half of the century. Strategy is being worked out for when India becomes a global superpower, for when the US and Europe have sunk so low they are third-rate backwaters.'

'This all sounds like some sort of bad conspiracy theory.'

'Possibly, but truth is stranger than fiction. Could you have predicted the fall of the Berlin Wall or the global financial crash or the Arab Spring? In any case it doesn't really matter. Weiss is setting the agenda and you'll do what he says or suffer the consequences.'

'Did he put you up to this just now or are you part of the whole thing?'

'He told me to try and persuade you. He mentioned a break-in at your father's house. There were gunshots and someone was hurt, possibly killed. He felt it might be time for the police to investigate.'

'How—'

'I've no idea.' Fairchild held his hands up. 'But Weiss deploys resources as and when needed. He probably had your father's place wired from the get-go.'

'This is crazy. Why me?'

'You remain the best person for the job. I can't imagine getting close to Hope is going to be any easier now she's been alerted to the fact she's a target, so a long-range shot will still be the method of choice. Simeon has assets aplenty he could deploy but I assume he feels you are a safe bet because you're personally involved. That gives you the motivation to carry out the job and zero reason to betray him. Especially after it's all over.'

Silva looked across the lawns. Near a boundary hedge a man with a German Shepherd walked his rounds. At the gatehouse another of Fairchild's staff stood on guard. What were her options? Get out of here and hide away somewhere? Hope would know about the death of Greg Mavers by now and Silva would be on her radar. She'd be even keener to track her down and shut her up. There was Haddad to consider too. Then there was the implicit threat from Weiss: help us or your father suffers. No, running wasn't the right move.

'It looks like I don't have much of a choice,' Silva said. 'Do I?'

'No.' Fairchild nodded and then handed Silva the plate of biscuits. 'Not really.'

–

Later they were in Fairchild's operations room. Screens and terminals. News reports from CNN, Al Jazeera and the BBC. A huge map of the world dominated one wall; when Silva looked closer she could see that, too, was a screen complete with little flashing icons.

'So.' Fairchild moved over to the map and jabbed a finger at North Africa. 'Contact will be initiated in Tunisia.'

'*Tunisia?*' Silva wondered if she'd heard correctly.

Fairchild looked apologetic. 'Yes. Apposite, if nothing else.'

'Tunisia.' Silva repeated the word. Fairchild was right. How apt. Hope's blood spilling on the same soil as her mother's had. Job done. The circle complete. Go home and sleep easy.

Who was she kidding?

Fairchild moved his finger down over the map. 'Brandon Hope owns an olive farm near the border with Algeria. According to Simeon, Karen Hope will be staying at the farm overnight next Thursday.'

'How the hell can he be sure?'

'Remember Brandon's charity and the rescue boat?' Fairchild inclined his head and Silva nodded. 'Well, the boat is going to be in the marina at the resort of al Hammamet. Brandon is throwing a fundraising party and various politicians and celebrities are going to be flying in or crossing the Med in their superyachts to attend.'

'Including Karen Hope?'

'Yes. There'll be massive security around the marina, but Simeon's source says Hope will be journeying to the farm at some point.'

'Forgive me if I'm sceptical.'

Fairchild glanced at the map screen, perhaps wishing Hope had her own icon. 'I'm sorry, but you'll have to trust Simeon on this one.'

Silva followed Fairchild's gaze to the screen. She had the sense she was a marionette. Little sticks attached to her arms and legs, pushing and pulling. Simeon Weiss the puppet master controlling her and just about everybody else on the stage.

She mentioned it to Fairchild and he shrugged.

'The analogy is perfect, my dear,' he said. 'But are any of us truly free to do as we please?'

Chapter Thirty-Three

Holm and Javed examined the shipping manifests for the *Excelsior*. The schedule suggested the weapons shipment would be on the boat and heading for Rotterdam on the following Monday. They had to factor in how long the drive would take from Rotterdam to Naples and the length of the crossing to the Tunisian marina where the *Angelo* had made repeated visits.

Holm was struggling to work out an ETA based on the speed of the yacht when Javed tapped him on the shoulder.

'Forget it, boss,' Javed said. 'The *Angelo* will be in al Hammamet on Thursday evening.'

'How the hell do you know that?'

'Because there's going to be a party on board to raise money for the charity. All sorts of celebrities are going to be there, many arriving in their own boats.' Javed pointed at his monitor. 'It's here in *La Stampa*. It just came up in a search. Stroke of luck really.'

Holm picked up his phone and called Palmer. 'We're on for dinner on Thursday at your place.'

'I'll look forward to it,' Palmer said and hung up.

They'd gone over the details at their previous meeting and Palmer agreed with Holm that the operation had to be kept hush-hush right up until the last possible moment.

'When we've found Taher and the weapons?' Holm said.

'Yes. Then you call me up and give me the location. I'll put plans in place so a force can be mobilised the instant you contact me. Probably some UK/Tunisian joint venture, maybe a drone strike. Whatever, as soon as I know I'll action my plan and hopefully we'll have Taher and the weapons.'

'Hopefully.'

At that point Palmer had reached out and put his hand on Holm's arm. 'But not a word before you are one hundred per cent sure, Stephen, OK? If you're right about a mole then this is much too big to risk a cock-up.'

'Boss?' Javed turned from his screen. 'What are we going to tell Huxtable? We can't exactly expect her to believe the Nazi story again, and I don't think the Tunisians have much of an animal rights movement.'

'We tell her nothing,' Holm said. 'I'll buy the tickets on my credit card and if anyone asks we're going on holiday together. If they enquire further then it's harassment.'

'I'll be the laughing stock,' Javed said. 'My reputation will take a dive.'

Holm raised an eyebrow. '*Your* reputation?'

–

The feeling of powerlessness came again when, on Thursday morning at a little after eleven, Silva found herself strapped into a seat in the same private charter jet that had flown them back from Italy. Itchy sat across the aisle, and opposite and facing her, Lona.

As the aircraft accelerated down the runway and rose into the air, Itchy leaned across.

'It'll be all right, Silvi,' he said. 'Karen Hope is going down.'

Itchy had been 'in' from the moment he'd known there was to be another chance to take out Hope. Loyalty to Silva and professional pride had seen to that. Silva insisted on another twenty-five K too. Fairchild had thrown his hands up, but she'd dug her heels in: no payment to Itchy, no Rebecca da Silva.

'You know,' Itchy continued as he broke into a bag of cashew nuts and gazed out of the window. 'I could get used to this lifestyle.'

'Don't,' Silva said.

She settled back in her seat and closed her eyes and there was Sean's face hovering in front of her. Over the past few days she'd tried not to think about him but he'd always been there like a dull ache. Perhaps more than an ache, perhaps a deeper malady spreading inside her, consuming her. She'd wanted to contact him so she could discover the truth about what had happened, but Fairchild had forbidden it and, in addition, he'd refused to answer any questions as to Sean's involvement.

'Operational details, Rebecca,' he said. 'We have people on the other side, so the less you know the better.'

Was that the real reason? More likely it was yet another underhand tactic devised by Simeon Weiss. Let her stew, let the anger build. The meaner she was, the better. Sean's face smiled in her dream. He laughed and Silva tensed. Angry wasn't the half of it.

They touched down at Tunis–Carthage International mid-afternoon, taxied to a spare slot and were met by a pair of customs officials at the foot of the boarding steps. Lona, all smiles and flirtation, handled the formalities in French, and within five minutes they were heading for the VIP arrivals lounge.

'Nothing is too much trouble these days,' Lona said. 'Tunisia relies on tourism and olives, and since the Bardo and Sousse atrocities tourism has been badly hit. People were just beginning to come back when the attack that killed your mother took place.'

A car stood waiting for them in the pick-up area, a Tunisian man at the wheel. Silva and Itchy loaded their bags into the boot and climbed into the back seat. Lona sat in the front.

'This is Nasim,' Lona said. 'He's our guide and driver.'

Nasim smiled in the rear-view mirror, said something to Lona in French, and then the car was nosing into the heavy traffic.

'We're staying in a town fifty miles from the farm,' Lona said. 'You'll head there first thing in the morning so you can arrive before it's light.'

As they sped out of the city along a busy three-lane highway, Silva remembered that when she'd arrived in Tunisia to visit her mother several months earlier it had appeared exotic. Now she stared out blankly at white low-rise apartments, the rubbish-strewn kerbs and the uninspiring monotony. Soon they were out into flat, arid country. The occasional olive plantation. The concrete shells of half-finished buildings. She dozed, awoken every now and then as they turned at a junction or hit a pothole at speed. After a while the flatness was replaced by rocky hills, sparse vegetation, anonymous towns. The road crested a ridge and swept left, a vast plain of undulating nothingness spread out to their right.

'Algeria,' Lona said. 'Nearly a million square miles. The olive farm is close to the border, perfect as a handover point for the smuggled weapons. They could be going to AQIM groups in Algeria or to Daesh in Sudan, perhaps even as far as al-Shabaab in Somalia. The whole of North Africa is a mess, to be honest.'

'But why on earth is Karen Hope going to be there?'

'That's just what I've been told.' Lona turned to the back. 'I follow orders and don't ask too many questions. Life's easier that way.'

Right, Silva thought. Or perhaps you know more than you're telling.

The sun burned red as it sank in the west, somewhere amid the vastness of Algeria, and as dusk fell they entered a large town. Vehicles were honking their horns, people everywhere until they turned down a small alley and drew up outside a house with a high concrete wall. Lona got out and opened a pair of heavy gates and the car eased in alongside a white Land Cruiser.

The house was newly built and cool inside. Lona gestured to a couple of doors off the hall.

'You'll sleep in there.' She turned. 'There's food in the kitchen, so eat and then rest. You leave at five a.m.'

'Not we?' Silva said.

'Nasim will take you out to the olive farm in the 4 × 4. The kit's already packed. When the job's done he'll drive you straight to the airport and you'll rendezvous with the jet. I'm going back via a different route. We won't meet again.'

'And you'll be somewhere safe in case anything goes wrong.'

'Nothing will go wrong, you'll make sure of that. You've got Nasim too. He can be trusted. He's one of ours.'

'One of ours?'

'Our assets.' Lona tilted her head. 'The UK's assets.'

Silva had it then. 'You're not with Fairchild, are you?'

'No, of course not. I work for Simeon Weiss. I was placed in Fairchild's organisation to watch over him, to make sure he did as he was told.'

'You can tell Mr Weiss I'm not happy at being duped like this.'

'Simeon has no regard for you emotional well-being.' Lona paused and smiled. She reached into a pocket and pulled out a small envelope. 'However, he did ask me to give you this. He called it a reward.'

'What?' Silva watched as Lona ripped the envelope open and extracted a photograph. The image was one Silva had seen before: Karen Hope and two men at the villa in Italy. One was Latif, the other unidentified. 'This is nothing new.'

'No, but the information that goes with it is.' Lona passed the photograph across. 'The other man is known as Taher. He's the terrorist who planned and carried out your mother's killing.'

'And how is that a reward?'

'Taher will be at the farm tomorrow.' Lona shrugged. 'Two birds, one stone, right?'

With that, Lona was gone.

'This bloody stinks,' Itchy said. He gestured after Lona. 'She's setting us up for something. One phone call by Mr Taxi out there and we could be in the hands of this Taher and his mates. Next thing there's a video on the evening news and then…' Itchy drew a finger across his throat. '*Schlick!*'

'Lona's on our side, remember?' Silva said. She looked at the photograph and wondered not about Taher, but Simeon Weiss. What his endgame was and how he'd managed to play her at every turn.

'I don't trust any of them.'

'Neither do I but now we're here we don't have much choice.'

Nasim came through from the rear of the house. 'You eat. Now, please.'

In a rear living room a low table had been set out with food. Large round flatbreads, slices of meat, a bowl of couscous garnished with slices of red pepper, some triangular pastries that looked similar to samosas.

Nasim left and they sat on cushions to eat.

'Looks great,' Silva said. 'He'd hardly prepare all this if he intended to shop us, would he?'

'He's fattening us up,' Itchy said, piling stuff into a bowl.

'Well, as a last meal you can't complain.'

Later, Nasim cleared away and Silva and Itchy went to their rooms. Itchy said something about taking it in turns to stand guard, but Silva disagreed. They were getting up before dawn and she wanted all the sleep she could have.

'See you in the morning, then,' Itchy said. 'Fingers crossed.'

–

Holm and Javed took a Lufthansa scheduled flight from Heathrow to Tunis. They were, Holm thought as they landed at Carthage International, woefully ill-equipped. He'd managed to blag a satellite phone, but they had no weapons, no surveillance gear, and no cover documents. They were relying entirely on Palmer's promise to provide in-country support should things go wrong.

Once they'd negotiated passport control, they hired a car and drove the short distance down the coast to their destination. Holm had been rather pleased with himself in that he'd managed to book a couple of rooms in a hotel on the seafront using a TripAdvisor app on his phone.

'A couple of rooms?' Javed said. 'That's our cover blown.'

Al Hammamet sat some twenty miles south of Tunis on a curve of sandy coastline. A jumble of white buildings surrounded a marina complex, and away from the coast the land stretched away, pan flat. There were hotels and plazas and, despite the terror attacks, a good smattering of tourists.

They checked in to the hotel and Javed opened his marine traffic app. The *Angelo* was three quarters of the way across the Med from Naples and looked as if it would arrive at some point in the evening.

'Let's take a recce,' Holm said. 'And get something to eat.'

'Maybe a club later?' Javed said. He puckered his lips and kissed the air. 'Just to embellish our cover story?'

'Fuck off.'

They strolled towards the marina area, past restaurants where staff attempted to entice them in.

'How the hell can a boat as big as the *Angelo* fit in here?' Holm said. As they approached the marina he could see an array of small yachts, but nothing approaching the size of the *Angelo*.

'There.' Javed pointed beyond the masts to where a breakwater provided protection from the open sea. Several large motor cruisers were berthed on the marina side. 'Those probably belong to some of the guests coming to the fundraiser.'

Holm turned his head. South of the marina a swathe of beach ran down the coast as far as the eye could see. Hotels lined the waterfront for a mile or so. A quiet and secluded spot for smuggling it was not. Plus they'd seen a good number of soldiers patrolling the streets, presumably there to reassure the tourists.

'This is too public,' Holm said. 'How are they going to get the weapons ashore?'

'Marine parts, remember?' Javed gestured across to where a large white van had parked near one of the cruisers. 'These boats require all manner of servicing. A few crates offloaded won't seem suspicious.'

'Let's pray you're right.'

They went for a stroll down the strip. Holm ducked into a minimarket and purchased a couple of bottles of water and some snacks in case they needed them later. The light eased away as dusk fell and the resort was transformed. Coloured lights flickered on and strobes flashed from several bars. There was a heavy *thump thump thump* of a bassline as an eager DJ began to play tunes to lure customers into his establishment. When they returned to the marina the place was lit up like a Christmas tree, and several of the motor cruisers had underwater lights that illuminated the water surrounding them. There were dozens of soldiers, and several police officers had set up a checkpoint at the entrance. On the far side of the marina a large white boat was making sternway into an alongside berth. Crew in smart uniforms threw ropes and marina staff made the craft secure.

'We're on,' Holm said. 'The *Angelo*.'

He found a restaurant which offered a good view of the *Angelo* while Javed fetched the car and parked it close by. Holm ordered food and drinks, and when Javed returned he pushed a Coke over to him.

'Now we wait,' he said.

'I don't think so, boss.' Javed took a quick sip of his drink and nodded towards the *Angelo*. 'Look, action.'

A series of deck lights had come on and the white van they'd seen earlier had pulled up close by. A derrick on the quayside swung its arm over the boat and hoisted a large wooden crate from the deck.

'The weapons,' Holm said. He began to rise. They needed to get to the car. 'Now all we have to do is follow them to Taher.'

'Hang on.' Javed's gaze went to a smart yellow SUV parked alongside the van. 'There's something else happening.'

An electric passerelle slid out from the side of the boat; in the shadows Holm could see a woman waiting on the deck as a member of the crew carried two bags down the passerelle and loaded them into the back of the SUV.

'That's…' Holm could hardly believe his eyes. He blinked, wondering if he needed glasses. Before he could speak the woman had walked down the passerelle and moved across to the car. One of the crew opened the door for her and she got in. The vehicle slipped away down the quayside, the white van following close behind. 'I wasn't expecting her to be mixed up in this.'

'Who, boss?' Javed said. 'I didn't see.'

'Karen Hope,' Holm said, grabbing a handful of banknotes from his pocket and shoving them on the table. 'Brandon Hope's sister and the next president of the United States of America.'

–

The yellow SUV cruised out of the marina gate with the van behind. Holm and Javed raced for their car and followed at a distance.

'What the hell is she doing here?' Holm said as they cruised down the main strip.

'Brandon's hosting a charity event, remember?' Javed nodded forward. 'Having his sister come along would certainly encourage guests to part with their cash. He's probably sold the seats at her table. Ten K to share a Pot Noodle with a future president.'

'But she's no longer at the charity event. She's in a convoy with a van containing a stack of smuggled weapons. Explain that, Farakh.'

'Perhaps she doesn't know what's in the crate.'

'Of course she doesn't know what's in the crate.'

They were leaving al Hammamet now, passing the last of the hotels on their right. Holm concentrated on following at a reasonable distance, trying to banish a niggling thought from his mind: what if Karen Hope *did* know what was in the crate?

They headed south for a few miles, hugging the coast before turning inland into what seemed to Holm to be wilderness. In the darkness there was only the intermittent flash of oncoming headlights and the occasional glimmer from a settlement off in the distance.

They drove for several hours, the road surface deteriorating until finally tarmac gave way to gravel. Ahead, the mini convoy continued to forge into the night and Holm was forced to stay well back and drive on dipped headlights. He grudgingly admitted to Javed that they could have done with his tracking device.

Javed nodded while reading a map on his phone. His finger hovered over the screen.

'Algeria,' he said. 'Just a few miles to the border.'

'Shit.' Holm glanced down. 'If they cross then we're done. This is dangerous enough as it is.'

His worries were ended when a few minutes later the SUV and the van turned off the road and headed up a rough track. Holm slowed the car to a stop and wound down the window. Off to the right, red tail lights were disappearing up a rising escarpment. Some kind of settlement sat on the ridge, silhouetted against a sky burning with a million stars.

Holm got out and after a moment so did Javed. He came round the car, stood next to Holm and peered into the blackness.

'Before you ask,' Holm said. 'I have no bloody idea what Karen Hope is doing up there.'

Chapter Thirty-Four

Silva didn't sleep much. There was some kind of festival taking place in the town, and car horns sounded throughout the night. There were fireworks too, the first of which brought Itchy scampering into her room, half asleep, almost as if he was suffering from combat stress.

It was still dark when Nasim tapped on the door.

'OK we go in thirty minutes, yes?'

Silva shouted out an acknowledgement and got up and washed. Nasim had packed breakfast in a basket and they ate as they cruised out of the town and onto a dirt road. The town sat on the edge of a desert plain, and as they left the last house behind the sun slipped over the horizon, illuminating a landscape of reddish-brown rock and low hills, a sea of sand dunes in the distance.

'One hour.' Nasim held up a single finger. 'Then we there.'

Silva recalled Itchy's words of the previous night: *This bloody stinks*. He was right. They had no idea where they were going, no idea of the terrain or the distance or anything. All they knew was Hope was supposed to be at their destination. She prayed that part was true and this time she could put an end to it all.

Nasim was as good as his word; at six they edged along a track that rose up the side of a stony hill. He stopped the Land Cruiser before they reached the top, wrenched on the handbrake, turned and nodded. No words were necessary. They were here.

Silva and Itchy climbed out and moved up the track towards the summit where a rocky outcrop cast a long shadow in the low morning sun. Over the crest the ground fell away to a deep ravine and on the far side of the chasm lay something like an oasis: a grove of ancient olive trees surrounding a number of buildings. Beyond the buildings a vast plateau spread into the distance and more olive trees marched in rows to the horizon.

They crouched next to a boulder and Silva noted the sun would swing round to their right, but never get behind them. She looked at the ground nearby where a few pieces of greenery sprouted from dry soil. She could lie there but they might need to rig some kind of camouflage screen. She peered through the low glare to the farm. Several buildings sat together but the biggest was obviously the farmhouse. There was a large white van and a yellow SUV parked on one side of the walled complex. She turned to Itchy.

'Three fifty.' Itchy stretched out his hand and raised his thumb. 'Tops.'

She'd guessed the same. Depending on exactly where Hope appeared, the shot was an easy one.

'Let's do it,' Silva said.

–

An hour later and they were set. Itchy had the spotting scope out and had ranged the distance to be three hundred and thirty nine metres to the front of the farmhouse. The rifle was lying on a mat and they'd arranged a desert cammo net on a couple of poles in front of their position. Through her binoculars Silva could see a veranda to one side of the house. A couple of tables sat beneath a billowing canvas awning. She pointed it out to Itchy.

'If Hope goes out there to eat or have something to drink it would be perfect.'

'Killing al fresco,' Itchy said, laughing at his own joke. 'Assassination au naturel.'

Silva winced. The humour wasn't appreciated. Not right now. She wanted Hope dead, but if it could be accomplished with a snap of her fingers she'd have taken that over having to sight through the scope and squeeze the trigger, wait a second and watch for the spray of blood as the bullet hit Karen Hope in the head.

They took it in turns to sit in the shade of the rocky outcrop while the other one kept watch. Itchy fiddled with a SIG pistol which had been in among the extensive array of equipment, while Nasim hovered near the car, the doors open for a quick getaway. If necessary they'd leave the gear behind; it was unlikely to fall into the hands of the authorities, not out here.

At a little after eight thirty, just when Itchy was beginning to annoy Silva with his constant shifting about, two men came out from the farmhouse, climbed into the white van and headed off down the track to the road. In the centre of the farmyard, previously hidden behind the van, stood an old pick-up truck. On the bed of the truck sat a large wooden crate.

'That's what we saw at RAF Wittering,' Silva said. 'Weapons from Allied American Armaments.'

'Unbelievable.' Itchy turned to Silva. 'If you had any doubts, the crate should banish them.'

'The only doubts I have are over the intel. There's no sign of Hope, is there?'

'The target's in there.' Nasim knelt behind them. He tapped a chunky fake Rolex on his wrist. 'You patient, please.'

They resigned themselves to waiting, ate some more food and kept hydrated. The van had been gone an hour now and Silva was beginning to wonder if they'd been sold some kind of dummy. Perhaps Hope had got wind she was in danger and had sneaked out in the back of the van. Perhaps she'd never been here at all.

Silva tried to relax. She shifted her position and peered through the rifle scope. She had a clear view of the rear veranda; if Hope came out it was a relatively simple shot. *If* she came out.

'What the...' Itchy prodded her arm and pointed. 'What the heck are *they* doing here?'

Halfway up the side of the ravine that cut below the farm-house, two figures were scrabbling across a scree face, small pieces of stone skittering down as they attempted to stay upright. Silva reached for her binoculars.

'Shit,' she said. 'It's the guys we saw at RAF Wittering.'

—

They'd kipped in the car, Holm having found another track running parallel to the one the van and the SUV had gone up. He reckoned they were well hidden from both the road and the settlement, but still the night was an uncomfortable one and neither he nor Javed had slept much. By six it was light and they could see the lie of the land. Fortuitously, they'd managed to park in a deep wadi that led in the general direction of what they could now see was a farmhouse with assorted buildings. Holm broke out the water and snacks and stood looking towards the farm. Karen Hope was up there. *Karen Hope.* Holm had to repeat the name to himself just to make sure he'd got it right and the whole thing hadn't been a bad dream.

'Now what?' Javed said, munching on a dry flatbread.

'We head up there.' Holm gestured to the valley. 'We need to get closer and we can't very well go sauntering along the track.'

'It's like the Grand Canyon.'

'Nonsense.' Holm quickly judged the distance to the farm and the depth of the rift. 'A mile along the bottom of the wadi and a short climb up. We'll be totally out of sight all the time.'

'And when we get to the top?'

'We spot the weapons and see if Taher's there. Then we call Palmer on the sat phone.' Holm cocked his head. 'You set?'

'Yes.'

'Good. Let's go.'

An hour and a half later Holm was regretting his earlier optimism. He'd seriously underestimated the amount of effort needed to navigate their chosen route. Low scrub filled the bottom of the wadi and every step was a fight against thorns and briars. Once they were through the scrub it was no better. The sun streamed in from the southern end of the ravine, leaving no shade, and the light shale reflected the glare into Holm's face. The heat was intense. A few metres away, Javed was moving easily across the slope of the ravine, sure-footed and seemingly expending little effort, while Holm was struggling to stay upright as the loose rock shifted beneath his feet. He turned and looked to his left where the gradient steepened. At some point they needed to go up there and he was beginning to wonder if he'd have to admit to Javed he wasn't going to make it.

Ahead, Javed stopped. A gully ran diagonally across the face of the slope before turning upwards and disappearing into the dark shadow of a series of rock pillars.

'There, boss.' Javed pointed to the top of the cliffs where a cluster of olive trees stood near the edge. 'Those trees are close to the farm. If we can manage to get up the gully we're home.'

Home. Bloody hell, Holm thought. That's where he'd like to be right now. Miles Davis floating through the speakers, a glass of something in his hand, a cool breeze coming in through the balcony windows of his flat.

'Right.' He staggered along until he was next to Javed and peered up the gully. Jagged towers of rock offered something to hold on to and provided some welcome shade. 'Of course if someone happens to be standing at the top we've had it.'

Javed shrugged. Self-evident. Nothing they could do. Go on or go back. He waited until Holm nodded and began to climb.

The going wasn't too bad to start with, but when they reached the section below the cliff face Holm found himself struggling. The rocks had appeared chunky from below, but now they were up close the hand holds were no longer so obvious. At one point he looked back the way they'd come and regretted it. Climbing down now would be next to impossible.

'You go first.' Javed flattened himself against a large boulder to let Holm climb past. 'I can guide your hands and feet.'

Holm stood with one hand jammed tight in a rock crack for support. Sweat ran down his face and his shirt was sodden. If he wasn't shot at the top or didn't fall to his death he figured he'd have a heart attack. He nodded at Javed again, unable to speak.

After a couple of minutes to get his breath back, Holm pressed on. One step at a time, one handhold at a time.

'A foot up and a little to your right.' Javed's encouragement was gentle. 'Just below your hip.' A nudge or a suggestion every few seconds. 'To the left of your shoulder there's a small ledge, see it?'

Holm nodded or grunted his replies. He focused on the rock within his immediate reach, only once making the mistake of looking down again.

'My God!' They were much higher now. A virtually sheer face dropping away until it met the scree slope a long, long way below. Holm closed his eyes as vertigo snatched the last of his courage from him. He imagined dropping from the cliff and falling until he was pulverised on the boulders littering the bottom of the ravine. He clutched at the rock in front of him. Wondered, perversely, how Huxtable would spin the news coverage of his death.

Stephen Holm was on extended leave and taking a walking holiday in Tunisia… he was a valued member of JTAC but hadn't been working in the field for several years… he will be missed greatly by his family and his many friends and colleagues…

'Boss!' Javed snapped him back into the present. 'We can make it. Look up!'

Holm opened his eyes and craned his neck, expecting to see nothing but a sheer wall of unclimbable rock. Instead he saw a sloping boulder dappled with sun and shade. Above the boulder hung the branches of an olive tree. He thought of olives now. Olives and a crisp white wine. Perhaps, after this was all over, he'd return to Italy and rent a villa on the Amalfi Coast. Sit and watch the sea.

'Right,' he said, reaching for the next handhold and pulling himself up. In another couple of moves, his head crested the clifftop and he wriggled over and lay in the shade of the tree. 'Thank God.'

Javed scrambled up and lay alongside him. For a moment they stayed still. Holm turned towards the farm. The little olive grove comprised half a dozen ancient trees. Each tree sat in a small depression and a black hose snaked between them. Water trickled from a hose end within arm's reach. Holm crawled over and put the hose to his mouth and took a drink. Then he splashed water on his face before handing the hose to Javed.

As Javed drank, Holm turned to the farm again. A low wall separated the olive grove from the farm. Beyond, several buildings surrounded a yard. The farmhouse stood to one side and there was a veranda at the rear. He eased himself up. The yellow SUV was parked next to a pick-up truck and on the back of the pick-up was the crate they'd seen loaded into the white van.

'The weapons,' Javed said. 'We need to call Palmer.'

'Yes, but I want to see what's going on in the farm first.' Holm swung his gaze to the main building. 'And find out what the hell Karen Hope is doing in there.'

–

Taher stood at the farmhouse window. On the far side of the room the future president of the United States of America sat at a small table eating breakfast.

'We're done,' Karen Hope said. 'You fulfilled your side of the deal and you've got the missiles and the money. Now we go our separate ways.'

'You think you can just walk away from this?' Taher turned from the window. Despite the large deposit sitting in his bank account, despite the missiles hiding in the loft space of his lock-up garage and the ones outside on the truck, he felt as if Hope had got the better of him. 'Your hands are stained with blood too.'

'It goes with the territory.'

'Perhaps, but there's always a price to pay, and I'm wondering, given the nature of the prize, if I wasn't short-changed.'

'Tough. You set the terms and I delivered.' Hope reached for a glass of orange juice and took a sip. 'My brother made a huge error of judgement and almost jeopardised my chance of becoming president. I don't intend to let anything else get in my way.' She slammed the glass down on the table and looked across at him. 'Including you.'

'Yes, but…' From the corner of his eye Taher spotted something through the window. *Someone.*

He held a hand up to Hope, edged up to the opening and peered down. Two men lay prone by the wall in the olive grove. One was brown-skinned, with short black hair, not much more than a boy. The other was older and white, a few strands of grey hair on his head, flabby features. Taher had seen the man before in a dossier given to him by his contact in London.

'MI5,' he whispered to himself.

Hope pushed her chair back and stood. 'Visitors?'

'Yes.' Taher moved back from the window and grabbed his AK-47 from where he'd propped it against the wall. He checked his Glock was secure in his shoulder holster and went to the door. 'I'll deal with them.'

Downstairs, he crept along the corridor which led to the veranda. A slit of light came through a narrow window. He peered out. The men were still there, hunched behind the stone wall. Neither looked armed.

Taher continued along the corridor. He stopped and listened before he stepped onto the veranda. Anybody approaching along the track would have triggered the PIR alarm, but the alarm was silent and apart from the wind there wasn't a sound. By the state of these two they must have climbed up from the ravine. This was amateur hour.

Taher slipped out onto the veranda and across to the steps that led down to the olive grove. He moved silently until he was within a few feet of the men and then cleared his throat.

'You've been after me, old man.' Taher raised his gun as the two men scrabbled upright. 'For a long time.'

'Taher.' The older man pushed himself up from the ground and beckoned his colleague to do the same. He didn't appear to be surprised.

'And now you've found me. Job done.'

'I'm not finished yet,' the man said. 'Not until you're behind bars.'

'You're out of touch. There are no bars these days. Missiles from the sky, helicopters bringing special forces – so much easier than all the legal problems imprisonment brings.' Taher gestured towards the steps with the barrel of his gun. 'And I'd welcome that. I wouldn't want to rot in a prison wearing a hessian hood and an orange jumpsuit. Wouldn't want to receive a daily waterboarding from my brave and fearless captors. No thanks. Give me martyrdom every time.'

'A British prison,' the man said. 'We do things differently.'

Taher lunged at the man and grabbed him by the shoulder. He jerked him round and at the same time brought the butt of the gun up and smashed it into the white, sweaty face. The man staggered backwards and tripped. He went down hard.

'You do things differently?' Taher spat on the ground. 'In the Iraq War my family was incinerated by a missile launched from a British ship by a British commander. A British prime minister gave the order to attack. Over the centuries you have decimated whole continents and then scuttled back home and ignored the mess you left behind.'

The younger man bent to help the older one. Taher waved his gun and gestured that they should climb the steps to the veranda.

'It's over, do you understand? We are in a new age now. No longer can you treat foreign policy like a game. There will be consequences to your actions.'

'Problems?' Hope slipped out of the door as they reached the veranda. Her gaze moved to the two men.

'They're from the UK.' Taher had to keep himself from laughing. If this was the state of the country's secret service it was no wonder they hadn't had much success in catching him. 'So-called British intelligence.'

'You were expecting them?' Hope's eyes showed a flare of anger. She lowered her voice so the men couldn't hear. 'You should have warned me. You know I like to be informed of everything. Especially with Greg out of the picture.'

Taher grimaced. The deputy ambassador, along with two of his bodyguards, had been involved in a car accident a few days ago. It appeared Mavers had been drinking and had insisted on driving. The car had left a winding country road and ended up upside down in a river. There'd been no survivors. Taher didn't buy the story, of course, but at this point the fate of Mavers was inconsequential. The man didn't know the details of the smuggling route, didn't know anything about Taher, and wasn't much more than Hope's well-paid lackey, someone who'd grovelled at her feet in expectation of a reward when she became president.

'Greg told me the girl must have had high-level backup.' Hope was speaking again, her voice harder and laced with anger. 'So these two could have been part of the team that tried to kill me in Italy.'

'It's possible.' Taher turned his head. The older man could barely stand. Blood ran from a cut above his left eye and he was breathing heavily. The younger man stood muscles taunt, like a cat about to pounce. Taher pulled out the Glock from his holster and handed it to Hope. 'Cover them.'

A couple of lengths of nylon twine hung near the doorway, part of the rigging used to hold the sun awning in place. Taher pulled them off and told the men to face away from the house. In turn he wrenched their hands behind their backs and bound their wrists tightly together. That done, he stood and stared at the men. Wondered what the hell he was supposed to do now.

'Remember what I said inside?' Hope's voice was not much more than a whisper, meant just for Taher's ears. 'About not letting anything stand in my way?'

'Yes.' Taher said. 'What of it?'

'Well, they've seen me, haven't they?' Hope was holding the weapon in both hands. There was a sheen of sweat on her face. 'We can't let them go.'

Hope's tone was insistent and menacing, and he realised he was right not to have crossed this woman. She'd stop at nothing to get what she wanted. Even if that meant executing an old man and a boy in cold blood.

'No,' he said softly. 'We can't.'

Chapter Thirty-Five

Silva and Itchy had watched the men clamber up the side of the ravine and edge up a gully towards the house. At one point she'd thought the older man would fall; he appeared frozen against the sheer rock face and through the binoculars she could see he'd closed his eyes and was clinging on for dear life. Eventually he began moving upwards and the pair crested the cliff top and crawled into the olive grove where they crouched behind a low wall.

Now, though, everything had gone pear-shaped.

'Fuck,' Itchy said. While Silva was looking through the scope at the veranda, Itchy was concentrating on the two men. 'They've been made.'

Silva pulled her eye from the scope and picked up the binoculars again. The two men were getting to their feet at the behest of a man with a smooth face and a wispy beard. The man from the photograph Lona had given her. Taher. He cradled a machine gun and jabbed it at the men as he marched them up to the veranda. Then he hit the older man in the face.

'We could take him,' Itchy said. 'Give them a chance to escape.'

Before Silva could think on that, Karen Hope walked out from the farmhouse. The billowing white sun awning flapped back and forth, obscuring the view every few seconds.

'It's Hope!' Silva slipped back down into a firing position and eased her right eye up to the scope. 'Tell me what's happening!'

'Taher's got some twine and he's tying the men's hands behind their backs. Whatever their stupid plan was it hasn't worked.'

'Perhaps they've got backup.' Silva's other eye glanced at the sky, hoping to see a smudge of distorted air and hear the *chop chop chop* of a helicopter. There was nothing.

'We're the only backup.'

'What the hell were they playing at?'

'Soldiers.' Itchy rolled on his side and glanced at Silva. 'Only you don't, do you? Play at it?'

'No.'

Now Taher was waving his gun at the two men, forcing them over to the edge of the veranda. They both knelt, the older man falling on his face before Taher pulled him up. Karen Hope advanced into view. She held a pistol with both hands and took up a position behind the old guy, raising the weapon to the man's head. Through the scope Silva could see Hope's arm muscles tense.

'Silva!' Itchy shouted, and Silva was aware of him scrabbling for his own pistol, useless at this range. 'We've got to do something!'

And then, for the briefest moment, the world dissolved away and Silva was gone, floating somewhere above the ravine and the house as if she was viewing an aerial photograph. As if she was in the heavens looking down. As if she was God.

Ever since Fairchild had come up with the plan to kill Karen Hope, Silva had wondered if she'd be able to pull the trigger when the moment came. In Positano she'd been so close, but circumstances had intervened. Here, they'd waited and waited. Still she'd been unsure. Now, though, there was no time to ponder or prevaricate. Whether her mother approved or not, whether Karen Hope deserved death or not, was irrelevant. The decision had been made for her. There was a second, perhaps two, and then the old man would die. The only person who could prevent that was Rebecca da Silva.

She was back on the ground, the hard rock under her body, the rifle in her hands. There was no time for composure, for steadying her breathing, for recalculating the ballistics in her head, for making a final adjustment to the scope. There was only time to move the rifle a fraction so Karen Hope was lined up in the reticle. If she missed, likely she'd hit the old man and he'd die anyway.

Which meant she couldn't miss.

'Silva!' This time Itchy's voice came distorted, as if in slow motion. 'Now!'

Hope stepped forward, both arms outstretched, the gun pushed hard against the old man's head. There was a look of utter determination on her face, and in that instant Silva realised this woman craved absolute power like a drug.

Silva touched the trigger.

The bullet took approximately half a second to reach Karen Hope. In that time she'd moved slightly and, although Silva couldn't see it, Hope's forefinger had already begun to squeeze the trigger on her own gun.

The bullet hit Hope just below her right eye. It exited through the back of her head, a spray of blood and brain matter splattering outwards. The head jerked back in a delayed response, the body arcing forward, the arms flying upwards, the effect like a crash test dummy flung from a moving car. Then came a double crack as the echo from Silva's gun came back along with the bang from Hope's pistol.

'Shot,' Itchy said in the same pan-flat manner he used when they were on the practice range. He reached out and patted Silva's back. 'Now the other one.'

Taher was moving fast towards the door to the house as Silva reloaded. She fired again but the shot smashed into the stone lintel and he was gone.

'Shit,' Silva said.

'Don't sweat it, we'll get another chance.'

Silva reloaded and raised her head. The two men had fallen over the edge of the veranda and into the olive grove. They were invisible beneath the trees.

'Are they alive?' Silva said.

'I don't know,' Itchy said. 'But Taher's going for the pick-up.'

Silva moved the rifle to the left. Taher had raced through the house and emerged at the other side. He clambered into the truck. She had a split second to act while the vehicle was stationary, because hitting a moving target with a rifle was next to impossible – something for the movies, not real life. Taher was in the vehicle now, but his head was partially obscured by the door pillar. Silva squeezed the trigger and a moment later the glass on the driver-side door crazed in a spiderweb pattern. Inside, Taher jerked sideways, but even as he did so the vehicle was moving forward, the back wheels spinning in the dry dirt. The pick-up slewed round in the yard and shot towards the gates to the complex, causing an explosion of wood as the bull bars smashed through. Then the truck was away and heading down the track, weaving back and forth, dust rising.

'Last chance,' Itchy said. 'But take your time.'

Silva already had the rifle aimed down the track way ahead of Taher, anticipating the moment when the vehicle would crest a small rise and she could get a shot in through the rear window. She couldn't see Taher's head because he was hunched down, but that wouldn't matter; the bullet would pass through the seat. Just a couple more seconds and—

And then she could see nothing. The dust had risen to obscure the track.

'Damn it!' Silva fired anyway, but the odds were minuscule and when the dust cleared the vehicle was gone.

–

When the shot cracked off Holm thought the report would be the final thing he'd hear, his last conscious thought. Death seemed to take a long time coming though, and in the seconds

331

remaining he considered his lot. He hadn't been a bad man. In fact, on balance, he'd done more good than evil. He regretted the way he'd treated his wife and was sorry he hadn't spent more time with his daughters. Some extra R & R with Billie Cornish would have been nice too, but she deserved happiness and it looked as if she'd found it. The one big regret he had was involving Farakh Javed in this mess. He was gay, he had annoying habits like slurping his coffee and cutting his fingernails, and was generally a right pain in the backside, but the lad, in a way, was the son Holm had never had.

Holm turned his head, surprised he was still lucid. There was no pain, no feeling at all. He reasoned the bullet must have destroyed his nervous system. And yet if that was the case, how come he was staring at Javed and thinking all these crazy thoughts?

'Boss!'

Javed moved sideways and bowled into Holm, knocking him over the edge of the veranda. They fell six feet onto hard earth, the landing knocking all the air out of Holm. Now he did feel pain. A sharp jolt up the side of his arm, his eyes blurring as he spun from consciousness for a second. He jerked his head. That hurt too, but not from a bullet. His forehead had collided with the trunk of a thousand-year-old olive tree.

'What the…?' Holm was back in the land of the living. He might not make one thousand years, but he reckoned he'd be good for a few more. 'What happened?'

'Sniper,' Javed said, sounding impressed. 'Took out Karen Hope. *Bam!*'

'Taher?'

'I heard a vehicle so I reckon he's gone.'

'Let's get up there.' Holm struggled to his knees and tried to pull his hands from the twine Taher had tightened round his wrists. It was impossible.

'We should stay out of sight.' Javed was kneeling too, straining against his bounds. 'There's a gunman out there somewhere.'

'If he was aiming at us, we'd be hit by now. He was either after Taher or Hope.' Holm paused and craned his neck to try and see onto the veranda. 'Is she dead?'

'If she isn't then I think it's still unlikely she'll be running for president. I saw half her brain hit the wall of the house. I don't think the bit remaining is going to be good for much.'

'It's not a joking matter, Farakh. You're talking about the woman who was going to be the leader of the free world.'

'And who was about to put a hole in our heads.'

'Yes, there is that.' Holm was struggling to come to terms with Karen Hope holding a gun. Well that part wasn't surprising; her family owned an arms company after all. But the future president of the US standing alongside one of the world's most notorious terrorists, about to help him commit murder? That was a little difficult to understand.

'Boss?' Javed's hands came from behind his back, the twine somehow severed. 'Your turn.'

Holm stared at the boy, wondering what miracle he had summoned and from where. Then he spotted the shiny object in Javed's hands. His nail clippers.

–

With their bonds removed, they made their way up from the olive grove back to the veranda. Holm stood over the body of Karen Hope. Bits of flesh and bone had splattered across the ground and there was a mark on the wall of the farmhouse where a stone had exploded.

'High-powered rifle,' Javed said. 'They were out there on that ridge. When Karen Hope came out... *boom!*'

'Don't.' Holm stepped back from the body, aware of a sticky residue on his shoes. He gazed down at what was now no more than a cadaver of a woman. Hope. So much of it gone. All that promise unfulfilled. And yet she'd been about to blow his head off. What was that about? However Holm tried to spin what he'd seen and heard, the end result didn't make sense. He turned to Javed. 'Come on, let's check inside and then we'll call Palmer. After him, Huxtable, although what the hell she's going to make of this, I have no idea.'

'Karen Hope tried to kill us, she got whacked and Taher got away with a load of weapons.' Javed came over and stood alongside Holm. He contemplated the body and shook his head. 'Good luck with that, sir.'

Inside the house was cool. Narrow corridors led between thick stone walls to airy rooms with rustic furniture. The large kitchen was well equipped and stocked with food. A dining hall had seating for twenty, and at one end of the building was a bunk house.

'Do you think this place is a training camp?' Javed said as they edged down yet another corridor.

'No idea.' Holm pushed through a curtain and out into a central courtyard. He leaned on a wall, feeling deflated. All this way and all this effort and the main prize had eluded them.

'We've disrupted the supply chain,' Javed said, sensing Holm's despair. 'Whatever that boat was up to it won't be doing it any more.'

'You're right.' Holm brightened. 'Let's check upstairs and then we'll work out what the hell to do.'

Holm let Javed lead the way and they went back inside and took a narrow spiral staircase to the upper floor. A corridor ran down one side and had windows every few steps, each offering a view over the vast olive plantation. Javed paused at one of the windows.

'Sir.' He pointed outside as Holm joined him. 'One man drove in the van and another chauffeured Karen Hope. They both left in the van. Taher escaped in the pick-up and presumably Hope was going to drive the yellow SUV out of here. Which leaves me wondering, whose vehicle is that?'

Holm peered down. A Jeep Wrangler was parked in the shade of a couple of olive trees, hidden from anywhere but the upstairs of the farmhouse. He turned from the window as footsteps tapped on the wooden flooring. A tall figure stood silhouetted at the end of the corridor.

'It's mine.' The figure was in shadow but Holm would recognise the stick-thin man anywhere. 'Hello, Stephen.'

'Hello, Harry.'

Chapter Thirty-Six

Nasim wasn't keen.

'Lona no order,' he said. 'We leave now. Go back to Tunis.'

'I don't care what Lona ordered you to do,' Silva said. 'I'm telling you we're going to the compound. You can wait here and we'll take your car or you can drive us there.'

'I no go and the car no go.'

'Yes you fucking do.' Itchy had loaded the equipment into the rear of the Land Cruiser and now he stood behind Nasim, the SIG in his hand. 'You go, we go, the car goes.'

Nasim protested again, but climbed into the car. They set off back down the mountain track. It was a mile to the end of the ravine where they joined the main road, and then almost immediately they turned off up the track to the farm. The dust from Taher's rapid exit still swirled in the air as they bounced along, Nasim growing increasingly agitated.

'I don't like it, I really don't like it,' he said. He glanced in the mirror as they pulled up and stopped at the battered gates to the complex. 'We stay only five minutes, OK?'

'Sure.' Silva got out, reached in through the driver's window and snatched the keys from the ignition. 'But just in case we go into the red, I'll take these.'

Nasim raised his hands in a gesture of despair and resignation.

'We've only got the one weapon.' Itchy patted the SIG. 'Let's be careful.'

They slipped in through the front gates, Itchy in the lead. Silva pointed to the right and Itchy nodded. He moved to the side of the yard. A small dust devil spun up and danced for a few moments before dying back down. Other than the gentle hiss of the wind and the occasional snap of the canvas awning at the side of the house, there was silence.

They reached the main building. A low wall ran from the building and ancient olive trees stood behind the wall in a small grove. Itchy jerked his gun in the direction of the grove.

Silva nodded. There was an opening in the wall and they could cross the grove and get to the veranda without having to go into the house.

They went through the opening and crept along the wall to where a series of steps led upwards. When they reached the steps they stopped again. Still no sound. Silva held out her arm. She'd go first, Itchy would cover.

She eased up the steps and onto the veranda. Karen Hope lay in the centre. She'd fallen backwards, her right leg contorted beneath her, the left stuck out at a weird angle. One hand clamped the pistol tight while the other hand had risen to her chin, a finger gracing her lower lip as if she was attempting to wipe away a morsel of food. The upper part of her face round the right eye had gone. Everything from there backwards had been ripped apart by the bullet. She was dead all right.

Silva paused for a moment, but she was still pumped. This wasn't the time for reflection. She moved to the edge of the veranda and looked over. Bare earth and some olive leaves that had been knocked off when the two men had fallen. She swung back to the house where an arch led into the building proper. No door, just a dark shadow.

'I'll go first.' Itchy had his hand on Silva's shoulder. 'You stay back.'

Itchy moved along the veranda towards the arch while Silva checked nobody was sneaking up behind them, before they slipped into the relative cool of the house. After the brightness outside, the interior was like ink. She slid her feet across the tiled floor and turned a corner. Ahead Itchy was waiting in another doorway, light flooding through from some sort of central courtyard behind him. As Silva approached, he held out a clenched fist, thumb down.

Enemy spotted…

Itchy pointed to the upper storey where a series of windows overlooked the courtyard. A shadow passed across one opening and then another. Itchy placed his hand in front of his face and pointed to the right of the door where a corridor ran parallel.

Form ambush…

–

Martin 'Harry' Palmer walked down the corridor towards them. Taher's AK-47 was cradled in his arms, the finger of his right hand on the trigger. Holm stepped back, aware of his damp shirt, the sweat cold and clammy on his back.

Palmer. Harry bloody Palmer.

The chill on his skin brought forth a shiver as realisation set in. How could he have been so stupid? So blind? All those briefings at Thames House, Palmer there with his dinky little visitor's pass bearing the highest security level. Worse than that, the years of personal friendship between the two of them. The curries, the nights out together, the drunken chats on the state of the security services or on the progress Holm was making in catching Taher.

I can't understand it, Harry. We were so close. He just seemed to slip away without a trace.

Never mind, Stephen. There's always a next time, eh?

Not with Palmer there wasn't. Not with Harry bloody Palmer.

'Hello, sir.' Javed, innocent of the true situation, smiled and put out a hand in greeting. 'A timely arrival if I might say so.'

'Farakh.' Holm touched Javed on the shoulder. In his head he played back the conversation he'd had with Palmer at the cafe in Battersea Park. 'There's nothing timely about it. He's been here a while. Isn't that right, Harry?'

'Yes.' Palmer stopped a few steps away. 'I was beginning to get bored of waiting for your call, to be honest.'

'Taher got away with the weapons.' Javed lowered his shoulders as if by way of an apology. He still hadn't got it. 'But the good news is we eyeballed him.'

'That's about the only good news though.' Palmer raised the gun a little. 'I mean, events have taken a turn, haven't they, Stephen? You come here to catch Taher and instead a president ends up dead.'

'She wasn't a president,' Holm said. 'Not yet.'

'But she would have been if somebody hadn't meddled.' The gun swung up and Palmer gestured for them to move down the corridor. 'Now everything's gone to shit.'

'Boss?' Javed turned to Holm for some kind of answer.

'Harry's not all he seems, Farakh.' Holm shook his head. 'He's played us, played everyone. All this time Taher managed to keep one step ahead of us and I couldn't work out how he did it. The answer is Martin Palmer.'

'What?' Javed looked at Holm. 'Are you saying—'

'Downstairs!' The gun jerked again. 'I don't know what you've got to do with the death of Karen Hope, but you've caused a whole lot of trouble.'

'Nothing, Harry.' Holm spread his hands wide as he walked to the end of the corridor. 'We're unarmed. An old guy who will shortly need a Zimmer frame and a young 'un who thinks tradecraft is an ethical food company. What on earth would we have to gain by killing Karen Hope?'

'I've no idea, but it's a bit of a coincidence that you turn up and Hope is shot.'

Holm shrugged. He began to descend the spiral staircase. Javed and Palmer clattered down behind him. When he was halfway to the ground floor he realised he could make a run for it. Palmer wouldn't be able to hit him, not with the tight angle and with Javed in the way. Of course Javed would take a spray of bullets in the back. Holm muttered a curse under his breath.

'What did you say?'

'I asked you why, Harry? Why Taher? Are you a convert?'

'A convert? Don't be crazy. I can't stand Taher's brand of Islam. To be honest I can't stand any brand of it or any other religion. All of them are prejudiced and bigoted. There's nothing worse than self-righteousness, and believers of any faith tend to have it in spades.'

'So it's the money.' Holm nodded to himself. 'Something for your retirement.'

'Ask yourself, Stephen, if you're happy with the way we're treated. Here we are, defending the realm, and what do we get for it? Bugger all. No thanks, low pay, the chance of a tribunal if we cock up, a slow decline if we don't.'

They reached the ground floor and Holm moved into the kitchen. Without being asked he went to the table and pulled out a chair.

'How much did they pay you?'

'You're mistaken – the money was good but it wasn't just about the financial rewards.' Palmer aimed the gun at Javed and encouraged him to sit too. 'I met Jawad al Haddad years ago and he offered me information on various terrorist groups. I used the information to save lives, understand?'

'I bet Haddad twisted what he gave you. Everything was designed to strengthen his own position and promote his own factions.'

'Sure, but the result was that individuals were taken out and plots were disrupted. Isn't that the point of what we do?'

'Means and ends, Harry. They have to match. Pocketing cash while looking the other way when some of the bombs go off doesn't work for me.'

'The problem with you, Stephen, is your idealism. This is the real world. Compromise. Two steps forward, one step back. Progress always has a price.'

'Paid in bodies and cash, right?' Holm shook his head. He was stalling, all the while trying to find some kind of angle. 'Tell me how this is going to end. I assume you can't let us live?'

'Sorry, Stephen, no, but you'll be heroes. You tried to save Karen Hope, but there were too many terrorists. In the end you went down in a blaze of gunfire.'

'Taher's AK-47.' Holm looked at the assault rifle. 'He left it for you.'

'There was no time to work out a plan after Hope was shot.' Palmer gave a flat smile. 'But it'll do.'

'Others know about this, know we're here, know you were instrumental in leading us to Taher. They'll be able to work out what happened.'

'Nice try, but you didn't tell anyone. You were too scared about blowing your chance at catching Taher off your own bat.' Palmer laughed. 'Not duty or loyalty to your country, was it? Vainglory, that's all.'

'Martin—'

'Enough,' Palmer said. 'Let's go back outside. You're going to be part of history. Your names alongside Hope's.'

Holm slowly pushed himself up. Their last chance would be on the way back to the veranda. He let Javed go first, thinking perhaps the young lad could make a run for it. They walked from the kitchen along a narrow corridor, bright sunlight at the end where the corridor joined a small inner atrium. As they crossed into the atrium a voice shouted out from one side.

'Stop there. And put your hands on your heads.'

–

Silva had slipped along the corridor and crouched behind a large carved wooden box. Then she'd waited. A minute slipped by and then another; then through an arch to her left she saw two men emerge into the glare of the courtyard.

'Stop there,' Itchy said. 'And put your hands on your heads.'

The next few moments passed like lightning. As Itchy stepped forward to cover the two men, a shot rang out from the darkness of the arch. Itchy collapsed to the floor, his hand to his right leg.

'Drop the fucking weapon!' A tall thin man emerged into the courtyard. He had an AK-47 in his hands and his finger tightened on the trigger. Itchy was half slumped on the floor, one hand on his knee and the other holding the SIG. 'Now!'

Itchy nodded and the gun fell from his hand, clattering on the floor.

'Stephen, kick it away!' The thin man thrust his own weapon towards the older man and made a sweeping motion. 'Do it!'

Silva knelt hidden from his view behind the box, but she had direct line of sight to Itchy and the other two men. The older man moved his foot next to the gun and, as he did so, his eyes flicked to her hiding place. For a moment he hesitated, but then he kicked the gun and it slid over the floor towards Silva.

'I'd say we're another step closer to solving this mystery, Stephen.' The tall man stooped out of the doorway. 'British intelligence comes up trumps once again.'

'Hope's dead, Harry,' the old guy said. 'I wouldn't count that as a success.'

'Don't knock it. The way this will play out, you'll still be the hero of the hour. A dead hero, yes, but a hero nonetheless.'

As the tall man moved to cover Itchy and the others, Silva reached for the SIG.

'Stop!' she shouted, holding the gun braced in two hands.

The man froze, his finger still touching the trigger.

'Or what?' He didn't seem surprised as he turned his head towards her. 'This is a Mexican stand-off, right? If you shoot me, I'll shoot at least one of them.'

'I'll take that chance if I have to.'

'It's Ms da Silva, isn't it?' He smiled. 'You see, Stephen, there is actually no mystery at all, no global conspiracy to assassinate a president, rather a cheap and dirty personal vendetta.'

Silva wondered how he knew who she was, and in that split second the man swung the machine gun and fired a burst. Silva was already moving, diving behind the wooden box and letting off a single shot as she rolled out the other side. This close she went for the body. This close there was no chance of missing.

The man staggered back as the bullet hit him in the chest, stopping his heart instantly. For a moment some part of his sympathetic nervous system continued to work and he stood balanced like a statue. Then he toppled backwards and folded to the floor.

Silence.

Silva stood and walked over to the body, gazing down. She had no idea who the man was except he was something to do with the weapons smuggling, something to do with Taher, ultimately something to do with the death of her mother. Yet, staring at the husk at her feet, she felt nothing. Neither was there much relief that Karen Hope was dead. There was no feeling of triumph, no sense of celebration. A sudden wash of despair overcame her and she wished she was away from here, away from everyone, up on the moor, just running, running, running until she'd sweated all the anger from her body.

She was brought back to her senses as Itchy uttered a groan. He grimaced and held his leg and turned to Silva. The grimace became a smile and he gave her a nod of respect.

'Shot,' he said.

Chapter Thirty-Seven

Holm and Javed arrived back in the UK in the early hours of the next morning. An MI5 detail met them at Heathrow and they were ferried into central London in the back of a windowless van. As the van's doors opened and they climbed out into the underground car park beneath Thames House, Javed looked across at Holm for reassurance.

'It'll be OK, lad,' Holm said. 'We're on the right side.'

His words, he knew, were rubbish. There was no right side, only the winning one, and the victor had yet to be decided.

Huxtable met them as they emerged from the lift.

'Stephen, Farakh,' she said. 'I'm glad you're both in one piece, but what a mess, hey?'

Holm nodded. Wondered if she was glad they were in one piece because it would mean she had more to tear apart when she got to work on them.

They stopped off in the situation room where chaos was emblazoned across a dozen screens. Every TV channel was covering the Karen Hope story, whether live from Tunisia, live from the Capitol or live from the Hope family home in Louisiana. Details were sketchy but so far the story was that Hope had been kidnapped by terrorists while attending a fundraising party on her brother's boat. A British agent had died trying to rescue her, but questions were already being asked: where was her own security detail? What was she doing in such a hotspot as Tunisia in the first place, and how on earth was the US going to recover from this tragedy?

Upstairs, alone with Huxtable in her office, Holm gave a summary of what had happened, starting with his decision to go after Taher and finishing with the death of Karen Hope and Martin Palmer. That done, he tried to absolve Javed from any responsibility.

'The boy,' Holm said. 'He did what I said. Whatever punishment is coming should be for me only.'

'He knows secrets,' Huxtable said. 'Big secrets.'

'And he'll keep them, ma'am. Just as I will.'

'Whatever the truth, the story for now is that Karen Hope died a hero, understand? British intelligence, fortuitously, were there to try and save her, but we failed. Palmer will get some kind of posthumous award no doubt.'

'He was a traitor.'

'A traitor is someone who goes over to the other side. Palmer was on a team of one.'

'He fooled me completely,' Holm said. 'No wonder we couldn't catch Taher.'

'Palmer was MI6's liaison officer within JTAC and had access to material from across the intelligence spectrum. That made it easy for him to prewarn the terrorists.'

'Did you know?'

'Not the name, no, but there were too many occasions when operations failed to produce results. Did you really think I shut you in that cupboard out of some form of spite?' Huxtable sat back in her chair, as if disappointed Holm hadn't worked it out himself. 'I instigated the whole thing.'

'I...' Holm hadn't seen that coming. 'You set me up? The tweet? The codes? Everything?'

'I was a little surprised you fell for it, actually.' Huxtable smiled. 'But in the end you did well.'

'The one-time pad? That was you?'

'I wanted to make sure the pointer to Western was absolutely secure. I have to say I thought it was rather clever.'

'Suppose Farakh had missed the tweet? Suppose he hadn't understood its significance?'

'No chance of that. Farakh Javed is a bright young man. Anyone else reading the first tweet wouldn't have had a clue and, even if they had, the contents of the second tweet were in an uncrackable code.'

'Wouldn't it have just been easier to tell me?'

'Not really. Say, for instance *you* had been the mole. Then you'd have known I knew. I also wanted you to work discreetly, and I was pretty sure you'd try to keep your hunt for Taher hidden from me as well as everyone else.'

'Right.' Holm conceded the point. 'But who put you on to Ben Western and SeaPak in the first place?'

'Jawad al Haddad's young wife, Deema. We recruited her years ago when she was at boarding school here and she's been feeding information to us ever since she was forced into the marriage with Haddad. The intelligence she provided has been limited to bits and pieces she managed to overhear, but one such snippet was the name Western in connection with Taher. However, there was no context until a flag came up a few weeks ago about a man of the same name going missing in Suffolk. The Western case seemed to me to be a long shot, but I backed you to discover if there was anything in it.'

'And Karen Hope?' Holm leaned forward and, without thinking, dropped his voice to a whisper. 'She was in cahoots with Taher, ma'am.'

'We don't need to explore that aspect, Stephen. Not for now. To be honest I haven't got my head round everything yet, but we'll see how things pan out. Take it from there.'

'What about the sniper? Palmer seemed to think Hope was killed by the people who rescued us, but they were British so it doesn't seem likely.'

'You didn't speak with them?'

'Only briefly. They gave us a lift back to our car and then high-tailed it.'

'Need to know, Stephen.' Huxtable tapped her nose with a finger. 'You know the why and the when. You don't need to know the who.'

'This was officially sanctioned, wasn't it?' Holm realised the question was one he should never have asked so he avoided her gaze. 'Bloody hell.'

'In the next few days Thomas Gillan will be tending his resignation. Ostensibly he's going for personal reasons, but in reality his departure is down to a misinterpretation of instructions from the cabinet secretary and the national security adviser.'

'They're passing the buck.'

'Put it this way, Thomas Gillan took one for the team, for the country. Something, I'm afraid, politicians almost never do.'

'A hero, then.'

'As much as anyone.' Huxtable smiled. 'As much as you and Farakh.'

'Taher got away.'

'Don't be hard on yourself. Your friend in Suffolk is obtaining warrants for the arrests of the SeaPak manager Paul Henderson and several of the *Excelsior*'s crew, and our Italian colleagues are awaiting the arrival of the *Angelo* in Naples. In addition to stopping the smuggling we flushed out Palmer, and with a bit of pressure the Saudis will remove Jawad al Haddad from the scene, meaning another source of funding for the terrorists will be cut. Catching Taher was always going to be a big ask, but we will get him.'

'We?' It was Holm's turn to give Huxtable a wry smile.

'Yes, Stephen.' Huxtable tapped the desk signalling the meeting was over. 'We.'

–

Silva and Itchy returned in the private jet. They were met by Simeon Weiss, and he whisked them away from the airport and off to Matthew Fairchild's place. After food and rest and some medical attention to Itchy's leg – which turned out to be a nasty flesh wound but no worse – Weiss conducted an initial debrief and gave them cover stories for their periods of absence in Italy and Tunisia. There was ample evidence to show they'd been in Wales on both occasions, he said. Somebody remembered seeing them on the slopes of Snowdon. There was CCTV footage of Itchy buying bread and milk in a shop in Betws-y-coed. A traffic camera on the A5 had caught Silva breaking the speed limit. A fine would be arriving in the post.

'Pity about the weather though,' Weiss said, winking.

Fairchild was the perfect host over the next couple of days but it felt as if they were under house arrest. They couldn't make calls out, although Fairchild told them Itchy's wife and Silva's father had been informed they were safe and well. Finally Weiss told Itchy he could leave but insisted Silva remain at the house for an additional debrief.

When Itchy had gone, Silva confronted Weiss.

'What is this?' she said. 'Why can't I go?'

'Because I say so.'

Later she was shown into the large drawing room where Weiss hovered near a table, uncharacteristically nervous. He fiddled with some papers while one of Fairchild's minions served her tea.

'Well?' Silva said after several minutes of silence.

'We're waiting for someone,' Weiss said. 'In the meantime I have been authorised to brief you further.'

'You mean tell me a little more of the truth?'

'Yes, if you want to put it like that.' Weiss ducked his head an inch. 'Your mother's files have been anonymised. Which is to say, all trace she had anything to do with the photographs, the research, any of it, has been removed.'

'But—'

'Karen Hope was undoubtedly a crook, a fraud and a murderer. However, in very few jurisdictions does that give you the right to execute her without trial.' Weiss lifted his shoulders in resignation. 'If we were to give your mother the credit she deserves it would be simple for anyone to work out you must have been the sniper, both in Positano and in Tunisia.'

'Some people know already.'

'Knowing is not the same as having the evidence.'

'They could still come after me. The US government. Haddad. Taher.'

'When we release your mother's material, which we will do shortly, the US will back off. Now Hope is dead, the rationale for any sort of coverup has gone. Haddad is likely to face trial in Saudia Arabia. The trial will be swift and the verdict is not in doubt. I imagine the punishment will be quite barbaric. As for Taher, well, we're closing in on him.'

'Right.' Silva wasn't convinced. 'And what about the Hope family? Brandon and the father. Those kinds of dynasties tend to bear grudges.'

'Brandon Hope has disappeared. If and when he surfaces he'll have a lot of explaining to do.'

Could her worries be dismissed so easily? It was noticeable that at no point since she'd returned from Tunisia had she been offered any kind of protection. There'd been no talk of a new identity or of relocation.

'One more thing – your motorbike.' Weiss pulled a set of keys from his pocket and placed them on the table. 'I had it brought here. It's in Fairchild's garage.'

'So I can go now?'

'In a bit.' Weiss slipped over to the window and peered out. A chauffeured car was rolling down the driveway.

'Who's that?' Silva craned her neck but Weiss stood blocking the view of the front steps. He turned and trotted to the door. As he reached it the door swung open, to reveal a woman standing there. Brown tweed. Glasses on a bony nose. Something like a character from an Agatha Christie novel.

'My boss.' Weiss almost seemed to bow his head in deference. 'The new Director General of MI5. Fiona Huxtable.'

'Ms da Silva.' Huxtable's hand was extended as she strode across the room. 'It's a pleasure.'

Silva shook Huxtable's hand. If the title was supposed to impress her it hadn't. If anything it had made her suspicious.

'What's this about?' she said.

'Loose ends,' Huxtable said. She gestured to the chairs near the fireplace. Silva went across and sat while Huxtable perched on the edge of her chair like a bird. 'I came here to thank you. You've done this country a great service, perhaps not just this country.'

'You used us,' Silva said. 'We were pawns on the board.'

'I don't like the word *used*,' Huxtable said. '*Utilised* is a better one. From what I understand we were running low on choices and you were the optimal bet. In a percentage game only a stubborn fool passes up the best chance of winning.'

'I should have been told from the start.'

'Look, Rebecca, I knew nothing of Simeon's operation. The activities of the Special Accounts Unit are a mystery to everyone but the director of MI5.' Huxtable shot Weiss a glance. 'To say there's been a lot to take in since I was appointed is a monumental understatement. To be honest I feel a little used myself.'

'Your head isn't on the line.'

'Simeon assures me everything is being done to remove you from the picture. We're all working to produce the best possible outcome, and that includes keeping your part in the operation under wraps.' Huxtable's lips slipped into a thin smile. 'Sadly that means no wider recognition or thanks for your actions. You see, if for some unfortunate reason your part in the assassination came out we'd have to deny you completely.'

A cough came from over by the table. Weiss raised a fist to his mouth.

'Thank you, Simeon.' Huxtable glanced across and then back at Silva. 'Do you understand what that means?'

'It means you'll kill me if I talk, right?'

'The safety of the sixty million citizens of this country comes before the welfare of any single individual. There's always a bigger picture.'

'It's a pity you lot didn't see the bigger picture before you started selling arms to the Saudis.'

'*We* did, Ms da Silva. The problem is, most of the time our masters don't want to hear the truth. Politicians are cowards, basically. It's people like you who have the bravery to act.'

'Don't patronise me. The army was my career, but I killed Hope because she murdered my mother, not through any desire to serve my country.'

'We're still grateful.' Huxtable nodded at Weiss and he came across bearing a manila folder. He placed it on the coffee table. 'And as a mark of our gratitude we'd like to offer you a position in Simeon's outfit.'

'*What?*'

'We need people like you, Rebecca. People who have the skill and courage to carry out extraordinary missions that can't—'

'I don't think so.' Silva pushed the envelope across the table towards Huxtable. She stood. 'If that's it, then I'll be off.'

Weiss moved swiftly, intercepting her as she reached the door.

'Let her go, Simeon,' Huxtable said. 'She'll come round, you'll see.'

The arrogance in the statement almost made Silva turn and scream, but she composed herself and walked from the room.

–

Her father sat on the rickety chair at the end of the jetty. He appeared to have given up on the fly rod and now held a long pole in his hands. The fluorescent tip of a fishing float bobbed in the water beneath the end of the pole. As Silva placed a foot on the jetty her father spoke.

'Stupid buggers.' He lifted the pole, swung the float in, and examined the hook. 'They've stolen the worm. I don't know how Matthew managed to catch those trout. I get nothing or a measly gudgeon. Waste of money stocking the bloody lake.'

'Hello, Dad.' Silva removed her foot from the jetty and waited for her father to rise. 'I'm back.'

'So I see.' Her father put the pole down and pushed himself up from the chair. Silva moved aside as he walked towards her. 'Matthew called to let me know you'd be coming. Itchy all right?'

'He's fine. Richer. Then again he's going to need the money with the kid on the way.'

'A kid, eh? Boy or girl?'

'Itchy wants a girl.' Silva smiled to herself as her father frowned.

'Right.' They strolled up towards the terrace. The table had three glasses. Lemonade. Just like before. He gestured for Silva to sit. 'We'll have tea later.'

'Will we?'

'Yes. I've made some sandwiches.'

Silva pointed at the third glass. 'Are we expecting a visitor?'

'We are.'

'Might I ask who it is?'

'You'll see presently.'

'Aren't you going to say anything? About what happened?'

'There's no need. Karen Hope is dead. It's over. Job done.'

Job done.

She wondered if it was 'job done'. If, now Hope was dead, she'd be able to return to some kind of normality. He father certainly seemed to have moved on. There were builders round the front of the house dealing with the damage from the fire and on the table she could see an index card with her father's handwriting scrawled on it. 'Housekeeper Wanted', it said at the top. Poor Mrs Collins wasn't long in the ground and he was already advertising for her replacement.

'Job done and you're home safe.' He looked over at her for the briefest of moments and then turned away. 'That's what matters.'

'Dad, I—'

'Rebecca?' A glass chinked and she was aware of her father pouring the lemonade. 'Our guest is here.'

She looked up as a figure passed in front of the sun.

'Becca?' An American accent. A hint of Irish. Whiskey, wood smoke, coffee, peach.

'Sean.' Silva answered flatly as she stood.

'I'm sorry.' Sean gave a tentative smile, putting out feelers.

'You told your boss about me and he shopped me to Mavers.'

'My head of station knew nothing about what Mavers was up to. Obviously he briefed the ambassador and the deputy ambassador, and that unfortunately put Mavers on to you. After I'd talked to my boss I tried to contact you, but couldn't. I was so worried.'

'*You* were worried? Mavers was going to torture me.' Silva looked away. 'Jesus, Sean, I was so scared.'

'Ahem.' Silva's father made a waving motion from the other side of the table. 'I'll leave you two alone, but I just want to say something about this young man.'

'Really, sir, there's no need.' Sean bowed his head.

'There is a need.' Silva's father looked across with a scowl. 'Rebecca is stubborn and difficult. She won't listen if you tell her.'

'Tell me what?' Silva said.

'Sean saved my life and probably saved yours too.'

'What on earth are you talking about? He nearly got me killed.'

'Perhaps, but after he failed to contact you he came here. Luckily those bunglers hadn't set the fire very well and it took a while to take hold. Even so, had he not turned up I'd have been fried.'

'Sean?'

Sean nodded.

'And,' Silva's father continued, 'he did something else. When I told him Mavers was involved he suggested we check out the black site, guessing you might have been taken there. I got the information to Matthew and he was able to effect a rescue.'

'Right.'

'So an apology is due.' Her father rose from the chair and patted Sean on the shoulder. Cast Silva a glance. 'OK?'

As her father walked off, Sean stepped forward. Silva held up her hands.

'I killed Hope,' she said.

'Is that hope with a capital H?' Sean said. 'Or are you playing with words?'

'No games. I need to know if you can accept what I did.'

'A week ago the answer would have been "no", but now I've been fully briefed and know the truth, yes I can. Karen Hope didn't offer any kind of hope. If she'd stood for president millions of people would have voted for her, but she was a con. Once elected she'd have been in the pocket of Haddad and the Saudis. US foreign policy would have been shot to pieces.' Sean tilted his head. 'Sorry, I didn't mean…'

'And she killed my mother.'

'That's worst of all. In your situation I'd have played it exactly the same.'

'Right.'

Silence for a beat and then a shrug from Sean.

'So, are you going to give me a sit rep? Or is that information classified?'

'The situation's not great, to be honest. The terrorists are still out there, Haddad or his allies probably have a death squad after me, and what's left of the Hope family will be seeking some kind of vengeance.'

'Have you got protection?'

'Nope.'

'Doesn't seem right after what you went through.'

'They offered me a job. I guess it's sort of carrot and stick. Take up their offer and stay safe, refuse and run the risk of getting popped.'

'And are you going to take it?'

'No.' Silva gave a half smile. 'Even though I am now unemployed.'

'How come?'

'I was sacked for taking too many days off. If only they knew.'

'What are you going to do?'

'I don't know.' Silva shrugged. 'Stay here for a bit maybe. Help my dad with some stuff. See if Itchy needs a hand decorating his house.'

'Doesn't sound very edifying.'

'After the last few weeks it's exactly what I need.'

'And when you've done helping and decorating?'

Silva didn't answer. Was she really going to return to her boat, get another crap job, and just carry on with her life as if nothing had happened? That didn't seem credible. What was the alternative though? Huxtable's job offer was out, but perhaps Fairchild could find her something to do. Then again, did she want to join his band of mercenaries and get paid for being shot at? Probably not.

'What about your side of things?' she said.

'All out damage control,' Sean said. 'The State Department are trying to placate our allies, while the Agency are coming to terms with the fact that they allowed this to happen in the first place. Operationally, Hope should never have been permitted to go off on her own in Tunisia, but the bigger issue is how she was ever allowed to rise to a position where she might become president. Of course the Agency isn't allowed to operate inside the US, but somebody should have been feeding intelligence on Brandon Hope back to the Director of National Intelligence.'

'And why weren't they?'

'Either nobody knew, which is bad enough, or somebody made the decision to keep quiet, which is worse. Heads will roll.'

'And your own position?'

'I hear I'm up for some internal commendation for helping to expose Mavers.' Sean grinned. 'What can I say? I'm just your average all American hero.'

'Then I guess I'd better do as my dad said and apologise.'

Silence for a moment before Sean moved a step closer.

'Rebecca?' he said. 'After all that's gone on, I need to know where we are.'

'We're quits, that's where we are. Same as before. No better no worse.'

'And what about the future?'

Silva smiled at Sean as she reached for a glass of lemonade. 'Let's just say I'm thinking about it, OK?'

Epilogue

Irene Caxwell had tried for ages to get a rental for the little annexe attached to the rear of her bungalow. The place was small, admittedly, and perhaps not ideally located for tenants who wanted easy access to the nearby town of Windsor. The lodgings were cold, too, but she'd had a wood burner installed and a big stack of logs sat ready for the fire. This winter the occupants would be toasty. Not that the summer was over yet, of course. September had so far been unseasonably warm, and the woods round her house still teemed with life. Swallows flitted back and forth, fattening themselves with the last of the season's bounties before their long flight south. She could see rabbits hopping at the edge of the field, and the squirrels were causing havoc when she put food out for the birds.

The two men turned up late one evening. At first she felt a little unsettled. They were... *not white*.

Her unease soon vanished. Sabin and Mohid were both so friendly, so erudite and Sabin was, well, so *beautiful*. His face was angelic, with piercing eyes and flawless skin, a wisp of beard on his chin. They were students, Sabin explained, and had recently returned from a study trip abroad. Now they needed solitude to complete their PhDs in time for the end-of-year deadline. What were they studying, she enquired. Mohid's PhD was to do with astro-something-or-other. Astrology? No, that didn't sound quite right. Never mind. She remembered Sabin had said he was examining the Islamic diaspora. She didn't know what diaspora meant, but Islam...

357

'What do you mean, not white?' her friend Sybil said when she told her about her new tenants.

'They're a couple of those…' Irene said. 'You know. *Muslims*.'

Sybil brushed aside Irene's concerns. 'I slept with one once. It was in Turkey. You remember the holiday I took a few years back? Well, it was then. A young Kurdish man. Very nice. Very… um… very… *good*.'

Irene's mouth dropped open. 'That was the holiday you took for your sixtieth!'

Sybil nodded, smiling. Something about her face. A warm glow. As if vitality could spring forth from a memory. 'Yes.'

Irene showed Sabin and Mohid the annexe and explained it was completely separate from the main house. They'd be able to come and go as they wished. They both seemed pleased and asked if they could move in right away. And they'd pay cash, if that was OK?

OK? It was fine!

'One thing,' she said when they were back outside but before she accepted the money. 'You wanted peace and quiet and solitude, but you do know what's just over there?'

She pointed over the roof of the bungalow and as if by magic a huge shape loomed in the air, engines on full power, the fuselage seemingly close enough to reach up and touch. As several hundred tonnes of aluminium and passengers and aviation fuel crawled into the sky above them, the windows rattled and the ground beneath their feet shook.

'Heathrow airport.' Irene cocked her head. 'Are you sure the planes won't worry you?'

'No,' Sabin said. He glanced at Mohid and smiled as he looked up. 'They won't worry us one little bit.'